Foreword

This unique novel is not only limited to the l facts and information about the City of Joy, along and to some extent, the country as a whole, but also is about the living conditions of people, especially the destitute children living on pavements, under bridges and shanties. Traffic snarls and pedestrian problems add up to the mess of faulty roads and encroachment of hawkers and peddlers on and around the streets. Environmental issues and other important issues like administration, police functioning, political quagmires and issues pertaining to judiciary and advocates are also highlighted, along with healthcare delivery system, private nursing homes, government facilities, etc.

Unethical matters as it pertains to few schools, doctors, accountants and some other professionals prevalent in the state are also revisited, along with views pertaining to matters of historical significances. Some thoughts relating to chauvinism, some popular jingoism and issues relating to xenophobia or ethnocentrism are also incorporated in the novel. It is pertinent to note that in light of the increasing over-action or inaction by self-proclaimed 'intellectual groups' (who prefer to call themselves as wise guys and try to impose their individual thoughts and preferences on masses, while many of them have vested interests behind their 'proclamation') in and around Kolkata, it might be a good idea to go through the novel in order to review where individual thoughts and ideas stand!

The novel is based on a fictitious character (based on real incidents), and it should be read as a fiction only. While every effort is made to change names and characters of people and entities in the entire novel, it should also be understood that no resemblance or similarity with any character or entity is intended, and accordingly, pertinent legal disclaimers are resorted to.

About the Author

The author is currently a twelfth grader in a reputable private school in Kolkata - she is a very aspiring, honest, hard-working and polite young lady, whose dream is to become an Anchor with CNN someday. Many internationally acclaimed journalists and reporters, whom she met serendipitously, have been in constant touch with the author, motivating and guiding her to the coveted destiny. Her pursuance of International Baccalaureate Program, along with her ongoing pursuit of Junior Fellowship Course (Young Global Leaders Program, Oxford, UK), will hopefully land her on smooth surface for her college years abroad, preferably in the USA, which has been her aspiration!

The first book composed by this minor girl, titled "From Wonderland To Reality" was published world-wide last year; the timing was propitious, as the author was blessed with five-star ratings from most of her readers across the globe, as also from reputed houses like Goodreads, IBNS et al. Hundreds of copies of the book were sold within the first couple of months after publication; very positive feedback, ratings & comments were received from all quarters. Renowned singer Shri Soumitra Ray publicly eulogized & extolled the book during a gala event on November 2018 & solicited sale of that book for charity.

As was promised through her first book, the author donated the entire sale-proceeds of her book to a few charitable trusts including Cry India, Akshay Patra Foundation and a lesser-publicised orphanage named Antyoday, located in Paushi (East Midnapore, West Bengal). Ten thousand rupees were donated for educational sponsorship of a girl child there for a year, with another ten thousand rupees donated for the general welfare of kids at Antyoday Orphanage – all donations were duly acknowledged by all and are available for viewing.

The budding author primarily gained her inspiration initially from visiting old-age homes, orphanage, homes of the differently-abled individuals, as well as experiencing first-hand the strained lives of the economically disadvantaged sections of our community (while she was imparting education to street-kids

Outline

Kolkata (erstwhile Calcutta) is the capital and heart of State of West Bengal - it is a lifeline to many places around Bengal. It used to be India's capital under the British Raj; it is believed by some that this great city was founded by East India Trading Company as a trading post.

Kolkata is commonly referred to as City of Joy, with rich culture, deep-rooted traditions, grand colonial architecture, enriched history, spectacular art galleries, ethical societies – the City may be termed as a hub of education, business, science and technology, fairs, commerce, agriculture, and various activities. The Port of Kolkata is India's oldest operating port, located on the east bank of the Hooghly River, about 47 miles west of Bangladesh. Kolkata is widely regarded as the cultural capital of India.

It is a City that is very famous for initiation of the freedom movement in India, which eventually led to ousting of British government from India. Many legends and heroes of not only the freedom struggle, but also almost all walks of life, were born in this great city.

A religiously and ethnically diverse centre of culture, literature, film, theatre, music, dance and performing arts, Kolkata culture features idiosyncrasies that include a distinctive feature which separates itself from most other cities – close-knit neighbourhoods and freestyle intellectual exchanges, which are respectively termed as 'para' and 'adda' locally.

There was a time when it was customary for guys, young and old, to hang out together and organize festivals, etc. in their neighbourhoods and compete with others, be it through Pujas or cultural programs or otherwise. The same group or a different one, consisting of guys from all ages will assemble at a pre-set place every evenings and weekend mornings, typically near some tea stalls, to discuss issues pertaining not only to their own city, but also of every place known to them in earth, with everyone rendering their opinions on matters of politics, sports, education, commerce, films, and what not!

during her junior school years) – with the extra delectation & motivation of being able to do something for the above-noted groups of people through sale of her first book, the author acquired enough inspiration to continue with her efforts, and thus, she composed this novel. She also plans to start scripting her third book once this second book is published, so as to serve the community through her creations, in whatever meagre manner she can, with limited resources, etc.

The author was felicitated with a Birangana (Bravery) Award from the Government of West Bengal during a convivial ceremony held at Eastern Zonal Cultural Centre, Salt Lake City on November 19th, 2018, where she received Certificates, Memento and cash prizes from the Minister of State, Women and Child Welfare Department, in the august presence of esteemed dignitaries from UNICEF, Justices from Kolkata High Court, reputed journalists, and others.

The award was accorded solely for the author's heroic plight & struggle to continue her education, career and life, despite repeated ignorance and torture by her biological father, who had eloped with a sleazy woman years after the author's mother died, leaving her practically an orphan. It was by God's grace that the young author had found a safe and normal home in her maternal grandmother, ably supported by an avuncular maternal uncle (an ex US Government Officer who emigrated back to India to take care of the author) – he regards the author as his own daughter, as she's the only family he got apart from his ailing old mother. The maternal aunt of the author also provides enough care and regular support to her.

The young author has been engaged in various societal developmental activities since her primary schooling days, when she was in a reputable Catholic School near Deshapriya Park, South Kolkata. She had been teaching economically disadvantaged sections of our community for a long time, continuing with her ongoing efforts at her High School located near Park Circus. As a part of the curriculum of IB Board, the author is also into various creativities, activities and service projects. She makes sure she fulfils all the laid down requirements of her pursuing program, apart from tedious studies in holistic approach, through effective time-management skills – she is fortunate to have compassionate teachers; some of them protect her like guardian angels from all evils.

The author regularly participates in Tennis Competitions, attends Guitar classes and Old Age Homes religiously on a routine manner – she's also active in networking with friends and outside world on her leisure time. She meticulously spends some time every weekend as well as during holidays on writing, apart from making career planning, helping with household chores, helping out kids in the neighbourhood with their studies and activities, etc.

The young author aspires to be a successful TV journalist with a world-famous news broadcasting corporation spread across all corners of the universe, to be a Senior Correspondent with them some day. She spent considerable time after her Board exam cogitating on her career plans - she desires to pursue courses in History, Law and Anthropology during her college years.

Losing her loving mother to an ill-diagnosed terminal disease when the author was only four years of age, she was painfully denied of paternal love from her own father, who leads an extravagant life with multiple paramours - he doesn't even visit or care for his own lovely daughter. The young author's maternal grandparents have been taking care of her since childhood days – the author got the second biggest shock of her life when her maternal grandpa passed away within a couple of years of her mother's untimely demise. The third rude awakening to the harsh & cruel world struck her like a lightning when her father abandoned her completely for a sleazy woman with chequered history.

However, despite all the evil spells during her tender age, the author has been able to muster up enough courage to face the world - to brazenly take up any challenge life poses on her. Despite being an innocent little girl with big dreams and ambitions, the author faces many untoward incidents routinely, primarily arising out of covetousness towards her by some. Her grandma, uncle and aunt on her mother's side try to protect her to the best of their abilities from all evil souls; they all are confident that the author will shine in her career someday soon

– she'll continue to be the great human being that she always has been. Her impeccable mannerism and politeness mesmerize all who knows her.

It can be claimed that the young author may be disparate from many kids in the sense that she attained mental maturity at an early age. She has made her best conscious efforts to jot down remarks in this book apropos of the circumstances only – offending others or insulting anyone is not her habit and is beyond her traits. Some of her statements and deliberations in her causerie about political or other persons are full of jokes, hyperbole, intentional disregard of linguistic and stylistic norms – she left room for the readers of the novel to read between the lines and make their own assertions.

It may be noted that the first book written by the author was a gran success, with many copies sold across continents. However, the royalties receive by the author was a meagre percentage of sales, as per terms and conditions the publisher. Therefore, efforts are now being made to ensure that sor reasonably fair amount of royalties are received this time, by publishing w Amazon Kindle Direct, so that more revenues can be generated from sales of book, which can further be channelized towards deserving orphanages and NG The author believes in being a change agent herself in her continuous st towards improvement, excelling in life and to contribute whatever little tow society.

As was promised in writing through her first book, the author her making the same exact pledge for this novel too; all sale proceeds received the sale of this book during the current year, will be donated to social through established charitable organisations, benefitting under-privileged

At the outset, the author wants to thank all her readers and patr supporting her just cause, in whatever manner they deemed fit – she garnish the same patronage and support for this novel, as in past. Any suggestions or comments are welcome, to be sent directly to the a bhatumukherjee@yahoo.com - all correspondences will be acknowledg

during her junior school years) – with the extra delectation & motivation of being able to do something for the above-noted groups of people through sale of her first book, the author acquired enough inspiration to continue with her efforts, and thus, she composed this novel. She also plans to start scripting her third book once this second book is published, so as to serve the community through her creations, in whatever meagre manner she can, with limited resources, etc.

The author was felicitated with a Birangana (Bravery) Award from the Government of West Bengal during a convivial ceremony held at Eastern Zonal Cultural Centre, Salt Lake City on November 19th, 2018, where she received Certificates, Memento and cash prizes from the Minister of State, Women and Child Welfare Department, in the august presence of esteemed dignitaries from UNICEF, Justices from Kolkata High Court, reputed journalists, and others.

The award was accorded solely for the author's heroic plight & struggle to continue her education, career and life, despite repeated ignorance and torture by her biological father, who had eloped with a sleazy woman years after the author's mother died, leaving her practically an orphan. It was by God's grace that the young author had found a safe and normal home in her maternal grandmother, ably supported by an avuncular maternal uncle (an ex US Government Officer who emigrated back to India to take care of the author) – he regards the author as his own daughter, as she's the only family he got apart from his ailing old mother. The maternal aunt of the author also provides enough care and regular support to her.

The young author has been engaged in various societal developmental activities since her primary schooling days, when she was in a reputable Catholic School near Deshapriya Park, South Kolkata. She had been teaching economically disadvantaged sections of our community for a long time, continuing with her ongoing efforts at her High School located near Park Circus. As a part of the curriculum of IB Board, the author is also into various creativities, activities and service projects. She makes sure she fulfils all the laid down requirements of her pursuing program, apart from tedious studies in holistic approach, through effective time-management skills – she is fortunate to have compassionate teachers; some of them protect her like guardian angels from all evils.

The author regularly participates in Tennis Competitions, attends Guitar classes and Old Age Homes religiously on a routine manner – she's also active in networking with friends and outside world on her leisure time. She meticulously spends some time every weekend as well as during holidays on writing, apart from making career planning, helping with household chores, helping out kids in the neighbourhood with their studies and activities, etc.

The young author aspires to be a successful TV journalist with a world-famous news broadcasting corporation spread across all corners of the universe, to be a Senior Correspondent with them some day. She spent considerable time after her Board exam cogitating on her career plans - she desires to pursue courses in History, Law and Anthropology during her college years.

Losing her loving mother to an ill-diagnosed terminal disease when the author was only four years of age, she was painfully denied of paternal love from her own father, who leads an extravagant life with multiple paramours - he doesn't even visit or care for his own lovely daughter. The young author's maternal grandparents have been taking care of her since childhood days – the author got the second biggest shock of her life when her maternal grandpa passed away within a couple of years of her mother's untimely demise. The third rude awakening to the harsh & cruel world struck her like a lightning when her father abandoned her completely for a sleazy woman with chequered history.

However, despite all the evil spells during her tender age, the author has been able to muster up enough courage to face the world - to brazenly take up any challenge life poses on her. Despite being an innocent little girl with big dreams and ambitions, the author faces many untoward incidents routinely, primarily arising out of covetousness towards her by some. Her grandma, uncle and aunt on her mother's side try to protect her to the best of their abilities from all evil souls; they all are confident that the author will shine in her career someday soon

– she'll continue to be the great human being that she always has been. Her impeccable mannerism and politeness mesmerize all who knows her.

It can be claimed that the young author may be disparate from many kids in the sense that she attained mental maturity at an early age. She has made her best conscious efforts to jot down remarks in this book apropos of the circumstances only – offending others or insulting anyone is not her habit and is beyond her traits. Some of her statements and deliberations in her causerie about political or other persons are full of jokes, hyperbole, intentional disregard of linguistic and stylistic norms – she left room for the readers of the novel to read between the lines and make their own assertions.

It may be noted that the first book written by the author was a grand success, with many copies sold across continents. However, the royalties received by the author was a meagre percentage of sales, as per terms and conditions of the publisher. Therefore, efforts are now being made to ensure that some reasonably fair amount of royalties are received this time, by publishing with Amazon Kindle Direct, so that more revenues can be generated from sales of the book, which can further be channelized towards deserving orphanages and NGOs. The author believes in being a change agent herself in her continuous strive towards improvement, excelling in life and to contribute whatever little towards society.

As was promised in writing through her first book, the author hereby is making the same exact pledge for this novel too; all sale proceeds received from the sale of this book during the current year, will be donated to social causes through established charitable organisations, benefitting under-privileged kids.

At the outset, the author wants to thank all her readers and patrons for supporting her just cause, in whatever manner they deemed fit – she hopes to garnish the same patronage and support for this novel, as in past. Any kinds of suggestions or comments are welcome, to be sent directly to the author at bhatumukherjee@yahoo.com - all correspondences will be acknowledged.

<u>Outline</u>

Kolkata (erstwhile Calcutta) is the capital and heart of State of West Bengal - it is a lifeline to many places around Bengal. It used to be India's capital under the British Raj; it is believed by some that this great city was founded by East India Trading Company as a trading post.

Kolkata is commonly referred to as City of Joy, with rich culture, deep-rooted traditions, grand colonial architecture, enriched history, spectacular art galleries, ethical societies – the City may be termed as a hub of education, business, science and technology, fairs, commerce, agriculture, and various activities. The Port of Kolkata is India's oldest operating port, located on the east bank of the Hooghly River, about 47 miles west of Bangladesh. Kolkata is widely regarded as the cultural capital of India.

It is a City that is very famous for initiation of the freedom movement in India, which eventually led to ousting of British government from India. Many legends and heroes of not only the freedom struggle, but also almost all walks of life, were born in this great city.

A religiously and ethnically diverse centre of culture, literature, film, theatre, music, dance and performing arts, Kolkata culture features idiosyncrasies that include a distinctive feature which separates itself from most other cities – close-knit neighbourhoods and freestyle intellectual exchanges, which are respectively termed as 'para' and 'adda' locally.

There was a time when it was customary for guys, young and old, to hang out together and organize festivals, etc. in their neighbourhoods and compete with others, be it through Pujas or cultural programs or otherwise. The same group or a different one, consisting of guys from all ages will assemble at a pre-set place every evenings and weekend mornings, typically near some tea stalls, to discuss issues pertaining not only to their own city, but also of every place known to them in earth, with everyone rendering their opinions on matters of politics, sports, education, commerce, films, and what not!

If you are a mute spectator, you would wonder if global decisions are made at this level on every possible issue related to Homo sapiens! Everyone seemed to be at top of the issues they discussed, which may entail anything and everything going on out there – most of the folks there would appear to be experts in analysing, criticizing or just being vocal at everything, irrespective of the fact that they might not be knowing anything in real sense!

People from Kolkata originally are hooked on to their chosen football clubs that they feel a part of – either East Bengal or Mohan Bagan, or in case of a particular community, Mohammedan Sporting. As a matter of fact, Kolkata is said to be the birthplace of football (soccer) in India. Fans of those clubs still clash with each other despite being century-old arch rivals. The spectators' vigour, exuberance and energy at any football match held in the City are worth noting, to be rarely found in other cities.

When it comes to football, even a guy who never played the game will offer his expert advice on strategies and game plans, at his para adda circle. This adda will not only involve football but will most definitely encircle all areas of life – including some incidents in far-away places that they have actually never been to! An illiterate guy with no education will tender his opinion on big scandals like Watergate, 2G, Bofors or Commonwealth Games in New Delhi (from what has been preached by mentors in some political group he is affiliated with).

A typical Bengali office Babu with a permanent government job (who may be routinely habituated in taking bribes from general public) will offer the best form of advice on corporate governance, at those addas! A phoochka wala vending on the street will discuss matters pertaining to rocket science, with no inhibitions! A guy manufacturing 'hooch' (illegally made country liquor) will try telling you what's really going on with Trump administration!

Street food and street-side vending in Kolkata can easily claim the top prize around the world in terms of variety, tastes, prices and availability. Many foreigners and dignitaries from around the world love the street food here, although they may not be very hygienically prepared – but, it will certainly satisfy your taste buds, thus regaling on anyone's humble fare!

Hawkers and peddlers encroaching pavements is the biggest problem in infrastructural development of the city, which are typically ignored for vote bank politics. Vehicles emitting carbon poison can easily be seen plying through the roads, despite the city recording poorest level of Air Quality Index over recent period; as a result, Kolkata tops the chart of cities with poor AQI consecutively.

Racing and over-taking contests that are routinely engaged by private buses, min-buses and auto-rickshaws in and around Kolkata kills and injures thousands of people each year. Administration and police personnel may be busy hatching or counting their eggs, instead of taking corrective actions - those vehicles pollute more air every day and kill more people through accidents in this beautiful city.

The incredible growth in population, migration from other states and countries, the scenario of global economy and drastic rise in consumption (all clumped together by scientists around the world to coin a term – the Great Acceleration), had a drastic impact not only for Kolkata, but also have altered our Earth's ecosystem and intrinsic system in a period of merely five or six decades.

Despite some positives resulting out of this (like increasing lifespans and a sharp rise in middle-class segments), this leap has come at a huge cost – especially in terms of loss of biodiversity, which should raise some serious bells, due to the fact that biodiversity is an essential element of survival of any life forms in earth. Human colonisation and expansion are stretching our Mother Nature too thin, thus jeopardising our biodiversity.

Bio capacity, which is measured in terms of global hectares, is an ability of an ecosystem to renew itself; on the other hand, ecological footprint is a measure of our consumption of natural resources. These two factors accounted together, allow us to compute whether humanity is living within the means and resources of our planet. Bio capacity has increased by around 30% during the past five decades, with the advent of new technology and improved land management systems around the globe.

However, Biodiversity has been going down drastically since the 70's The largest contribution to ecological footprint has been identified as carbon emissions from fossil fuel burning, followed by other threats like destruction of grazing land for animals, deforestation, excessive fishing, large-scale farming and land-conversion; all these contribute together for extinction and destruction of many species including birds, mammals, amphibians, plants, corals, etc. – if not controlled globally starting right now, those will have adverse effect on us.

Kolkata is no exception to the above, still contributing to global warming at an alarming rate, with carbon emissions by vehicles and machines in and around the city, increased toxic fumes in the industrial belts, coupled with problems associated with burning of leaves, wastes, etc. While the wonderful city is currently vying for a UNESCO Heritage tag, showcasing the Central and North Kolkata for its rich history, more emphasis should be laid by all concerned not to destroy the city.

It used to be a great centre of business and life before we got our Independence from the British Raj. Following Independence, the City suffered several decades of economic stagnation, although it used to be a hotbed of modern education, science, culture and politics amongst others, especially during pre-Independence period.

Closure of industries still haunt the city big time, as industrialists are denied free hand by all the local governments that were ever elected in power, with no exception – all of them want vested interests to make undue gains out of any industry which sets foot here, turning the industrialists frustrated. Now, it has ridiculously come to the point where fried brinjals & fried onions sold at every neck of the woods are surprisingly being termed as cottage industries, apparently to shift public attention to the epic problem created by the vacuum!

Durga Puja festivals across Kolkata and the adjoining areas are renowned all over the world; this festival is now vying for a UNESCO World Heritage tag for intangible heritage. The Puja, that theoretically should last four or five days each September or October (depending on the Bengali calendar), extends well beyond the actual dates of Pujas; it has turned to be spearheading into crowd-pulling competitions amongst various organisers of Pujas.

The entire city is illuminated and glows beautifully at night times – crores of people assemble in the City from all over, for pandal hopping, deriving pleasure, and having unlimited enjoyment during the days of the festivities. The immersion of Goddess Durga along with her children on River Ganges (or other rivers, depending on the venue of the Puja and proximity to waterbodies), lakes around the City is mindboggling.

It was a very noble idea of the state administration to showcase this event during the last few years through a procession held at Red Road on a specified date, where tourists and locals flock together to get a glimpse of the procession. There are also other festivals and other pujas celebrated round the year, some hosted in lavish manner, others in less extravagant manner, varying with budgeted expenses and potential for revenue generation of the local puja committees and paras.

Some organizers of Pujas and other festivities in Kolkata spend millions of rupees over just a few days; they turn it into a fiasco with glamorous cultural programs, etc. thus spending crores of rupees they have collected. Officially, collections are made through subscriptions and donations from local residents and business organisations conducting businesses there. However, it is a well-known fact that a bulk of the chunk comes through extortion and muscle-flexing from affluent sections & businesses, whereas the other huge chunk is derived through blessings of local MLA, MP (who in turn, pressurizes others to pitch-in). Political donations to festivities have been a boon to many of those organisers in recent days. The amount of money spent on those festivities could easily feed all the hungry or starving kids out on the streets of Kolkata year-round! But vote bank politics and polarisation takes the front seat.

It is quite strange that the current administration benevolently contributes to financial welfare of a certain 'privileged' section, through grants to local clubs, flurry of donations to associations whose members are affiliated with ruling party, ad hoc payments to certain sections, etc. On the flip side, the administration appears to adopt an apathetical attitude towards people who may be in dire need of funds – the economically disadvantaged sections! Very little are being done to eradicate our primary social evil – poverty. It appears that whoever do not have voting rights are not entitled to benefits or care. Who's going to say that those people have fundamental rights too?

Kolkata is home to Kolkata Knight Riders, an IPL franchise - Eden Gardens revives its old spirits and switch the city to festive moods during the times that cricket matches are played here. Billions of rupees are also spent on IPL matches across the country where some people die out of hunger still now!

Amongst the hundreds of places of interests in and around Kolkata, some are located on the south, some on the outskirts, while most are on the central and northern sides. One can easily spend five to six days in the city to catch a glimpse of their most favourite destinations - Google Maps contain various pertinent information and reviews of all those places, which can be readily accessed by travellers to plan their itineraries around Kolkata.

Another fascinating feature of Kolkata is its availability of multi-specialty clinics, professionals and shops on almost all corners of streets of Kolkata – starting from chiropractor and physiotherapists (especially around Princep Ghat, where some of those people will torment your full body with their technical know-how!), dentists (tooth-extraction on pavement nary the most hygienic atmosphere), hair-dressers and beauticians (vendors functioning as barbers, sitting along pavements), shoe-polish, umbrella-repairs, key-makers, stamp-sellers, astrologers, indigenous ice-cream vendors, all the way to podiatrists (clipping of nails, etc.) and advocates (practising on street-sides under make-shift chambers adjacent to courthouses) – all kinds of expert advices and services may be availed right on the streets! Where else can anyone find those?

On a serious note, streets of Kolkata have been beautified and improved substantially in recent times, although the quality of repairs and patchwork done on the roads are really shabby and inferior in terms of quality. Many useful flyovers and bridges have been constructed in order to ease the flow of traffic, but poor maintenance and lack of proper inspection have resulted in devastating collapses of some of the bridges, killing many and injuring more. In addition, any collapse of a flyover or a bridge has chain-saw effect on commuters and general public, due to the fact that bureaucratic red-tapes and corruptive practices prolong the renovation and repair processes, thereby making commuters and other people's daily lives miserable, painful and stressful.

Subways (referred as metro in common terms) below the streets of Kolkata make life easy for lakhs of commuters and passengers throughout the city, although there have been some concerns in areas of fire-safety and attempted suicidal bids many times. The City of Joy is full of multiplexes, shopping centres, malls and outlets of international brands, spread across the city, and fine dining restaurants, fast food restaurants and renowned franchisee outlets make the city a shopper's paradise as well as a toothsome destination.

However, incipient scandals have erupted where dead animals' meat were procured from wastelands by certain sections of crooked profit-minded evil people, which were subsequently sold to many outlets and restaurants in the city, some of which included branded restaurant chains – thus thwarting the real progress of Kolkata; maybe, turning it into a hell for innocent bystanders and commoners. And not surprisingly, many culprits arrested in those ghastly acts were subsequently released on bail, and some are even back on the streets, thus countermanding public health and judiciary actions.

Another burning problem very typical with the City of Joy (entir
West Bengal, to be precise) is the violence that comes hand in hand with
be that a local Panchayat election when a bulk percentage of seats
uncontested (due to the apparent claim of ruling party with asperity
failure of opposition parties to field their candidates, either because of
ruling party members, or physical harm & property-damage of anyone
field candidates for the opposition), or Assembly or Parliamentary el
anyone dares to file nomination, they would immediately ransack the
houses or kidnap their loved ones, in order to force the candidate to wit
nomination within a circadian cycle of 24 hours; thereafter, the candid
be described as fogey or valetudinarian or otherwise, to avoid public in

Media gets unduly coerced or economically influenced (through
advertisements of 'projects' which would never materialise, or through
yapping of 'achievements') – thus, the matter will never surface event

Local goons and musclemen backed by ruling party footle aroun
fair & peaceful voting, as a stratagem to induce booth-jamming, r
forced voting! If Election Commission of India take a stringent actio
party will cry foul play, thus trying to draw public sympathy, musing
others should join in their fight against the constitutional body (althoug
can be ephemeral to last)! They may believe in 'Qui perd gagne!
translated as 'loser take all' with some show of hypomnesia, as l
memory isn't meant to daunt them serving their purposes!

Elections in even local school or college committees are not sp
not to mention elections in corporations or local statutory bodies – :
election is marred by non-ending violence in Bengal, which is kind c
the state. Many people die, more people are wounded, and even mor
properties due to vandalism or organised crime. Police authorities ci
primarily because they are not allowed to work independently, which
fundamental problem in the whole country.

Kolkata Police used to be revered as one of the top-most law enforcement ncies in the world, ranking next to Scotland Yard. However, their functioning ecent periods may make them look ridiculous in public eyes – they cannot n protect their own yards. Police stations are attacked by mob backed by ruling ty rowdies, when police officers were seen hiding under their desks or crying loud, through national television channels! Some of their top brass were seen ying the role of servants to the supremo of the ruling party, which is a real me for such educated and meritorious candidates of Indian Police Service. ny top bureaucrats also give away their pride and self-respect to become a y' to various half-educated, stumblebum and lummox ministers of states, who 't even belong there! Fearing transfers to less lucrative assignments, many of se bureaucrats give in to unfair demands of their 'superiors', thus exposing r backboneless traits!

Be that as it may, Kolkata is the pride of Bengal and to some extent, to the ntry - its streets are holding up its reputation pretty well, despite certain dents and lapses on the part of administrative bodies. Boom barriers were lled at huge costs at some intersections like Exide more, which became nct within a span of a year- but the City is booming and let's hope that it will.

And so, will its wonderful and vibrant streets for years to come. Amidst ical slugfest and educational drains, backed by unemployment, lack of proper thcare and real development, the streets of Kolkata will definitely spring back here it was, in the same fashion as the streets have always done in the past!

The impetus and onus will be on us, the commoners and everyone else, to l up and make our streets less clumsy, less risky and less unhygienic – so that ext generation can breathe fresh air, walk and commute more safely, enjoy hospitality trademarked to Kolkata only, drink pure water, eat edible & enic food, rest properly and maintain peace across the horizon   - so that all njoy a better life in general.

Each one of us are responsible for upkeep and development of our streets; we can begin by not spitting or dirtying or publicly urinating on streets! We can pave in change by acting as change agents, so that the younger generations do not blame us to have caused irreparable damages to their future! Let's all be responsible and accountable to the society in general.

Backdrop

Streets of Kolkata are culturally woven into the own fabric of City Of Joy, presenting a rich and diverse history of yesteryears. It is often claimed that Kolkata lives on its streets! The city unfolds many stories through its streets – the chaotic cacophony of hawkers, vehicles and pedestrians mixed with errant auto-rickshaw drivers, and carefree attitude of bus drivers honking incessantly – all these make one wonder if it is truly a reflection of the rich Bengali culture and tradition. Bengali people used to be renowned as peace-loving, sober and educated with extremely rich cultural & social past.

Aroma of typical Bengali fries and roadside phoocka-walas and jhaal-muri walas remain there for ages; it is rightly said that anyone can fall in love with varieties of street-side food in Kolkata, which is also known as the City of Joy.

According to some, the name Kolkata, formerly known as Kalikata, later changed to Calcutta, was originally derived from the word Kalikshetra (place of Goddess Kali, located in Kalighat). The city has various sobriquets like Cultural capital of the country, City of Palaces, Land of Joy, City of Processions, and more lately, City of Dharnas (Metro Channel now being a hotspot for staging dharnas by ruling party, typically denied to oppositions)!

Kolkata has always intrigued visitors with its never-ending charm, warmth, affection, rich cultural heritage and even as breeding ground for national movements. The streets of Kolkata have been able to shine in glory over the years -it is a melting pot of tradition, rich heritage, glory and modernity. The streets have impeccably adopted to changing times and needs, camouflaging itself as much as possible, to present its vibrant colours to outsiders.

There are innumerable streets and lanes in Kolkata, some very popular and some little known. Amongst the most famous ones are Dalhousie Square (Binay Badal Dinesh Bag, or in short BBD Bag), Park Street, Camac Street, Chowringhee

Road or Jawaharlal Nehru Road, Alipore, Strand Road, Barrack pore Trunk Road, Grand Trunk Road, College Street, New Market, Shyambazar, Maniktala, Burra Bazar, Gariahat, Hatibagan, Free School Street, Park Circus, etc. With modernisation and expansion, Salt Lake, New Town, Rajarhat, Garia, Kasba, Jadavpur, Eastern Metropolitan Bypass, Behala, Howrah and Ultadanga and other places have cropped up as popular destinations.

With population explosion, many chose to move out to fringes and outskirts of the City – thus, places like Joka, Sonarpur, Baruipur, Barrackpore, Dum Dum, Barasat and adjoining areas have flourished over the recent years. The famous Park Street located at the heart of the city, still commands highest footfalls, excepting busy railway stations like Sealdah, Howrah, etc. and the business districts.

Park Street is not only popular amongst foodies and party-mongers but is also a very busy office para and lovers' paradise. Restaurants and resto-bars here truly international in essence – one can find the old joints like Trincas, Peter Cat, Kwality, Moulin Rogue, Mogambo, et al dancing in sync with modern joints like Barbeque Nation, Flurry's, Marco Polo, Don Giovanni's, Paris Café, Carpe Diem, Hard Rock Café, Burgrill, Mamagoto, Olypub, Starbucks, KFC, What's In D Name, Arsalan, 1000 BC, Hakuna Matata, Domino's, Wattle Wallah, The Bridge and Someplace Else at Park Hotel, London Bubble Co. – amongst a host of other popular restaurants.

During Christmas and New Year's Eve, Park Street becomes a hot destination for locals and tourists alike. Carols playing in various places, lighting and illumination in and around all the structures as well as on the streets, hustle and bustle of moving traffic, hundreds of street vendors; massive crowd, young and old – all flock to Park Street especially during evening and night hours. It is practically a street that never sleeps. Cops there manage traffic and pedestrians equally well during rush hours, although there are always an element of rotten egg spoiling the basket. Park Street is also visited by celebrities, the rich and famous of Kolkata, as also by commoners, and this unique blend makes this place a little different.

Another hot spot in the City is College Street – apart from the fact that the famous Indian Coffee House and several reputed institutions of higher learning are located here, it is also a place for bookworms; the book stores here can match or even exceed any expectations of book lovers around the globe. One can find any book here with the ease of buying new or used versions - one can spend days here just browsing through the wide collections of books and magazines.

Places like Gariahat, Shyambazar, Maniktala, Hatibagan, and Burra Bazar (wholesale market, specifically Nandram Market), Chandni Chowk (electronics and appliances), Bow Bazar (ornaments and other items), New Market etc. are shoppers' paradise. The only factor shoppers need to consider while shopping in any of these famous markets is their bargaining skills – although there may be signs posted in any shop that it's a one-price shop, but one needs to keep bargaining for lower prices; this is typical of India and more specifically, of Kolkata. Although some shops in metro cities throughout India are likely to rip customers off with any chance they get, but Kolkata has evolved to be on the top of such notoriety, with influx of few unscrupulous traders from other states.

It's a true wonder how some of the streets of Kolkata have metamorphosed themselves from being somewhat dreaded places just a few decades ago, to places of interests and tourist attractions now. To name just a few, James Long Sarani (a lifeline for residents in and around Behala now) used to be infested with criminals and anti-socials even as late as in the 1980's – nobody could venture out in the evening on the stretch of road connecting Joka and Chowrasta; even taxi-drivers used to refuse passengers blatantly if the destination was anyplace past Behala Tram Depot.

Vast stretches of vacant low-lying lands there gradually gave in to promoters and developers for converting those lands to homestead, as people started to move in gradually there – at present, most properties in those areas sell at prime rates. Pailan and Amtala used to be totally villages, and now who could tell that foxes and wild animals used to roam free there just as late as early 1990s!

Speaking of central Kolkata, the distinguished street connecting Jawaharlal Nehru Road and Park Circus, known as the famous Park Street, used to be mostly burial grounds for Kolkata's Muslim and Christian population just a century ago. Other than St. Xavier's College, a shopping mall named Hall & Anderson, Magnolia Ice-Cream Parlour, few night clubs and Asiatic Society, there were nothing much there.

The heritage place which defines fine dining and upscale living these days used to be a name associated only with few elite classes who took a great pride walking down the streets there; this famous street of Kolkata has managed to retain its original flavour among the elite and upper middle-class people, as well as enthusiasts, party-lovers, night-club frequenters and office-goers.

The entire stretch of land past Golpark in South Kolkata used to be jungles, where military camps were set up by the British, primarily in the area where Rabindra Sarobar is located. Dhakuria Bridge was built in the late 60's connecting Ballygunge with southern fringes like Jadavpur, Garia, etc. As late as during the 80's, prime places like Santoshpur, Sonarpur and Baruipur were undeveloped with very little infrastructure. The Eastern Metropolitan Bypass used to be dumping ground for solid wastes - now it is the lifeline of the City, connecting VIP Road with far-away places like Canning and Sunderbans.

There are a bundle of tourist attractions in and around Kolkata - places like Victoria Memorial, Indian Museum, Birla Planetarium, Maidan, Fort Williams, Princep Ghat, Dalhousie Square, Chandni Chawk, New Market, Park Street are all located within a few square kilometres' area, well connected through the subway system, popularly known as Metro, as well as public transportation and private taxis. In the southern section of the City, Kalighat is one of the prime tourist attractions, where Goddess Kali's temple is located. One can take Metro to the next stop at Rabindra Sarobar, which has great waterbodies and walking trail - one can spend half a day taking a serene stroll along the Lake area, watching migratory birds or just playing or sitting idle.

The next station is Tollygunge, where the renowned film studios are located. After that, Metro runs all the way to the outskirts of south-eastern Kolkata. Commuters' from all across the places have found great ease in travelling to and fro work, business or otherwise through the regularly operating metro trains.

In the northern part of the City, more heritage and culturally diverse sites like College Street, Beadon Street, Shyambazar, Tala Tank (used to be the only source of drinking water for Kolkatans in the past), Sovabazar, Maniktala and Sealdah are located. The northern part is more congested than the southern part of Kolkata, mainly due to the fact that people started building houses in Kolkata during the initial periods of industrialisation here.

Heritage places like the house of Rabindra Nath Tagore (Jorasanko), Swami Vivekananda (Simla), Shri Ramakrishna and abodes of stalwarts of India's revolution in the fields of education, culture, spiritual and freedom-movement are mostly located in North Kolkata. Bankim Chandra (the great Bengali novelist) also used to live in north Kolkata.

Few exceptions to the above are Mother House (St. Teresa), house of Netaji Subhas Chandra Bose (real unsung hero of India's freedom from British rule), house of Mahanayak Uttam Kumar (now converted into a bungalow) are located in Central Kolkata and adjacent areas.

Streets of Kolkata have metamorphosed into quite accessible and infrastructural developments over the years, as foreign cars have replaced futon gaaris (horse carriage vans) and electric buses are taking over pre-historic buses and trams. However, trams plying through Red Road are still considered a major tourist attraction - the journey is quite an experience. Red Road is the place where Republic Day parades and other important events like Immersion Procession (Durga Puja) takes place.

The famous East Bengal Club, Mohun Bagan Club and Md. Sporting Club are all located here, within walking distances, and so is Eden Gardens, which houses maximum capacity of crowd. Kolkata High Court and Netaji Indoor Stadium are located very close, along with Raj Bhawan (Governor's House), GPO (Head Post Office in Kolkata), Customs House, Fairley Place, Writer's Building and Lalbazar (Headquarters of Kolkata Police) are all situated in close proximity.

Boat-ride along Ganges or just a simple walk along the banks of Hooghly River will definitely be worthwhile for anyone, especially in the evening, with Howrah Bridge and Vidyasagar Setu well-lit; the beautiful Millennium Park on the other side provides entertainment for all ages. These places have seen much lesser crime these days, thanks to the safety and precautionary measures adopted by the current local administration.

There are hundreds of popular destinations in and around Kolkata - some of them are Belur Math, Dakshineswar Temple, Kashipur Uddyan Bati, et al on northern fringes, and Swaminarayan Temple, Diamond Harbour, Ganga Sagar, Bakkhali, Raichak, etc. on the south-western fringes and beyond. The famous Tarakeswar Temple, Maithon Dam, Bakreswar, and other attractions are hours' drive from the City, and so are the renovated beaches of Digha, the gorgeous hills of Darjeeling, as also other wonderful sites in North Bengal like Dooars, Kalimpong, Alipurduar, Jayanti, Jaldapara, Hasimara and various wild life sanctuaries spread all over North Bengal. The home to Royal Bengal Tigers, that is Sunderbans, can also be toured either by private vehicles and vessels, or through conducted tours by Govt. Of West Bengal for a day or two.

As a matter of fact, Government of West Bengal has revamped and redefined tourism in the State by various positive measures - the package tours offered by West Bengal Tourism Department to many places of importance in an efficient, safe and enjoyable manner have really picked up lately. Bookings can be made online to any place like Sunderbans, Murshidabad, Jhargram and beyond. Accommodations are provided in reasonably clean and safe resorts and hotels, food is hygienic, tour guides describe relevant points; no nuisances are tolerated by the authorities.

In the same token, many lapses have been noticed through inactions by inept politicians and some of their 'pet' administrators in Kolkata in recent days. There have been too many incidents of bridge collapses in Kolkata lately, which may be result of a complete failure of the statutory bodies in terms of inspection, maintenance and up keeping – dereliction of duties and politicisation of vendors and contractors may be couple of the causes behind such gross negligence - a surprising comment from a MoS, after Majerhat Bridge collapsed some time back, as to the ownership of agencies under him, makes one wonder how efficient some of these people in power really are!

Be that is it may, it is often debated if our streets are wide enough to capacity at current levels. It is hardly argued if we should focus on using environment-friendly means of communication, more and often, than cluttering our streets with trillions of carbon-emitting vehicles. There are many households these days where each member of the household has one or more cars at their disposal – can't they think of carpool or any alternate means like sharing app cabs to work or any other destinations?

Kolkata has been already on top of the chart of maximum level of pollution amongst any major city in the country – our AQI has been alarming. But we still see vehicles plying on roads emitting black smoke. Many Pollution Control centres use unholy means to issue fit certificates to vehicles – they should be closely monitored, and strict disciplinary actions should be taken against any offender. Let's think more about our children for a moment, and let's gift them the most precious gift any parent can give – the gift of healthy life!

Factories, waste dump yards and cowsheds have been moved way beyond city perimeters, thankfully. But do we act in a cohesive manner to ensure that we don't dirty our streets? We go to clean lakes, waterbodies and even rivers and oceans, and dump plastics on it, either willingly or as part of rituals. Is it right? Guess so!

Before we blame the governments and our machineries, we need to make sure that all of us are doing our own part right. If I can't change people, why can't I change myself and be a leader by example? What if each one of us do some introspection with brooding over the adverse repercussions if we don't act timely – before it is too late to change for betterment of mankind? Let's resolve and act fast; if we can't change someone, let's try to be a change agent ourselves and lead by example!

Streets of Kolkata – The Novel

It was little past six in the evening on a wintry night near Princep Ghat, not very far from the busy hustling and bustling Esplanade, Dalhousie or Park Street areas of Kolkata. The taxi driver in his late thirties stopped there briefly to get some fresh air and detox his mind from what he had experienced minutes before, on Strand Road – he had to drop a dying woman in her mid-nineties near a shanty there, as she had apparently no other places to go!

Diana was her name, as the taxi driver recalled. She appeared to be on the brink of geezer hood; despite her apparent senility, she didn't forget to pay for her trip – she took out a very expensive purse she was carrying with her to pay the fare, before she leaped towards the shanty in a mysterious fashion; he wasn't willing to leave her there; but being a law-abiding citizen, the taxi driver realised that it was a 'no parking zone' – so, he had to leave the spot quickly without any hue and cry. After all, Kolkata Police was ostensibly reputed to be very efficient in collecting paybacks lickety-split, for any opportunity they got!

He didn't forget to stop at the nearby traffic kiosk of Kolkata Police; within minutes after Diana got off his cab, he stopped at the kiosk to inform the officer on duty there about a very sick and frail elderly woman, possibly hailing from a very affluent background, who insisted on getting dropped off in front of a shabby shanty minutes from there – the taxi driver sought his help. Sadly, the officer rudely asked him to leave law and order matters to the Police; he asked the taxi driver to vacate the spot immediately - so, he had no option but to leave with a heavy heart. However, he decided to make a stop at Princep Ghat to catch an air of fresh breath, in order to cool down his mind – he was absolutely perplexed, shaken and traumatised by what transpired in his cab that evening.

The cab driver had picked Diana up from Tollygunge around five pm, when a middle-aged man hired his taxi, to transport his mother to her daughter's house located in Kidderpore – the passenger, Diana later told the cab driver that the gentleman who hired the cab was her son; since she had already spent a month with her son in Tollygunge, she was travelling to her daughter's house in Kidderpore, because she had to rotate her stays between her son and daughter each month - it was too much for either of them to handle her expenses, etc.!

The taxi driver didn't forget to ask Diana why she wanted to get dropped in that dark and dirty area, when she was in such pain it seemed – all he got back from the old lady was a rebuke – "this was the place where I found my kids. You don't dare to call it dirty or use any bad adjective to describe it. This is my heaven…." So, the driver didn't even dare to ask further questions; he was upset a tad as his taxi didn't have air-conditioning – the lady rider seemed to be a lady from an affluent family who weren't used to travelling by non-ac vehicles. He noticed that lady was very uncomfortable in the sweltering heat.

He found a parking space near Princep Ghat on the other side (area designated for holding rituals by the banks of Ganges); so, he pulled over, locked the taxi, went down the stairs leading to the river, and put water on his face – he needed to calm down after he got a hunch that something big was amiss with his last passenger!

She looked so gorgeous, seemed to be a lady from high society, with impeccable mannerism, so soft-spoken – she even asked him while they were stuck at a traffic jam (with processions from a political party causing bottleneck on the road) if he ever read any article on streets of Kolkata in newspaper – this was after the cab driver told her that he was a literate person who couldn't find a suitable job, resulting in picking up his profession as a driver; however, he was an avid reader of the same newspaper that the lady was referring to!

The lady seemed to be a putative author of few books, as he guessed during their intermittent conversation during the ride! He felt rueful and somewhat deprecatory about her children's disdainful attitude to their aged mother at that stage. Maybe that was usual with the moneyed, hoity-toity privileged class – he exclaimed after splashing water all over his head, face, neck and arms. The Ganges water was hallowed as a holy, cleansing river – so, he could not wet his feet, although he needed it to heal his accumulated pain and penitent looks.

He let his breath out in a long exhalation of relief from his heavy chest, especially as he looked so contrite that some people there known to him relented – he was almost a regular there, stopping in between his trips to purify his soul and body from the daily torment he had to put up with during his trips. Many passengers did wrong things in his cab, most of which he used to protest; some he couldn't protest, if the passengers flexed their muscles claiming to be associated with the ruling political party! It seemed all rowdy young men at that time were affiliated with the ruling party, as they derived many unholy benefits through such association. So, he had to endure the abuses, for which he later felt conscience-stricken over his sheepish silence.

Yes, heaven it seemed to Diana alias Di at that point, after the hell she had been through during the last several hours, especially with her adopted son and daughter arguing over phone to force their frail mother on each other's custody for few more days.

Her son insisted that he had already fulfilled his obligation by letting Di stay (by enslaving his mother, in other words) for a month - now it was his sister's turn to take care of her for the next month. Her daughter was yelling at the top of her voice that she was going to attend a very important party that evening - she couldn't leave her sick mother at home unattended for hours! What if she died at her custody – the whole world will accuse her….

Diana's son, Subir screamed at his sister, Mary: "why can't you tell your daughter to stay back with mom while you're attending the darn party?" Mary replied that her daughter Ruby needed to go out with her friends for their own party at the same time; the quarrel never ended – it seemed that Di was a becoming a burden on her children; the very same children she loved and cared for throughout her life! Maybe she was better off dying, rather than facing the routine feud by her children as to who should be obligated to perform for Di!

Di couldn't blame Subir as he was taking his family for a vacation to Andaman for a week - there would've been no one else in the house to take care of her medicines, food, etc. Mary on the other hand, could not be blamed either as she had her program arranged in advance; she even forgot that Di would be arriving that evening. It was her own fate that had to be blamed, Diana felt.

As there were no one present in the shanty she entered either, Di decided to sit down on the guard rail next to the shanty; but she couldn't – she fell down on the street; although she suffered some minor injuries, but she managed to slowly crawl inside the shanty. She was too weak in mind and body, both!

The front portion was stuffed with kitsch knick-knacks, little & dirty aluminium utensils, torn clothes, modest but gilt ornaments – the floor was a palimpsest of rugs, torn pieces of clothes, used dirty clothes and broken pieces of old furniture. A malodorous and fetid smell was emanating from the place, with foul smell of urine and human defecation or feculence from someplace else in close proximity – it was murky, nebulous, although the other side of the small, crudely built shack appeared crepuscular.

Di laid down on her back on the grungy floor – such a venerable statesman, charismatic and energetic, exalted and eminent personality – she had to take comfort in wherever she was lying! She was a very malleable and pliant lady with lots of class – she learnt from her childhood days how to be adaptive of every possible situation in life; so, she didn't mind!

After all, that place seemed to be where she apparently got a new life years ago. As she rested her head on the guard rail on the back of the shanty wall, Diana started hallucinating - seeing stars in her eyes, with numbness of shoulders and excruciating pain on her chest. She felt thirsty, but there was no water around – her vision became blurry and her thought process started wandering off to the time she can remember when she first met Mary – her loving adopted daughter.

Around forty years back, it was a beautiful summer morning when Mary was playing at the same place Di was laying down, with a ragged doll her mother collected from a nearby dumpster for her – Mary was about three years old. Her mother used to be beautiful, although it was extremely difficult to visualise that, based on her ragged and torn clothes, wrapped around her body just enough to cover herself from praying eyes.

Diana had just returned from USA after spending nearly four decades there – she was a very renowned anchor of a world-famous news TV channel. She got fed up living an elite life there and wanted to return back to India to do something for the underprivileged kids back home, who often didn't even get two square meals a day. She was a venerable statesman with lots of wisdom and vast experience.

She was in her late fifties by then – she had seen the best that life had to offer to any fortunate person in this world, with chauffeur–driven latest model of Mercedes, two Porsche and a Lamborghini parked at her driveway, a palatial house spread over acres of land with sixteen bedrooms, a private golf course, a helipad and three gigantic swimming pools. Eight people were employed by Diana who took care of horses, gardening, maintenance of golf course, pools and house – her mansion used to be frequented by celebrities - she had six security guards working round the clock in shifts for her.

Di used to hire choppers whenever she wanted to fly to the nearest airport, in order to avoid congestion in traffic. Her employer used to take care of all her travel expenses, right from arranging first-class tickets in premier airlines for her, to accommodations in five star hotels whenever she used to travel for business – other times, she will have her employer's car pick her up and drop her back as per her show timings. The fat pay cheque that she earned from her job kept adding funds to her savings, as her allowances took care of almost all other expenses. She was in fact a millionaire in terms of her vastly accumulated wealth; she was living a life most people could possibly dream of!

However, unlike some of the rich and famous around, Diana always made sure that she spent enough on kids' welfare and charity - she did donate regularly to various charitable organisations of repute and participated in many fund-raising events for many of them routinely. She was a single working lady; she chose to remain single after some failed attempts in her younger years to settle down with someone she could trust her heart with – alas, she couldn't find anyone meeting her standards in terms of in-built quality.

Although she had dated few guys here and there but gave up on them. Di had her mind set to concentrate on building her career – she always wanted to be a noble, kind-hearted and supportive lady who could do something for the society in general.

At that time, Diana felt the urge to give it back to the society what God had bestowed upon her. Although she always got involved in social causes right from her childhood, but she felt that the homeless children she used to see on the streets of Kolkata during her childhood days, needed her the most. So, she decided to sell off everything she had acquired over years, all her movable and immovable properties, and return back to India.

It didn't go well initially upon her emigrating back though – some people thought that she returned back to enjoy an extravagant retired life; some thought she was planning to run for political parties' nomination as a leader; some even thought that she came back to flaunt her immense wealth to everyone she knew, to gain popularity.

However, no one realised that she already could have done better with any of those in the US itself, if any of those were her true priorities. Di always preferred to maintain a low profile; thus, she chose silence rather than answering to inquisitive people about her real plans.

Initially, Diana visited some Homes for distressed children around Kolkata; she also started making financial contributions for developing infrastructure and facilities of those Homes, which were often run by NGOs (non-governmental organisations) and state-aided agencies. However, she soon discovered that many kids, especially girls were regularly tormented or physically abused by the staff and employees of many Homes, and often by people in power.

Certain officials there had vested interests - they had unholy nexus with some outsiders, and in return, extended favours to those outsiders by 'gifting' the girls for a night or two. Local police seemed to know of such unlawful activities - some media tried to bring up those illegal matters to limelight – however, with less than qualified people running the local administration in several instances, and Justice System running in snail's pace, nothing seemed to work in favour of those distressed children for good.

Diana started approaching various authorities and Commissions pleading with them to alleviate the wrongdoings and provide safe shelters to children – she found out soon that things in India were not half as transparent or fair, as in the US or in any developed countries. Despite India being a developing nation, mind-sets of some people there, especially those in power, were primitive and somewhat disgraceful.

Most people in power were either corrupt, or chose to be mute spectators – media was easily purchased through various perks and unethical dealings, the most common being big-budget advertisements accorded by those affected by any newspaper clippings or television show, to the concerned media houses who were printing/airing news about corruption involving those, in order to force them to stop circulating factual news and reports – thus, they chose to lay blind-eyes to any such corruptive practices.

Members of various Commissions were like prized seats for political party's blind supporters – they came from various facets of academic, cultural and social brilliance; most of them were kind of celebrities in their own fields, be it film stars or authors, singers, painters, social activists, dancers or performers – but, what many of them lacked was adequate skills to run their offices. With change of Bengal's political regime after a certain political party ruled or ruined West Bengal for more than three decades, a new party came into power with many promises and many colourful dreams of a new Bengal.

In reality, the only colour that emerged out of that 'change' was blue and white, as all governmental and civic buildings, bridges, roads and structures were painted blue and white. One of the leader's relative soon became a billionaire from a pauper in just few years, selling those paints to the civic bodies! More scams and shams started to pop up across the state soon after that party came into power - those scams claimed thousands of crores of rupees to the exchequer, going right from the savings accounts in banks and post offices of ordinary people to the pockets of those people running the scams, most of them being associated with the party in some way or another.

Lakhs of poor people lost their life savings to those fraudsters, aided and abetted by many Ministers and people in power, as chit funds started cropping up like mushrooms across the state, promising a return which was too good to be true. It also cost the exchequer a lot in terms of lost flow of money. It was a sordid example of bribes and scams taking over administration and local government.

The modus operandi was very simple – due to lack of proper monitoring by central institutions, anyone could venture into money market offering triple or quadruple returns within a short period of time for an investment into their 'window-dressed' operations. While most companies started working as non-banking financial institution outside the ambit of then-existing laws in real estate, others ventured into time sharing or gold or educations or shopping malls, amongst milliards of other frivolous operations.

Some started issuing preference shares and debentures to public without even registering with the regulatory bodies - SEBI or RBI; those share certificates and deeds of title were openly issued in favour of the unsuspecting depositors, right under the noses of administration; it was ludicrous that in many social or cultural gatherings hosted by owners of these chit funds, state level ministers and high ranking police officials would be guest speakers (of course with payback) – there, they would add the desired trust in the minds of the general public about the authenticity of those pyramid 'gypsies', which would entice the public to invest more in their fake companies.

Those companies would initially give a fat pay out to certain investors, only with the objective of luring them into not liquidating their positions, but instead add more to their existing investments - the dreamt or promised amount of return remained only on paper.

Lakhs of agents and intermediaries employed by these companies would entice more customers in their respective localities or circles, in return of huge amount of commission to the agents' - people known to those agents glanced at the changing affluent lifestyle, which acted as a motivation for those people to tread the path shown by those agents, who were thus entrapped as depositors.

The agents often knew themselves that the company they were procuring businesses for, won't be able to pay promised return to investors ever, because the pyramid was bound to collapse at one point; then they will have to leave their own homes, and take shelter away from their homes in order to avoid retribution. However, the fortune they will make before the collapse would attract more and more of those agents to keep on deceiving their neighbours, relatives, friends and even co-workers.

Those shady companies often offered luxury cars and other prizes to the top agents periodically; they would be often flown to some exotic location for seminars and meetings – thus, it was sort of a win-win situation for the agents. So, money market in Bengal and adjoining states became a huge national phenomenon, a sort of a leviathan, bringing in stashed cash for the perpetrators of economic offence in volumes nearing billions of rupees.

Company officials, however, knew of the imminent risks associated with those private investments very well. When there was not even a single stock which can guarantee a 300 per cent return within a short period of time, then on what basis the owners and management of those companies boldly went on collecting more and more investments from general public, assuring a return of 300% per annum?

No psychiatrist will ever be able to resolve what exactly went in the grey-matters of brains of those crooked individuals (other than pure greed), when they offered such return consistently, barring the universally accepted truth that fraud and deception were their ultimate intent.

That was especially true if one factored in the 40% or 50% agents' commission, and another 30 to 40% overhead expenses coming out of the equation of the very first year's collection! Pay-outs to administrative bodies and political parties in power were not even accounted in the above maths – so, where will the money for redemption come from when the policies matured?

Many people blamed the investors who got duped or cheated, coining them as ignoramus; they concluded that those people were more gullible than others, based on their cultural beliefs. However, in the scientific world, it's pitted against another widely believed paradigm, shaped by several counterintuitive studies that indicated that we all are equally biased, irrational and likely to fall for propaganda, sales pitches and general nonsense. Thus, many investors were shanghaied by propaganda spread in presence of ministers of states & other influential buffoon personalities, to ultimately get duped.

The inevitable happened soon - most of the agents had to flee to other states or unknown locations as soon as the spam was unearthed. Mary's biological father was an agent with one of such fraud companies, named Bishal Group of Companies.

The owner of that shabby company was a retired highly positioned CRPF officer, who used his clout to set up a chit fund which collapsed within seven years of inception - he was subsequently jailed, but millions lost their fortunes before the scam came into limelight.

He roped in his entire family into his fraudulent operations – his ailing mother, a lady of 86 years of age, was shown on the corporate records as one of the Directors; his wife who used to be a typical Bengali housewife was shown as another Director, with expertise in tea plantations (as tea plantation was one of the fronts used by the Company to siphon off illegally collected deposits).

His unemployed son-in-law was made another Director, who was put to head the bottling and packaging unit of the company, whereas no such units existed at all, except on paper! That son-in-law was just a local hooligan who had eloped with the daughter of the owner of Bishal earlier. So, Madan Chaudhuri, the owner, considered it safe to bring in that guy – he was also made a Director of Real Estate operations. The only objective of the unit was to buy as much land as possible with the duped investors' money, in the name of fictitious persons or someone distantly related to them.

One of the brothers-in-law of Madan used to work for a government agency in the past – his name was Sisir Bhaduri. Sisir was never an accomplished sportsman, although he got the coveted job in sports quota, by dint of close contacts with one of the ministers from erstwhile government. Once joining Bishal, Sisir became a Director of Legal and HR departments – there was not even a single employee under him; as a matter of fact, none of the Directors there had any employees who actually worked for them, other than on papers.

All employees of that company were clubbed in two huge rooms in an office initially located at Jadavpur, later shifting to Minto Park area – one room was full of data entry operators, who used to type in depositor's details on pre-formatted 'fake' certificates to be issued to the unsuspecting depositors. The other room was occupied by computer folks who played around with programming various false identities for the company – the remaining few in that room kept records, etc.

The main entrance at the Minto Park Office had great designs, architecture and furnishings – expensive wall paintings, chandeliers and glass-enclosed cubicles around the reception area gave it a grandeur look, especially with a very pretty receptionist with skimpy dresses.

Madan would regularly hire gorgeous young girls as his personal secretary, offering lucrative salary and attractive packages. While many of those girls innocently walked in after getting hired (the only criterion for hiring would be looks and sizes), some girls voluntarily offered their personal service to the old beast Madan. Sisir would call those girls at his chamber sometimes, on the false pretext of bringing out certain files from the cabinets, waiting anxiously for any free sneaky peek accidentally – he was in his eighties; so, he couldn't possibly do anything except fantasising!

However, Madan would take those girls to dinners alternatively, choosing as per his own whims or wild fantasy – an extravagant dinner will definitely be followed by an offer to go to a nice hotel to relax! If the girl was innocent, she will quit the job and will never even come back for her salary. Due to the intense unholy relationship Madan enjoyed with local police, no girls will dare to lodge any complaint against him.

If his female assistants were contentious, it was a different story. Madan also used to advertise on the local newspaper every now and then, looking for gorgeous young secretaries. After he was done with them, he would offer their services to his esteemed clients and highest producing agents. In a nutshell, Madan and his troop were using all kinds of unfair means to procure and increase their illegal business, enjoying life with the hard-earned money of lakhs of middle-class wage earners or sometimes, poor peasants who wanted to save for rainy days, or for their daughter's wedding, etc.

Until he got caught after one of the top companies in chit fund scam got embroiled in legal system following some hoopla, Madan engaged in all kinds of unscrupulous activities. A Company named Shraddha was duping investors all over the country, operating from Salt Lake, until the owner of the company almost became defunct trying to pay off ministers of local governments, bureaucrats and police officers. Since other states were involved in the scam, the company got busted by central authorities, following which the State had to take him in custody, fearing that he might leak out privileged information!

The duped investors filed lawsuits against Shraddha, when it became obvious that it wasn't the only company robbing investors. A hundred and twenty chit fund companies started operating in full fledge right after the change in regime in Bengal, taking advantage of the greed of some of the ministers and other people in power. Supreme Court of India had to issue a directive to CBI to unearth all chit fund scams in Bengal subsequently, and that was how Bishal also got entangled - Madan and his associates were all caught and put in jail.

However, the money that the agents had collected from public vanished – thus, agents had no other option to flee from their situs of residence, to hide from public ire. Similarly, Mary's father had to abandon his newly purchased posh bungalow and fleet of cars overnight, as he had to flee to unknown destination immediately after the pyramid scheme overturned. He was being 'shown' by police as absconding in court cases, after they got substantial sums from him as cut money – very typical of Police from Kolkata at that time!

Mary's mother was one of the innocent victims of that scam, as she got married to this guy just a year after his sprouting business with Bishal started – he promised his bride the world; little did the lady knew about her fate changing so soon. Neighbours and all depositors chased away Mary's mother with her new-born – since the lady didn't have any place to go to (her parents were deceased and she was the only child), this poor woman ended up on the streets of Kolkata with her infant girl.

Mary galumphed along beside the frail mother who was boiling some leaves for her daughter – the kid had a quick mind and a splendid gift of repartee, as she immediately asked Diana: "grandma, do you need any help?" The innocent words coming out of the kid mesmerized the veteran celebrity – she sat down!

Di was taken aback by the plight of the little girl and her young mother, after the latter narrated her daily ordeal to Diana, while the kid was playing with a stuffed animal that this rich grandma brought her. Her mom had to submit herself to a local pimp, who would get customers for her, and take half of what she earned. In addition, that pimp used to beat her up mercilessly at any opportunity he got, trying to command his control over the ill-feted girl. Diana didn't think twice before asking her to come and stay with her, so that the mother and her kid can be properly taken care of, to get out of their misery – to lead a decent life.

But alas, the ill-feted mother had contracted AIDS from her forced profession earlier - she died within a year after her beautiful daughter started a new life in Diana's house- she was hospitalised for treatment for a long time though!

Di bought a sprawling bungalow at Alipore, the place where most prominent industrialists and celebrities of Kolkata called their neighbourhood. She converted the five bedrooms and two living rooms on the ground floor into a single huge hall, with beds laid in a row on one side, and study tables and play areas on the other side. She had intended to bring home some of the distressed kids from praying hands of monsters walking on some streets of Kolkata, so that those kids can call her house as home – a safe place for them to stay, eat, play and study.

Di had no other option to exercise than forming a NGO with the help of some of her ex-colleagues back in the US, along with a few of her childhood friends at home – the authorities concerned couldn't ask her to pay any munificence or cause much hindrances, after Di was kind of forced to let them know who she was! She hated doing it, as she always liked to maintain a low-profile; but sometimes, society may take undue advantage from nice people, especially if the person returned from countries like USA, UK and the likes!

That was after her failed attempts to rescue girls from some Homes, as prevailing laws won't permit a single lady to adopt a child - the Commission for Protection of Child Rights Diana had visited multiple times failed to provide any feasible solution to her noble efforts. The officers in their legal cell were apparently law graduates; but their knowledge and application of law were not an iota better than average people with average brain – in addition, some of them were egoistic with complex mind-set. So, Diana gave up on them, and started working out a plan of her own. She named her NGO after her late mother Gita – she chose Gitalaya as its name, meaning abode of Gita!

After bringing Mary home along with her sick mother, Diana felt little gratified that she has been able to save both the infant and her mother. However, her satisfaction was short-lived, as Mary's mother died shortly, after a prolonged hospitalisation in a private nursing home adjacent to Dhakuria Bridge.

Mary did not know that this hospital had a horrible reputation; they were engaged in imprudent business practices, like many nursing homes in the City, of inflating bills and neglecting patients. Having spent nearly fifty years in the US, little did Di know that hospitals can get away with such unethical practices and more often than not, with totally unlawful activities – unreal, she exclaimed!

Upon admitting her patient there, Diana found out that one of the owners of that place (who also happened to be a practising physician), Dr. T.K. Modi was himself a crook, who allotted targets to all doctors engaged therein for minimum number of admissions on a monthly basis, pending which the doctors won't be able to collect their commissions on tests and other diagnostic procedures to which patients were tormented with routinely.

Physicians used to get around 25% commission on most diagnostic tests and treatments on top of standard commission on medicines prescribed by them.

In addition, many pharmaceutical companies offered most doctors special incentives like Europe tour (all-expense paid) if they met the target set by those companies, especially for new and overpriced medicines. Although that kind of unlawful practice had been recently prohibited, but many companies started to circumvent this in their own ways.

In that hospital in Dhakuria, Dr. Modi had successfully managed to employ two specialists, one in Oncology named B.P. Majumder and another nephrologist named B. Majumder, who specialised in deceiving helpless patients and their next of kin by prescribing tests and medications not at all required for that particular patient, but which were absolutely required to earn foreign tours and financial incentives for those doctors, as well as for Dr. Modi.

In less than three months' time, Diana ended up footing a bill of two crores for Mary's mother, who was being given a very expensive injection twice a week for eight weeks - that injection alone earned those doctors US trips but ended up hastening demise of Mary's mother!

Diana did complain to the Association of doctors, as well as to the regulatory bodies overseeing private hospitals, but it was just a waste of time and energy. When that same hospital, as Di learnt afterwards, caught rapid fire due to negligence of their maintenance guys several years ago, the first thing that cropped up in the hospital authorities' minds while the building was being gutted, was to close the exit doors so that no patient can leave without paying the bills!

As a result, more than hundred patients died of asphyxiations and burn injuries, against which the administration didn't take any concrete action, except a momentary eyewash, by closing it down for a year or so as vox populi. This was the state of famous and expensive private hospitals in this part of the world, exclaimed Di!

After the sudden sojourn to heavenly abode of Mary's mother, Diana started treating the fateful kid as her own daughter; she hoped that Mary won't remember her biological mother when she grew up – that way, the traumatised infant can look forward to a new beginning in a sentient house; at least, that's what Diana had hoped.

She also started looking for a few more destitute children, so that Mary can get to enjoy the precious companies of own siblings, and Diana can parent them as well for their better future. She heard from a local friend that there was a very good orphanage in Paushi, East Midnapore, operated by a dedicated family. So, she contacted the owner, visited the place a few times, and then convinced him to send a boy under Di's custody, based on written undertakings, etc.

During her visit to Paushi, Diana was very impressed with the ambience and facilities offered by the hosts to their children. When told to choose a child, Di wanted to hear out the background of the residents there, meaning what type of situations they faced before being rescued by the Orphanage. This was because she wanted to take home the worst affected children, and thus give the kids the very best opportunities to grow up with Mary.

So, the lady in charge narrated the ordeal in details of all the residents there - Diana chose a four year old boy named Subir, who had speech impairment since he watched his father beaten mercilessly and killed by a mob, who then brutally vandalised their house, after which they ruthlessly violated and viciously killed her mother in front of his eyes! All these because of a false rumour spread by certain individuals in the locality that his mother was a child-lifter!

Subir was born in Kolkata to a father who used to be a hawker – a street vendor who earned a halfway decent living. His mother was a housewife until the time that Subir's father lost his 'dala' due to change in political regime – he used to be a close associate with a Union leader of the erstwhile ruling party. The newly formed government was quick to ascertain his affinity to their arch-rivals, displaced him immediately by forcefully occupying his shop and evicting him out of there. He took to peddling in buses as an occupation, selling incense sticks and other items. However, a bus ran over his leg and with that, he lost his left leg - the family was pushed into abject penury.

Subir's father was getting off the bus when the fatal accident happened – he had alighted from the bus by stepping down, when the gormless conductor pushed him - the driver didn't wait for him to get down and step aside. He was lying on the road, blood spattered as he was crying out for help – the severed leg laid beside him!

Traumatized, he was pleading for passers-by to take him to a hospital; in fact, that moment of horror left an indelible scar on his psyche. What followed was even worse – owing to a long-drawn medical negligence, gangrene developed on his left leg, above the severed portion. A critical operation in a government hospital subsequently helped save his life, but his entire left leg, thigh-down, had to be amputated.

The medical bill from previous hospitalization along with costs of medicines, diagnostic tests, etc. had already exhausted the family's small savings which they had managed to put together for years, mainly earmarked for Subir's future educational purposes. Now they had to borrow from relatives, friends and even from moneylenders, at high rates of interests. After bleeding physically, Subir's father started bleeding financially.

People around them helped him a lot - even some strangers pitched in, reading about the tragedy in local newspapers. But, as media in Kolkata were found to be somewhat biased and profit-oriented, the plight of the family was not detailed after finding out that the bus-driver was related to a local councillor of the ruling political party.

Di decided to act on the various irregularities, malfeasance or venality, so that a break can be applied on profiteering or nepotism, to stop political interventions and fiddling with public money and life – she chose social media as she hoped that some king of uproar from public may lead to stop said practices.

She was more frustrated to discover that television channels and print media had turned sordid and vile. Owners of TV channels and print media were being indirectly pressurized by local administration to engage in biased circulation of news, which had debauched the morals of general public.

Print-media, televisions and even some radio channels in India were not what they were supposed to be, on many occasions. The moment they started writing or televising about any corruption, or unlawful activities involving local ruling parties, they immediately started receiving flaks and facing chin music from the henchmen affiliated to such parties.

That was being followed by a rising trend – whenever ruling party wanted to cover up their acts from circulation or publication, they started awarding their advertisements and commercials to the media concerned, on a regular basis, trying to portray some unrelated 'apparently good work' done by them. It may include inaugural ceremony or laying of foundation stone to gazillions of events, starting from projects which will never materialize, to building hospitals, to even public toilets! All those advertisements brought in quick cash inflows to the concerned media – out of gratitude or something else, they stop televising or circulating authentic news against the party involved. Coercions in many forms were some of the other common tactics followed if the former didn't work!

It was no wonder that the term 'fake news' had evolved, emancipating from one particular corner far down on the west! Many reporters over time became experts in 'newspeak, that is, propagandistic language marked by euphemism, circumlocution and the inversion of customary meanings, as a tactical attempt to diminish the range of thought in the readers' minds.

As had been noted in one of the most popular English dailies in Kolkata, the newspeak attempts were characterized by elimination or alteration of certain words, or substitution of one word for another, or interchanging the parts of speech, and thus create certain words for political purposes.

Incidentally, that newspaper got thousands of advertisements for daily print from the local ruling party, months leading into the Parliamentary Elections! Thus, they reap benefits by creating a hoopla involving the oppositions, which sometimes even extended to a national political party who have ruled or ruined the country for over 70 years.

Di selected her favourite social media platform where she had the greatest number of followers, in excess of few lakhs, to launch an attack on the system, by posting the following article, based on her own experiences:

"India being the world's largest democracy, goes to vote every five years with the hope that the next government, be it in State or in the Centre, will be able to eradicate the ills, so as to lead our country to become a developed nation.

The problem lies in the way elections are contested and nominations are made by inept bunch of people without adequate education or experience – this is true of electoral candidates throughout our country! People with multiple convictions and ongoing pendency of criminal cases against them are not barred from contesting polls. People with a simple matriculation can stand elected as Member of Parliament. If lawmakers have no education and expertise in running an administration, then how can citizens expect service? If blowing communal tension becomes the ideology of winning elections, then how can the country progress?

One particular Dynasty has ruled us too many years since Independence – where that has led to? If a common man becomes a Prime Minister and tries to instil values and induce changes, then all the thieves congregate together to displace him – is this the way our forefathers dreamt of? Instead of voting for a particular political party, thereby enforcing your own prehistoric notions and beliefs, why can't we vote for a good person notwithstanding his/her political affiliation, by researching well into his education, career, past history and activities engaged by him/her in the past?

The question will be daunting to answer, and it is up to the Generation X to choose who they want their leader to be – is it going to be a decent, qualified and honest individual or a hooligan – they have to ask themselves these questions and then cast their votes, after weighing out the available options with great mental legerity.

A big problem faced by many politicians is, politics of appeasement and coalition – if someone wins the electoral process and becomes a minister, s/he should not be allowed to bring in people of their choice to run the administration. The minister shouldn't be empowered to get involved in the process of choosing various portfolios in various Commissions and other important places. A folk singer with limited education becomes a Member of an important Commission deciding on peoples' fate, merely by buttering the minister concerned – is it a prudent practice?

The same logic applies to dispensation of public money by elected officials to moneys at their disposal, by their own whims and bias/favouritism with such largesse – the magnanimity often wends towards wrong recipient, thereby depriving those for whom the fund was to be allocated to. The improper recipients return their lagniappe to those unethical and corrupt benefactors in bribes, munificence or paybacks! Some malefactor, felon or thug should not be allowed to sit in our Parliament to decide nation's destiny!

Similarly, important institutions like Intelligence, Taxation, Police, etc. should be freed from the ambit of political control and whims of vested interest groups. Three important pillars of our Constitution (Judiciary, Legislative and Executive bodies) should be allowed to work independently, without curbing each other's functions to fit political wishes. India is the world's largest democracy, which is still ravaged by corruption and ill-wills!

Although media is considered as the fourth pillar of our largest democracy in the world, but the authentic, veritable or bona fide distribution of news has taken a toll on public images about media during recent times in Kolkata. Reliability of news circulated by many television channels and news media in this part of India has been put into question by 'fake' or incomplete news, especially during the runaway times leading to the exercise of voting rights in the Parliamentary elections.

If required, some prehistoric provisions of laws and regulations need to be repealed, and if required, boxed-out provisions in our Constitution may be amended or revisited judiciously, for greater interests of the people. It should really be governments by the people, of the people and for the people, instead of apparent government against its people. Vote-bank politics has been a major devastation in our politics, especially during recent times. A repulsively obsequious person is better fitted as a follower, than a true leader. Exhibitionism should be better displayed in other areas barring leadership roles.

As for Bengal, it is a shame how we turned from 'bhadrolok' (sober people) to hooligans. West Bengal used to be India's one of the most important industrial hubs, just a notch below Mumbai. Now it has slipped to a middling position in the national league. Similar slippage has been taking place in the fields of education – entire middleclass localities are witnessing the continuous exodus of educated youth to other states.

Their children and grandchildren will never return to Bengal due to the inactive administration led by inefficacious politicians at every level – people are getting unhappy day by day about the maladroit and cloddish way things have been handled at the top.

Sadly enough, there is considerable activity and boisterousness in the state-subsidised club culture that have been evolving like mushroom at every corner of the hapless state – while there used to be one or two clubs at the most in the past in one area, now you can find four or five of them, sometimes sharing premises with other 'sister-clubs'.

Routine inflows of taxpayers' money into those clubs have not only resulted in an economy with 'chop & muri' (deep fried snacks & puffed rice) and carom boards & festivities, instead of meaningful productivity to contribute to our gross domestic product.

Every conceivable puja in our calendar are now being celebrated with great fanfare – apart from helping those clubs to host pujas of some Gods not very deep-rooted in Bengali culture, the government is returning to fiscal profligacy by donating in immoderation to clubs and other groups grossly loyal to it. The prodigality is going to cost our nation in the long run, if not controlled immediately. Due to the excessive number of pujas and other occasions, the State has more public holidays every year than ever before; sometimes the government offices are shut down for weeks, causing great inconvenience and lack of service to general public.

Of course, income is also being generated in other ways – it is actually an organised extortion controlled by politicians. Literally nothing is possible to be done by a homemaker for matters like home improvements, let alone buying new homes, without the hawk-eyed leader in your area (who has been assigned the important task of reporting every single move to his master) not asking you for a 'tola'. Syndicates have sprung up in every locality, with the responsibility to supply everything from cement to iron rods – with the backing of political leaders, those syndicates are multi-functional.

First, they fund the politics of the ruling party, and second, they maintain the cadres (who are usually idling away their time, except during election times, when they act as foot-soldiers).

The erstwhile ruling party started this practice of 'tola' on local businesses – it was very tightly monitored by the local party units. However, with the present ruling party, the term got a whole new meaning, ranging from domestic work to industries. The single-window system under the previous regime has been replaced with multiple payment points, resulting in turf wars and clashes involving different factions of the same political party! Local leaders now dominate their individual localities, thus making the citizens live in anxiety and fear of humiliation.

What is happening in Bengal is the systematic debasement and criminalisation of public life. The local police have been rendered useless & ineffective, while there are serious allegations of criminal complicity against their top brass. The higher levels in police are apparently becoming domestic servants of the politicians, as Kolkata Police's once highly regarded reputation is being tarnished.

In admission rackets for college entrance, a different type of 'tola' system works – student union leaders seek humongous donation from prospective students, in return of assuring a seat. Once the seat is procured by paying the bribe, the student has to guaranty his allegiance to the party in every manner, which may sometimes be additional contribution to party fund, etc. The repercussions of not following orders or stepping out of line may even be murder.

The cumulative effect of this debasement of public life is collapse of morale – a Board examination at class ten level has witnessed leak of questions for all the seven papers, thereby turning the entire exercise as a farce. Many out-of-state colleges are now beginning to decline candidature of Bengal students, because the authenticity of their mark-sheets is not always found to be fair. However, it was very sad to note that this type of assault on our education system did not result in any kind of protest or outrage – Bengali people who hitherto attached an exceptional premium on education and knowledge, grumbled in private – they meekly digested the disgrace!

Fortunately, there is some light at the end of the tunnel. Earlier, even during the turbulent 1970's, the 'bhadrolok' classes loathe to accept anything disparaging being said of their state - many of them even glorified the romantic nihilism. At present, a mood of resignation is also accompanied by a sense of shame. There even seems to be an impatience towards the current regime's disingenuous attempts to camouflage the social and political decline, with contrived Bengali pride based on emotional separatism.

It is up to the honest and unbiased functioning of our Election Commission to find out if free and fair elections can take place in Bengal, after years of forced decisions on voters by the current regime – people were unable to cast their votes during the municipal polls held last; as for the last assembly polls, there were widespread reports of 'booth-jams' and 'chhappa-votes', which are indigenous forms of rigging and false casting of vote by agents of ruling party.

God willing, if any neutral observer appointed by the Election Commission to our State to ensure overseeing free and fair election makes any adverse comments on the state of conditions, lakhs of cadres and party-workers will block streets of Kolkata, accusing the observer to be biased. Same goes with statements of any Governor or other constitutional bodies – it will be dealt with the same furore and brouhaha. The resulting pandemonium may cripple the City, but who cares! Even the CEO of the Election Commission of India is not spared from wrath of vested interests, and it is a shame when the head of the state decides to call the official names."

The preceding post by Di was indeed liked and shared by many across the country and even beyond, as Diana had a fan following around the globe during her hay days. She was happy that positive vibes can be generated amongst likeminded people, which may contribute to overall development in some ways or other. She also thought that both Maya's deceased mother, as well as Subir's victim father could obtain some peace, seeing that some actions have been taken on the issues that cost Maya's mother her life, and Subir's father his profession!

Anyways, Subir's father had to incur huge medical expenses for his treatment, and gradually they were pushed neck-deep into debts. Also, the heavy medication prescribed on him eventually led to his liver dysfunction. He also suffered from excruciating nerve pain routinely, for which he failed to take up any means for generating income for the family.

Lack of proper education also didn't help the victim's causes, and he became unemployed – however, to the administration, he was simply an addition to the number of unemployed youth across the State; the authorities were more careful to deflate the total number of unemployment, as this would have an adverse effect on the ruling party on upcoming elections!

Their suffering could have been mitigated to some extent if they received compensation from motor accident claim they filed, but due to typical adjournments and delays in trial, they were forced to explore alternative means of earning for the family. The local councillor, Biswa Chatterjee was quick to put a rubber stamp on the application Subir's dad filled in to qualify for disability, indicating that he belonged to the opposition party, and thus the chances of getting any aid went out of the roof!

Biswa Chatterjee rose from status of a vagabond lawyer with no clients, to MIC in the Metropolitan Corporation of Kolkata – he served a full term initially after winning the Corporation election, and was quick to make his wife as his succeeding councillor, in order to ensure that the largesse cash flow from various sources didn't stop. He didn't care for public image, as he had the blessing of the supremo of the party – he had enhanced his position by having some ruffian, keelie, larrikin and rambunctious followers from local slums and pavement-dwellers.

The lumpenproletariat public were not interested in any social advancement or any development of the State; they kept on blowing the shofar to the tune of the ruling party brazenly – so, people like him flourished across Bengal! The educated mass, however, felt the strong urge to bring in a change in regime, in order to save the glorious State from ruination – choices weren't that great either; so, the same old and same old!

Subir's mother was not literate – so she couldn't opt for a gainful employment or something which will provide a decent earning. Although she tried her best to earn a living by serving as a domestic help, but the money wasn't sufficient to pay off the rents of their flat, located at a low-income group housing estate in Ultadanga, as also to sustain a family of three.

A guy living in the vicinity offered her a job for which she needed to travel twice a week to Siliguri and if needed, to Nepal. Subir's father didn't have any other option but to express his gratitude to the guy for standing by the family at the difficult time. He had to send his wife along with him, knowing fully well that this guy would most likely violate and exploit his wife!

The role in which Subir's mom worked was just a small-time smuggler – she had to cross over to Bangladesh or Nepal, deliver Indian goods there, and bring in foreign goods on her way back. The job was very risky; but she had an innocent look on her face - no one suspected her. If she got caught while crossing the border, her masters will bribe the officials to arrange for a safe passage for her.

However, she will lose a part of her earnings if she got caught – this was the only impediment in her mind when the guy who gave her the job asked her for advanced physical favour; she reluctantly had to agree, as her life and her family's life depended on her coerced consent.

It started as a onetime thing, but ended up as a routine, not only from the guy here, but also from his associates. Maybe that they hoped she would agree to such heinous acts of cowardice by those guys eventually – however, the lady didn't; as a result, she was rendered jobless soon. She also dared to lodge a written complaint to the police, complaining against her torment and assault, for which the officer on duty immediately descried her helplessness with legerity.

Although the victim had been chary of telling the whole truth, but the duty officer decided to overtly persuade her to narrate every-minute details of her ordeal. He also wanted the victim to enact the sequence of events, by pretending himself to be the culprit molester, and in the process, ending up violating her himself!

That was during the days when people used to get bombarded with false claims from those in power, saying that they won't interfere in police investigations, and will let law take its own course! Many policemen acted in shilly-shally manner pertaining to most complaints from ordinary citizens.

And God forbade if someone ever raised their voices anent police inaction, or against police brutality or lack of political will – they will soon be framed or reified as Naxalite, to be put behind bars! Anyone portraying much gumption or sharing jocosely remarks against those in power will be subject to acuity, affliction or anguish.

When she returned home devastated, Subir's father took her to a local party office, in an attempt to get justice. The lollygaggers and touts of Biswa Chatterjee instantly branded them as opposition party-members in a consorted way out to demolish the reputation of the ruling party. They started putting the hapless couple through hell!

Media were quick to jump on the occasion, portraying her as a morally corrupt young lady, and her husband as an accomplice to crime, following which a mob gathered in less than few minutes (all pre-planned, as political vendetta) and lynched Subir's father. A section of the crowd first paraded Subir's mother unclad on the streets, then violated her and choked her to death – local media in a slapdash, portrayed the incident as a mob retaliation against alleged child-lifters!

Subir became extremely traumatized at the sight – he became partially speech impaired from that point on. Thank God that he was finally brought in there at Paushi by a widowed septuagenarian lady. Diana was told that Subir still woke up from his sleep sporadically at nights, crying loud and shaking in fear, for which he was put under medication.

Di chose Subir over others, as he was the only one not looking up amongst all the kids standing there in queue for food – his eyes were focused on a stray dog; as soon as he got food on his plate, he offered a part of it to that dog - Diana decided that he's the one going with her. That image itself tugged at her heartstrings.

She had also visited certain orphanage of children to speak to various public and private bodies engaged in the welfare activities of children around the State – she managed to act as a saviour to many kids by bringing them home with her, after due process, to eventually enable them to lead a happy and normal life. This was her dream from a long time, remember?

However, most of the kids she had brought home, later left for higher studies to different cities across India, depending on their merits and also on the amount of donations Diana provided to the Colleges for their admission there.

Many of them duly graduated from their colleges and became gainfully employed or became successful businesspersons. They never stopped showing their gratitude to their 'grandma' Di – they would make it a point to write to her or call her periodically; occasionally, they will send in some gifts for her. All of the kids had special places in Diana's heart.

But, the two kids who she rescued from total destruction, Mary and Subir, who used to call her 'mom', and stayed with her till her end – maybe they led her to the end!

What transpired next in the lives of the little kids rescued by Diana from the streets of Kolkata fell short of a fairy tale, in the sense that Mary and Subir soon started attending a top-notch nursery school in Park Street, which can only be accessed by the children of who's who in the City due to the extortionate fees and related expenses. The newly founded little fairies in Diana's life, meaning Mary and Subir, brought in tremendous joy and happiness in the house.

The kids used to recite an abecedarian chant every now and then, taught by their foster mother, beginning with "A for apple" and ending with "Z for zebra", filled the atmosphere with heavenly tranquillity and aroma. Other kids also pitched in, and they all had fun together.

Some of the kids were soon adopted by people known to Diana in the US; they were extremely delighted to board their flights at Dum Dum NSC Bose International Airport – they lived happily thereafter in the 'land of the free and the home of the brave'. One kid though, decided to return back to her motherland to be on the side of children of sex workers in Kolkata – her name was Alicia.

Alicia was named after the cyclone Aila, as she was rescued on that day from a brothel in Kalighat. Aila was a severe cyclonic storm which devastated India and Bangladesh on May 23rd several years back, killing more than 340 people in just three minutes of intensified wind gush of 110 km an hour, along with an one-minute sustained wind speed of 120 km / hour – more than one million people were rendered homeless, with a total loss of property in excess of three hundred million US dollars.

Di had named the little girl Aila, which was changed to Alicia by her foster parents in USA, upon her immigration there later. Aila was born and raised in a brothel in Kalighat – her natural mother used to be a sex worker there. If she had surrendered to the system that ruled the red-light areas of Kolkata, she would have probably fallen prey to the trade, like most girls in those dark alleys.

The little girl had other plans, as she fought tooth and nail with the unwritten laws prevalent in red-light areas, to come out of brothel through her strong willpower backed by confidence and determination. Born in that area, no one knew better than Aila about the vulnerability that stared at children of sex workers. While many children were forced to take up their mothers' profession, Aila was not the one to follow the beaten tracks.

Initially, she severed ties with the red-light area and kept herself out of the profession, by going to school regularly, excelling in education, and spending time at home doing homework and constructive work. Having faced abuse by her mother's clients, she realised how painful the experience might be for a kid! She didn't want other kids to suffer like she did initially.

It all started when Aila had dragged her alcoholic father, who used to be a pimp, to the police station after he beat her mother up one day, as her mother had protested against his stealing the money she kept aside for Aila's education, and spent it on gambling and liquor. Aila decided that it was enough – she dialled the emergency number of police and child helpline, accompanied his mother to the police station and filed a written complaint.

A lady from a local NGO was present there at the police station, who decided to take Aila out of her misery, and placed her under their care at a Home. It was from that home where Di had adopted Aila, when she went to visit that home during her search for distressed kids. Di loved her innocent looks and the straight talks between her and Aila led to the latter's subsequent adoption at Gitalaya.

Di had put in details of all the kids on Gitalaya's website – it was from the portal that Aila's foster parents, who were known to Di from her past, decided to adopt her and fly her back to USA sometime later. Alicia finished her high school from Minneapolis with great grades – she was accepted by some of the very reputable colleges in the US, but she had other plans in her mind.

Aila never forgot her past – what pained her most was the conditions of the kids she knew while she herself was there in Kalighat. So, she convinced her foster parents to travel back to Kolkata for few years, in order to save the children from exploitation and abuse.

After she returned back, the first thing Aila did was to meet Di and pretty soon, she was able to open a school for the girls living in red-light areas of Kolkata. She remembered how she used to be taunted at school during her early childhood days – her friends at school used to ridicule her by calling her sex-worker's daughter. No one protested, and Aila decided to be her own saviour instead of waiting for a messiah to save her!

She started counselling mothers of the girls enrolled in her school, owned and set up by Diana, so that they stop accepting sexual abuse of their children by some of their clients as normal. She gave the victims hope, firmly stating that she would arrive herself if any mother or her daughter called her at any time of the day or at night, anticipating any kind of abuse. Gradually, many kids from the red-light areas became aware of their rights after seeking help from Aila.

Aila had helped many kids lodge complaints against the predators, to get them arrested and prosecuted. She even accompanied victims to the Courts, always encouraging them to protest against any violation of their rights. She even decided to include boys as well in her scheme; she roped in retired sex workers to keep a round-the-clock vigil on abuse and violation of rights of children.

The red-light areas of Kalighat stretched out on a long alley and by-lanes; so, Di encouraged Aila to divide the area into five zones – the five elderly women helping her out, who used to be sex workers in their prime, would get assigned to each of the five zones. A night-shelter was set up by Di for the children of the brothel; she would visit often during nights to see if everything was alright. She would also organise camps meant for young girls in the area, to create awareness on abuse.

When all the girls and boys of the red-light area of Kalighat got enrolled at her school, Aila expanded her horizon to include territories of Kidderpore red-light area. Di was always very supportive to her in every manner – pretty soon, Aila was able to accomplish what she dreamt of – she wanted to see that every child in the brothels going to school and having a respectable livelihood, so that they did not have to take to the inhuman profession of being a sex worker!

Children as well as their mothers loved Di and Aila for what they did – they used to say that those ladies are role models for them; if it weren't for them, the world would have been the same for the kids of sex workers there even at present days. Many of those kids started seeing lights at the end of the tunnel, and eventually left the area along with their mothers. It was extremely tragic when Aila got hit by a bus when she was crossing the Hazra More one fine evening, resulting in devastation to all.

Di was struck again by the severity of that blow – how can God be so cruel, she wondered. But, as always, she became steadfast in ensuring that the noble efforts of that great child of God didn't go in vain. She roped in support from some of her acquaintances, who subsequently took over the school Aila set up.

During the initial stages when Di was contemplating adopting infants from streets of Kolkata, she was gravely concerned about the well-beings of those infants, especially in the light of prevailing norms, practices and schools of thoughts. It was a prevalent belief at that time that infants lack the abilities to form complex ideas – most psychologists accepted the traditional thesis that a new-born's mind was a blank slate (tabula rasa), on which records of experiences are gradually impressed. It was further thought that language is an obvious prerequisite for abstract thought; in its absence, a baby could not have knowledge.

Because of the fact that babies are born with limited repertoire of behaviours, spending most of their early months sleeping, they certainly appear passive and unaware of the surroundings. Until the time Di was questioning herself if she should adopt infants, there wasn't any obvious way for those psychologists to demonstrate otherwise.

It gradually became evident with advent of new technologies that, with carefully designed methods, one could find ways to pose rather complex questions about what infants and young children know and are capable of doing. Substantial quantity of data was gathered by the professionals about the remarkable abilities that young children possess, which stood in stark contrast to the older emphases on what they lacked. It was getting clear that very young children are competent – they are active agents of their own conceptual development.

A major move away from the tabula rasa view of infant minds was adopted, where psychologists argued that young human minds can best be described in terms of complex cognitive structures. Cognitive development proceeds through certain stages, each involving radically different cognitive schemes – it was revealed.

The famous Swiss psychologist, Jean Piaget observed that the world of young infants is an egocentric fusion of internal and external worlds; development of an accurate representation of physical reality depends on the gradual coordination of schemes of looking, listening and touching.

As for the theorists of perceptual learning, learning was considered to proceed rapidly due to the initial availability of exploration patterns that infants use to obtain information about the objects & events of their perceptual worlds. As information processing theories began to emerge, the metaphor of mind as computer, information processor and problem-solver came into widespread usages and was quickly applied to the study of cognitive development.

Although those theories differed in many ways, but they shared an emphasis on considering children as active learners who are able to set goals, plan and revise. Children are seen as learners who assemble and organize material – as such, cognitive development involves the acquisition of organised knowledge structures, including biological concepts, early number senses, and early understanding of basic physics. Apart from that, cognitive development also involves the gradual acquisition of strategies for remembering, understanding and solving problems.

Di was quick to recognize the great strides made in studying young children's learning capacity as a result of theoretical and methodological developments, followed by lots of research which all indicated that complex processes are involved in nurturing and upbringing infants.

However, due to her marital status as a 'single' lady, it was impossible for her to provide a home for infants in order to raise them to near perfection, because of limitations under prevailing laws as to adoption, etc. Therefore, she decided to opt for children little grown up, instead of infants, in order to provide foster care to them.

Diana initially thought of sending the kids to reputed schools in foreign countries, as she was financially unlevered of bearing the expenses. That way, they could be more versatile, educated and noble down the road, as many schools in India were marred by favouritism, nepotism and various practices which did not lead to value-addition to kids at schools.

But after a lot of brainstorming, she chose to send them to local reputed schools, as she wanted them to grow up with positive characteristic traits and deep-rooted Bengali culture imbibed in them. Di felt that the kids should complete schooling in India, and then go for college education in the US, thus deriving the benefits of the best of both worlds!

Many colleges across India, and especially in Bengal during the period involved, engaged in accepting donations and deploying bigoted & partisan approach, with unfair means for student enrolment. In Bengal, the situation had been made worse by almost all colleges forming unions under political shelter bolstered by the ruling party - those unions typically asked applicants to deposit a lump-sum money with them before seeking admissions.

Despite the administration's effort to cope with that malpractice by instituting online admissions, the college unions still predominantly played a pivotal role; faction-feuds and clashes with opposing unions and student bodies were a very common feature in that part of India.

In addition, the quality of professors across Colleges in West Bengal had gone down substantially for various factors, politicisation of education being one of them. So, Diana wasn't going to let her kids go through the chaos and trauma in Colleges in India, in future.

The kids' typical days will start from getting up early, taking some music lessons from private tutor in classical songs, getting dressed for pre-school after a sumptuous breakfast, having Di drop them off and picking them up around mid-afternoon; they will sleep for few hours, then go to parks for children and have lots of fun, return home and watch cartoons on television, attend yoga sessions at home in the evening, have gala dinner and then go to bed.

On weekends and holidays, they will attend swimming classes at Dalhousie Club, play tennis at Dakshin Kolkata Sansad (DKS) at Deshapriya Park, visit Quest Mall or Forum in Elgin for shopping and fun; they used to play with the pet dogs at home, as soon as they finished their homework, or mingle with friends.

It was only during bed time that Diana had to diligently spend an hour or two after dinner with Mary, Subir and other kids, telling them stories of her life – each day Di had to narrate to the kids how she herself grew up - everything about her parents, grandparents, education, career and almost everything that Diana remembered about herself. She was a beautiful lady and her tear-drops used to drip down her cheeks when she recollected the story of her life and narrate those to the young listeners, in a manner that wouldn't cause any harm to their emotions – Di's life was not a bed of roses after all!

Diana was the only daughter born out of a wedlock between the youngest daughter Gita (daughter of Biman and Ritu) and her miserable husband, Randip. Biman and Ritu were born in Bangladesh and repatriated to Kolkata during the Partitions when they were kids. Biman hailed from Narayangunj near Dhaka and his father Danish had eleven kids – four sons and seven daughters.

Ritu, on the other hand, hailed from Bikrampur district of Dhaka; her father was a medical practitioner. She had a brother and sister each, named Konika and Avik. Both Biman and Ritu's mothers were typical Bengali housewives, taking care of domestic fronts, upbringing of children, etc. as was prevalent during that era. It was much before women's liberation or rights movements started in this part of Asia; it was even before the yeasty days of suffragettes, demanding the right to vote through organized protests.

A suffragette was a member of a militant women's organization, founded by Emmeline Pankhurst in the early 20th century, who fought for the right to vote in public elections, under their banner 'Votes for Women'.

Di had heard stories from her grandma Ritu how she and other female members of her family used to hide in water reservoirs on the roof of their house in Dhaka in the year 1942, when riots started in India and Bangladesh between two communal groups, all of whom spoke the same language – both the groups had all kinds of similarities in traits, customs, manners and everything else between them, except their religion – one belonged to Bengali Hindus (most of whom repatriated to West Bengal after Partition), and the other to Bengali Muslims (majority of whom remained in Bangladesh).

The group speaking Bengali was further divided into two sub-categories: a faction belonging to East Pakistan, the other being to West Bengal. Those two separate factions of Bengalis from erstwhile East Pakistan (now Bangladesh) and West Bengal, as also the Bengali Muslims from Bangladesh – they used to be all a part of undivided India, before the British conspired with Nehru and Jinnah to divide India into two countries – a new India and Pakistan.

Pakistan was further divided into East and West, after their cruel leaders and dictators unleashed a wrath of violence and crimes against people residing in formerly East Pakistan, occupying territories earmarked for Bengali Hindus and Muslims, inflicting inhuman tortures on the peace-loving citizens.

Pakistani army at that time didn't even spare children and women, the manner in which they kept on butchering innocent civilians were not only ghastly and unthinkable of, but also can be compared with the concentration camps run under Hitler's regime.

Many were annihilated or were desecrated into pieces, through piercing bayonets of Pakistani soldiers' and extremists' rifles following widespread rape and inhuman brutality. Adolescent girls would be violated by groups of men in uniforms in front of their mothers and sisters; those men will take turns in violating all of them, not even sparing their grandmothers or other relatives, eventually killing all those innocent victims, in order to wipe out evidences of their barbaric acts, which in itself is quintessence of their moral turpitude.

Those were the same people who believed in deification of jihadist, most of whom blow themselves up to kill other human beings – no wonder why Pakistan was infamous for harbouring terrorism and was instrumental in spreading violence all over the world through their cacophonous words of wisdom! Such a place should naturally be teemed with terrorists!

A brave heart named Sheik Mujibar Rahaman from East Pakistan decided to stand up against the barbaric raids of West Pakistan armies often; he garnished resistance to thwart the aggressors (military invasion by Pakistan in the year 1971); he formed a regiment called Mukti Joddha Bahini (freedom fighters), recruiting men and women from all spheres and disciplines of lives, in the form of volunteers.

Rahaman, later named as Banga-bondhu (friend of Bengal) and his men trained those new recruits thoroughly, to fight against the Pakistani aggressors with anything and everything. His sonorous & orotund voice, along with his impelling speeches stimulated, actuated & mesmerized a huge population of East Pakistan. Very soon, they mustered up enough courage to stand tall against men in uniform, alias the Pakistani crusaders to chase them off, many times by sacrificing their own lives in order to free their country from Pakistani rule.

Diana heard a story about one such lion-hearted teenage girl named Roshenara Khatun, who didn't think twice to wrap herself up with mines, climbed up to a lamp-post on a major street in Dhaka, waited for Pakistani tank to arrive below, and then jumped off, thereby destroying the tank and killing herself as well as all the Pakistani soldiers in and around the tank. There were thousands of incidents like that whispering on each dust of the great country and its any brave-hearts, which inspired millions of others to join in the movement under Banga-bondhu.

It became so abstruse to Diana to recondite why the entire world and its super-powers were silently watching the mass devastation by the satanic infiltrators, other than a word or two of official condemnation or vocal warnings, etc. – they prescinded from the massacre happening in cross-border terrorism, although there was no dearth of wiseacres in Pentagon at that time.

That was especially true of the American government, since they were well-known to lead the strongest army in the world, with latest warfare techniques and ammunitions. Pakistan used to be one of the largest buyers of US made weapons and artilleries – that was probably why USA decided to keep mum during the Pakistani aggression - that may have been their chain of thought or reasoning or ratiocination.

Soviet Union, former USSR, couldn't have come up to the rescue operations, fearing retaliation from USA with probable start of a third World War!

China, on the other hand, decided to keep a lid on their lips in Pakistani matters. The former preferred to be a mute spectator on issues on foreign soils, as long as it didn't invade their business parameters or interests - the government who blatantly opened fire and crushed its citizens in Tiananmen Square in Beijing can be the apotheosis of any horror movie genre!

Tiananmen Square is a city square in the heart of Beijing, China, named after the Tiananmen, located towards the northern side, separating it from the Forbidden City. In the year 1989, within a span of only 18 years from the massacre in Bangladesh by Pakistan, Chinese troops opened fire at protestors agitating against undemocratic activities of the Government in China, killing and arresting thousands of those pro-democracy protestors in a most horrific and brutal manner – it shocked the entire world and brought denunciations and sanctions from the US. However, this same US was tight-lipped earlier over Pakistani brutalities inflicted on innocent civilians in the year 1971.

The savagery of the Pakistani forces along with several terror outfits in Pakistan joining hands with armed forces shocked its neighbour India; an iron-lady was the head of State in India at that time – upon her directive, Indian Army soon marched in Pakistani soil, in order to stop the infiltrators, aggressors and perpetrators of widespread violence in East Pakistan.

Although Diana did not like the political party that Mrs. Indira Gandhi belonged to, as Di and her parents always maintained a position against the concept of "one family ruling the world's largest democracy perpetually", however, Di was a great fan of that mettlesome lady, who didn't think twice to order the great Indian Armed Forces to march into Pakistan and its occupied territories, in order to show them the reality – to where they belonged!

The surrender of Pakistan's notorious & infamous President Yahiya Khan's military to the Indian Army Chief General Sam Manekshaw along with 93,000 Pakistani troops headed by General Niazi finally ushered in a new dawn of civilisation in Bangladesh, where the Mukti Bahini claimed victory over Pakistan with direct support from its greatest neighbour, India and subsequently became a free country - now Bangladesh.

The party led by Mrs. Gandhi apparently crumbled under global pressure at that time and signed the Simla Agreement. Prisoners captured and land occupied by Indian Army were released, whereas it was a golden opportunity to resolve the Kashmir issue (creation of Nehru) in lieu of the prisoners of war.

As the children grew older, Diana also explained to them why the rift between people hailing from Bangladesh (settled in Kolkata) and people whose ancestors belonged to West Bengal still existed to some extent, in her own fashion.

Di's paternal grandparents hailed from Diamond Harbour, a small rural area at that time mainly used for fishing and transporting goods brought on shore by vessels plying through Bay of Bengal. In other words, they were 'ghoti', meaning hailing from West Bengal by origin, contrary to Diana's maternal grandparents who were 'Bangal' - meaning hailing from East Pakistan by origin.

The sentimental and ideological conflict between people who were born or had parents hailing from erstwhile East Bengal (now Bangladesh) to descendants of the State of West Bengal, also commonly referred to as Ghoti (while Bangal was the common term associated with the former group of people), may be compared to those existing between Russia and USA, especially during the pre-

Cold War era. Ghoti and Bangal are the sub-groups of Bengali Hindus in India, categorized as those originating from West Bengal in India vis-à-vis those with ancestral origin in East Bengal (Bangladesh).

People hailing from Bangladesh, or direct descendants of Bengali population in East Pakistan had no choice but to migrate to India following colonisation towards the end of British raj in India (after widespread riots broke out between Hindu and Muslim population of Bangladesh following partitions). The Partitions were enforced after a debatable tripartite agreement to divide India into two countries – India and Pakistan in the year 1947.

However, many residents of erstwhile East Pakistan chose to move to undivided India before this, fearing backlash from other communities in their own homeland; so, with winds of change, came along conflicts and disputes.

Di tried explaining the differences to the foster children, as they were growing up, because the kids heard the terms 'ghoti' & 'bangal' at school without having any idea what those terms meant at all. So, they were pestering their mom to explain the differences in detail, which Di had to oblige! She did the narration quite well, as per the kids' level of maturity with growing ages!

In fact, it was a detailed lecture that the kids didn't understand much anyway!

Ideological differences:

People whose ancestral origin lies in West Bengal tend to think that the State belonged to them; they believed that the East Bengal (Bangladeshi refugees before, during or after partition) repatriates have caused them misery in all respects – socially, economically, culturally and in terms of employment opportunities.

Political parties across the line, in their opinion, supported the ingress of those refugees for their advantages in vote-bank politics; thus, the disposable resources had taken a direct hit – it was wasted for those refugees. Many of them tend to believe that some of those refugees came from inferior background with foul mouth; they believed that Bangals had polluted the atmosphere!

Some hard-liners even pointed out that crime had increased in West Bengal after people from East Bengal migrated there, over the dispute arising from the Partition during the year 1947. Some even went to the extent of alleging that the Bangals lacked mannerism and courtesy - they were quarrelsome and often engaged in disruptive services.

Those Ghoti hard-liners' rage was primarily aimed at the governmental agencies that offered those Bangals permanent residence or citizenship status in India. The bulk of their anger towards Bangal population resulted out of frustration, as most of those repatriates had strong educational, cultural and social backgrounds, which infuriated those aggrieved!

On the other hand, people whose ancestral origin was in East Bengal tend to think that it was only because of their migration that West Bengal has developed over time, with many renaissances there can only be attributed to their influx. There was nothing much left of West Bengal after Independence - it was the migrating Bengali Hindus from Bangladesh that brought in a wave of positive changes in terms of land development, buildings and infrastructure, as also the overall economy.

Many of those sub-group of Bengali population thought that Ghotis were very jealous of them, who looked down upon Bangals in many spheres of life initially – however, when those Ghotis saw the wind of change the Bangals brought in, they got overly zealous and started bad-mouthing them.

Hard work, dedication, honesty and courage were the four ingredients that Bangals ushered in Bengal. The hardliners alleged that the Ghotis were only sweet-talkers – they were shrewd and uncompassionate. According to them, Ghotis were very selfish and compartmentalised group of people, who didn't care much for others.

Differences in Food habits:

The cuisine of current day West Bengal is a derivation of that of East Bengal. The form of starch is common to both. A meal has rice and fish at the heart of it and ends with sweet chutney, but the similarity ends there. Bangal dish is not complete without Hilsa fish, shutki (dried) fish, or other fishes like koi, pabda, tengra, mourala, etc., while the Ghoti dish is not complete without shrimp / lobster, bhetki, pomfret, etc. Sesame seed is one of the main ingredients used in Ghoti cuisine, while red chilli forms an integral part of Bangal culinary items.

The approach towards food is also quite different. Ghoti food is influenced by the Colonial era and is quite regal in appearance. The ingredients and methods show the affluence of the region and the influences of the era gone by. The cooks who would prepare the meals ran the kitchen - the owners of the house had little to do with it.

Whereas in East Bengal, the women of the house used to be in charge of the kitchen, with ladies starting from grandmother to daughter-in-law, sisters, aunts and even sometimes widowed females of households – all mingling in the common kitchen to plan menus, discuss cooking styles, options & implementation. Often the functions in the kitchen were delegated amongst the ladies, depending on various factors like specialty items, experience and even some experimentation.

Modern Bengali households reflect this distinction even to this day – Ghoti homemakers in West Bengal rely more on cooks - this can lead to the lack of a personal touch. Whereas, Bangal households rely mostly on the members of the household to cook food, even after the concept of joint families gave in to the modern ways of nuclear families. This is another area of cultural and sentimental conflict between the two sub-groups, one claiming their superiority over the other.

Differences in Dialect:

While Ghoti people speak traditional Bengali language, Bangal dialect is typical in the sense that most words end with 'sey' sounds. However, the third generation Bangals mostly use the dialect used by Ghoti population - presently, there's not much difference in spoken language between them.

Fashion and lifestyle differences:

While Ghoti women love to show off their heavy gold ornaments at any opportunity they get, be it festivals, celebrations or simple get-togethers, Bangal women love to flaunt their expensive Sarees and fabrics. Men, on the other hand, like to wear Dhoti Panjabi, if they are Ghoti, and Pajama Panjabi, if they are Bangal. However, with passage of time, dress codes and fashions are not that different between the two sub-groups of Bengali population.

The elite Babus, that is Ghoti men, traditionally liked to visit clubs and associations more often than Bangal men, who preferred to stay at home with families or visit places. It is also claimed that Bangal men are more extravagant in spending money in shopping, food and lifestyle, unlike their Ghoti counterpart who prefers spending on houses, and may be little miser when it comes to gifts, etc. – Ghotis used to be good in saving money, while Bangals used to spend till it ends.

It is also said that Bangals are more hardworking than Ghotis, as most of the Bangals used to have vast agricultural lands with multi-crop yields in East Pakistan, before they were forced to leave everything and migrate to India. They had to start from scratch upon entering West Bengal.

Many of them had to build their own houses or sheds in various parts, many even setting up their own colonies in Bagha Jatin, Garia, Jadavpur, Tollygunge, Ballygunge and most places in South Kolkata; whereas Ghotis preferred to stay in the vicinity of North Kolkata, which has less open spaces due to heavily congested roads and buildings. With modernisation, things have changed quite a bit; now there are Ghoti and Bangal cohabitants in most areas, although Northern part of Kolkata is still a strong bastion of Ghoti population.

Many Bangals claimed that they brought in educational, social and cultural revolution in West Bengal through influx of eminent personalities in science, literature, music, acting, sports, religious leaders, etc. – Ghotis continued to believe that they already had their share of eminent personalities.

However, when it comes to sports, the rivalry between the two sub-groups of Bengali population spread across the globe becomes imminent - it sometimes takes ugly turns in conflicts between the two giant clubs – Mohun Bagan, a traditionally Ghoti club, and East Bengal, a purely Bangal club. Those clubs also play other sports, but it is Soccer (commonly referred as Football in this part of the globe) where the rivalry takes its ultimate form.

Although bloodsheds and hooliganism between rival factions of their supporters have drastically reduced from what it used to be in the 20th century, but the factional feuds and flaunting of powers after a win or lose between East Bengal and Mohun Bagan soccer tournaments continue to flex its muscles till this day.

Diana had to interview two persons from each group of supporters during her sophomore years, as part of her school project, on the condition of anonymity, during a derby match between the two clubs.

The following were her findings, which she submitted for her project:

1) Person A (supporter of Mohun Bagan Club), an Octogenarian gentleman: 'Mohun Bagan (MB) is the most prestigious name in football all over Asia. We are the ones that defeated the mighty British club in IFA Shield in the year 1911. We believe in peace and harmony, unlike East Bengal (EB) supporters. We have won many prestigious tournaments all over Asia; we continue to be the best club in the country in football.'

2) Person B (supporter of East Bengal Club), a septuagenarian gentleman: 'EB has won many more tournaments than MB, although they started playing football years before us – doesn't it tell you the whole story? We defeated them 5 to nil in Kolkata; how can they forget that? We have produced more national footballers than them. They survived on recruiting our footballers in

the 70's and 80's – we produced the best players, and they lured many of those players to their tent by unfair means. And speaking of hooliganism, who used to vandalise cars on Red Road after losing to us? Peace is something we crave for, not them.'

3) Person C (supporter of MB), a lady in her early 30's: 'It's very difficult to talk about this, as my husband is seating next to me in MB enclosure. I belong to a family of EB diehard fans but got married to a family of MB supporter. I watch matches in this gallery as I don't want to sit alone in EB gallery. I feel helpless not being able to cheer for my favourite team from here. It's only when I reach home and call my parents that I get to enjoy our victory, and that too, silently (laughter). Today we are winning; so, I'll clap after the game to pretend that I'm cheering MB up, while I'll be actually saying kudos to EB (laughter).'

4) Person D (supporter of EB), a lady in her late 20's: 'Although my favourite team is MB, but my fiancé here is an EB fan; so, I'm compelled to watch the match here (in EB enclosure). Every time MB players are near the EB nets, my heart starts beating and I end up standing when my fiancé pulls my hands down to make me sit. People sitting around me will kill me if they knew that I'm actually a MB fan (whispering); so, I lay low. Today we're out of luck, but what makes it worse for me is the continuous applaud and supporters' cheers for my enemy team - I have to digest everything quietly! But we'll take our revenge on the next game.'

Thus, it was quite apparent that the conflict and rivalry between EB and MB will continue to exist in the future, as generations pass on their stories, pride and prejudice to their next generations.

It may be worthwhile to note that Diana found out, during conversation with some other people, that there were even divisions in certain families as to their choice of teams – a guy whose father used to be EB supporter and mother used to be a MB supporter, chose to support the team of his mother's choice.

That selection was not based on anything else than his pure love towards his mom, which apparently outweighed his love towards his father. When Di asked him how he celebrated the wins, he smilingly said he got treated either way!

Another young girl in almost similar situation said she preferred it when the team ended up in tie, as she can't bear the thought of having to see any of her parents sad. However, that girl didn't make her own selection of team to support – she preferred it to remain unbiased and non-judgemental.

The fine line was slowly changing, and maybe with the generation Y becoming less addicted to sports and more leaned towards gadgets, the conflict will limit itself down the road. Be that as it may, some conflict will still be there as long as soccer in Bengal is associated with EB and MB Clubs in Kolkata.

Both the Clubs enjoy international reputation, in terms of winning tournaments, hosting many star-studded European and other great teams in Kolkata, sending their players to play for UK and other teams, as also having recruited many foreign players in their teams.

Those clubs historically ranked very high on national tournaments and have produced many legendary players. However, some of the officials of those clubs along with many of their hardliner supporters had contributed towards the animosity or conflict between the two clubs & their supporters. Hopefully someday, all the supporters and fans of both clubs will learn to see soccer as their common game of pride – they will someday try to look beyond the performances 7 debates over the local clubs.

Diana's paternal grandfather, Harini Das, was an advocate by profession, practising civil law in Diamond Harbour Civil Court. His father was also an advocate in Alipore Civil Court; it was Harini's father who cheated a lonely widow of her three-storied house in Fern Road, through manufactured documents, and by producing fake witnesses before the Learned Court, to throw the widow out of her own house, in order to occupy that prime property located very close to Ballygunge Railway Station.

Di's paternal grandmother, Lila Das was a mentally sick and pervert lady, who used to think of everybody as thief. In reality, she used to steal unaccounted money from her husband's pocket every Saturdays when Harini returned to their Ballygunge house (where his wife and children stayed).

Harini had various ladies (unrelated to him by blood) spend time with him at Diamond Harbour during weekdays; Lila also had a few paramours in and around Fern Road – like husband, like wife!

They had one son, Randip and two daughters – both the daughters were married off at early ages in order to save them from 'predators' inside the family – it was a very nasty background of the entire Das family, that was kept a tight secret from everyone outside the family.

Harini, a curmudgeonly old man, used to be a good lawyer. He used to refer his lost cases to his son, who was an advocate of Kolkata High Court, with very little knowledge and sense of application of law. Randip (Randi) was extremely poor in studies, and his mother had a paramour who worked for a reputed School in Ballygunge Place – that paramour helped Randi to appear for Secondary Board Exam as an external candidate of the reputed School – although he scored poor marks, but he passed the Board.

The standards and quality of education of West Bengal Board drastically went down over time, as a ruling party in the 70's took away English as a compulsory subject from syllabus. The Chief Minister of that party was quick to send his own son to study in UK, right after abolishing English as a medium of instruction in government schools! The same party also barred entry of computers in the State for a long time, thus rewinding back the clock of progress to many years.

Anyways, Randi somehow managed to pass the Higher Secondary (senior school) as external candidate of some other institution; thereafter, he took to study Law at a College in Hazra. He chose Law because his scored marks in the Higher Secondary examination were too low to pursue other major subjects in one hand;

and, Law was probably the only course in India where you appear for tests on open-book basis, on the other hand.

He somehow managed his degree in Law and started practising under advocates known to his father. He couldn't manage to practice independently for a long period of time due to incompetence, lack of proper knowledge in legal areas, coupled with poor English skills. His father used to pass on cases he had lost to Randi; a close friend of Harini in Diamond Harbour named Sudip also helped Randi with clients, thereby enabling him to start his practice independently.

Randip's mode of operation was preposterous, spurious, bamboozling and slimy – he will inevitably lose cases in single bench in High Court, and then convince his clients to go for an appeal in division bench, thereby doubling his fees. He will again lose in Division Bench and will tell his clients that High Court Judges are incompetent and corrupt – if the client moves to Supreme Court, that will ensure that justice will be served to them.

He had pre-set arrangements with an advocate of Supreme Court named Rajan Mukherjee, who used to charge Rs. 10,000 from Randi for each client's case. Randi lied to his clients stating that Rajan Mukherjee charged Rs.30,000 thereby pocketing the difference in fees to Mr. Mukherjee for each client.

In addition, he consoled the clients by stating that he won't charge any fees in single bench case for them in Supreme Court as the client had already paid for his fees twice before – the fees being around Rs.15,000 for single bench and Rs.25,000 for Division Bench hearings in High Court!

Clients used to feel little better that way, for not having to bear that loser advocate's fees anymore; but they were in for more surprises if he lost his case in Supreme Court initially. This time, he will bring up a multitude pf false excuses for losing in Single Bench in Supreme Court – then, he will advise for an Appeal again. As his compensation for appeal, he charged Rs.50,000 (out of which he paid Rs.20,000 to Mr. Mukherjee) – thus it was a win-win situation for the crooked lawyer!

If somehow, he won in his lawsuit in Supreme Court, Randi will invariably hold on to the Court documents (like Certified Copies of Orders) before squeezing another several thousands of rupees from them, in addition to airfare, hotel, food and shopping. He often used to have few ladies (from his several illicit affairs) accompany him to New Delhi, portraying the ladies as his wife to unsuspecting clients – they had to bear her expenses too!

Randip also tried cases in Diamond Harbour Court sometimes, inevitably losing the case in order to force his clients to go through the cycle noted above. In addition, he practised in Salt Lake Tribunal, Alipore Court and Bankhall Court.

His clients typically consisted of land-owners, farmers and fishing trawler owners, all of whom had lots of extra cash to spend on court cases, in attempts to bend the law towards their ill will – many times they succeeded, taking advantage of loopholes, missing files, inabilities of opponent parties to run the high costs associated with court cases, death in family, and several other factors. Sounds very strange, but that was the reality!

Despite all his routine inflows of liquid cash, crotchety Randi always acted as a pauper, lying to people about how poor his practice was getting due to this and that – all cooked up stories to keep away glaring eyes on his income, to keep competition at lowest possible level, and to obtain sympathy from others. Even some of the Judges in High Court used to award him cases pertaining to Liquidation or Receivership out of sheer sympathy – distorted truth that he didn't have success in his profession.

He was an irascible and cantankerous person with split personality; he used to act very decent, quiet and sober in front of general public - but to people who really knew him, Randi was a monster in every literal sense of the word, a moody and petulant person with waspish tongue, smutty & filthy mouth, with a vicious mind full of nefariousness, malevolence and debauchery.

Randip and his parents successfully suppressed a previous marriage he consummated in the past, while dealing with Diana's mother and her parents, while trying hard to arrange his marriage with Gita. Little did the latter or her parents realised that Randi tried to kill his ex-wife, who had left him and filed a criminal case including section 498A of IPC (dowry torture, etc.).

As luck would have it for the Das family, one of the Officers in Gariahat Police Station at that time used to have unholy relations with Lila, by dint of which Randi didn't even get charge sheeted! Anything was possible in Bengal – Diana thought. Randip also had many affairs with several ladies – like father, like son!

Diana's maternal grandparents, on the other hand, were really a boon in her life. Biman used to be a very honest Accounts Officer with A.G. Bengal – he was indeed a very meritorious student all along. He used to stand first in class throughout his school years, despite having no private tutors. He studied in a Bengali medium school in Fern Road but had sound knowledge of English – his grammar was impeccable. He scored very high in his School Leaving matriculate examination in all the subjects and secured letter marks in all Science subjects.

Biman even stood first in the Entrance Examination of Jadavpur University, for pursuing his dream course in Engineering; however, as luck would have it, his father couldn't afford the extra fees associated with that branch of science; instead, with a broken heart, Biman got admitted into St. Xavier's College in Park Street, with pure science subjects.

After graduating, he successfully passed the recruitment examination for the Office of the Accountant General of India – he got posted in Bengal. Biman was well-known amongst his peers for his uprightness, probity, rectitude and candor character. He had lots of self-respect and moral values for which he was admired by all.

He was soft-spoken and polite too – hardly anyone saw him getting angry over something easily; he carried a smiling face wherever he went, and hardly lost his temper. He was extremely bright and intelligent at the same time – calm but cautious, and never gave in to unholy pressure.

Biman had three brothers and seven sisters – his father Danish used to be a postal officer in GPO, Kolkata, after emigrating from East Pakistan. Biman was the eldest amongst the sons and fifth youngest among the siblings – he had four sisters elder to him, and three youngers to him.

Danish bought a piece of land measuring four cottahs near Golpark, adjacent to where the present Dhakuria Bridge is, and constructed a two storied house. He had his eldest daughter married off to an Air Force captain, the second to a Revenue Officer, third to a LIC officer, fourth to a government engineer, fifth to an officer of FCI, sixth to an officer of AG, Central and the youngest to a Purchase Officer in Bata India.

So, all of his daughters except his youngest were government officers - he was indeed a happy man with his family, except with his third son, a perpetual troublemaker. His second son was a naval officer and the third son was a Motor Vehicles Inspector; the youngest was an employee of FCI – Biman arranged for employment of his youngest brother there as the latter failed to obtain a gainful employment anywhere else.

Danish was a loveable person but was quite strict as a guardian – no hanky punky was allowed in the house. He had his notorious third son thrown out of his house twice due to heinous acts once - for accepting bribes, on the second occasion, for dereliction of duties. Danish used to tell his wife that she should have gotten an abortion when she was pregnant with that third son, out of sheer frustration with Sunny, the third son with ugly habits – he was full of depravity, infamy & corrupt at work, possessing a mind full of degeneracy and malignity.

It was Diana's grandma Ritu who begged Danish to let Sunny back in, after he was thrown out of the house for the second time, following his marriage – that decision of Ritu proved to be very costly for her during her later years! She did it with all good intentions; but the recipient of her sympathy was a born criminal – a villainy person with lots of perversity and sinfulness.

Biman's immediate younger brother, Aloke was a miser, egocentric, acquisitive & carpetbagger type of person – he was not only extremely opportunistic and insensitive from his childhood, but also used to be quite deceptive and shrewd guy. He married an old lady hailing from the outskirts of Krishnanagar, who used to practice witchcraft. Her sorcery, necromancy and deep knowledge of demonology casted a spell on Aloke, who became practically her servant for ever.

The couple used to be routinely buttered by some greedy, avaricious and covetous relatives, who used to blatantly praise them in brazen manners for almost everything the couple did, right or wrong – those greedy and materialistic relatives thought that by pleasing Aloke and his witchy wife, they would be able to obtain expensive gifts, etc. from them during family ceremonies like wedding, birthday, etc.

Ritu got married to Biman when she was appearing for her matriculation examination – she was only 17 years of age. Danish was looking for a proper match for his eldest son, when he came to know from someone that there was a very decent young girl living in Jadu Colony, Behala, who would be a perfect match for Biman.

Danish didn't waste no time; he showed up at the paternal residence of Ritu the next morning, when she was studying for her upcoming examination.
She had no idea that her life was going to change drastically over the next few months.

Her elder sister Konika got married to a Judicial Magistrate just six months back; so, her father was in no shape to arrange for a second wedding reception in such a short gap!

However, Danish was very persistent - he told Ritu's parents that he was not going to leave until they promised their daughter's marriage with his eldest son – he assured them that the groom was someone they will be very proud of, and, their daughter will be very happy with. Ritu's parents were reluctant initially, primarily out of concern for Ritu going into such a huge family!

They expressed their concern to Danish by stating that their little daughter would have to deal with such a huge family after her marriage. But they felt little relaxed to learn that all the four daughters of Danish who were elder to the prospective groom, were already married off.

In addition, Biman was posted out of Bengal at that time, as a Junior Accounts Officer – so they thought that Ritu will be lucky to have such a nice groom with no baggage there with him. Danish took a peek at the prospective bride, asked her to sing a song for him, and gave his word to the parents that wedding was final. The date was fixed later as the following month, on January 19th.

Ritu was the second child of Dr. Moni Chatterjee and Mrs. Santi Chatterjee. Her elder sister, Konika was two years older to her – Avik, her only brother was three years younger to her. They hailed from Bangladesh, where Moni was a surgeon by profession.

One of his younger brothers named Amiya Chatterjee was a Colonel with INA, led by Netaji Subhas Chandra Bose, who later got married to another young cadet of INA – Mrs. Aruna Chatterjee, who rose to a level of Captain in INA Jhansi Brigade during later years. That couple had routine contact and interaction with INA's chief Netaji; they were loved by the Great Man! After Independence, Amiya Chatterjee served the Indian Military as Lt. Colonel. They were survived by a daughter named Esha, who was married to a British groom.

Ritu and Aruna became very close as they grew older, due to the fact that Aruna's only daughter Esha wasn't around when Aruna fell sick. It was Ritu who used to visit her aunt regularly at her Deshapriya Park apartment and took care of her as own daughter until Aruna died. Diana used to accompany her grandma to Aruna's house during school breaks, when she was startled to know who the great aunt associated with during her younger years. Di became very fond of her – she used to call on her every now and then to find if everything were alright for Aruna.

Aruna had gifted two books she wrote on Netaji to Diana; she also shared many of her fond memories with Netaji to her. Aruna used to recall the day

Japanese fighter planes were bombing incessantly on INA's bunkers in Burma, when she was barely 14 years of age!

Their group captain, one Hyder Ali, rushed to save Aruna and her female companions under instruction by Netaji, and took them through the woods and hilly slopes to a tent where Netaji was supervising his forces. They all had moved to a different location after Japs stopped bombing; then they proceeded to have lunch with Netaji.

Aruna always had tearful eyes when she described Netaji as a man first and a soldier next. She never had a feeling that Netaji was the Commander in Chief, as he always made everyone feel at home. He was more of a father to the girls, and an elder brother to his soldiers. But his discipline and mannerism were very strict – always punctual, had mesmerizing tone of voice, smiled intermittently during conversations, and was a complete man in every sense of the word.

Di never forgot how Aruna cried when she asked her great aunt why Netaji didn't return to India after Independence! She cried like a baby for long period of time, and then gave her response. Diana never asked her the same question ever again to her grandma's aunt.

Netaji knew very well that Nehru would inform the British the moment he gained any knowledge regarding Netaji's whereabouts – Nehru suffered from inferiority complex anytime Netaji used to be around, be it on a meeting of Congress Party or when Gandhi used to summon them. Nehru's trait in terms of his characteristics was full of arrogance, stubbornness and rude; on the other hand, Netaji was full of vigour and charismatic, flexible, open to discussion, very soft-spoken and polite. Netaji didn't like to be called a leader, whereas Nehru vied for it all the time.

When Diana asked for the first time about Netaji's real cause of death, Aruna told her in teary eyes that such a legend can never be dead. He lived in the minds of all INA members and other patriotic people around the world forever – he will be in peoples' minds forever, despite Nehru's vile attempts to track his descendants down, and run a 24x7 vigil on them, even few decades after Netaji's mysterious disappearance. Aruna refuted all points raised through plane-crash theories in Taiwan, promulgated by some.

It was some imbecile at the helm of India post-Independence period who was scared that if Netaji ever came back to India, he would be unanimously elected as the leader of our nation, only because of the fact that Netaji was a born patriot, a true champion of our causes and a natural leader.

Therefore, in order to keep the Great Man in abeyance, that lunatic power-crazy Prime Minister set up round-the-clock vigil on all of the relatives, friends, associates and the brave men and women of INA who were still surviving. That vigil under the disguise of protection was carried on by various intelligence wings of the Government of India, who had to obey the PM.

It was also claimed by some that the imbecile, whose family had been ruling our country for generations, had ordered immediate arrest of Netaji if he ever returned to India – he was sceptical about his ill-devised plans' failure to track Netaji, and therefore, was paranoid.

Many believed that Netaji did return to India at a later period under the name Gumnami (unnamed) Baba, to spend his final years in the country for which he devoted everything he had! But, families of that lunatic PM kept disavowing the fact that Gumnami Baba was indeed Netaji.

Di found out later through someone that, a leading American hand-writing expert concluded that Netaji did live in India for several decades after Independence, under the identity of a reclusive ascetic who used to be called as Gumnami Baba by others. The expert, named Carl Baggett, reached the conclusion after scrutinising the letters written by Netaji before his mysterious disappearance, and by Gumnami Baba.

With over 40 year of professional experience, Baggett who was certified by the American Bureau of Document Examiners, handled more than 5,000 cases in authenticating documents based on hand-writing analyses; he had also testified Pan US as a handwriting expert in the Courts located across all the states.

Baggett was given the two sets of letters (one set written by Netaji before his disappearance, and the other written by Gumnami Baba), in order to analyse them, without being informed about the real identities of the writers. After he concluded that both the sets of letters were written by the same man, Baggett was informed that the person whose letters the examiner was none other than Netaji Subhas Chandra Bose.

Since he was absolutely certain about his findings based on his education, experience and recognised talents, Baggett stood by his decision that it was Netaji who scripted both sets of letters – he issued a signed statement to such effect.

According to official records promulgated by the crooked PM at that time, Netaji was killed in an air crash in Taiwan (although no evidence could be ever found of such crash anywhere near the airport of Taihoku) in August of 1945 – his 'ashes' were later preserved in Rankoji Temple in Tokyo – the Japanese had strong liking of the Great Man; they were fooled into believing the concocted story at the behest of the imbecile PM.

However, general public and his close associates never believed that theory; their beliefs were supported by theories that Netaji survived the crashes, made his way to India, and lived as Gumnami Baba for several decades in Uttar Pradesh's Faizabad.

There were innumerable evidences that the Baba was none other than Netaji, when he was seen in light outfits inside his room in a freezing temperature, after he gave away his blanket and warm clothes to his aid there, so that the latter could feel warm. When the aid asked Baba how he can survive the extreme cold temperature without warm clothes or blankets, Baba had replied that he was used to it during his stays at Siberia!

There were many books and personal effects that belonged to Netaji which were seen to be in possession of Baba. In addition, his stature, tonal quality, stern nature – all pointed out that Baba was in fact Netaji – all of those were ignored and overlooked, for reasons not difficult to guess!

Around 130 letters written by Netaji from 1962 to 1985 addressed to one of his very trusted associates in INA, Pabitra Mohan Roy, under the disguise of Gumnami Baba were released by the former's family after Roy was gone.

A book published much later on Netaji's life provided evidence that Roy used to meet Baba often – a Commission formed much later in response to public outrage surrounding Netaji's disappearance, under the chairmanship of Justice Mukherjee, had incriminating evidence through more than 10,000 pages of journals written by other INA members, that Netaji returned back to India. Those documents were collected through Right to Information Act and given to Baggett for further examinations.

In his testimony, Baggett had said: "Based upon thorough analysis of those items and application of accepted forensic examination tools, principles and techniques, it is my professional expert opinion that the same person authored both the writing on the known (proved as letters written by Netaji) and on the questioned documents (accessed from Roy and other revolutionaries)."

Some may argue that Netaji did suffer from psychological trauma apparently from his captivity and torture while in Russian custody, and that was why he chose to remain secluded from public.

If that theory was true, then it further explained why the government led by that lunatic PM, and his successors (daughter, son, son-in-law and now grandson and granddaughter) always maintained 'friendly ties' with Russia, at the cost of enmity with the US in the past – such questionable decision to stick with the Russians as ally may have caused India lagging behind as an under-developed country for so long!

The decision to remain underground by Netaji may have been fuelled by a mental imbalance, which manifested in occasional false memories and delusions (paranoid & grandiose) in him. Those disturbing signs could not be detected or discussed by those confidants of Netaji, as to them, he was nothing short of a God!

And that he was indeed, felt Di always – he was a God who saved Indians from foreign oppression and tyranny; but we forgot him, just as many people tend to forget the sacrifice made by Jesus for mankind!

That was how Di used to narrate to her kids the valiant efforts and incredible sacrifices made by Netaji! She always wondered why no government, either at Centre or at state, succeeding the 'dynastical regime' made no efforts to unearth the real facts behind Netaji's disappearance.

Some leaders momentarily assured public (especially before any election) that if they came to power, they will reveal the truth. However, once they came to power, they chose to remain tight-lipped – maybe politics of appeasement or vote bank politics result in such 'forgetfulness' – wondered Di.

She didn't get to vote in India (fortunately for her, as all parties seemed to be the same), because she attained majority at a time when elections weren't forthcoming, and she had to leave for College abroad.

Another direct associate of Netaji, Jatin Das's sister-in-law Kamala Das (wife of Kiran Das, who was Santi's best friend from School) did concur with statements by Aruna on a separate occasion, when Ritu took Diana to her house years later. Kamala Das's son Milan Das and daughter Minoti Das (Mithu) were very good friends with Di's grandma, Ritu.

Minoti resided in a posh apartment near Buddha Temple in Lake area; she taught kids from the adjacent slums in Gobindopur and Panchanantala – she used to be thrilled to see Ritu every time Di visited her, along with her dear grandma.

Di also heard stories of a few young lion-hearted girls who didn't care for their lives in the movement to oust the British from Indian soils. One of them was Bina Das – daughter of a schoolteacher from Cuttack named Beni Madhab Das. Netaji was amongst one of his students in Ravenshaw Collegiate School, while he was teaching there – later, he moved to Krishnanagar where Bina was born.

Bina was preparing for her matriculation examination from Bethune School, when she came across Pather Dabi, an epic by Sarat Chandra Chattopadhyay. It was a banned book, but somehow Bina managed to get a copy of the book and started reading it over and over, thus sacrificing her study time in preparation for her upcoming examination.

During her English test, students appearing for matriculate examination were asked to write an essay – Bina instantly decided to write the essay on Pather Dabi, the great novel. However, despite being a first girl from her school, Bina didn't fare well in English! It didn't take her a second to realise that she was discriminated for writing her essay on that banned book. She later told her close associates that it was her first sacrifice for India's freedom, which she was proud, and not repentant at all!

Bina later attempted to assassinate the Governor of Bengal, Stanley Jackson, when she was just 21 years of age, during the convocation ceremony at the University of Calcutta. As Stanley was going to take his seat, Bina rose up from the chair she was seated on and approached one of her teachers there with a request for a glass of water.

No one suspected that the timid looking innocent girl had a revolver concealed under her gown – when the teacher instructed Bina to wait till the Governor was done with his speech, she didn't go back to her original seat - she intentionally took a vacant seat nearby, in close proximity to where Stanley was.

After few minutes, she got up, took out the revolver and shot at Stanley multiple times – unfortunately, the bullets missed the target - Stanley was unharmed. Seeing that, Bina again fired a couple of rounds, which again missed Stanley by a whisker.

Bina was overpowered initially by Suhrawardy, the Vice Chancellor of C.U., and later arrested and imprisoned for nine years for attempt to murder charges.

Her statements to the Magistrate during her trial went down in history; she said "I fired on the governor, impelled by love for my country, which is repressed. I sought only a way to death by offering myself at my country's feet and thus end my suffering. I invite the attention of all to the situation created by the measures of the government. This can upset even a frail woman like myself, brought in all the best traditions of Indian womanhood. I can assure all that I have no personal feelings against the Governor. As a man, he is as good as my father. But as a governor of Bengal, he represents a system which has kept enslaved 300,000,000 men and women of my country".

Following her release from prison, she participated in the Quit India Movement, for which she was sent back to jail for another three years. After Independence, she got married to another freedom fighter named Jyotish Bhowmick, who happened to be a close friend of Di's grandpa Biman – the world is small, thought Di!

Bina started teaching by profession, but since she had her graduation certificate revoked by CU, she suffered a lot – she didn't accept the pension provided by the Government to freedom fighters. Actually, very few of the real freedom fighters of India accepted the pension, as they never risked their lives for money; freedom to them had a different meaning! Bina subsequently shifted to Hardwar where she died – her body was later identified by a distant relative.

The story of legendary women, Suniti Choudhury and Santi Ghosh, fascinated Diana every time she heard it first-hand from freedom fighters' direct descendants like Minoti and Aruna. Both Suniti and Santi were teenage girls, who opened fire at Charles Geoffrey Buckland Stevens, a British bureaucrat and District Magistrate posted at Comilla, then a part of undivided India, killing him on the spot.

The young girls, one of them 14 and the other 15 years of age, were sentenced to life imprisonment – after eight years, they were subsequently released from jail. After independence, both the Congress party at the Centre, as well as the Communist Party at the State, offered those brave hearts pensions for freedom fighters, which they blatantly refused to accept.

Moni's father, Dr. Manmohan Chatterjee was an attending physician at a Dhaka Government hospital. The eldest of his four sons was a Professor of Physics in Dhaka University. Moni was the second son, and Amiya the third. The youngest son, Bimal Chatterjee was a top executive with Bata Corporation's head office in Canada – he later went on to become the second in command of Bata worldwide, and retired in style!

Moni was called on military duty to Singapore during the World War, where he was subsequently imprisoned by occupying forces for several years. He had gotten married to Santi many years ago - they already had three children at home. It was at that time that Kamala Das provided all kinds of moral and other support to Santi and her family, until Moni was released after the war was over. The kids missed their dad for many years - Ritu always lamented about that period when her dad was kept in prison, many times during her conversation with others, many years after the fact.

Santi was a quiet person and raised three kids successfully. She left for India along with the rest of the family during the Partition, taking refuge with a relative in Kalighat, until she managed to build a house in Jadu Colony, Behala. The house was named after her, as Moni never stopped to appreciate how challenging it was for his young wife to raise three kids all by herself, amongst slaughters and all kinds of crimes by some of the Muslim communities in Bangladesh, against the Hindus there.

Santi's only son Avik completed his B.E. from Shibpur and M.E. from Jadavpur University; he became the Chief Engineer of CMDA, as it was called at that time, later known as KMDA.

Avik got married to a lawyer whom she met during his college years; however, he decided to move out of his paternal residence in Behala. His parents and sisters were devastated, but accepted his will, so that their only son / brother can live peacefully. However, Santi never forgot her son, as she always used to cry out loud every time his name cropped up, even decades later. After Moni's peaceful death, Santi couldn't live in the same house she spent so many years with her love – she was missing her husband so much.

She soon sold her house to a promoter and moved in a nice flat close to where Ritu lived. She decided to move in close to Ritu's house only because Ritu was the most devoted and loving child amongst all her children, who always took care of her parents.

Santi loved Diana so dearly that even during her final years, when she can hardly walk, she would get up from her bed at the sound of the little kid entering the flat with her grandma, Ritu.

Avik and his wife both would later die prematurely of fatal diseases – probably their inhuman actions to abandon aging parents (without any reason), and the pain inflicted on Avik's parents, came back to haunt them, and curse them! They were survived by a daughter who used to be an air hostess, but became a ground staff for a famous airline, posted in Doha, along with her husband and two girl children.

Going back to Ritu's marriage with Biman on January 19th, it took Ritu just few days to realise that she would be eventually left behind at her in-law's residence - as she was very young, her in-laws advised her to stay back at Kolkata; Biman would come home every weekend.

Three unmarried sisters-in-law with crooked brains, three brothers-in-law with opportunistic behaviour, along with a selfish, cruel and nosy mother-in-law made her life miserable soon. The whole family except Danish and his eldest son Biman were barbarous and spiteful – they evolved some fiendish methods of torture to the young newly-married housewife. At times, Ritu vacillated between leaving her in-law's house and continuing rendering her service as unpaid maid of the household! Such was her untold misery – she couldn't talk about it to anyone, because she was a shy type of young girl who confided in herself all her grief.

Ritu had to get up at 5 am every day, start fire in charcoal-filled huge earthen fire-pot emitting thick smoke for several minutes until fire would start, prepare tea for everyone in the house, and then take individual cups of tea to each king and queen's bed, who would still be snoring then. After that, she had to bathe, changed her clothes, freshen up and cook varied breakfast for members of the 'royal' family on a-la-carte basis, depending on what mood the princes and princesses were in, so as to serve them their royal breakfast on time!

The devilish in-laws will always come up with excuses for being late to school or college (because of their own fault in getting up late); then, they will definitely blame it on the newest addition to their house as a 'maid-servant for free (Ritu)' – then her highness, Ritu's demonly mother-in-law will vent out her anger (frustrated soul for producing so many kids every alternate year – she probably made more friends at the hospital than anywhere else, as she spent most of her time there delivering the by-products) against the poor young housewife on some pretext or other –she was simply jealous of Ritu.

Danish was the only one in the entire family who will speak out for Ritu, but then flow of information to him was skewed through manipulations most of the time through the hard drives of circus party there! The three cunning unmarried sisters-in-law will make up some devilish plans to embarrass and harass Ritu in front of others, and then go on to badmouth her, in her absence to other adulatory relatives and sycophants.

After breakfast, Ritu had to collect used utensils from each prince and princess's rooms, bring those under a tap located outside the kitchen, wash all cooking and serving wares, and get ready for her next assignment – preparing lunch for the royals. Although there was a paid domestic help in the house, but the lady ended up running errands from all corners, more than having the time to attend to her own pre-assigned chores. Ritu's wicked mother-in-law made sure that the domestic help was attending to anything else, excepting helping out the poor bride.

Ritu never even boiled rice while she was in her paternal home before marriage; now she had to cook square meals for an entire football team! Sometimes, with arrival of the married sister-in-law along with their nth number of by-products, things got out of hand for Ritu; this was when all the chin music used to be played against her by everyone. She used to silently cry, wipe out her tears with corners of her saree, move on to finishing her pending assignments. She had to make sure that no one noticed her crying, lest she would be scolded further.

Some of the evil husbands of those married samples of visitors showed false pity towards Ritu – but they had ulterior motives behind such sympathy and false care for her. She refused to be touched inappropriately by them, and then situations would turn ugly – all the battalion will team up together against Ritu, start blaming her character, her upbringing and everything about her, not even sparing calling names towards her innocent parents and siblings!

She had to digest everything and confine her feelings deep down her heart, as Biman would not believe that his entire family were at fault, and she was the only one who was innocent. Ritu couldn't narrate anything to her parents either, fearing that her military-trained father wouldn't tolerate any of those non-senses; he would definitely bring her back to his house. Divorce at those times were unthinkable, kind of jarring halt - there were no laws to protect women.

Domestic violence was some foreign concept back then; it was customary that all women needed to be like blunt disciples of Gandhi – tolerate everything - don't speak up - get beaten, don't raise your voice - get abused, don't protest. Women kept their veils up - still they used to get violated (unlike now when many women can't buy enough clothes to cover up themselves properly, go to hang out with unknown guys and then complain of getting violated after a few hard drinks and smoking stuff....).

Ritu used to wonder why her beloved father agreed to get her married at such tender age; but she couldn't blame him, as he had no idea that Ravana's family was awaiting her arrival there. Biman was the only person in the entire family who was different from the rest of the sample-pieces. He didn't even get to see his prospective bride before wedding day- he accepted the fact that his father could do no wrong.

Fortunately for Ritu, at that boiling point, Biman realised that something wasn't right; he decided to take her along with him to Kalyani – thank God, or else Ritu would probably be charred to death or would have committed suicide!

Trouble brewed in for Ritu in Kalyani too, as that was where her sister's in-laws' house was - Naresh (Konika's husband) had a wicked and loose character brother, who would try sneaking in during the time Biman was at work, to make an attempt. Eventually that news reached Biman through his neighbours - there were more troubles in the conjugal life. Fortunately for the poor bride, Biman got transferred to Berhampore little later, when dusts finally seemed to settle from that point of time.

Riya was born in Kalyani – nearly two years later, Vikram was born, when the couple were at Berhampore – so Biman and Ritu became parents of two beautiful kids. Life was indeed fair to Ritu after that time, because there were no more disruptions and interruptions in their family life; pretty soon, she became closely acquainted with the neighbours there.

She spent lots of time hanging around with wives of Biman's colleagues, who all lived in the same compound meant for government officers - their children too played together on a huge field in front of the Jailhouse there - a place called Square Field.

Ritu would spend the morning getting breakfast ready for the family, then feed the kids – after Biman left for work, Ritu would listen to music, ran some errands, cooked lunch for the family and then waited till Biman came over to have lunch. After Biman left for work again, Ritu would put the kids to sleep, took a nap herself, met up with ladies around, and then waited till the kids got up.

All the kids from the compound used to play in the huge field in front of their quarters; the mothers yapped between themselves occasionally bursting into laughter with some stories narrated by some of them, while keeping a close vigil on the kids.

Lucy, a pet Alsatian brought in as a puppy to the residence of Biman, used to love the kids – she kept a close watch on her sister (Riya) and brother (Vicky) playing on the field with other kids – since Lucy was kept leashed during daytime by the main entrance, it might take a while to reach to her siblings, God forbid if they ever had some trouble! She had complained about it in her own ways to her master Biman as well as to her chef Ritu; but alas, they didn't seem to appreciate her grave concerns.

Sure enough, Lucy's concerns about the safety of the kids were not unfounded – pretty soon, a day arrived when Lucy saw another kid built stronger than Vicky pushing him – Vicky fell down on the ground and was crying! The kid who pushed him was the son of one of Biman's co-worker, living close to Lucy's house; so, she knew him, but couldn't bear the fact that his very own brother Vicky be shoved or pushed by any outsider!

So, in a blink of an eye, everyone present in the vicinity witnessed something that rarely happened – Lucy forcefully unleashed her chain, vehemently pulling her necks through the strap, and ran like an Olympian to the field, to save Vicky from 'assault'. She was barking loud while she gave a fiercely chase to the kid who pushed Vicky; all the people present there were shouting at the top of their lungs, because they feared that the huge dog was going to bite the kid who pushed Vicky.

But Lucy didn't bite him – she just chased him down and pushed him with her back; the poor kid was already crying out loud in fear – his cries escalated after Lucy made him fall down!

People present on the scene talked about the incident for years to come. It was simply an act of a true friend – a selfless and honest act to extend support when someone you call a friend, needed it – thought Lucy! Unfortunately, her endless love and spirited chase didn't win her any recognition from anyone outside the household of her master that day!

She died years later out of natural causes, making everyone around her really sad; her family remembered her forever though – stories of her bravery and loyalty spread across generations in the family she belonged to! Di also knew Lucy from what she heard about her.

During the weekends or holidays, Biman would take his family to neighbouring areas of interests, like Plassey, Hazar Duari, etc. – the family had great times together; they used to have lots of fun. Biman and Rekha would sometimes go to watch movies at nearby movie theatres - the kids would accompany them, especially because Vicky was very close to his mother – he would definitely raise the pitch of his cries if he didn't see Ritu for a while. He was very fond of his dad too; he used his dad as a shield to protect himself from his mother's occasional fit of rage – he would simply caution Ritu that he would complain to his dad, if she raised her hands on him!

Riya, on the other hand, used to be a quiet little sweet girl, who loved her brother and tried her best to be his guardian. She used to pick raw apple from the orchard nearby whenever she visited the place with family; then she would ask her dad if she plucked the right ones or not! Biman used to smile and tell her not to pluck anything without permission from the gardener, to which she smilingly agreed.

The gardener though was a very kind person, as he would always make sure that Riya would have at least a dozen apple to carry with her back home – the apples were ready to eat too – not raw or ripe! Everyone seemed to wonder about her dissimilitude from her brother, in terms of habits.

While Riya was a shy and quiet little girl, Vicky was a talkative naughty guy – she was not half as loquacious or garrulous as her brother. Even as she grew up, she was extremely reticent about her personal affairs. Sometimes they used to attend formal get-togethers of family or friends; although Riya would be very excited to go to any party (she eventually became a party-monger later in life, attending all types of events and ceremonies), but while there as a kid, she would be reticent, with her face looking more lugubrious than usual.

As was revealed at a much later time, she used to be worried about her loving brother getting into some kind of mischief, which he normally would, resulting in some harsh words showered at him.

Any rebuke to Vicky would be unbearable for Riya – she loved him dearly. As a matter of fact, there were times when her brother had to cheer her up by saying: "don't look so woebegone Didi" – she was his elder sister, referred to as didi. Riya would then be cheerful and happy. Vicky didn't mind the reprimand or admonition though – he always wanted to explore the unknown and question anything which didn't make sense to him. He was extremely bold and adventurous too, unlike his timid sister.

During a vacation of the family to Betla forest near Ranchi, Vicky wanted to find out why everyone needed armed escort for forest safari – he thought in his little mind that animals don't harm human normally; Biman also told him the same exact thing.

But, then why would people need armed escort to roam the forest? Some of the answers provided to him by the forest guards didn't satisfy his curiosity – so, he decided to venture out there all by himself to find out.

The family was staying in an Inspection Bungalow owned by the Forest Department – it was located in the middle of the forest with barbed wire and other fencings all around the property. The only gate for ingress and egress was manned by armed security guards, as there were some disturbances arising out of Naxalite movements back then.

There was also a watch tower adjacent to the bungalow, where 24 X 7 vigil was maintained by the guards. So, the expedition planned by little Vicky was no piece of cake – he would definitely be caught if he wanted to sneak out during the daytime; at nights, there were flood-lights all around the place – so, he had to literally pluck his brains out to be able to come up with a tangible or feasible escape plan.

He thought about it all night long as everyone else were in deep sleep; he had to get out to see what happened if he walked through the jungle all by himself, without any guard present. Vicky was around nine years of age – he wasn't very tall. The only way to sneak out of the place was to tip toe to the back side of the bungalow (covered with long trees), crawl under the wires quickly enough to evade eyes of the security guys and walk right out. So, there was no stopping that intrepid valorous kid.

A little past five in the morning the next day, the daredevil kid slowly crawled out of the fencing as everyone inside the bungalow were sleeping. He exhibited unflinching determination in making sure that the guard on the tower didn't notice him, by playing a coy – he picked up a brick laying around the ground, threw it towards the other side, so that the guard will be alarmed by the sound of the falling brick, and will focus on that part where the sound came from – that will give the undaunted kid enough chance to get out.

The plan was carried out with surgical precision – later in life, Vicky would be a very successful manager with top-notch planning and execution skills. Anyways, as soon as he was able to get to his feet, Vicky started running deep inside the woods. He loved the smell of the jungle, its freshness and almost everything about it.

He desperately wanted to see wild animals there, which happened within a few minutes – he saw a gang of bison chewing grass, twigs and shrubs nearby. The one which appeared to be the matriarch lifted his head to take a deep look into the invader, stared at him while continuing to munch his food, and decided to ignore the miniscule figure on the other side!

Vicky later learnt from zoologists that bison can be extremely fierce, despite the fact that they are herbivores, and can chase down any enemy with a violent end. But, at that time, not only was he completely oblivious, or even aware of the potential danger arising out of his adventurous mind, but he also chose to ignore any imminent threat for reasons understandable best by him.

He may have been a tad crazy in his earlier days too, thought Di upon hearing the story from Ritu and Riya.

In the meantime, Ritu woke up to attend nature's call – she screamed out Vicky's name as soon as she saw that he was not there on the bed. Being a very caring and affectionate mother, she had a hunch that something was amiss.

Everyone got up immediately, called out for Vicky and began to run around to look for him. The guard posted inside the bungalow instantly rang the alarm bell; Biman instructed the manager there to get their car ready, ran around the open fields inside the bungalow, and hopped on to the car as soon as it was ready to roll.

Security guards scrambled with their guns, and soon the search started for Vicky, with his parents desperately looking around for him, frantically calling out his name every few seconds.

The Happy Prince was taking a stroll alongside the hill towards the backside of the bungalow, watching some deer galloping – their fawns were so cute, trying to hide behind their mothers; they were probably stags, as he discovered when he grew up. He wanted to see more wildlife, but couldn't see much except the bison, deer and a couple of wild boars; a few red jungle fowls and a peacock were some of his other sightings there.

He eventually heard the commotion, the ruckus and honking of the car; but he couldn't see much due to the dense vegetation, until the car came closer. He shouted back to assure his parents that everything was fine – wow, what a relief it was for the parents. The forest ranger who accompanied his parents immediately got off the moving vehicle and picked Vicky up to 'load him' back to the car – what he said next was really unnerving to everyone there.

The ranger promptly pointed at some fresh elephant dungs along the trail and exclaimed that a herd must have passed the path few minutes back. Sure enough, as everyone started to look around, there was an elegant and gigantic herd of elephants crossing the hill atop. They didn't even care to stop or look at those gathered around the bottom of the hill, and to Vicky's utter dismay, they disappeared quickly into the bushes – there seemed to be few calves with the herd; probably that's why the elephant herd didn't waste any time to get out of human views.

What Ritu didn't tell Di was the resultant punitive measures adopted by the parents on their over-smart son! He was locked inside the bedroom for the rest of the day at the bungalow, and his dad held his hand tight (like a police officer arresting a criminal) all the way to the car during the time they were leaving the forest; inside the car, Vicky ended up losing the window seat, as he was forced to sit in between his parents – what a tragic ending for the kid!

Di used to mischievously bring up that incident to her dear uncle many a times upon hearing about it from her granny, when she will definitely add some adjectives aimed at her uncle – he used to smile or blush sometimes; apparently, he preferred to maintain silence over the issue. He probably realised at a later time that what he did that day wasn't right!

Back to the days at Berhampore, the siblings were growing up; it was time to put them to school. During those times, pre-school or nursery school concept of education wasn't common, especially in small towns. Biman wanted to take a transfer to Kolkata for the betterment of his kids (education prospects), but there wasn't any opening for him down there yet. Ritu was also better off staying away from her devilish in-law's family, as much as she could, for the sake of mental sanity, at the least!

It was only during their infrequent trips to Kolkata when the rugged old form of monster-like extended family surfaced for a few days. The sister-in-law will conspire to steal Ritu's clothes and blamed it on the domestic help, her mother-in-law will force her to dispose of her ornaments to her daughters, her brother-in-law will work out a plan to embarrass her in front of others, etc. Ritu breathed a huge sigh of relief each time they boarded the train back to Berhampore. It seemed to her that she was again breathing normally!

The same went on for few years until it was time for the kids to start attending schools – at that time, no schools will admit students below six years of age. So, Biman had to take a transfer to Kolkata in order to make sure that his kids got proper education in good institutions, as there weren't any reputable schools in Berhampore during those days. The family bid adieu to all with teary eyes – they kept in touch with others for a very long time, and many of the old neighbours and friends from Berhampore visited Biman and his family numerous times.

Vikram got admitted to a very reputable English-medium school at Ballygunge Place (the primary section was located at Hindustan Park then, to move to Ekdalia later on). His elder sister Riya was admitted to a very good school in Lord Sinha Road - things were perfect, other than some family tiff here and there.

However, by then, Danish had died leaving the ground floor to Biman, and the first and second floors to his monster-brothers; Biman was the one who paid his father for building the second floor, but he kept mum as his father made out the Living Testament on his dying beds, leaving his elder son with the ground floor. Biman was always a happy go lucky type of person and avoided trouble at any cost.

Sunny would resort to criminal and vicious acts down the road to forcefully persuade Aloke and their youngest brother to vacate their portions of the ancestral property, after which they started living somewhere else. Aloke had built a nice house at Salt Lake and lived there till he died of horrible disease when he was 88 years of age. His only daughter turned out to be a lunatic; she could not settle down in life – Aloke got his punishment for his evil act through his daughter. Biman's youngest brother had died of liver dysfunction much earlier, which was quite anticipated, as he was an alcoholic for a long time.

Within a year of Danish's death, Di's mother Gita was born – she became a darling to the family instantly, as she was always a jovial and energetic type of personality; Vikram and Riya treated Gita as their own kids, being quite elder to the latest addition to the family in terms of age.

Biman's demon mother subsequently passed away; the evil brothers were all separate by then – all of them got settled with their families. The remaining three witch sister-in-law were married by that time, as they got new assignments from hell – to destroy lives of their husbands and in-laws, which they successfully completed with full marks subsequently.

Time flew thereafter, and soon Gita got admitted into a very prestigious girls' school between Gurusaday Dutta Road and Beckbagan. It has been one of the best schools for girls since its inception; as such, the family was so happy. However, school fees for three kids at reputable schools plus books and stationeries were proving to be beyond the means of a single wage-earner; so, Biman had no other choice but to change School for Gita, to get her admitted into the same school where Riya was going.

Gita accepted the change with a heavy heart – however, she did confide in her dear brother Vikram about her grief, by saying jokingly that her daughter will someday go to that particular school, which she couldn't any longer! Atta girl – God must have listened to Gita then, and after nearly forty years, Gita's daughter Diana was indeed admitted there in senior section, in pursuance of her dreams! That dream would turn into a nightmare for Di later!

Riya got married early too, when she was in High School, as a very decent proposal for marriage cropped up through a friend of Vicky's. Sam (Riya's husband) was distantly related to a friend of Vicky. One day, when that friend was all dressed-up in an unusual manner, Vicky asked him where he was going at that odd hour dressed up like that! The friend replied that he was going to go to a house with his aunt to find a bride for his cousin brother.

Vikram had always been a humorous person throughout his entire life, even in ups and downs; so, he jokingly told his friend that he didn't need to waste time searching for a bride, as his own sister Riya was there!

That same evening, a beautiful and gorgeous lady with lots of class knocked on the doors of Diana's grandparents' house - when her grandma opened the door, she was in for a real shock. The lady was wearing very expensive saree, with lots of flamboyant jewelleries; a very strong perfume she was wearing filled the air with beautiful smell – there she was - Nelly, Sam's mother, who instinctively showed up at the would-be in-law's house at the behest of his distant relative's friend, Vicky!

Within a few seconds, Ritu realised that what she did was a big mistake – she didn't believe her son when Vicky told her earlier during the day that one of his friend's aunt was going to come that evening to see Riya, as a prospective bride for Sam. What happened next was kind of a fairy tale, as Riya and Sam got married the same winter; they relocated to New York after a few years, where a beautiful girl child was born out of the wedlock – her name was Rina.

By virtue of being a born US citizen, Rina got the benefits of free schooling. She used to be a fairly good student till her senior years, when she chose wrong friends and began late night partying and other stuff that hampered her education. Riya and Sam were upset about it but couldn't help – that's the price of wrong friendship that many kids across the world end up paying, without realising it until it was too late – same happened with Rina, after her fate ran havoc on her career.

Late night partying, skipping school for attending to parties, under-age drinking and smoking, use of unlawful objects, etc. were all causes of bright kids getting distracted from what their primary focus should be on, during that vital juncture of life in early teenage years, for which the implications were far too higher than what most kids realised at that point of time. They used to think that it was fun to engage in those sorts of things; but what they didn't realise was, they were wasting the most valuable time of their lives by concentrating on almost everything material, except studying.

Anyone can hold off to those 'fun things' that please them till later years, when they were through the phase of character-building and career-planning. Life isn't short for having fun – all kinds of fun can be had after a concrete foundation has been built, on which the future 'fun' or 'misery' may depend – some kids didn't seem to realise it; maybe it had something to do with parenting too!

Anyways, Rina couldn't complete her college due to setbacks in her early life. Pretty soon she realised that many of her erstwhile batch-mates had completed their college successfully and moved on. She tried obtaining a degree in nursing, but couldn't stick to it; so, she entered the job-market with less than accepted qualifications – as a result, it took her many strenuous years at work before she got up the ladder, because she had to start from scratch. Rina chose not to start a family - she was a bachelor living with her parents.

Riya initially used to be a typical Bengali housewife, taking care of her extended family – she had a spirited and funny brother-in-law, three sister-in-law (all married, by the grace of God!) and her husband Sam's parents. They initially used to reside at a rented accommodation near Park Circus, then moved to another rented one in South End Park, before Sanjay, the spouse of the eldest sister-in-law bought a three-storied huge house in Keyatala, to let his in-law's families stay there. Sanjay's epic success in life can make a great story by itself!

Sanjay used to belong to a very mediocre family from Jadavpur; his father didn't make enough money to allow his son to pursue his dream career in Engineering, due to many constraints. He had scored exceedingly well in the entrance examination, after which he was offered full scholarship to study Civil Engineering in Kharagpur IIT. He received a Gold Medal after securing the first position in first class thereafter – soon, he was offered a lucrative job at a multinational company. But Sanjay had other ideas in mind.

He contacted some US universities where he could pursue his Masters, and based on his performances and superb college application, etc., he surely got admitted for pursuing MBA from a top college in the east coast. Although he got partial scholarships and financial aid for his studies in the USA, but he needed to earn money to pay off other dues, apart from meeting up his living expenses. So, Sanjay took a night-shift job in a posh condominium complex in Manhattan as security person.

Sanjay diligently spent all day at his school, running to professors for clarifications and further explanations than already provided in the classes for different subjects. Then he will rush back to his job which started at 6 in the evening – it was a 12 hours' shift. Sanjay rushed back to his hostel from school, change over and grabbed something to eat on the run, and would take the subway to reach his workplace on time. There, he would perform his assigned duties till midnight; he had to open electronic gates for residents, log in any visitors and log them out, man the computer at his desk with CCTV images of the building displaying there, etc.

During the evenings, Sanjay didn't get any chance to go over his study materials due to heavy ingress and egress – he didn't have the resource to buy all the required books; so, he had to lend books from library, read those, take notes and return those on time.

After midnight, Sanjay made time for his studies for several hours while keeping an eye on the TV monitor at work – he went straight back to his hostel in the morning after grabbing some cheap breakfast, put alarm on his clock, and take a nap for few hours, until it was time to get up and go back to school. Such was his hectic life that many couldn't possibly even think of, let alone trying it out!

Literary, Sanjay didn't have more than three to four hours' time (at the maximum) for sleeping during weekdays – he tried to make it up on weekends, but his heavy schedule hardly let him relax even a little bit. It was some extraordinary willpower and strong determination that eventually led his path to succeed in life; Sanjay came out first again on his final and got an immediate job offer as Marketing Manager of a reputable company, as his first placement.

Within a timeframe of less than three years, Sanjay got hired by J.P. Morgan as Vice President. He bought a nice house at a prime location in New Jersey and got married with the eldest daughter of Sam in Kolkata. His wife obtained her visa really quick, as Sanjay had already obtained US citizenship by then. The newlywed couple flew back to US together shortly after their marriage was consummated.

Sanjay joined American Express as Senior VP shortly thereafter; within a few years, he got promoted to the position of President. His career was unstoppable, as he soon joined Citibank NA as Executive Director! What else can anyone dream of?

It was only due to Sanjay's unselfish love and his graciousness that the entire in-law's family of Riya were able to procure their alien cards for travel to the USA shortly - all of them eventually got naturalized as US citizens. The remaining two sister-in-law of Riya got married to academically brilliant guys from Kolkata, who migrated to USA after their marriages by dint of their spousal alien cards.

Those brothers-in-law also subsequently sponsored their own families for travel to US. Thus, around 150 people, who were related somehow to Sanjay's in-law's family, moved down to US – the chain reaction continued, and much later in life, Diana found out that there were at least 75 Bengali families in the USA who were direct beneficiaries of Sanjay's noble and generous actions!

Riya went to US with her husband Sam within few months of their marriage, where they rented an apartment at Queens, NY; they lived with Sam's brother, Bob. Rina was born there - Bob also got married with a close relative of the then CM of West Bengal. Panchali, his wife, was a beautiful young lady from a very cultured and educated background - she became friends with Riya in no time; the duo sister-in-law used to have great time together.

Bob used to be extremely handsome – fair complexion, well built, sharp features, beautiful eyes and manly voice; it seemed like God gave him all the qualities relating to beauty quite generously. But he was a womaniser, flirting with almost every beautiful woman out there; his whereabouts were unknown to his wife initially.

But eventually, the news reached her - Panchali tried to persuade Bob to lead a devoted life. She tried extremely hard to desist him from engaging in actions which would finally end up in breaking such a wonderful marriage; but she couldn't.

Bob had multiple affairs; girls used to be all around him; it was impossible for him to sacrifice all the beauties to be faithful to one – so, his wife was left with absolutely no option but to divorce him. She later got married to a guy from Punjab to lead a normal and happy conjugal life in CA.

Bob, on the other hand, got remarried twice, but failed to establish trust on his partners' minds, resulting in two more annulments of marriage. He did have a daughter from his third marriage - she turned out to be a popular Tollywood actress down the road.

Sadly though, Bob died a pathetic death from short circuit of air-conditioner placed at his bedroom years later, when he was merely 55 years of age. Irrespective of his character, Bob used to be a great person, smart, witty, humorous and lively. Diana fondly remembered him from her early childhood years – uncle Bob used to love her too.

Riya realised after some time that she needed to work, not only for financial independence, but also in order to stop being forced to act as baby-sitters for her three sister-in-law's family – they used to assemble together on long weekends and holidays at Riya's house, have fun all day without helping out Riya in any manner. They would then leave their rotten kids at Riya's safe custody, while they went out partying with their brothers and other friends.

This became a routine gradually - Riya got over-worked; not only she had to clean the house before the group of around 12 arrived at her place, but she also had to cook, clean, take care of the spoiled brats, and then clean all the messes they left behind – it was getting on her nerves. She couldn't take it no more; that's when she decided to start working.

In the meantime, her brother Vicky had also arrived at NY, encouraging her to take up a gainful employment. Vicky also brought his parents to NY within a year of his arrival there. Biman insisted that Riya started learning how to drive.

Without a driver's license, it was difficult to get a decent job, unless one restricted himself to working around his locality. Biman started accompanying Riya on her driving lessons – he felt ecstatic when Riya finally got herself a licence and eventually, a job at a supermarket as cashier.

Riya worked very hard between her job and her household chores but was able to maintain a healthy balance. Sam was working for an Indian firm; he was content there, as he was getting more money in cash! In addition, he was unwilling to work for any American company due to his inherent shyness. They bought a house in Hicksville, Long Island after ten years or so, and moved out there. Riya had already secured herself a decent job at a local bank by then, and it was easy for her to get transferred to the bank's branch at Long Island. Riya used to drive to work, after dropping off her daughter at school. She used to pick up her daughter Rina from her school after work.

Hicksville was the town from where Rina completed her schooling. As she was getting involved with bad company there, Riya and Sam decided to sell off their house to move to Florida, far from where they lived. So, they bought a nice house in Cape Coral, not far from Miami – Riya got a great job with a famous bank there, where she was liked by everyone, including her customers.

Sam decided to sit back at his new house and enjoy life; he was little lazy at working, although he had great inherent talent of singing. He spent his old days watching sports – he was a die-hard fan of New York Yankees! He also used to spend time recording songs for his relatives and friends; he would use full use of his karaoke and loads of musical instruments that he had purchased over time – then, he would upload his songs on YouTube.

Rina began to comprehend the value of her lost time and opportunities; she started focusing on a carefully selected career. She went on to become a good nurse later on in life; she was eventually successful at her profession, although she always repented her lost golden days!

After Diana's mother and her parents unknowingly fell into the trap laid by Randip and his parents, Gita got married to Randi without realising that he was not only a psychopath liar and a guy with no moral values or character, but also a criminal who had tortured his first wife for dowry. He finally got a nasty divorce from his first wife – he got away with his crimes throwing his clout around as a High Court lawyer.

Gita and her parents were kept in complete dark by Randi and his family as regards the chequered past of that notorious son of Das family. He used to carry an innocent look on his face, mostly hiding behind occasional quiet nod if someone asked him any question! He was too cunning to expose his cunning attitude to outsiders; some people thought him to be a decent guy!

Upon learning all the grave facts about her husband several months after her marriage, from a neighbour of her in-laws, Gita was devastated - she wanted to return back to her parents' house. But the entire in-law's family literally fell on her feet, apologised for not being honest and truthful to her and her parents, by failing to divulge the horrible past of Randi.

Gita had a soft heart and believed in the old saying which states that "to forgive and forget is a virtue", and thus forgave the sinful in-law – Randi also shed crocodile tears, fell on her feet, and apologised for hiding the truth from her, thus making Gita forgive the dubious guy!

However, trouble started brewing right after Gita got pregnant with Diana – Randi and his mother Lila would not take Gita for routine medical check-ups and diagnostic tests, hearing which her parents and brother got really upset. Her parents insisted that Gita started staying at her parent's house till she delivered the baby, for safety of the mother and the child.

Randi jumped at that lucrative offer – he didn't have to make up more excuses for not having money, citing lack of regular income. And, he didn't have to spend time trying to think of making up excuses for his various ill habits.

He even refused to accompany his lovely and honest bride to the various chambers of medical professionals she used to attend, in order to get treated during her prenatal stage, not even during her post-natal stages later.

Gita was made to believe that Randi didn't make enough money at his profession – so, she felt compassion and sympathy for that devious guy. She did return to her in-law's house after a month of her delivering Diana; she thought that a father's care was essential for a kid, and thus she chose to go back to her house in Fern Road, when Di was a month old.

Di was born on a bright sunny summer day in May, at CMRI Hospital in Ekbalpore. Gita's parents and siblings were so happy and thrilled to have the most invaluable addition to the family - Diana was jovial right from the time of her birth, as she hardly cried.

As a matter of fact, she used to open her eyes and make faces – everyone around her used to love it and burst in laughter. She used to throw her arms and legs up and down sometimes, making a round face – the scene got scripted in the hearts of her grandparents (maternal) and uncle and aunt. It used to be so much fun just to be around that beautiful god-gifted child!

Randi and his virile mother weren't happy at all by the fact that a baby girl was born – they expected a boy! Maybe that would entice them with a prospect of turning the kid into a money-machine someday, as money was of utmost importance to Das family.

Das family used to fight amongst themselves frequently for money matters - issues relating to money was of primal importance in their hearts, if they had any! In fact, their world revolved around money - there was no place for love, affection, care, values or principles to them.

Vicky used to say often that his loving younger sister got married to the worst family in the universe! Vicky's life was full of ups and downs, as he was a person with zero tolerance with corruptive or immoral practices; he hated liars. He would often get into fight with others if he ever felt that anyone was harming innocent people. His innocent and childish face wrongly gave the signal to others that Vicky was a timid man, which he wasn't at all.

He would not give nuisance to anyone and would not take any from others. He mostly made sure that legitimate interests of people around him were protected; he wouldn't allow others to ride roughshod over his principles. Vicky was somewhat different from most of his contemporaries in the sense that he would question any imprudent or unethical activity, without adopting the 'go with the flow' type philosophy. He rocked many boats during his lifetime, although that caused him enough stress, anxiety and sufferings.

He was spending his retired life in Puri, after his mom and niece moved to the USA. They would maintain daily contact over phone, WhatsApp, Skype and Instagram with each other, as the trio were very closely knit by heart. As Vicky got fed up with decaying moral values amongst many people in Kolkata, with more and more corruptive practices cropping up in most spheres of life, he decided to move to Puri – that way, he could at least lead a peaceful life without any aggravation or mental unrest. He penned down the following paragraphs over his frustration in Bengal and sent it to Di – she loved it.

"It was a gloomy Sunday morning in Kolkata – incessant rain due to low pressure and depression over Bay of Bengal during a fine winter season was spoiling the mood for everyone, from students to retired people, to kids and their parents to professionals, from daily-wage earners to industrialists – of course, for different reasons applicable to the pertinent individuals.

Many students wanted to get to private coaching classes hosted by their school teachers – it is almost customary in this part of the globe that you take private tuitions from your subject teachers at school, paying hefty fees; it doesn't matter if your parents can afford it or not. If they can, its fine; if not, be prepared to be singled out and end up with poor marks. The period being the examination season, with the finals coming up shortly, the students were expecting to get some 'insights' into the questions to be answered during the finals. And, if you're a college student, your plans to hang out with your friends or your special ones seems ruined now.

As regards many of the retired middle-class people, you're upset as you couldn't get the bargain at the local fish market over the weekends, and your spouse is going to be in a fit of rage if you don't end up with some tasty food items – this is a Sunday, remember? I deserve to be treated a little better today! The old bugger needs to dig in the closet to pull out his raincoat and woollen scarf to venture out to grab something to please his wife with. And, if you're the unlucky one without the wife, then your daughter-in-law is going to mar your mood by insisting that you do your part of the chores, as if you're duty bound to do so.

This is in addition to your complimentary baby-sitting of your grand-kids and your ferrying them to and fro school and tuition classes – you get to eat some leftovers at the end of the day. This is your deal – don't complain, as you're lucky that they didn't take you out for a holy dip on the Ganges during Ganga Sagar Mela or Kumbh Mela and didn't abandon you there. In case your husband has departed for his heavenly sojourn already, be prepared to cook and clean the dishes too! At least you have a bedroom of your own below the staircase, even though it's a makeshift one with no fans or lights, barely fitting your cot in it.

And, more importantly, please don't come out of your 'shell' when guests are around, as they'll either mistake you as maid, or your son is going to be embarrassed to call you his mom. You gave him birth alright; but that was your duty – you were duty bound to raise him and sacrifice everything good in life for his well-being. You were always a maid servant anyways – either cooking or cleaning or dusting or wiping floors or some other household chores. So, you're depressed too today, if not because of anything else, but due to the fact that you don't have a wearable woollen cloth to shield you from the cold. That's okay – you gotta bear it.

Speaking of some parents from well to do classes, they were upset that day as their plans to eat out in the fancy restaurant were marred by no mercy from the rain-god. The driver didn't come, and the car wasn't cleaned enough to be driven through the elite driveway leading to the valet parking! So, you've to end up calling in for home-delivery, and that was going to be outrageous, as you'll end up having to spill some food for your in-laws, alias free domestic helps. That was gonna be costly! Then, there were some who lived and grifted, lived for the day – as soon as they got some money by any shady deal or whatever he was involved in, they just spent it obnoxiously – it was a bad day for them too!

Some professionals were angry as their scheduled trip to beauty parlours for pedicure, manicure, shaving and dyeing hairs were all in jeopardy. In addition, your invitation to your peer's party at the rooftop was cancelled due to that unholy rain! Gosh! Booze and smoke would've filled up your appetite if the sky held up a little bit – but no, it had to be today. Worse was the situation of the middle-aged men (should I dare to say those in mid-life crises) who were supposed to take their good-looking female secretary or some other traveling colleague's wife to the secluded resort down on the south-suburban fringes! They already promised their innocent wives at home, that they'll get her nice diamond rings on their way back from that 'important meeting' with the boss, who's flying in for a special occasion! All lies may get caught!

In case you were one of those holding an important government portfolio, especially in the police or some civic bodies, your plan to take the lady-complainant or male-complainant's wife for a bar-be-cue party (all expenses paid) with music and dancing (may be something more) looked dim. You had been holding off to her complaint (or her husband's complaint) on the false pretence of having to discuss the matter in detail! Now, you'll end up with asking for the cash reward only – this isn't a bribe, as you were doing them a favour by pressing false charges on the accused, right? It didn't matter who had purported the crime; all it mattered was how much you individually gained out of it, correct Sir? You're not a con artist grifting millions of rupees from unwary peace-loving citizens of Kolkata, are you?

Situation was grimmer if you were one of those politicians. You came into power by promising people all kinds of changes – the changes don't have to be for the betterment; it's perfectly acceptable if the change is worse for them – after all, it is a change, isn't it?

You were all set to attend the public rally at the famous ground this afternoon, and paid few crores to your agents for ensuring that a minimum five lakhs' turnout there; the money part you're least bothered – it came from the land-sharks, promoters, supply-syndicates and brokers of land anyway. The part that came from the industrialists are already in your pocket, or in the safe custody of your brother's in-laws (so that it can't be traced) – you aren't worried about that part.

The part that was bothering you the most was, what will happen to the promised sums of money that those illegal traders and hosts of your other 'beneficiaries' were to pay you in disguised cloth-packets after the rally? How can God be so unkind to me? I had been regularly donating to the mosques under my jurisdiction, so as to kill two birds at one stone – one, to show my party's solidarity to them for encashing during the votes, and two, to take deductions under income taxes after paying a tad bit to the party fund.

Other leaders of your party need not be paid much by you – you can redirect those asking for new permissions for buildings, etc. to channelize their energies (in the form of cash and kind) to those leaders, not to mention those unwarranted below-the-table tender papers that you had personally ordered to be signed. Roads and infrastructural developments should never be done permanently; engineers and contractors have already been instructed to do 'temporary' repairs unofficially, so that next year's funding doesn't fall short. If audit caught up, you can easily manoeuvre in your typical ways. So, in a nutshell, you had plenty of reasons to be upset too – let's not harp on that further, which may cause embarrassment and wastage of your valuable time!

Daily wage-earners had a completely different ball game to play. If you were a rickshaw-puller or labourer, there won't be any gainful work today. Who cares if you had ten rupees in your pocket to feed your hungry family some breadcrumbs with or not? The world had enough problems already – you didn't need to add up to it. Just go home and drink country liquor and have your family skip a day's meal, alright?

In case you were some of the street peddlers or hawkers, you were worried that you'll have to pay your local councillor's men a daily pre-determined amount every day; if your total sales didn't add up to the number, how can you make-up the deficit amount with? Just borrow from someone at a high rate on interest. Don't brag about it – you guys are destined that way. Only time you were needed in society was when the voting time came, understand?

Problems that some of the elite class, some industrialists faced that day was havoc. Their penultimate meeting with the corrupt (or should I say prevailing standards) powerhouse had to be postponed, as many influential people will like to spend the gloomy day on your heated pool in your basement, in the company with some celebrity hot-shots, with expensive dining and imported wine or scotch whiskey. Rather than meeting you at the top-class city club today, they'll like to share the luxury you were endowed with – at least they got a perfect opportunity today.

You couldn't say no to them, as your business will definitely suffer otherwise! And what if any of those bureaucrats or ministers got drunk with your chardonnay and high-flying drinks, and forgot that the nice young lady they saw in your house was your own daughter? Why did it had to rain today? If it was any other day, I could've walked straight into their office and gave them whatever 'token of appreciation' to them! That would've taken care of that immense earth-shattering problem of pleasing them!"

Di giggled a lot after reading the lines sent by her uncle, as she knew very well what Vicky had in his mind while writing the passages. He was fed up with the 'system'; so, he chose a reclusive life to stay away from all the hoopla. To Di, Vicky seemed to be a lone rider – a person to whom moral values, ethics, principles, honesty and straight-talk meant more than anything in this universe.

He was a septuagenarian by the time Di got settled in life, to become a hotshot anchor of one of the most renowned television channels in the USA. Vicky spent nearly a quarter of his life in the US himself, from his mid-twenties till his early forties. Those two decades of time he had spent out of his country of birth had moulded him into a very different person than most seen those days. His belief and character may be antiquated, but it was the inner peace that mattered the most to him.

Vicky was born to a very honest father – Biman, who used to work for the Government. Vicky's mother Ritu was a typical housewife who completed her Board exam at the same time as her son and elder daughter were graduating from school. Vicky's elder sister got married at an early age, like their mother, to a guy based in New York. The younger sister and Vicky used to be like best friends till Vicky immigrated to USA after graduating from college – he did work a few years before that in India. The younger sister Gita got married to Randip at home, and had a beautiful baby, named Diana.

Vicky graduated from one of the best schools and colleges in that neck of the woods from where he belonged. As a kid, he was average in studies, but an all-square in other fields, starting from sporting events to social and cultural life. His father always inculcated some value-systems in the siblings from early childhood days, leading by example.

While being stationed at an ongoing structure of dam in Kolaghat, with a view to inspect records and accounts, Vicky's father was offered bribe by unscrupulous contractors, in connivance with some engineers, for passing a bill (for erection of pillars on the dam, which actually were never constructed at all), which he refused right away, resulting from his transfer to other department by dint of exercising of undue influence by the vested interest groups. Vicky was a witness to the incident, as he was vacationing with his father during his school break. This incident, amongst others, influenced Vicky a lot during his later years.

On the other hand, Vicky's uncle Sunny, who used to be an Inspector for local Motor Vehicles Department, used to issue licenses and permits to almost anyone who will pay hefty sums to him. Vicky witnessed many such incidents when visitors with briefcases (stashed with money) used to visit their ancestral house. The obvious happened, with his uncle living upstairs leading a lavish life, while Vicky and his family led a very modest life. But, as luck would have it, none of the two sons of Vicky's dishonest uncle got beyond school, and eventually turned out to be small time criminals languishing their father's ill-gotten money, engaging in frequent brawls and various criminal activities.

While Vicky and his sisters became well-settled in life, but those paternal cousin brothers became social menaces. After the death of their father, those two brothers started fighting each other for extracting money their father had left behind. That saga eventually led to the untimely demise of their mother, out of trauma and shock. Those two brothers always fought amongst themselves and were a big menace to Vicky and his family.

Vicky, on the other hand, went to the US, worked hard between jobs to get a degree from there; he soon got himself a decent Government job, offering nice benefits and perks. Since the Government there reimbursed tuition expenses for higher education related to the field of work, Vicky got six more post graduate degrees from institutes of international repute, within a span of ten years. He was then promoted consecutively, to soon head the team he was earlier subordinate to.

His dream career let him travel across US on government business; all his expenses were billed to the corporations he was auditing. He bought a nice farmhouse with acres of land, and spent the weekends gardening, mowing, etc.

He used to enjoy a very decent and peaceful life there. He also took his younger sister and his parents to US several times - he wanted them to stay with him; but they preferred the lifestyle they were used to back home, and thus returned back to India after spending few months with Vicky each time they had visited.

During one such visit to the US, Vicky's father developed a heart problem, for which he had to be hospitalised right away. As they lived in a small town far from the City (Vicky had the privilege of using his home as office-address, meaning he would get reimbursed for all flights to work and back), the family was very scared thinking it might be too time-consuming for the ailing father to reach hospital. However, to everyone's pleasant surprise, a chopper landed on Vicky's lawn after he had called the emergency number, which flew his father to the hospital, accompanied by medics and paramedical staff.

They were constantly in touch with Vicky on the ground (for learning about his father's medical history) on the one hand, and with the doctors in Syracuse Hospital on the other over phone. By the time Vicky reached the hospital along with his mother and sister, his father had already been operated on and a stent had been implanted successfully! In other words, the hospital authorities didn't even care to find out about billing for expenses – their only prerogative was the patient's survival. One Dr. Caputto was the surgeon in charge of the operation, that doctor became so friendly with the family later on!

Around ten years later, when some unethical doctors in India's premier hospital in the capital insisted that the stent be replaced, during a routine check-up there, Vicky contacted that doctor over phone; Dr. Caputto immediately recognized him - after hearing what doctors in India were saying, he just smiled and told Vicky to get his father out of there, as his stent was permanent!

Vicky used to fly back home every year to see his parents and younger sister, if they didn't visit him on any particular year – they spent three weeks traveling together to exotic destinations. He also kept close contacts with his elder sister Riya who used to live in New York with her husband Sam and daughter Rina, up until they moved to Florida quite a while after living in the US. They bought a beautiful house there; they used to meet up with the family as much as possible.

Many people thought that Vicky had made a big mistake by marrying a wrong kind of woman, who succeeded in squeezing out almost his last breath, during the small amount of time they stayed married. Soon, Vicky had to divorce his wife and preferred to stay single, after a few attempts to get remarried fell apart.

He decided to return back to India, sacrificing his esteemed job and luscious properties, as he realised one day that despite of having the most coveted material things in life, he was missing out on taking care of his ailing parents back home, apart from the fact that his evil uncle Sunny and his two sons were making life miserable for his parents, trying to evict them from the ancestral house, after successfully evicting the other two uncles.

Sunny was a very greedy person, to whom money mattered the most – he even tried to fly out to Bangladesh, to their ancestral home, many times in order to see if he could get the sale proceeds of the big land his grandparents used to own there, before the entire family had to flee the country after Partition. Sunny always poked his nose into other people's businesses, to gain popularity in one hand, and to find out if he can gain economically by any unlawful means. He used fictitious names to deposit his ill-gotten money in various banks, all of which got confiscated by the government after his death many years later, as none of those depositors actually existed – they were fake; Sunny thought in his evil mind that he will live many years than he actually did, so as to enjoy his high life with those money.

Alas, God had other punishments in queue for him. Sunny was so cruel and notorious that his wife tried to commit suicide twice by consuming poison – she survived on both the occasion though, once at RKMS hospital, and once at EEDF where doctors washed her stomach instantly. Sunny quarrelled with his brothers living on the first floor of his father's house – he used to beat them up frequently. They got so disgusted with Sunny's routine abuse and torture that they sold off their shares of the house to him at a nominal price, to be able to get out of there for a better life.

However, Biman and his family were the only ones standing in the way to Sunny's evil intentions to occupy the entire house and give it to a promoter known to him, thereby getting refurbished posh apartments and huge amount of money. His elder brother Biman, on the other hand, used to love his parents and had a strong sentiment attached to the house - therefore, he wasn't willing to budge in to Sunny's unholy desires.

The travesty was that, Danish had earlier thrown out Sunny from his house three times, as the latter was a cause of constant nuisance for everyone. Sunny was forced to live in South End Park and other areas in rented houses during those times – but, Biman and Ritu had very soft hearts - they requested Danish on all those three occasions to pardon Sunny and let him move back in – Danish loved his eldest son Biman, as also his wife Ritu; so, he agreed to let the evil son back in. He always used to curse Sunny and tell him that his mother was better off going for abortion when she got pregnant with him, had the family knew how evil and notorious Sunny would become later!

Vicky's parents were not willing to leave the house, due to the sentiments attached with it, and also because of the fact that Vicky's grandfather had requested his dad and mom not to abandon that house. Therefore, Vicky thought it was best to return to the land he came from, so that he can protect his parents from routine verbal and physical abuses by the culprits. He had all his furniture and appliances packed in a 40 feet container and shipped to his port.

Thus, Vicky returned back, bidding adieu to the land which gave him all the success, all the glory and all the best that anyone could have dreamt for.

Soon after his return, Diana was born to Vicky's younger sister Gita and her husband Randi. She became the prime attraction of the family right away, with her giggles, her loving caresses and her funny activities. Vicky became very close to Di - the two of them bonded very easily. Her mother used to be a government schoolteacher; she used to drop Di at the beautiful bungalow that Vicky had constructed upon his return and pick her back in the evening.

However, Diana was getting much closer to Vicky and his parents than her own family. She soon started staying with them, taking turns between their ancestral house in Golpark and Vicky's bungalow located in the fringes of the city. Di's father was always a very selfish and miser person - he never was able to obtain his daughter's love and affection due to his own fault. His wife had to accept it the way it was, as they didn't want another divorce in the family.

Vicky's younger sister was wrongly diagnosed and treated by a doctor in a very reputable private nursing home located very close to their ancestral house. Although Vicky took her to all the best hospitals across various cities in India, it was too late - she passed away at an early age of just 37 years.

Vicky's father couldn't cope with the untimely loss; he too passed away after medical negligence by doctors in two top-of-the-line private nursing homes. This was following another series of torture by Vicky's notorious uncle and his two criminal sons. Vicky was broken-hearted after the two subsequent losses in his immediate family, and before he could recuperate, he was entangled in a legal battle fighting a false lawsuit filed by those same miscreants against him.

However, God was merciful to Vicky's family for a change, as the notorious uncle Sunny died in a brutal road accident after his sons abandoned him on the streets, when they failed to persuade him to sign over all tangible and intangible properties in their names. As they had very good connections with the local police station, they got away with their crimes; even after their mother's death soon thereafter, they continued to harass Vicky and his widowed mother so that they leave the house.

Those two uneducated and unemployed creatures made their lives miserable by routine physical assault, verbal abuse and threats to the peace-loving family. At the same time, those two evil cousins will file false complaint against Vicky and his family at the local police station and even at Alipore Court, so that they get disgusted and leave their ancestral house too!

So, Vicky decided to stay away from his ancestral house, after his successive attempts to get legal help went unheeded (due to the unholy nexus between the two evil cousins and the local police personnel). He would visit his mother and Di for few hours during weekdays.

On weekends, they will spend great time at Vicky's – as Diana's school and all other classes she were going through were located in close proximity of their ancestral house, the mother and the niece used to return back Sunday evenings. There were no good schools in the area where Vicky had built his posh bungalow - his huge house was inhabited only by him till school closed for summer, winter etc.

Vicky had tried out many jobs in his hometown since his return to India, including as Head of one of the most prestigious B-schools in the country, located close to his bungalow. But they all had something in common, something that Vicky could not compromise with – that was, corruptive practices.

While working for the US Government, Vicky used to be in charge of anti-corruption; now, his values were being vindicated by constantly having to deal with corruption at all levels. He had even written to the top government official with corroborating evidences against the corruption at this premier B-school but was told to turn his head around!

He couldn't do it, and as a result, he was getting very unpopular with the trade unions and some of the faculty-members who used unfair means to deprive the school of legitimate fees-sharing on consultancy services to external bodies, etc. Vicky had no other option but to resign after his discussion with the Director there revealed that he knew everything that was going on but wasn't willing to resort to any positive actions against those corrupt individuals, apparently due to influence of cut-money.

Vicky tried private sectors too, but same old, same old story even there. They were either getting into unauthorised collection of deposits from common people (promising hefty and quick returns), or were using unfair means to circumvent laws and regulations, or evade taxes by illegal means, etc. Vicky got so depressed that he decided to call it quits for his professional career.

He started working in his own garden – this was after his individually set-up consultancy services ended up being not paid timely by the clients on false pretexts - Vicky decided it was best to stay away from people as much as he could, just in order to have peace in life. But, his ongoing court cases and legal battles with the two criminal cousins caused a lot of drainage of his savings; soon, he needed to sell the house to fund Diana's undergraduate studies.

Di was a very good student all along - she got excellent grades in her Board examinations at school levels; she aspired to be a journalist when she grew up. The family decided that it was best for Di to pursue her undergraduate courses in a reputed US college, as opposed to local colleges in their own country, not only for her better prospect, but also to ensure her smooth transition to becoming a decent individual.

The period of time when Diana was completing her junior school at a time when the State was marred with political turmoil and vendetta politics, which directly hampered the educational institutions adversely. Also, Vicky wanted his most favourite girl in the world, Diana to undergo her college and post-graduate courses in foreign land, for better prospect and lucrative career, most preferably from one of the Ivy-league colleges in the USA or in UK.

Diana started her pre-nursery school when she was only two and a half years of age. Gita used to drop her off in the morning on her way to work; Ritu or Biman used to pick her up after school. Di seemed to be very happy with friends there playing with her, learning nursery rhymes, little bit of recitations and singing. The way she used to enact what went on at her preschool in front of her maternal grandparents and uncle were something so hilarious and cute!

Most of the time, especially when her school was closed for holiday or weekends, Di will pretend to be a teacher herself, with a saree wrapped around her neck (hanging out all over the place, sometimes making her trip on loose ends of the saree), while she was still wearing frock with diapers wrapped around – she'll compel Biman, Ritu and Vicky to stand up as soon as she entered her 'classroom' (usually the family room) and say 'good morning miss' (it didn't matter what time of the day it was) with an insouciant face. Then she'll say 'good morning students' in a rhythmic manner.

God forbade if any of her 'students' inadvertently got seated before she sat down on a baby chair with a small table and blackboard attached to it, which Biman had bought for her dear grand-daughter. Then, Di will really appear upset, tell the errant student to get out of the classroom and stand outside for ten minutes, with poker-faced seriousness! However, she will definitely call the student standing outside back by calling his/her name out loudly, in less than a minute, apparently as the little girl didn't learn to read hands on clocks yet!

After that, she will start singing some nursery rhymes in her cuckoo voice; then she'll instruct the 'students' to emulate her in every possible manner, irrespective of situations when her students sometimes felt that the verse defied scansion! If anyone made the heinous mistake of laughing or smiling at her 'classroom', Di will scream at the top of her lungs and ended up bursting in laughter herself. She soon will get back to her role, by warning students to fall in line, and not to disrupt her class!

As she started attending her nursery classes couple of years later, Di would pick one of the several broken pieces of chalks from her study-table (she ended up breaking each chalk into several pieces by mistakenly applying more force than the poor things could take); then she would write 2 plus 2 on her blackboard attached to the table, draw a line below it, and ask her 'students' to raise hands if they knew the answer. In case one of her students failed to raise a hand, she will make sure to throw some pieces of caution to that student, sometimes warning against a 'guardian call' to school!

Biman wilfully tried to answer some of the questions relating to addition, subtraction, multiplication or division wrong, as Di started learning those gradually, mainly in order to test his grand-daughter's own expertise! If Di knew the answer to which her grandpa responded accurately, she'll praise Biman with a pat on his shoulder with a staid face.

But, heaven forbade if Di' did know the correct answer, and Biman gave wrong answer intentionally, in order to ensure that the kid learned properly – she will become incandescent and enraged through her facial expressions; she will appear to be apoplectic with rage; she'll scream at the poor old septuagenarian fellow, telling him to stand up holding his ears, for the 'mistake'. Furthermore, she'll instruct her student to write down the correct answer ten times, more if he was giggling!

Di was an avid learner with inquisitive mind and soon developed flairs for writing, public speaking, debates, quiz – she used to participate in all kinds of quizzes in maths, English, general knowledge, science and other topics, and brought in numerous medals, awards and certificates from national and international organizations of repute.

She turned out to be a very decent individual – honest, hardworking, caring, sharing, innovative and active with pleasant personality. In the words of one of her class teachers (comment made on her report card while Di was in sixth grade), she was "a gregarious, exuberant, generous, impartial, passionate, dedicated and unassuming young girl".

When she was ready to go to regular school, Gita got her dear daughter admitted to the same school from where her brother Vicky had passed out decades back – it was a new building at Mandeville Garden - Diana got admitted in Class 1 there. It was a coeducational school where she soon started having the sweet company of so many friends. The manner in which the little kids held hands together to form a queue when the classes ended was so enthralling!

They all looked like tiny fairies and most of them used to giggle or be in naughty modes most of the time, and all it took for them to straighten out their mischievous acts was a stern look from their class teacher, who used to be a fine young lady with lots of grace. The toddlers loved her and stormed her with barrage of silly questions – but that amazing teacher never lost her calm and responded to all the questions smilingly. The kids used to wave goodbyes to her and other teachers before leaving school premises, and also didn't forget to wave and say byes to their tiny winy friends during closing hours.

The efficiency and patience with which that School handled children were really supercalifragilisticexpialidocious! The management was run by one Mrs. Kohli, who had initially refused Di's admission into the school, probably being perplexed by the ill mannerism of her father (during interview of parents). Gita didn't want to harm feelings of her husband by avoiding him during the interview process, although Vicky had warned her in advance about probable ramifications of letting him appear for the interview, which Gita chose to ignore. Thereafter, Vicky went in to see Mrs. Kohli, asked her a simple question, and got his dear niece admitted there.

The question that Vicky asked was very simple – why should a bright kid be denied admission on the ground of her father's traits; it wasn't the father who was seeking admission – so, where did the School's scope of nurturing bright students stood, if all their students seeking admission were born out of great men? Iswar Chandra Vidyasagar or Rabindra Nath Tagore didn't belong to triumphant fathers! Quoting the great Malcolm Forbes, Vicky wanted to say that "failure is success if we learn from it." Or, as Maya Angelou had stated: "success is liking yourself, liking what you do, and liking how you do it."

The Principal got the message quite good that Vicky was a hard nut to crack; she decided to let Di appear for the final test to seek admission therein. As Vicky already knew very well, Di' did exceedingly well and got admitted into that School. Mrs. Kohli didn't forget to apologise to Vicky at the end of the year when Di stood first in the promotion exam and said that she was proud of Di. Vicky had also stated to the lady earlier that he was an alumnus of the school, and what if Di was his daughter, instead of Randi's? Mrs. Kohli didn't want to rock the boat further – matter was already settled.

The parents of kids studying in that school used to mingle together sometimes - two picnics were hosted by them during the two years that Di studied there. The first one held at a secluded hicktown called Bira, near Barasat, was attended by at least 20 kids and another 40/50 parents. It was a day full of fun, not only to the kids, but also for the parents. Diana's grandparents and her uncle Vicky joined there too and had a time of their life.

Vicky played badminton with a very pretty mother of one of Diana's friend there for some time - this gorgeous young lady fell for him quickly, as Vicky used to be a very handsome, smart and intelligent young guy. She was married to a popstar, who used to be nice too – so, Vicky refused the proposal very politely, which infuriated the young lady. Anyways, it was a great day of outing for all on that special day, during Christmas vacation.

Diana was in for the first fatal shock of her life, when her mother got diagnosed with a terminally ill disease. The carcinogenic lump that Gita developed in her breast soon spread and became malignant. It was during a visit to her in-law's house by Vicky on a fateful January afternoon, when he noticed a small lump on Gita's face near her eardrums. Vicky immediately advised his sister to get it seen by a medical professional, especially after hearing Gita was having pain on her face, along with her ears, for the last few weeks.

Gita was employed at a government school in Behala as a geography teacher. She refused to stay with her brother in USA years ago, when her brother took her there for a pleasure trip during summer vacation of her school. Vicky wanted his sister to obtain a teaching license in New York State, so that she can immigrate there and continue her teaching – he even sponsored his sister and got her a permanent resident status very quick, after sponsoring his parents for the green card. Call it fate or anything else, Gita insisted that she go back to Kolkata and continue her job there, as she was reluctant to learn the typical American accent.

Vicky couldn't convince his sister to stay, especially after his elder sister Riya got Gita a part time job at a shopping mall in Long Island as sales girl – Gita felt that her job description was way too inferior – it fell far short of her qualifications and work experiences in India; so, she quit her job there in no time, and left US for good, not paying any heed to Vicky's continuous assurances that it was not going to take more than a few months for her to obtain teaching license there, especially since he already had Gita's credentials evaluated and certified by a team of expert professionals in the US who specialized in world education field.

The tragedy was, Gita's teaching license was obtained from NY within a month after she left US, as she had earlier successfully taken the requisite tests, etc. But it was too late, and Gita had already resumed her job in her school at Behala. She had a bunch of peers there who were nothing but opportunists, without Gita realising it – they used to exploit Gita for their own needs.

One of them, Sumedha pretended to be Gita's best friend and got her convinced to take Sumedha's classes when she would leave early or avail of any leaves, thus making sure that she herself didn't lag behind in her own schedule, not caring at all about Gita's schedule or her own inconveniences.

Another teacher, Kalpana used to share her lunch with Gita and befriended her – Gita hardly got to prepare her lunch, leaving her in-law's in haste after getting up early, taking care of her new-born, boiling the bottles for her, preparing food for the in-law family, taking care of household chores and barely having time to take a nice cold shower. So, Gita wouldn't mind sharing the food happily which Kalpana brought at school, thus falling in her traps.

Kalpana had Gita review the answer-scripts of students from Kalpana's classes, and it was really cumbersome for Gita, as she barely had any spare time. She would take a bus to her paternal home, had to opt for a late lunch there, picked up Diana, and took rickshaw-rides back to Fern Road. Then, she had to clean the utensils the monsters used during the day, clean the rooms, prepare dinner for the abhorrent family, and take care of the baby too.

During the weekends, she used to scrutinise the answer sheets of students in her class first, and then review the answer sheets of Kalpana's students. Although the subjects were different, but Gita was an excellent academician with brilliant records at school, college and university levels; she browsed through the textbooks quickly and had a full grasp of the subject in no time.

So, Gita had practically no time for herself; during holidays and breaks, she would be shopping for the baby, the abominable in-law's family and her dreadful husband; or else, her husband will shamelessly ask her to take them out for dinner to somewhere nice, where he would gobble the food served in a matter of minutes and asked for more. He even used to grab the leftovers from his family-members; he didn't even refrain from grabbing food from his daughter's dishes, munch them quickly, and then started looking around if there was anything else left for him to quench his ever-increasing monstrous appetite with.

Gita didn't object, sensing trouble had she raised any objection; she also realised that inherent bad mannerisms or habits can hardly be changed for someone as old as he was. She even treated the harrowing in-laws with exotic vacations at her own expense, and the shameless family didn't even ask her if they should pitch in or not. If they hired a taxi to go someplace on their own with Gita taking care of household chores, they would wait for her to come down and pay their fares – such heinous minds and evil thoughts can only culminate from poor upbringing and evil surroundings, Gita felt.

Anyways, when her brother insisted that Gita should seek medical advice on the lump on her face, she went to the private hospital near her parental house on a weekend morning, to consult a lady doctor there, who said there was nothing to worry – it was supposedly an infection resulting from cold temperatures prevailing at that time. Vicky called up Gita and told her to get it seen by someone at Dale View Clinic near Minto Park, as they had pretty decent medical professionals there.

But Gita said she couldn't take a day off to go there, due to the upcoming Board and Higher Secondary examinations – she used to be an enlisted examiner for the Board, and a paper-setter for the Higher Secondary examination in Geography. In addition, her duties as invigilator and acting teacher-in-charge at her school would pose real problems if she went to Dale View. So, Gita sat on it till she started feeling pain on the left breast; it was again her pure negligence and lack of love for herself that led her to suffer from the pain for another month or so, when it finally became unbearable.

She always brought up her school-related issues and her lack of time at every attempt of her parents and siblings to convince her to seek proper care for her physical condition. What most people didn't realise at that time was the apathy and ignorance of her husband and his parents towards her, which put kind of pressure on her mind, thinking that "if they didn't care, I don't – I'm the one feeding them, running the household for them, caring for the baby and managing my duties professionally. If they don't want me, that's fine" – a kind of depressive mood she fell in, quite tragically.

It was mid-April some day when Gita's mother wanted to take her to a reputed doctor and went to Gita's in-law's house; they openly said that six hundred rupees of fees of that doctor was way too much for Gita to spare, as costs of living were on the rise, for which they were even unable to employ a domestic help at their household! When Gita's mom volunteered to stay there to perform the chores assigned to Gita on her behalf, they bluntly said that they won't be able to feed one more mouth! Vicky called up his mom from work – he was working for a top B-school in Joka as Head of Management Development Programs and Consultancy.

Vicky got so angry that he called up Randi and asked him to see him the same evening at Fern Road – Vicky busted their chops that evening, saying that he would file a criminal case against the whole Das family for torturing and abusing his sister, and put all of them in jail. Gita was crying but Vicky took his sister out of that living hell instantly - he booked two tickets to Chennai on the next available flight.

He went to his Chairman and narrated the ordeal, and the Chairman instantly promised any assistance he would require down the road – this gentleman had earlier given a superb letter of recommendation to Vicky praising his work ethics, dedications, sincerity and integrity, as also highlighting the positive outcome the Institute derived by virtue of his employment there.

Vicky and Gita reached Chennai the next evening and hired a car to Vellore. Upon reaching Christian Medical College campus at Vellore, Vicky got his sister admitted there in the Emergency Department, as this was the only way to expedite her treatment. He stayed with his beloved sister all night long and came back to a hotel in the morning after Gita got a cabin assigned there.

Doctors in CMC formed a Board to review Gita's medical conditions, after they found out that major lapses were observed during the earlier surgery for removal of her left breast few weeks ago, at the same private hospital where Gita was operated on towards end of March, upon diagnosing her with carcinoma, eventually spreading from her left breast – a perfect case of medical malpractice by the hospital in Dhakuria where Gita had her surgery done earlier!

Such surgery was done at the behest of Gita's parents and siblings, once they took her for an autopsy there forcefully, against the wishes of her demon husband and his parents. The doctor there, while operating on Gita, was teaching his junior staff intricate details of oncological surgery, turning Gita to almost a Guinea pig, and filming the operation at the cost of the patient's safety and breach of privacy. But, there again, this was India - who cared if rights were violated – so thought the patient party! Had it been any developed country, the darn private hospital would have been shut off by government.

Once doctors in Vellore determined that tissues were not removed accurately by the oncologist at Kolkata, they wanted to make sure their findings were correct and wanted to corroborate the evidences with actual slides of the surgery. So, Vicky called Randi after sending him a return air-ticket the same day to collect the slides from the private hospital and get it to CMC Vellore. However, the son of a gun refused saying he had urgent cases to litigate in High Court – so, he couldn't make it.

However, he kept the air ticket and since it was purchased with full fare by Vicky, he preferred to change the date to the following Saturday's arrival and next day's departure – he arrived there to enjoy a paid vacation for a day, ran up the food bills sky high by gobbling four meals (didn't even spare to finish everything during the complimentary breakfast slot next morning, forcing other boarders to go fast!), and returned to the laps of his devil mother.

In the meantime, since Vicky could not take a risk of leaving his sister at Vellore alone, and his parents were getting very anxious with Gita's health, he bought three tickets for his family to come up to Vellore the same evening; he went to Chennai to take flight to Kolkata after his parents reached there. He returned with the slides from the hospital where Gita had her surgery done and handed over those to physicians at CMC next afternoon.

It was on that fateful evening when the family learnt from the Board formed by doctors there, that it was a metastatic carcinoma, which was spreading to her brains due to negligence of the operating surgeon, one Dr. A.K. Majumder that the tissues around her affected breast were not removed correctly, resulting in the spreading of the killer disease to other parts of Gita's body – the doctors there gave a two months' window for the patient to survive.

The whole family was devastated; Gita's parents cried incessantly - the little kid couldn't understand why they were all crying. She asked her uncle why they were crying, as she saw her mother at the hospital and thought she was just doing fine – there was no reply that Vicky could possibly think of, other than merely telling Di that her grandparents loved her mother so much that they were missing her, as she was in the hospital at that time!

Vicky went to the roof of the hotel and started crying too, all by himself – he had been a very strong guy all along, who didn't break down under any circumstances thus far; but that time, when he realised that the sister he had practically raised along with his parents, who was seven years younger to him, was going to leave him for good in just two months' time – how can he face his sister at the hospital, when she was going to inquire about what the doctors said relating to her treatment? Vicky felt helpless for the very first time in his life, feeling completely shattered and heart broken.

But he mustered enough courage soon, to get over the grim situation - he made up his mind to sue the killer doctor upon his return to Kolkata. Little did he comprehend the nexus between the Associations of Doctors & regulatory bodies of doctors in India, which would not yield any fair resolution, unless he got extremely lucky, which he didn't eventually!

The family met that unfortunate 37-years old innocent victim of social and medical malpractice at the hospital the next morning, when they were stunned to find out that Gita already knew about her fate – she had even wrote a letter addressing Diana all night long, with a heart-breaking title of "Final letter of a dying mother to her only daughter" – she handed over this letter to her favourite brother, with an earnest request to hand over the letter to Diana once she attained majority!

The letter was carefully preserved in a hidden briefcase at Vicky's bedroom till his niece turned 18, when Di did well to control her emotions in front of others, or at least didn't break down openly.

Di was somewhat of an eccedentesiast from her childhood days, apparently very good at hiding her sadness behind a sweet smile, even at times when she had viable reasons to be extremely sad. She was getting struck with lightening-type shocks from early days in her tender life – so, she had to be strong; she had sheer determination to overcome all odds, to become happy in whatever life had to offer to her.

Her classmates in senior school shunned her from participating in any group activity or even from mere discussions, because they had certain complex, reservations and jealousy of that newcomer to 'their school' – Di didn't argue with any of them; she used to smile back at each one of those psycho girls, pretending that nothing had happened.

Much later in life, Di used to tell her friends, colleagues and almost anyone who she came across, if they ever felt sadness or appeared to be in some kind of pain, to "head up, stay strong, fake a smile, move on. World always looks brighter from behind a smile – although someone can never understand what really the feeling behind the smile was. I smile a lot to all I meet, because I never want them to feel like I do – I wouldn't wish this on anyone, not even to my worst enemies. A smile is the best way to get rid of trouble, although it can be a fake one. You walk through life much easier with a smile on your face."

All Gita had said that dreadful day to her dear family was, she wanted to return to earth to the same exact parents, siblings and daughter some time, with a different husband and in-law. She expressed her gratitude to her parents and her brother for everything they had done for her. She kissed her cutie pie little daughter, telling her to always listen to the grandparents, uncle and aunt. Then, she made a special request to them to take care of her baby for her, in the same manner they took care of Gita all her life!

Her brother scolded her for being so negative about the outcome, and to carry a positive vibe through a fighting attitude till the end – Vicky said that the inevitable cannot be stopped; but it could be prolonged and delayed. Instead of giving up so easy, he urged his loving sister to be strong and ride the waves to the best of her abilities.

Gita asked a question to Vicky next, which will keep haunting Vicky for the rest of his life, and used to cause him a lot of grief and suffering each time he thought about it later – she said that when she was little, she observed her friends playing in swimming pools in their houses, and she wanted to do the same thing as her friends did – she wanted a swimming pool in her house! She was about five years of age and Vicky was twelve.

Without even blinking for a moment, Vicky promised her that he will have a swimming pool made for Gita the next day, although it was impossible in terms of financial viability, feasibility, limitation of space, etc.

However, when Gita returned from her school next day in the afternoon (she used to go to the same school where Diana would go years later, but had to be transferred to a government school from class V onwards due to financial constraints of the family), she was dumbstruck to see her brother around, as he would be normally at his school during that time - Vicky never absented except the day his grandfather died when he was in third grade, and the day when the Principal's wife of his school was found murdered mysteriously – the authorities declared a holiday that fateful day.

It was a scandal which rocked the State later, upon revelations that the Principal conspired with his paramour to get rid of his beautiful wife – he was let go later, as almost everything could be purchased in Bengal at that time, and even later.

When Gita asked Vicky why he didn't go to school that day, Vicky reminded her of his promise the day before; he then took Gita on his shoulders and went to the veranda at the back of the house. Gita started shouting at the top of her voice to notice a swimming pool cropping up there! She could never forget that day till she closed her beautiful eyes – she used to talk about it to almost anyone near and dear to her, praising her brother's willpower and determination, coupled with strong love for his younger sister.

What Vicky did that day in reality was incredible; he started collecting a lot of mud from the adjacent field all morning long - then he barricaded the floor of the veranda by building mud-wall across it, sealed its drain with mud, kept pouring hundreds of buckets of water from the reservoir located adjacent to the veranda. He kept repairing the mud-walls if there was any leak, until the water-level was few inches deep, with its edges touching the iron grills installed on the sides.

That was nothing even close to a swimming pool by any wildest imagination; but it was enough to bring big smile and happiness in the young girl's mind – the girl who looked upon her elder brother as a real hero, in every sense.

Vicky had forgotten all about the incident until Gita reminded him about it, on that horrible day at the hospital, stating that when she wanted a swimming pool as a kid, he had indeed gotten one made for her; when she wanted to get an American teacher's license later in life, he got it for her; even when the school where her daughter got admitted initially refused her admission at parent's interview (when her half-literate husband spoke unforgiving English in a despicable manner), Vicky finally made it happen for her – he went there after their initial refusal, and stated that he was an alumni and was guaranteeing his niece's performance there. The office staff indicated that the last day for form dispersal had elapsed and he shall have to try next year.

Vicky made some phone calls to a few of his ex-teachers at the Senior Section who were still there, and some of them called the Principal, who met Vicky after a couple of hours and said she was helpless. Vicky told her politely that she would have to get security to forcefully remove him from her office, as he didn't think that victimising a young girl for lacuna on the part of her father was anything but prudent practice.

The Principal thereafter reluctantly told Vicky to fill up the form to seek admission through proper channel. Diana did great at the entrance test, and the rest was history – she stood first in her class later that very year.

Back to Gita's question to Vicky at the hospital bed, after reminding Vicky of all the incredible things he had done for her throughout her life, Gita said she had one final request for Vicky - she needed him to do it for her desperately. After some pause, what Gita said, stunned all - it appeared to come out of clear blue; it shook everyone present there.

She said:' whenever I wanted something in life, you always gave it to me. Now I want to live – so please get my final wish fulfilled! I don't want to die leaving you all, especially my beautiful Di behind – do something for me please.'

The lightning-struck family decided to go to Mumbai and get their loved member seen at Tata Memorial Hospital, as a matter of seeking a second opinion. So, after a few more days at Vellore, they caught a flight from Chennai on a Monday morning, and went to Parel straight from the airport. Gita's name was registered there duly after which the attending physician prescribed inpatient treatment for Gita at their facilities, upon seeing the patient and all her medical records.

The family admitted Gita there as per the physician's recommendations; they went to a decent hotel near the bridge where they spent few anxious nights, visiting Gita during the scheduled visiting hours, and consoling her that she might get better. Deep inside their hearts, they knew that Gita's end was drawing near - but they chose to believe that she will heal.

The first dosages of chemotherapy and radiation were administered there with a gap of couple of days; then the Head of the Department there finally met with Vicky and his parents one fine morning, during which he advised Gita to undergo chemo and radiation three times a week – the doctor suggested that it would be better for the family if they returned back to Kolkata, arrange for Gita's routine chemo and radiation at a local hospital, get her back to normal life, as much as practicable, and leave everything else to God.

Accordingly, the family returned to their home after which they arranged for chemo and radiation for Gita at Chittaranjan Hospital at Hazra three times a week. They also decided that Gita would stay with her parents, as the last thing she needed at that time was agony and aggravation, which was a normal course of affair at her in-law.

That arrangement worked out better for Diana, as she loved her grandpa, grandma & uncle so much that she used to miss them at her paternal home; plus, no one except her mother there would even play with her or speak to her – her wicked father tactfully managed to stay out as much as possible, and enjoy slimy companies with some dirt bags, some of whom were his female clients who filed for divorce, etc. – he used them to his advantages in his own ways.

Fortunately, Gita was able to go back to her teaching profession from July onwards - she started going for chemo and radiation twice during weekdays after school, and once on Saturdays. She did have some discomfort and uneasiness with her vanishing hairlines, but soon she went for wigs to wear outside her house. She was worried that students won't give her due respect with thinning hairs and partially bald head – it was a matter of her own self-esteem, and the family stood by her, respecting her decision.

During the following Durga Puja holidays, Vicky booked a five-star resort near Puri for four days, when the shameless, greedy and pauper brother-in-law, Randi accompanied them without any hesitation, anticipating free boarding, food and air tickets to and fro, as usual. Vicky wanted Gita along with her family to get out of the shock they had to bear lately, so that a nice trip could bring freshness, energy and vitality back to the family.

But, Vicky had tolerated enough nonsense from his evil brother-in-law by then; being disgusted, he told Randi straight on his face that he himself needed to bear the airfare if he wanted to go, as Vicky had already spent enough money on that piece of junk – however, as it later turned out, Vicky did not charge anything for boarding and food from that self-professed pauper, because of humanitarian grounds.

Randi was so cheap that he stated he was going to go by train and would return by train too - indeed, it was later revealed that he travelled second class – he was so miser that he couldn't even buy tickets in air-conditioned sleeper class!

At the same token, he ate so much that he threw up twice – as Vicky had him in the same suite he was staying, he warned Randi that if he threw up one more time, Randi shall have to foot the expenses of his food himself – sure enough, he stopped vomiting and started taking antacids after elephant-sized meals.

But, Vicky ended up spending sleepless nights there as the lion-like snoring by Randi all nights used to keep Vicky up – sometimes, the latter will take a walk on the beaches past midnight, just to feel sleepy enough to overcome the monster dinosaur's snoring like hell, just so that he can have a good night's sleep himself.

It was there on the beaches on a nice windy morning that the entire family was watching Vicky ride the waves on the ocean and having some long-awaited fun. He had earlier told Di to sit with her grandparents and mother on chairs alongside the water-edges, to watch her uncle, so that she can learn how to overcome fears in life. That was after a few bold moves by Vicky in their resort's swimming pool to take Diana on his back, when he swam through deep water, then taking a plunge into the water, when Diana would try to stay afloat by techniques Vicky had shown her multiple times earlier.

Sometimes, Vicky will rescue her – other times, he will let her drink some water, so that she would be forced to move her arms and legs, in the manner her uncle showed to her. Although Diana loved it, but her mom and others will make a hue and cry of it saying that such daredevil moves might be harmful for the kid.

But, that's how Vicky became an expert swimmer himself - he knew what he was doing.

Randi got bored watching his brother-in-law swim so proficiently and smoothly in deep waters - since he didn't know how to swim, he started entering the waters until it reached his shinbone; he would be fleeing back each time a wave would come in.

He was more than 6 feet tall weighing around 120 kg; so, no force of water could possibly wash him away! After a few streaks of running towards an incoming wave defiantly, he would soon be running back as soon as the waves neared him; all of a sudden, Randi told Diana to come with him, probably to exhibit that he was no less courageous than Di's idol – Vicky.

Before anyone could realise what was going on, Randi and Diana were standing side by side in about six inches of water! Gita and her parents were screaming on the top of their voices to bring Di back, but the sound of the waves and gusty wind overpowered their voices.

Vicky was getting ready to catch a huge wave that was beginning to form in some distance, when he turned around to see if his family was watching – there he saw Di and knew of the imminent danger immediately. He started swimming back as fast as he could, probably faster than his prize-winning swimming competitions at school levels during his hay days! He used to represent his school in swimming, cricket and football, and was a captain of his college football team.

Before anyone except Vicky could anticipate the force of the next big wave, it smashed on the shore; Randi immediately started running back for safety, towards the beaches – he let go of his own daughter in order to save his own huge hindquarter!

He did the exact same thing when Diana was coming to visit her grandparents with her mom and dad few years ago, after a fire broke out in the plywood shop located close to her grandparents' house – everybody were running around and Gita got stuck in the melee with her infant daughter on her arms on one side, and a medium-sized bag on her other arm, with feeding bottles, baby food, diapers, wash clothes, baby shampoo, oil and other items required for a baby's day-to-day life.

Randi was walking in arms' length, smoking cigarette, despite the warning given to him by Vicky earlier not to smoke anywhere near the baby! As soon as he heard the commotion, Randi started running towards safety - his wife and kid were left behind for unknown outcome!

Fortunately, Vicky was around - he knew that his sister and his world's most favourite niece were en route to their house – hearing the public screaming and loud noises, he ran towards the road which was supposedly going to be taken by his sister; sure enough, they were in the middle of it all, confused and bewildered – Vicky took the bag and the baby, pushed his sister forward, and shouted to her to run for cover. That's how they got saved that time!

Another time, during a trip to Sunderbans by vessel, Randi was asked by his wife to change Di's diapers, Gita was getting her baby food ready. Vicky suddenly noticed that instead of changing the diaper where he was standing, Randi decided to walk towards the rear of the vessel with his infant daughter on his arms, taking her almost to the edges of the vessel.

Vicky ran immediately, without a second thought, snatched the baby from Randi's arms and gave him some hard talks; he later changed Di's diapers himself. He also scolded his sister for telling the ignorant giant to change the diaper, as where he was standing was dangerously close to that croc infested river – a little jerk on the vessel would have definitely shaken him, after which, being such a coward, he would surely drop the infant in order to save himself.

That time in Puri, as soon as Vicky saw his niece on the water, he knew of the probable danger – but, shore was quite far from where he was. Fortunately, the giant wave moved in within a few seconds, and he caught it for a faster ride to the shore. When he was few metres away from shore, the wave had already made a landfall catching everyone off-guard. Randi was halfway out of the water;

but there was this little baby standing in waist-deep water with no knowledge or hint of the clear and imminent danger!

As soon as water started to recede, it shook off the little feet - there she was, drowning and being swept into the ocean. It was just sheer good fortune coupled with quick presence of mind that Vicky seemed to have been endowed with, that saved the imminent death!

Vicky took Diana out of the water just in time, waited till the water receded, and carried her on shore; first thing he did after giving the infant to her mother for drying and solace, was a huge slap on the face of the monster dragon, with some choicest words. Gita's parents almost fainted when the infant was being swept away; as soon as they got their senses back, they burst out at Randi venting their accumulated anger and frustration out on the devilish father.

Dark and thick cloud was accumulating on the family's horizon, as Gita fell sick again – this time she apparently lost her faith in life; her confidence in herself was visibly shattered. After the trip, she had to be hospitalized intermittently for the remaining four months.

The family chose Cancer Hospital near Joka for her next stop for receiving treatments, because Vicky could take care of all her medical and other needs on a timely manner there, due to the close proximity of the hospital from his house. In addition, this was apparently the only specialized private hospital at that time in Kolkata - Vicky knew Dr. Gupta, their founder, through a mutual friend.

Expensive medicines and injections kept Gita out of the acute pain associated with the disease, although she became more of a patient with limited abilities at that time, rather than a fighting spirit that she used to carry during the recent past.

Randi didn't even bother to visit his wife at all during weekdays, citing court cases – he only visited her for few minutes on some Sundays – on Saturdays, he used to go to Diamond Harbour where his father used to be in a dirty relationship with the domestic help he had engaged at his house-cum-chamber there; Randi chose the daughter of the maid for fulfilling his ulterior fantasies.

So, the father son duo ran a havoc on the mother daughter duo there, for which both those Das guys had to pay substantial amount to their partners in bed, to make sure that they don't approach the police, or don't spread the news! In the meantime, the bride of that household was on deathbed. Harini's wife had her share of affairs too earlier - so, it was kind of a mutual understanding and cooperation in unholy manner, where everyone strangely kept mum!

Gita headed for her heavenly sojourn on the 13th of February, when Diana had resumed her school in second grade. The family immediately decided that it was high time that Di be transferred to a good 'girls only' school, as she was getting more and more beautiful day by day; there were horrible stories coming out from her present-day school, relating to abuses of kids – even students in third and fourth grades were not spared by predators, as insanity took place in minds of certain people.

Apart from that, a motherless kid wouldn't be able to confide in her grandma or anyone else relating to any possible victimization or offences, God forbade if that had ever occurred. So, the family decided to change Di's school shortly after her mother's untimely demise.

Vicky approached the authorities of a very reputable Catholic convent located near Deshapriya Park but was told that the last date of form submission had already been over; the entrance exam date was scheduled for the following weak. Vicky met the Headmistress there, Sister Maria Reshma A.C., who was a heavenly lady with so much grace, charm and softness.

She listened very patiently to all that Vicky had to say - although a little reluctant initially, she finally agreed to let Diana take the test on conditional basis – if she scored high marks, she might be admitted – she will then be allowed to fill in the application form and comply with other formalities; or else, end of story. Vicky agreed to the stipulated conditions, as he knew that was a very fair offer.

He thanked Sister Reshma and prayed for her well-being at the Chapel in the school, from deep down his heart – they eventually became quite friendly, until Sister moved to another branch of the same school in Bengaluru – they always held high regards in their minds for each other.

As anticipated by her uncle, Diana scored 48 out of 50 on her entrance test, failing to correctly answer the last question because of her in-borne haste and freckle-mindedness. Sister Reshma always made fun of the fact that Di had answered the easiest question wrong – perfect example of careless mistake! Diana was extremely fortunate to have such a wonderful headmistress in her primary school like Sister Reshma.

Unfortunately for the family, the great Sister left for Bengaluru the same year Di moved to the Secondary section of that school, located in a different place called Jodhpur Park, She had very pleasant memories of her primary school lasting in her mind all her life. Sister Reshma was a name that Di remembered throughout her life, telling her friends and loved ones about the great sister she was fortunate to have for a short while.

When she got promoted to fifth grade, Diana had to move to a separate section of this same school, which was meant for higher classes. Initially, she kept enjoying her childhood and student life, despite her loosing mother when she was in Class I, followed by another big loss when Di was in the third grade, when she lost her dear grandpa Biman.

Teachers and other staff at that new building were pretty nice; but, since this was a catholic convent school, fresh influx of students from economically disadvantaged sections of a particular community with lesser values and discipline joined the old students, many of whom were very cordial and good. Some of these girls from other schools who joined Diana's school in fifth grade quickly noticed that Di was loved by all, and they wanted to be close to Diana – she reciprocated, feeling sympathetic to the new students, which somehow infuriated a section of the old students.

Some of those old students stopped talking to Diana for being over-friendly with those 'nasty' newcomers; a few of them even used to torment Di some time. Di had become iron-hearted over time, having to deal with the heavy blow life had offered her from her tender age. So, she ignored everything smilingly, and eventually things fell back into normal.

But by then, some of those newer entrants started badmouthing Diana to others accusing her falsely, probably in order to hastily gain undue fame – so, Di decided to maintain a low profile in order to weather out the constantly brewing cloud over her life. She continued to fare very well in her studies, as well as many extra-curricular activities.

Diana developed a flair for writing from her early childhood days, and wrote many essays and narratives, some of which were recognised by internationally reputed bodies like Commonwealth Society, Tata and Times of India. She took part in many writing competitions and won awards from Scholastics India, Goodreads and Litteratti Foundation.

She even started composing a book when she was in eighth grade, which was eventually published after her Secondary examinations (Board). Diana also participated in many international and nation-wide competitions on maths, spelling and science, and won prestigious awards from Spell Bee International, Wiz National Spell Bee, etc.

Di also developed a special feeling towards economically and physically disadvantaged kids from her junior school days – so, she started teaching some of those kids at her spare time – her passion was aided by her school's activities in imparting knowledge to kids as well as adult literacy programs through a famous organisation.

Some of Di's students subsequently completed their schooling later, for which she always took great pride and derived greatest satisfaction whenever she met those kids at later point of times. She considered herself fortunate to have been able to continue working on her passion even in her Senior School, when she was visiting recognised organisations for kids' learning routinely, imparting education and training to them.

It used to be almost a ritual for Di and her friends from junior school to congregate on Poila Baisakh, which marked beginning of the Bengali calendar, usually falling on either the 14th or 15th of every April. They used to meet at a pre-designated spot, from where they'll throng to some nice restaurants for lunch, or maybe convene at South City Mall close to their school, to go for a rendezvous at their food court.

The girls used to have lots of fun and entertainment, which they carried on to their classrooms sometimes, resulting in some teachers' wrath for excessive talking! But many teachers liked the girls from Gen Next due to their familiarity with Bengali traditions and cultures, unlike many of their counterparts in other English medium schools.

Akbar had invented a new calendar upon his crowning as a Mughal Emperor in the year 1556, which was actually Islamic year 963. The calculation of Bengali New Year was thus simple – add 963 to 1556 and subtract the result from the current Gregorian solar year; the result would be the current Bengali year.

Akbar infused Hindu and Islamic dating systems to create the calendar – it was imperative to clear all dues by the last day of the Bengali month Chaitra; it is still a norm for traders and business houses with origin in Bengal to start a new accounting period, popularly known as 'haal-khata' for offering credits and other facilities to customers, after writing off past debts or having cleared all the receivables from earlier years by the last day of Chaitra.

The celebrations thus begun during Akbar's reign for Poila Baisakh, although the calendar itself didn't last much beyond his lifetime, except in Bengal, where it became integral to agriculture and Hindu religion. Most Bengali-speaking people in West Bengal continue to celebrate this day in the manner that please them the most, frequently by eating out, sending flowers to friends &

families, wishing them happy new year, queuing up in temples and shrines to offer pujas, visit friends and relatives with sweets and yoghurt, etc.

Di was a great sportswoman too, as she started playing tennis from her fifth grade at a very reputed club in south Kolkata. She soon became very proficient in tennis. She won champion's trophy on few domestic competitions and regularly participated in all the tournaments, not for winning the game, but for enjoying it.

She also used to be a great swimmer, practising in a very famous swimming club in Lake Area – unfortunately, she started gaining some weight, due to excessive intake of fat, which acted as an impediment to participate in swimming competitions; but she enjoyed it. Diana also played table tennis, carom and badminton very well – in short, she was a nonpareil enthusiast!

When she was in eighth grade, fresh waves of trouble started hitting Diana at school, when her maths teacher, science teacher and Bengali teacher insisted that she attend their coaching classes off campus, like other girls.

Imparting private tuition by schoolteachers was theoretically prohibited by the school authorities officially - a warning to such effect was clearly printed on the School Diary – but in practice, many teachers in higher classes of that school used to organise private coaching classes for students at various locations. Many of those teachers always compelled their students to enrol in their coaching classes, for monetary gain.

When Di refused to join any of the coaching classes as a matter of principle, many of those teachers started taking revenge against Di, by lowering her scores written on her answer sheets. Her uncle Vikram complained about this malpractice to the school authorities, immediately after he found out the unscrupulous practice. Things became alright after that, although those teachers concerned would always wait for opportunities to get back at Diana at any cost, like poisonous vermin.

Di's father used to visit her most evenings, on his way back from court, to spend five or ten minutes with her. He was more interested about tuition costs, etc. than his daughter's result; every time Diana got promoted to higher classes, Randi would never look at her result. He would ask Vicky how much the tuition had become, as money mattered to him more than anything else. When Di got excellent marks in her Board examinations in almost all subjects barring one, her father didn't want to pursue the matter further with the Board or in other legal forums, fearing additional expenses involved in such processes.

While Diana's grandpa Biman was alive, all the expenses relating to living and education of Di were borne between his son and himself, out of his pension and savings. However, after his death, Vicky told Randi that from that point on, he needed to pitch in for some educational expenses for his daughter, as Vicky felt that Randi shouldn't be allowed to relinquish his legal duty towards his daughter. Fearing court cases, especially as Randi was pocketing the full family pension of Diana's mother, he agreed.

Vikram used to pay for all expenses on behalf of Di's father initially - then Randi used to reimburse him the money at a much later date, citing no income, and further upon furnishing all the receipts for payments made for Di. Vicky consistently put pressure on his evil brother-in-law so that he didn't get away with not paying for educational expenses incurred on his behalf by Vicky, until a certain point.

However, soon after Randi's father died, he stopped paying for Diana, as the evil lady Suparnakha he met in Diamond Harbour, had a huge influence and grasp on his life – she soon started controlling Randi in every way. Vicky and his mother had to bear all expenses for Di from that point on, although they filed complaints with various commissions, apart from initiating lawsuits against Randi.

All the Commissions that they approached were quick to issue very strong recommendations against Randi for ignoring his only daughter, but he chose to sit tight-lipped, shamelessly claiming in total disregards to law, affection or humanity, that he didn't have the money to afford his daughter's education. The Commissions in Bengal were like toothless and clawless tigers – their recommendations were not enforceable. Courts couldn't do much other than arresting a defaulter either – so it was a win-win situation for wilful defaulters on child support cases.

Ritu and Diana visited Riya in the USA when Diana was in sixth grade. They flew down to JFK through Heathrow where Riya and Rina were waiting for them. They stayed a couple of days in NYC, then drove to DC, Virginia and through mid-west, they travelled all the way to Cape Coral. Diana visited places like Boca Raton, Cape Canaveral, Orlando, Miami, Key West, Fort Lauderdale and Tampa in Florida, as also LA, San Francisco, San Diego and other places of interests in California.

During the three weeks' time that Di stayed in the US, she made up her mind that she would definitely attend college in the US – she was thrilled with the sizes of campus, infrastructure, security arrangements, facilities and overall great ambience and reputations of great campuses like UCLA, Stanford et al, and started dreaming big since then.

Diana also had the privilege of visiting many countries in the world as she was growing up, including France, Germany, Switzerland, Holland, England, Thailand, Bangkok, etc. - Ritu and Riya accompanied her everywhere.

She used to love those foreign trips that Vicky would arrange for his family; Di loved Vicky for that. Other times, she wouldn't be paying much attention to her dear uncle, making it seem like he was the one who she didn't care much about. However, in reality she loved him a lot. But Vicky always missed the expression of love from Di, as she hardly uttered the magic word to him - that she loved him!

Di took a gap year after successfully completing her junior school, when she published her first book, which was a huge success. She donated all the royalties received from sale of her book to recognised social organisations and orphanages, for benefit of kids.

Her book was sold all over the world – sadly enough, her family found it very difficult to convince relatives and friends to buy a copy each of the book at a nominal price, despite specifically stating to all that proceeds from sale of that book would go to charitable organisations. People's reaction was like a forced decision on them – very few actually got thrilled at the idea – thus, there was little encouragement for the gifted kid to pursue her noble cause!

All the friends from Vicky's school were very established in life, like Vicky used to be! One was the Chief Financial Officer of IG Airport in Delhi; another a very famous scientist; others very successful engineers, accountants, professors, Directors and Presidents of various organisations, earning seven digits' salaries per month, all leading highly lavish lifestyles.

One of those friends used to own a sixteen bedroom mansion in Silicon Valley - another one used to fly first class internationally on business every week – none of them bought a single copy of the book, which costs only a hundred rupees (author's discounted price) – the funniest part was that, one of Vicky's former classmates who had a flourishing software business, with a two-acres' villa near Bengaluru, ended up browsing the first few pages of the book in free kindle edition through a portal, then lying to Vicky that he actually bought the book!

Vicky observed with utmost frustration a peculiar trend - each time he spoke to his school friends, either over telephone or through personal meetings, about his niece's noble effort behind the book, most of those friends started talking about their own kids - how successful in life they were becoming.

Vicky praised them all, wished the best to all of them, as he considered his friends' kids like his own, but the same generosity was not reciprocated. Finally, he got the essence when the scientist friend told him that he was going to write a book himself– Vicky understood the real reasons for their abstinence from buying his niece's book – pure jealousy!

He soon ceased all kinds communications or any effort in keeping in touch with all of them, except a very few who could manage to buy the book after some time. He even quit the WhatsApp and Facebook groups, in order to make them realise what great friends Vicky considered them to be for him. Many of them tried to apologise, but Vicky's heart was already tested out to the maximum.

Di developed a special affinity towards writing from her childhood days, when she would scrabble few sentences on her rough copy – her maternal relatives would encourage her every time, thus helping her to be a proficient writer. During her sophomore years, Diana had written an essay on her motherland which immediately received recognition from the Postal Department of Government of India – the essay was titled 'Letter to My Motherland.'

"Hello, my loving and beautiful Mother India. I hope all is well, and you are taking good care of yourself. Please don't worry about your children, because our superb mother has done everything to make all her children grow on the lap of this outstanding country to turn out as the very best there is!

You have graciously given us the fertile land, the vibrant oceans, the ever-strong mountains and the clear blue skies above our head. We are trying to make best use of all our resources you have endowed upon us so sparingly. Although most of us try to protect our environment and save our mother, however, like in many families, not each one is the same. Few of your children try to take advantage of your gifts and exploit natural resource for more desired personal objectives. But we try to convince them not to go hard on wasting resources, in order to save those for next generations who're going to come from your children in the future.

You have been so tolerant of blood-spills and struggle for power, from good causes like freedom-struggle, establishing democracy, etc. to evil causes like terrorism, religious battle, etc. Your golden soils were ravaged at times with bloodbath - you endured it all. We try our best to maintain harmony across religion, caste, creed and power-struggle, but sometimes it takes a toll, rather unfortunately. We're slowly moving towards becoming a developed nation after years of rifts and difficulties; we are trying to attain zero tolerance for corruptive practices and political backlashes, although it's going to take some more time.

Like you have taught us from our childhood days, we try to be brave and confident of our abilities, with all that you have vested upon us, not bowing down to any kind of undue pressure. We try to be ethical at work, diligent in studies; we have inculcated the moral values that your other great children have taught us.

Your great sons like Swami Vivekananda, Rabindranath Tagore, Subhas Chandra Bose, Gandhi Ji and others have instilled amazing values and directions to our souls. We are trying to the best of our abilities to become good Samaritans, to be real children of God – children of our beloved mother India, whom we all are really proud of.

We believe in unity in diversity - that's why we stand tall amidst so many different dialects, differing beliefs and practices. Please look at us – we have so many verities of food habits prevalent in different parts of your lap; but it doesn't matter, as most of us like to share food from your other children, living hundreds of miles from our individual home or offices, through online or otherwise. We are gradually moving towards Digital India; we have already started efforts to reduce pollutions and clean up our environments.

We have grown stronger over the years - we are now capable of defending you from any foreign aggressor. We have learnt lessons from our past mistakes and are not going to let it happen again. We are financially become stronger and stronger; our relations with other motherlands are becoming friendlier. We export the excess of our requirements to others around the globe, also importing their excesses in, for fair & equal distribution. We are working really hard to eliminate poverty from grass-root level; we are trying to fund education for all your children, so that no unfair discrimination recurs.

Your female children are finally trying to come out of historical abuse and exploitations – they are now mostly educated and are trying to become self-sufficient. Women empowerment is on the rise; we are working to eradicate all forms of abuses from their lives. Their healthcare and other incentives are ensuring that they get pre-natal and post-natal cares, which is essential not only for lactating mothers, but also for the babies they're carrying. I'm sure you will be happy to know this. Hygienic toilets are being built even in remote villages, so that women can preserve their modesty – a move towards a better & safer environment too.

Our infrastructure and living conditions are also gradually improving, although we still have miles to go to reach out to the needy children in remote areas. Child-labour has been banned along with many other reforms taken to protect your small children and women, like early marriage banning, etc. When I drive along some beautiful highways (a brainchild of another great child of yours, recently deceased), I see crop-yielding beautiful farms and greeneries, I see small children going to school in villages across those highways, I see rural electrification and other infrastructural developments – it makes me feel so happy. You will be happier to know that we have made substantial developments in sciences and technology, Research and Development and innovative plans to improve our standards of living.

When I, as one of your children grow, my dependants also grow; other people associated with us grow - thereby having a chain-effect on the society as a whole. This growth culminated to our national growth, which will really make you prouder of your children. We have tourists from other motherlands visit us and appreciate your beauty - we also gain from their influx of foreign currency which adds to our Balance of Payment. Many foreign companies have invested in our motherland - more are coming, thus giving us a very strong economic position.

I feel very happy when foreign dignitaries praise my motherland during their presentation across seven seas and thirteen rivers away from us. Aren't you feeling very happy too? I'm sure you are, dear motherland, as your dreams are gradually on their way to be becoming true, in every essence – we are slow, but we are steady. So, have faith in us, the exact way you always have; I promise we won't let you down - we're already shining.

I will now have to wrap it up, since I need to go to my school – my exams are starting in a day. Please bless me, wish me best of luck. A mother's blessing is the most valuable gift a child can ever possess. I lost my biological mother when I was four years of age, but I have you. So, no worries at all. I know you'll be on my side till the end; I will always love you. Take care – Yours Diana".

As she was growing up, Di was turning out to be a fantastic tennis player. She played tennis regularly from her fifth grade onwards, up until she left India for college – she received many awards and accolades in many national competitions; her strong forehand and agile backhand smashes gave her an edge over many competitors, along with fine servicing qualities. Her idol was Novak Djokovic amongst men, and Monica Seles among women.

Monica Seles looked poised to rule women's tennis during the early 1990s, becoming the youngest woman to reach the world number one ranking in the year 1991, before winning three out of four grand slam singles titles the following year, with victories at the Australian, US and French Open. In the year 1993, she again looked all set to dominate the courts, opening that year by winning Australian Open with the defeat of German rival Steffi Graf.

However, in April that year, Seles was stabbed by a deranged spectator while playing a tournament in Hamburg; although she recovered from her injuries soon, Seles would not be able to play for two more years. She returned to turf in the year 1995 to win her tenth Grand Slam singles title the following year, with a victory at the Australian Open. Her courage and tenacity were admired by most people around the world, to which Di was no exception.

There was another award-winning essay Diana had written during her gap-year after Secondary (Board) examination, as to the reasons of Indians' celebrating their Republic Days. She started receiving many positive comments and praises from various quarters after her essay was published in a renowned journal in wide circulation across Bengal.

"Why do we celebrate 26th January every year since Independence? This is something that not too many people may ponder over while celebrating the one of the greatest days in our history; others will merely say that oh well, we obtained our independence formally through our Constitution on this day! Let's examine what history taught us first.

We all know that our great motherland celebrated her freedom from British colonisation on August 15, 1947; however, a sovereign state was formally formed on January 26, 1950. India had to fight really hard to drive the British out of the country for great many years, which eventually materialised on 15th August 1947.

However, even though we became independent, we did not have a constitution of our own – we were going by Indian Independence Act, with no formally adopted Constitution. Theoretically, a Constitution has the basic rules and principles laid down for running a nation. India did have a government at the time of Independence - but we did not have a Constitution.

26th January was the day when our constitution came into existence, around 67 years ago. The chief architect of our Constitution was Dr Bhim Rao Ambedkar, who headed the drafting committee that prepared a 'draft constitution' in November 1947; it eventually took little over a couple of years to take a final shape.

The Constituent Assembly formally adopted our Constitution on January 26, 1950, a date which was specially chosen to coincide with the twentieth anniversary of 'Purna Swaraj Diwas'. January 26, 1930 was marked as 'Purna Swaraj Diwas', or the day the nation would attain complete freedom from its colonisers, by the Congress. Indian National Congress had proclaimed goal for India's independence on that very significant day, back in the year 1930.

The members of the drafting committee felt that the birth of the constitution should be observed on a special day that held some significance in their fight for independence. When India was ultimately granted freedom by the British in the year 1947, on August 15th - not on January 26th, the latter date was instead assigned for celebrating India's Republic Day.

That was the day when the Indian Independence Act was consequently repealed; thus, India was established as a democratic republic; she was no longer a dominion of the British Crown! Thus, British Imperial Rule imposed forcefully over our predecessors ceased to exist!

Therefore, one may claim that special day to be the actual day when British raj ended through the enforcement of our own Constitution, in its truest sense, and we started a new dawn as a great nation, as Republic of India, making India a sovereign, secular, and democratic nation. It may also be more than a coincidence that Hindi was declared as an official language on that very same day, in the year 1965. Therefore, we may conclude that the Day has tremendous significance in shaping our nation over the years.

Dr. Rajendra Prasad took the solemn oath as the first President of independent India at the Durbar Hall in the Government House, Delhi, on that very day. It was followed by a Presidential drive along a 5 miles route to the Irwin Stadium, where Dr. Prasad hoisted our National Flag, after 21-gun salute; the seeds of our annual tradition of flag hoisting and parade was sown this way on the 26th of January 1950. The following are some of the excerpts of our First President's speech:

'We must re-dedicate ourselves on this day to the peaceful but sure realization of the dream that had inspired the Father of our Nation and the other captains and soldiers of our freedom struggle, the dream of establishing a classless, co-operative, free and happy society in 'his country'. We must remember that this is more a day of dedications than of rejoicing - dedication to the glorious task of making the peasants and workers the toilers and the thinkers fully free, happy and cultured.'

Unfortunately, very few of us today realize the inherent significance of India becoming a republic: that we, the citizens of India, have the power to govern ourselves by choosing our very own government. This is something which didn't come easy, although we seem to have taken it for granted - not to mention if we started realising the value of our independence - to what was bestowed upon us by all those great souls and martyrs of our country, the freedom fighters!

They didn't think twice before sacrificing their own lives, careers, families and prospects for attaining only one objective: to free our nation from enslavement; but, did we really get rid of all those social ills and negative vibes? Are we really free from those evils those great souls gave up their lives for, just in order to eradicate those ills, which also give us the chance to breathe free air? Well, the answer is yet to be unilaterally accepted.

Be that as it may, 26th January is a date which is like a birthday for every Indian roaming on the face of earth. Actually, it is more than our birthday itself. As found in a democracy, the people elect representatives to run the government, in a republic also. This government can't take away our rights, which are protected by the Constitution. This is one of the differences between a democracy and a republic.

Imagine what would have been the scenario if we left our fundamental rights to the whims of the governments! Term of any government is five years – they come and go; but we, the pillars of our country, live and pass on our virtues and benefits to the next generations. This is one of the greatest gifts any normal citizen can ask for; or else, we would be living the lives of any third-class prisoner rotting in jail for some crimes, committed or not.

People are the blood and chief resource of any country – without people, there could not be any development of any kind. So, if political leaders, bureaucrats, police authorities or other executive, judiciary or legislative bodies had the absolute power to define our lives, without a Constitution, we will be like flocks of sheep in a barren land, left at the mercy of the hoarders. Some may argue about certain flaws inherent in our Constitution, or someone else may claim that certain matters are outdated, etc.

Without going into any kind of debate over those issues, won't it suffice to conclude that our Constitution, framed on the 26th of January 1950 has been our umbrella over half a century? Shouldn't that fact alone may deem to make this day one of the greatest days in our history?

No matter how much wise and educated we may claim ourselves to be, it wouldn't be an overstatement if one claimed our predecessors as equally wise, if not more, to have thought of the future generations - to have given them a place to call our own country? Just like a baby finds comfort in his/her mother's laps, we find comfort in our motherland's soil, which is entirely attributable to this special Republic Day of India.

That matter alone may be enough for us to rejoice, to honour the great souls and martyrs of freedom movement, to salute our armed forces under our President, to watch the great parades, to listen to the visionaries and leaders, and above all, to stand up and say 'Thank you ALL.'

Nonetheless, Republic Day is not only celebrated in our great country; some of our neighbouring countries also celebrate their own Republic Days on different dates – China on 1st October, Pakistan on 23rd March, Nepal on 28th May. Italy and Turkey also have their own Republic Days.

Awards and medals are given to members of the Indian Armed Forces, as also to civilians, in our country on our Republic Day – it is a gazetted holiday; many shops and establishments are closed that special day, to honour the brave and bold souls, living as well as deceased.

Our Prime Ministers lay wreath on Amar Jawan Jyoti in India Gate, Presidents take salute from the military in our capital, state governors take salute from military at their respective state capitals, and school children participate in parades and various programmes all over the country. It is a beautiful sight everywhere; it is one of the proudest days in terms of history, heritage, culture and social uplifting for all of us in India.

Thus, our Republic Day, celebrated on the 26th of January every year, may be considered a national birthday to all of us - Indians living here or elsewhere - it will always be celebrated with great pride, pleasure, gratitude, respect and love to everyone – just our way of saying thank you from the bottom of our hearts to all our fellow men and women concerned, living and dead. It is truly a day of happiness for all of us – happy for what we are getting to enjoy today.

Our future generations will be duty bound and morally bound to celebrate this Day with great vigour, as long as we call ourselves Indians."

Di also wrote routinely for an annual magazine brought out by the housing society which Vicky was a member of, as well as for various souvenirs printed after Durga Puja in many localities across Kolkata. Many didn't know how she looked, but most knew her by name – through her writings!

Diana scored very well in her Secondary examination, although she expected much higher marks in almost all subjects. Vicky had initiated a lawsuit against the Board for failing to accurately award marks to answers given by her niece in the final exam, after walking the nine yards complying with required formalities - the routine reviews and procedures; however, Randi didn't pursue the case as he got involved with a sleazy woman named Suparnakha Pramanik, who started commanding her newly-found paramour's life; one of the very first thing she did, was to detach Randi completely from his biological daughter in a whisker.

Suparnakha was married thrice earlier with many children from her previous marriages. Taking advantage of loopholes in section 498A of IPC, she successfully chased off her first and second husbands and got away with their tangible and intangible properties at Haldia and Diamond Harbour, respectively. She also got married with some anti-social later, thus becoming notorious infamous and fiercely in her locality. One of her sons was married three times by the time he was 32 years old – one of her daughters from her second marriage used to be an escort for visiting businessmen and influential people. Suparnakha used to lure wealthy guys into relationships with her; she managed to master the art of seduction.

She used to lay traps for people in everyday life, like a spider-web, then suck out the resources and throw the remains to trash. She would often buy fish or other items from local traders, inviting them over to her house at nights; that way, she didn't have to pay for her merchandise; at the same time, the traders got one-night's stand – however, if any of those traders ever approached her again, she will use her resources at the local police station to lodge a false case against the person, and squeezed out everything from him.

Randi stopped visiting his daughter soon after falling in the traps of Suparnakha; he completely abstained from incurring even a paisa towards Di's education and other daily essentials. Vicky dragged him to Chid Protection Commission, where he lied and even tried to snatch important piece of evidence against him.

The Commission took a strong exception to his evil actions; they issued a nasty letter or recommendation against Randi; however, it was soon revealed that the Commission, although a quasi-legal entity, had very limited powers - its recommendations were advisory in nature, without actually having the power to enforce or implement its recommendations. This was probably known to Randi, being a lawyer by profession.

Multiple cases were initiated against the defunct and default father in Alipore Court; in a suit involving maintenance of Di, an interim order was issued by learned court to pay a specified amount per month to Diana. But Randi falsely filed an income tax return just four days before the date of hearing at court, understating his income to an unimaginable amount.

In some other cases, like in most court cases across the country, repeated adjournments, postponements and pleas for delaying the dates all resulted in waste of time, energy and more monetary drainage of the surviving grandma and uncle.

Police were reluctant to take a concrete action fearing lash back from a section of the bar association members, who stand divided all the time, but reunite the moment any stone is pelted at their beehives. Lawyers were the only section of professionals who got to enjoy full family pension of deceased wives and husbands, although their income was very high and they maintained a lavish lifestyle – law is law, and there's no working around it – so be it, felt Vicky.

Randi even pocketed the full pension of Diana's mom - letters to the authorities, to Chief Justice of High Court at Kolkata and even Supreme Court of India went unheeded. Some of the meetings she and her immediate family members had with some sitting HC and lower court judges relating to her misery appeared to be hopeless, as Randi and his paramour had good connections – political and legal!

Randi used his clout as an advocate of High Court for many years; on the other hand, Suparnakha used her feminine tactics to influence police and other local authorities. As some of the judges turned politicians were already known to Randi, he managed to exercise unlawful influence over some facets which led to repeated delays and dilemmas. Di got so upset with her real-life experience dealing with those inconsistencies that she wrote a review on the matter of mixing of politics and judiciary, after some research.

"Politics and legal profession in India seemed to run alongside from the dawn of colonisation. From freedom struggle to framing of the Constitution of India, lawyers Lala Lajpat Rai, Bal Ganagadhar Tilak, Gandhi, Nehru, Rajendra Prasad, C.R. Das, Ambedkar, and the likes played stellar roles. Lawyer-politicians like Arun Jaitley, Abhishek Manu Singhvi, P. Chidambaram, Kapil Sibbal and many others continued to fight for the political parties they were affiliated to, and many a times, for wrong causes. There were many occasions when Judges also turned politicians, including Judges from many High Courts and Supreme Courts.

As for some High Court judges, Justice Masoodi, a former J&K HC Judge, was fielded from Anantnag constituency by the National Conference Party, after Justice Masoodi had ruled by a bench headed by him that Article 370 of the Constitution, giving special status to Jammu & Kashmir, couldn't be 'abrogated, repealed or even amended'!

Another Justice Thipsay had also plunged into politics after retirement, joining the Congress Party, and so did Justice Bahuguna, who changed affiliation later. Former Chief Justice of Punjab and Haryana, Justice Rama Jois joined RSS after his retirement and eventually became a Governor.

As for some Supreme Court judges, there was a rich legacy of some of the best SC judges getting swept off their feet by politics, before and after their stints in the constitutional courts, and entering the political arena. Justice Mahajan of Lahore HC became a judge of the East Punjab HC in Shimla post-independence. At the behest of Maharaja of Shimla at that time, goaded by Sardar Patel (Home Minister), Justice Mahajan became the Prime Minister of the state – he witnesses the state's accession to India later. Justice Mahajan went on to become the Judge of the Federal Court, and after Independence, he became the third Chief Justice of India in the year 1954. He may not officially had entered politics, but surely, he was very close to the top politicians of Congress Party.

The ninth CJI, Justice Subba Rao, resigned from his position months before his scheduled retirement to contest for Presidential election, accepting such proposition initiated from Minoo Masani, the leader of the opposition at that time, thus becoming the first CJI to resign and enter politics immediately. Justice Subba Rao was renowned for his impeccable judiciary leadership, especially on contexts of fundamental rights issues, etc. However, the proximity of his resignation and contesting for Presidential election would have left no doubts to any minds that while discharging his duties as CJI, Justice Subba Rao was in active confabulations with political leaders.

If it was at current days, Justice Subba Rao would have been trolled on social media, and condemned by activist lawyers, who would have definitely fished out his earlier judgements against the government in order to mathematically prove his unholy nexus with politicians and leaders of the oppositions.

Another judge, Justice Hidayatullah, the eleventh CJI, used to be a member of Nagpur Municipal Corporation before he assumed the position of CJI in the year 1968. A day before his scheduled retirement, Justice Hidayatullah wrote the majority opinion and quashed the presidential order abolishing titles, privileges and privy purses for former princes, which included Madhavrao Scindia. His ruling against the Indira Gandhi led government's decision resulted in him getting no assignments to head any commissions of inquiry, etc.

Justice Sadananda Hegde was a prime example of a justice seeing politics and judiciary so closely. Hegde joined Indian National Congress in the year 1935, to be elected to Rajya Sabha consecutively from the year 1952 – however, he continued to practice in courts. In the year 1977, Hegde was elected to Lok Sabha in Bangalore, from Janata Dal, and became the Speaker of Lok Sabha after the resignation of Sanjeeva Reddy. He became one of the vice presidents of the BJP from the year 1980 for seven years.

Another remarkable fiasco relating to tangibility in politics by a Supreme Court Judge was that of Justice Khanna, who tilted the balance in a seven to six majority that coined 'inviolability of basic structure of Constitution' in a landmark case in the year 1973, soon became a beacon of judicial independence after refusing to bend before Indira Gandhi government's dictatorial regime during the Emergency declared in India. He resigned in the year 1977 like a true judicial warrior after he was suspended after the ruling party led by Mrs. Gandhi nominated Justice Beg as the CJI. Justice Khanna never bowed before any pressure and was admired by common people as one of the truest heroes at that time.

Justice Khanna spurned offers from Mrs. Gandhi-led government to head various commissions for two years in a row, which included his refusal to probe into the Maruti affairs, which was subsequently headed by Justice Shah. However, Justice Khanna later accepted the offer by the next PM, Chaudhury Charan Singh to become the Law Minister in the year 1979, which was a big surprise to many at that time, although he resigned merely after three days at Office, apparently as politics and governance became too much for Justice Khanna to handle.

After three years, Justice Khanna contested for the Presidential election, at the behest of the opposition parties, and lost. Such was the outcome for an independent and outright judge in the dirty game of politics in India! Examples like that aren't very common in Indian politics. On the same token, Justice Beg was later conferred Padma Vibhushan Award (India's second-highest civilian award) in the year 1988 by Rajiv Gandhi government for his "contribution to law and jurisprudence" – it is worthy to note in this context that Justice Beg, in his role as a SC judge, was part of the constitutional bench that had supported the government's stand in the same case in which Justice Khanna had tilted the balance in a 7-6 majority vote stated in the aforementioned case!

Another notable personality from SC who didn't bow under political pressure was Justice Iyer, who was quoted as stating "law without politics is blind, politics without law is deaf." Justice Iyer was known to possess a heart which bled for the economically downtrodden people. His brain was in continuous flux in order to justify his way of dishing out justice, with or without the backing of law. Some of his iconic judgements went off like a sonic boom in the country's judiciary, reverberating to the highest levels at times. Few of his landmark judgements included matters normally outside the purview of SC rulings.

Early during his career, Justice Iyer was more of a political figure than a lawyer. His political career ran from the year 1952 to later parts of the 60's – he was elected a member of the legislative assembly from Kerala and went on to become a Minister. After some time, he returned to judiciary, and was appointed as Kerala HC Judge in July 1968. With the help of machinations from friendly politicians at the Centre, he soon became a SC Judge, which was widely criticised due to his short tenure as a HC judge.

But, his workaholic attitude, coupled with his poor-friendly judgements soon dissipated all the criticisms, and he retired in the year 1980 as a towering personality – however, his inborne passion for politics was still simmering within his mind, and in the year 1987, Justice Iyer contested the Presidential election but lost. Thereafter, he turned an author and a critic for government policies.

At the other extreme of a SC judge getting prized was Justice Islam, who hailed from Assam and was considered an out and out congress-minded person. He was elected to Rajya Sabha in the year 1962, after which he contested unsuccessfully for Assam assembly polls while still a RS member! After Congress party split in the year 1969, Justice Islam decided to align with Mrs. Gandhi. He resigned from the RS in 1972 to become a Judge in Guwahati HC and retired in 1980 as Chief Justice, after which his political hunger rode him and rowelled him back to politics.

Nine months after his retirement, Justice Islam was made an SC Judge in the year 1980 - he resigned on January 13, 1983 and immediately, on the very next day, he obtained ticket from Congress party to contest for Lok Sabha! Just a month before his resignation date, Justice Islam gave a reprieve to Bihar CM from an ongoing trial of forgery and criminal misconduct! After the election was countermanded, Justice Islam became a member of the RS uncontested for a third term from 1983 to 1989.

Another prime example of politician-judge dilemma could be observed in case of Justice Misra, who became a SC Judge on March 15, 1983 and became the head of a commission formed to inquire into the alleged organised violence and rioting leading to widespread massacre of Sikhs in the capital in the year 1984. His report was released three years later, and it vaguely blamed the police for riots, failed to identify anyone involved in the massacre, and absolved some Congress leaders from complicity in the riots, which was deemed to be a perfect cover-up job for the Rajiv Gandhi-led government.

Justice Misra was later sworn in as the 21st CJI of India in the year 1990 and he retired within a year, to become the first chairman of National Human Rights Commission – what a travesty! He remained the chairman of NHRC till the year 1996, and later elected to the RS as a Congress candidate and became chairman of the All India Congress Committee on Human Rights! He also headed two more important national commissions after his party came back into power in the year 2005!

In 1990s, the vicious cycle of politician-lawyer-judge-politician-administrator stopped apparently, with the collegium system instituted for the task of selecting persons for appointments as constitutional court judges. However, post retirement, the Judges can still return to politics and contest in elections, thus revealing their own political colours which stayed hibernated during tenure of their judiciary postings. Thus, transparency in its truest sense is still a dream!"

An eminent personality from the judiciary, who was already retired from active service but did not choose politics, praised Di's writings very much – he inspired her and motivated her to opt for journalism as a career. The gentleman also gave her written acknowledgement of Di's work on his letterhead; the latter chose to keep the matter a secret, as she loved maintaining a low profile!

Di had also observed that many HC Judges in Bengal during those times were elated to receive 'rewards' for some judgments passed by them by ruling party, by way of subsequent appointments as heads of various committees and commissions, many of which were merely eye-washes!

A sitting HC Judge in Kolkata who served as acting Chief Justice for some time became a political person right after his retirement, and some of his judgements as HC Judge or Acting CJ remains questionable as to their fairness and freeness, be it for matters relating to violations in election campaign (model code of conduct which was typically overseen by Election Commission through its own machineries, but may be referred to HC by any aggrieved persons), or for matters relating to constitutional crises arising out of a Commissioner of Police and DGP sitting in uniforms with a protesting CM (protesting over a CBI raid directed by the SC to unearth chit fund scams) at a political dais, or other matters.

A District Judge from Alipore ordered an ex parte stay on the Order issued by lower court, without even giving any opportunity to the opposite party to respond. The stay was on an interim order of maintenance, which was vital to save a minor girl from vagrancy; lower court reviewed all available documents and had ordered for a certain amount of maintenance. However, the crooked father of the child involved exerted unholy pressure and influence on the District Judge, to successfully reduce the amount ordered earlier to half!

Thereafter, a complaint was lodged against the District Judge to higher authorities, which resulted in promotion of that judge as Registrar General of High Court! Thus, it can be clearly seen how much prudent practices some judiciary functions. At the same token, when an honest Judge of the High Court took exception in the case of malpractices by local administration pertaining to municipal election, the public prosecutors on the government's side defiantly decided to abstain from any hearing in the learned court of that sitting Judge in High Court! They subsequently had to back off within a day, after the government pleaders lost election-battle in High Court bar council elections – it appears that sense of shame doesn't touch some professionals!

It was not only the judiciary who got tangled sometimes in politics – many retired chiefs of armed forces of our country, who were responsible for protecting the country, subsequently got involved in politics after retirement, taking one side or the other. Therefore, their impartiality or unbiasedness during active military service may also be under the scanner questionably.

Di always felt that her great motherland has historically been infested with corruption, dirty politics full with appeasement or polarisation or incumbency – she felt that things were not about to change drastically in a short span of time; therefore, deep down her mind, she brewed the prospect of leaving India for higher studies.

Thus, Di and her guardians thought it was in the best interests of the child that she pursued her career in a truly free country, where democracy didn't have to stay boxed in some cold storages confiscated by a politically motivated group of people or others associated with them for vested interests.

In addition, the scope and development of technologies and artificial intelligence in western countries far exceeded the best available in countries ravaged by corruption like India; that way, Diana could use her great computing skills to her advantage – her guardians thought!

As for example, the US Food and Drug Administration approved a device that captured an image of retina and automatically detected signs of diabetic blindness. That new breed of artificial intelligence (AI) was rapidly spreading across medical fields, as scientists started developing systems that can identify signs of diseases in a wide variety of images, starting from X-rays to CAT scans. Those systems promised to help doctors evaluate their patients more effectively in a less expensive manner.

Diana's most loved person in the world, her grandma Ritu, was suffering from retina problems for quite some time; local ophthalmologists and other healthcare professionals couldn't find an immediate cure – Diana was disgusted. She had always been great in computing and was instrumental in developing some sort of artificial intelligence before; so, she started weighing out her options.

The forces of AI were most likely to move beyond hospitals into the computer systems used by healthcare regulators, billing companies and insurance providers. Just as AI helped doctors check patients' eyes, lungs and other organs, it also helped insurance providers to determine reimbursement payments, policy fees and costs. Ideally, such systems would improve the efficiency of healthcare systems; but Diana thought that they may carry unintended adverse consequences - manipulations that can change the behaviour of AI systems using any piece of digital data.

By changing a few pixels in a lung scan, for example, someone with vested interests can fool the AI system into seeing an illness that wasn't really there. Software developers and regulators should consider such scenarios as they build AI technologies – Diana thought. Many doctors, hospitals and other organisations could manipulate AI in their billing or insurance software with a view to maximise their profits, and that can jeopardise the patients' conditions.

As because so much money changed hands across the healthcare industry, stakeholders may start bilking the system by subtly changing billing codes and other data in the computer systems that track healthcare related visits. AI could exacerbate the problem – Diana felt that more staying in India, where healthcare was viewed more as a potential for easy money-making, than rendering services.

An adversarial attack can exploit a fundamental aspect of the way many AI systems got designed and built. AI was typically driven by neural networks, complex mathematical systems that learnt tasks largely on their own, by analysing huge amount of data. By analysing thousands of eye-scans, for example, a neural network can learn to detect signs of diabetic blindness. This 'machine learning' happened on such an enormous scale that it can produce some unexpected behaviour of its own.

The implications were profound, given the increasing prevalence of biometric security and other AI systems, and thus AI can save life faster, but was not immune against bids or concerted efforts to fleece people. Be that as it may, Diana still felt that the positive outcome of artificial intelligence will far outweigh any of its abuses, if controlled properly, and thus she vouched for working towards development of AI in her field of studies in future. As far as Ritu's treatment for her retina, they chose an eye hospital in Salt Lake, where optometrists recommended change of power for her bifocal glasses.

Unfortunately for Diana, that particular school she chose to pursue her path towards foreign education did not offer computer as an available option – so, she was forced to pick Social and Cultural Anthropology instead! Vicky encouraged her to go ahead with that subject, because it offered many attractive career choices, apart from its potential use in the field of journalism and mass communication. Diana being a very obedient and amicable young lady, agreed to change her preferred subject accordingly.

Diana got admitted in a highly reputable school near Park Circus for pursuing her International Baccalaureate Diploma Program. The head of IB program for the program in this school was a person with split personality, which neither Di nor her guardians could notice initially. On one hand, she was gracious, well-mannered, revered and highly educated lady, as well as the spouse of a Diplomat posted in foreign soils.

Her name was Mrs. Raha – she was the one who selected Diana, as she recognised her potential, qualities and intellect. The Principal there was more inclined towards selecting a girl who couldn't last in northern India due to her poor mannerisms and lacklustre attitude towards studies – that girl was recommended by an official of the school who knew her parents, by dint of serving in the armed forces.

Another girl whose mother used to be an alumnus of that school was also selected by the Principal– thus, for that school's IB program that particular year, which also happened to be the first year of IB offered from that school, three girls were chosen from outside the school, and ten girls were selected from that school.

Out of those 13 girls, Di was the only one who was selected by Mrs. Raha, to whom merit, talents and background were the main criteria for admission, not anything else, in sharp contrast to the criteria set by Principal of that school (who was more interested in 'return on investment' theory of economics, than developing or promoting talent-based search criterion).

Di had earlier got selected for admission at two other very reputed schools for IB program, prior to her seeking admission to that School near Park Circus – Heritage and CIS. The school authorities in both the IB Schools liked Diana very much - she scored highest on the entrance tests of both those reputed institutions in Kolkata; the authorities were really inclined on welcoming her on board at both of those esteemed institutions.

The primary reason Di preferred that other school near Park Circus was because her mother Gita used to study in that same school till fourth grade - she used to speak highly of that school to Di's maternal grandparents.

Another reason of choosing that particular school was, both Diana and her grandma Ritu were overwhelmed with joy and pleasure after meeting Mrs. Raha there – the lady gave out an air of great personality; it seemed that her surroundings glow with her presence, without any hoopla associated with some of the other biggies in businesses! She appeared to be a great lady with very pleasing personality – at least that's how she carried her to deceive others. That evil lady had a huge impact on Di's life at a later stage.

After Vicky met Mrs. Raha and the officials of the school, he concurred with his niece and mom regarding their assessments of Mrs. Raha; he didn't even take a second to decide to admit Diana there. Vicky made the most significant mistake of his life by not being able to assess the true colour of Raha – this eventually had led to tremendous amount of shock and unpleasant consequences towards the end of high school life for Di and her guardians.

The tuition and other expenses there were more than the other two schools, but since Randi assured Vicky to pay the tuition fees, he was very happy that Diana was going to attend the same school where his deceased sister used to study for some time.

However, Randi didn't honour the cheque he gave to Vicky for first quarter's tuition fees here - Vicky had to exhaust most of his savings in the process of having to bear all educational expenses associated with his dear niece from that point on.

Soon after the new session started in her senior school, Diana found one of her classmates there, who lived near Kidderpore to be very crooked; she was also an expert in hatching conspiracy and lies against whoever she chose, to fulfil her ulterior motives. That girl manipulated Diana from day one and also tried to harm her in as many ways as she could. Her mother was a nice lady, and so was her brother – Di didn't understand how a girl with such a nice mother can turn out to be as horrible as that spiteful girl!

The girl, named Bistha, spread false rumours about Diana that she was seeking help with tutorials, etc. constantly. When it was ultimately revealed that Di didn't actually seek any help from her at all, Bistha started playing dirty tricks on Diana.

At first, she badmouthed Di to all the other students, by circulating false and fabricated propaganda, so that all the classmates be alienated by Diana. Most of those girls belonged to reputed business houses in Kolkata - it appeared very strange to Diana as to how kids with good family backgrounds be so indifferent, selfish and careless – they soon segregated Diana into a separate compartment and didn't even share their seats or talk to her. They all probably fell for lies spread by Bistha about something Diana wasn't even aware of! The fact of the matter was, none of those girls had the privilege of enriching their lives neither through good family background, nor any moral values – manipulation was probably the only word that existed in their dictionary!

Some of those girls even went to the extent of reaching out to various teachers and even to Mrs. Raha, in a consorted effort to make Diana's life miserable at their school – it seemed Di wasn't welcome there. When the evil intentions to cause harm to Diana didn't work well with Mrs. Raha, some of those girls ran to the Principal to make false accusations about Diana – it was extremely strange that a few parents of some of those girls also joined the campaign to boycott Di and cause harm to her. The dubious parents also formed a WhatsApp group between them, in order to get a platform to hatch ongoing conspiracy and assault against the innocent little girl!

Most of those girls usually skipped school on Fridays, so that they can go partying early. Although none of them attained the age of majority, they used to be served with alcoholic beverages by various places in Park Street, one N Bar & Kitchen being infamously notorious for such unlawful practices. Or else, they will take turns to host liquor parties at their homes and spend the weekend drinking and partying – when they returned to school on Mondays with hangover from the excessive drinking, they acted incoherently, mostly behaving in strange manners. Vicky had informed the Principal as well as Raha about those incidents, along with other unlawful actions by those IB girls, but they chose to turn their heads away, claiming that they weren't aware of any such matters, despite having closed circuit cameras installed at classrooms!

One day, a girl named Malini was quoted as saying: "I drank too much on last Friday night and woke up submerged in a post-wine katzenjammer on Saturday morning. My head was buzzing, and every fibre of my body slowly shrivelled and wilted as the alcohol exited it." Di used to chuckle with those kinds of stupidity the girls exhibited at class many a times.

The principal, who seemed to be a nice lady at first glance, was actually a double-faced person, who quickly got poisoned by those girls with ulterior motives, led by Bistha. Without getting to the bottom of the veracity of a false and frivolous complaint against Di by those few girls, the Principal decided to call Diana's parents after sending an email full of inaccurate accusations and bunch of misrepresentation of facts.

Vicky was already accustomed to those kinds of dirty politics during his vast and varied exposure at all levels of management, in public and private institutions – he quickly assessed the situation and sent out a befitting reply via email to the Principal, with carbon copy to Mrs. Raha right away – the evil-minded officials chose to remain silent by not responding to the counter-allegations and several matters of grave concerns against those girls, sent through email by Vicky, along with corroborative evidences.

After speaking to Di, Vicky responded to all the false accusations point by point, proving all the allegations fake and untrue – thereafter, he and his octogenarian widowed ailing mother went to see the Principal, who didn't even discuss a single point previously raised by her through her email, nor did she bother to rebut any of the major accusations specified against the other girls by Vicky through his email earlier – instead, she chose to throw harsh words towards Di's guardians, from the moment they stepped in her office.

She started the discussion by stating that Diana lacked the qualities required for pursuing IB; she alleged that Di was lagging behind in all the subjects – all her teachers were complaining against her, and even the students were disgusted with her attitude towards them!

The Principal even warned the shocked parents that Diana would be removed from IB program the following month. She also said that Vicky and his mow were wasting money on Di – they were better off putting Diana for a regular course. And, she would wait till results of the first semester came out, so that she will have enough ammunitions to transfer Di from IB to a certificate course.

A born fighter like Vicky got startled at those kinds of baseless and false allegations initially - all he requested to the Principal was to wait for the result of the first semester which was forthcoming the following month. He knew very well that Diana had always been a bright student, against whom no teacher ever complained at any level. His mom was extremely sad and was crying – she was stunned that anyone with half a brain could bring in such untrue and serious allegations at her innocent, pure, simple, kind-hearted and bright granddaughter! Both Vicky and his mom felt humiliated, insulted and angry though, but didn't say much at that point, as Di was fairly new at that school – they didn't want to start rocking the boat at that very moment.

To rub salt to injuries, the Principal also called Di from her class in front of her guardians and instructed her to 'stop playing victim' – it was clearly evident at that point that the Principal was being influenced and poisoned. That finding became more obvious when Mrs. Raha came in the room later on - she had such a guilty-looking face when she walked in! She gave out impression of a truly wonderful person with great heart and sincere attitude; but, her face that day looked completely different – on one hand, she was quite embarrassed for having to deal with undue pressure in joining hands to accuse an innocent girl like Diana, and on the other, her evil politics to put the Principal as a 'front', just so that she can maintain her outwardly 'nice' image, was about to get shattered, especially with the turn of events to follow later.

The remorse Mrs. Raha had on her face that day spoke a million words. Vicky decided to strike back by informing the IB Board what was going on – he wanted to inform them about everything; but Diana persuaded him to refrain from any such action, as she had full faith in Mrs. Raha; Di said that she wanted to find out matters in detail, and then decide on the future course of action. Vicky went ahead with Di's proposal, as he had faith in his niece too.

It was revealed soon that no teacher actually complained against Diana – only one girl was spreading false rumours against Di, by convincing her other partners in crimes to spread the word. Di felt that since the Lord, Jesus Christ himself, silently faced his crucifixion by evil-minded soul centuries ago, she could easily endure & bear all pain momentarily, instead of falling into evil traps set by those warmongers. She chose peace over war, although that was not typical of her.

Nor was it something acceptable by Di's favourite uncle Vicky – he found it extremely difficult to come to terms with illegal acts; he believed in the theory that offense is the best way to defend. But he agreed to keep silent on the matter, unless extra action would likely to be warranted down the road - his avuncular and supportive feelings for his dear niece was always a steadying force in Diana's life, although she hardly admitted it.

Although many uncles around the universe are generally seen as affable and benevolent, if at times a bit patronizing, but not all uncles are likeable fellows, like Hamlet's murderous uncle Claudius, or even Vicky's own uncle Sunny! There were worse examples, like Vicky's cousin brothers, who were uncles to Diana – they had tried to outrage her modesty, against which no action was taken by local cops, as both those guys paid hefty sums to the officers of the police stations where complaints were lodged by Diana.

But Vicky was much more than an uncle to Diana – he was more of a father figure to her, a caring, loving and affectionate one, who was ready to give up his life to protect his niece. Diana on the other hand, never expressed to her uncle how much she loved him – she hardly recognised anything her dear uncle did for her ever, as she was different! She was great in hiding emotions and feelings – she managed to hide her true love for her dear Dada!

Back to the senior school episode, as it was compulsory for the IB students to actively participate in an out-of-town trip related to one compulsory subject, the first year's trip was selected for the 13 girls, although one of them couldn't go due to sickness. Diana went ahead with the planned trip, not caring about the probable humiliation and ignorance of her peers; her grandma and uncle helped her pack her bags for a ten days' trip to Pune.

The teacher-in-charge of the trip, Dr. Mukherjee was a lady full of vigour and positive vibes. She welcomed Diana at Netaji Subhas Bose Airport at Dum Dum, the moment Di and her guardians arrived there to depart for Pune, so that Di and her guardians do not feel unwelcome amongst the obnoxious and snob crowd present there – parents of other students!

What was ludicrous was the attitude towards Diana by her classmates from the moment Diana arrived at the airport – they moved away from where Diana was standing, assembled in a group by themselves, and started whispering; probably they were making fun of Di as she was overweight, or were criticising her dress, etc.

However, it was revealed later that Diana went by the books regarding instructions from her School to carry specified number of clothes, stationery and other items for the trip – many of her classmates didn't bring specified clothes or inner wears; a few of them used the same inner garment for the entire duration of the trip!

Some of those girls used to borrow deodorants from none other than Diana frequently to remove the odour around them, for not wearing clean clothes. Di smilingly shared her belongings to others, without even a frown at those girls who had nothing other than untrue allegations, criticisms, spite and mockery against her.

Di enjoyed her trip very much, although she was over-worked. At home, she used to be kind of lazy, as her loving grandma Ritu would pamper her for almost everything. This was the first time in her life till then that Diana had to wash her clothes, pack her bags, carry stuff by herself, make her bed and turn it, etcetera.

At home, when Di would be around, Ritu used to get up early in the morning, made breakfast for Diana, packed her tiffin, filled her water-bottle, made sure that Di wasn't leaving anything behind, hand her over ironed skirts and blouses, etc. Di used to call Ritu from one end of the house they lived to the other, even for silly requests like handing her the laptop, to fetch water for her or even to put her phone on charger.

After she returned from school, Ritu used to take out the tiffin box from Diana's bag, pick up her clothes she left on floor, warm up food and serve those to the Queen! Practically, Di was getting spoiled by her dearest grandma's love and affection – so, Di missed her very much during the trip.

The organisation which was selected by the School for the trip was quite reputed with a superb bunch of lady guides – they were very friendly and caring to all the girls and took care of all their needs. Still, a few of the wiseacre girls became a pain in the neck for those nice ladies, by various nasty habits like indulging their taste-buds into menus preserved for other groups at the venue, acting mischievously, demanding favours, etc. Those ladies became very fond of Di, as she stood out from the crowd - they maintained periodic contacts with her long after the trip ended. They even selected Di for 'bravery award' for her courage and stamina during an adventure sports event.

The girls shared modernised tents at the campsite although they stayed at decent hotels at airports. The environment around the campsite was marvellous and awesome – Di loved it there, except the choice of food, as vegetarian food was served mainly there at camp, which wasn't to her liking. Diana loved chicken, mutton, egg and fish – so, she lost some weight there, which was good for her!

One of the feisty girls there made up a concocted story after the trip ended, when she went to Mrs. Raha and complained against Diana and her uncle – that crooked girl claimed that Diana showed video of her classmates changing inside the tent to her uncle, while they were on video calls, during the camping! That particular girl was apparently under duress from Bistha – the ringleader and the mastermind of many evils perpetrated against Di later.

The truth was, Vicky was aware that when he and his mother would speak to Diana through video calls at permitted hours (which was either after dinner or before breakfast) during the trip, girls will be in their night suits; so, it wouldn't be fair for a man to look at grown up girls at night time; therefore, he made sure that every time they were on video calls, he would step out in the garden, on the pretext of smoking, after handing over the phone to Ritu. Moreover, Diana made sure she was out of her tent while she spoke with her guardians, mainly to get away from the cacophony and melodrama inside the tent – just to have normalcy and privacy.

Vicky was around 57 years of age at that time - Diana's friends would be like his grandkids, if he got married at the right time. He had never looked at any friends of his niece in indecent manner ever; but it didn't hold the girl from Di's class to make that kind of false allegation. Probably she wanted to get back at Diana for the latter's protest against an indecent act by that girl earlier.

When Diana and another classmate were called to that lying perpetrator's house earlier to complete a school project, the latter's father was walking around clad only in an underwear - the girl wore a skimpy outfit too, exposing some private areas of her body. Just out of pure innocence and curiosity, Diana asked that girl if she or her father didn't feel ashamed to walk around like that, with guests in the house. It probably infuriated the girl in question, and she wanted to take a revenge, proportionately aided & abetted by Bistha and some of her evil company at that school!

Mrs. Raha didn't believe the cooked-up story that girl propagated against Di during the school trip. She didn't even mention the 'story' to Diana until a much later time – finally when she heard it, Di fell from the sky wondering how anyone in their right minds can make up such heinous story involving her uncle! It was an apparent effort of character-assassination of Di too, as any third person would think why Diana would show pictures of her friends to a male guardian while out on a trip?

Vicky contemplated sending a legal notice to that girl's father, but Diana and Ritu compelled him to calm down and ignore the devil. Vicky felt so insulted that he never even looked at that girl ever in the future, during parents-teachers meeting or any common social events – he hated her! He also wondered what type of lady that girl will turn out to be at a later period of time! She would probably exploit many innocent guys down the road, malign them or even engage in mass extortion attempts through false threats, etc.

Diana scored highest marks in many subjects of IB in not only the first semester, but consistently throughout the first year of her IBDP. After her first term results were out, Vicky sent a very strong email to the Director of that school, with copies to the evil Principal as also to Mrs. Raha, putting down everything the Principal had earlier stated on papers, in order to keep records of the officials' attempted sins, to be used against them down the road – Vicky planned to send details of modus operandi of that school to IB Board later, so that other external students were not harmed further, which he finally did at a later time.

The School was extremely reputed in Kolkata; however, as Vicky learnt, that evil lady took over as DPC of that school just a year back. The Principal was kind of new too. Since then, performance of the school overall was deteriorating, as those ladies neither knew anything about managerial practices, nor did they possess any management skills. English was apparently the only forte of the Principal, although she spoke grammatically incorrect English many times in public. Neither she nor the DPC had any expertise in handling HR – they lacked most skills required or expected of a Principal or DPC in any good school.

The problem with this school was, it was owned and operated by an affluent industrial group whose top priority was maximisation of profit. There wasn't much set procedures or governance to go by, as the group apparently didn't believe in improving educational system much – commercial operation of the school was eyed in over years, although by dint of sheer luck, the school did command good reputation in the past. However, change in management without proper homework or vision resulted in poor standard of practices evolving pretty soon. Window-dressing was accorded higher priority than infrastructural, logistical or other developments, which obviously resulted in mismanagement, instead of streamlining of activities.

The upper edge enjoyed by the new Principal was, she was very close to a Principal of another reputable School owned by the same industrialists who owned Di's school. The other school was located in Moira Street, opposite the house where the legend of Bengali movies, Uttam Kumar lived. Since the Principal of that other school in Moira Street was a favourite of the industrialist who also owned Di's school, it became very easy for the incompetent Principal to get a job there. The group who owned both the schools didn't care much about performance of students, as they were more focused on their revenue aspects. Similar practices were very common in Bengal at that time.

Similarly, the Diploma Program Coordinator, Raha was selected by the group for reasons known best to them. It was later revealed upon further inquiry by Vicky that, the DPC had an adverse work record in Singapore, for which she was compelled to return to India. She was looking for a suitable job, and there it was for her to grab – birds of a feather, flock together! Like school management, like DPC; money was the sole consideration to both eying for their own interests.

The DPC of Di's school was inept, as she ended up selecting subjects and courses which were not too useful for any student wanting to go to USA or UK for college. For example, in History, no American or European topics were selected, whereas all the students enrolled for IB there wanted to go there. Instead, oriental history topics were selected, when not even a single girl there had any plans to study at China, Taiwan, Singapore or Bangkok. Had it been any average academician, students' interests and their prospects would have been the prime concern while choosing topics for them – in IB, schools can select topics amongst a host of available options, which was great!

However, the students of that school who chose history and some other subjects had to suffer a lot, not only having to study history of those countries where they will not even spend a day, but also by virtue of missing out on learning about American History or history of any European nation.

In addition, since it was the first IB batch for the school, the DPC wanted to show to the IB Board how efficient they were by suppressing material facts, engaging in imprudent practices, encouraging cheating and deceptive practices, indulging in hiking up of minimum attendance of certain students by falsifying data, raising marks obtained by few students in examinations unethically, etc.

At least two students failed to obtain the minimum marks required to continue IB at the end of the first year. And, three girls had less than minimum required attendance to be eligible for promotion. Exceptions were made unscrupulously in the above cases, probably in an effort to hide the inefficiency of the DPC – all girls were duly promoted by the school!

What was most amazing was the award of prizes to some girls who failed or fared very poorly on their tests throughout the year. Some girls selected for prize by the school probably paid off some person in authority, maybe an invisible hand, to magically become a prize-winner from a failed candidate. Merit certificates were presented to some girls who didn't even pass the internal assessments many a times in the past year!

As Vicky found out through extensive work and research, one person in the entire school was making all the apples in the basket rot. But nothing could have been done, as she knew some people in power. That was not a very uncommon trend in the State at that time, even much later. Despite being a born protestor against improper actions, Vicky could not do anything there, because of obvious reasons, until he was pushed to the wall at a later stage.

Bistha played another nasty game against Di towards the end of the first year, by conspiring with the girl who joined the school from north India, along with another Bengali student in their class (Diana and this girl were the two Bengali girls in IB – others were either from Rajasthan or from other parts of India by origin).

Bistha convinced that girl to send a WhatsApp text message to the other girl with lousy comments about teachers, and had this other girl (receiver of the message) change the sender's name to Diana, so that it appears to naked eyes that Di sent those comments about teachers – this girl who received the message went to all the teachers of their class and showed them the message, containing lousy and nasty comments about all those teachers.

The time was carefully chosen when Mrs. Raha was out of town on official business – that heinous crime of forgery, misrepresentation, libel, slander, defamation and fraud was strangely perpetrated by a group of teenage girls from supposedly decent families, and was planned, designed and implemented in a flawless manner. Some of the worst criminals and fraudsters in the country can be put to shame by those girls, although the mastermind was Bistha. Raha was an abettor, as she was well aware of what was going to happen; she might have spearheaded the poison – who knows!

A few weeks before the above incident, some of the students in Diana's class were posting very nasty comments and adjectives targeting the teachers and officials of the school, apparently as their various efforts to get rid of Di didn't work out – all the teachers in her class loved Di very much, and even those teachers who didn't teach Diana at any time, used to say loving things and render valuable advice to her whenever they saw Di anywhere.

Even the Principal was beginning to like Diana, realising her fault of pre-judging her in the past, and encouraged her to score higher. The office staff used to be very friendly and cooperating with Di, and so were all the students from other classes – that obviously had a ripple effect on evil minds, as they failed to maintain their vox populi, and started pouring out hate comments towards teachers and officials of the school, posting those comments on school WhatsApp group that was created for the IB students, with only the students in the group.

On the New Year's Day that year, one girl from IB posted a negative comment about the school authority's decision to reopen from the 2nd of January, calling it a four-letter decision by the Principal, addressing her with choicest of words; another girl replied to that post by writing that the Director can 'suck it', addressing the Director by name, without any prefix like Mrs or Madam. Bistha posted 'ya that' to those messages, although she was the group administrator.

Bistha herself made a comment about Mrs. Raha earlier in the WA Group, referring her as 'fat a.s' Diana was so shocked to see those posts that she couldn't sleep properly that night – she kept asking her grandma that how can girls who studied in that famous school from childhood use such horrible phrases against teachers and officials! Her grandma couldn't console her enough, other than suggesting that Diana should ignore those girls, as ignorance was bliss.

Before the above-noted incidents, some girls used horrible adjectives about their class teacher, Pampa Sanyal, who joined the school from one of the best IB schools in India; she was an extremely pleasant lady with motherly care and affection, especially towards Di. She had publicly stated on a number of occasions that she had full faith and confidence on Diana's abilities, and she believed that Di would indeed excel in life. Another teacher who taught German – Ms. Mita Banerjee also openly praised Diana many times for picking up the language so fast, which some of the other girls who had the same language in their junior school years, couldn't. The SCA teacher, Dr. Mukherjee had also publicly lauded Di's efforts and capabilities on many occasions, although the Dr. was an expert in doctoring materials, rather than being a good teacher!

Mrs. Srabani Chakraborty who taught mathematics to Di, was another great lady – she always smiled while speaking to Diana and loved her very much. There were many occasions when Mrs. Chakraborty would console Di and act towards her in a motherly fashion. Another teacher by the name of Ms. South, who taught ESS was also a good person, although she fell short of being a good teacher. In fact, many of the teachers in that school were pleasant, well-mannered, courteous, and with so much love and care for Diana at all times!

The best subject-teacher that Di had the privilege of having at that school was Mrs. Pampa Sanyal – Di used to feel as if Sanyal Maa'm was her best friend, or sometimes her sister. Diana remembered her favourite teachers there for the rest of her life – she was so ever grateful to them for how they interacted with her. In fact, Diana's success later on life may be directly attributed to few of the great ladies in that horrible school, amongst all the negativities and ragging, etc.

Many of Di's classmates were routinely posting derogatory comments about all the teachers, non-IB students and even the Director on various social platforms, which Di considered as being very disrespectful, rude and nasty.

When Diana objected to such posts, Bistha and someone else told her to mind her own business, using foul adjectives. However, when the girls were worried about the following year's IB batch coming in and performing better than them, they started posting their ragging plans and other plans to discourage those students from pursuing IB – this was approximately the same time when the school organised a seminar for IB for prospective students, where Diana had managed to explain benefits of IB to many parents of prospective students present there, on two different subjects, for which she received a special recognition from Mrs. Raha in writing.

So, as those girls started making evil plans to keep those prospective students at bay and were even posting nasty comments about their chosen subjects of studies, Di informed her uncle about the conspiracy being hatched, and Vicky suggested that she overlook those as trash momentarily!

Finally, Diana couldn't take the repeated abuse and cursing of teachers and officials of the school from those feisty girls anymore, and as per Vicky's advice later, she quit the WhatsApp Group by stating that she was fed up with such objectionable acts by few students of her class – she showed the message she had posted in the Group to Mrs. Raha, in order to get her nod; Mrs. Raha gave her the permission to quit the Group, which became a blessing in disguise to Diana, as she didn't have to deal with mental agony, pain or aggravation. However, as it turned out later, this was another evil ploy by Raha to crucify Di, as she couldn't come to terms with the fact that Diana was becoming so proficient and expert in history topics, and thus was becoming an eye-soar for an evil person like Raha.

Raha's own daughter, whose face and physique resembled Di in many ways, chose to take art as her career, instead of her mother's subject – history. Raha couldn't forgive her daughter for 'not living up to her expectation' when she decided not to pursue history during her undergraduate studies. She just didn't have any passion for the subject, which was beyond the comprehension of a dictator mother, or more accurately an autocrat or tyrant lady. Raha was a perfect example of despotic power ruling not only during ancient times, but also in other manner even in recent times.

Bistha apparently got mad at Diana after she quit the Group – she decided to go to the teachers to inform them of Di's quitting school group, without realising that Diana had sought required permission in advance - all the teachers already knew of the reason she quit the Group. Mrs. Raha and others told Bistha to stop poking in others' affairs and concentrate on her own behaviour – she also wrote to Bistha a comment stating that Bistha herself was her own biggest enemy! Thereafter, there was no stopping the evil-minded and gormless girl to hatch a virile conspiracy against Di, to prove to the teachers that she was a double-faced girl (which she proved her own self to be later).

One of the teachers called Diana one fine afternoon and expressed her resentment for horrible comments that she thought Di had posted, based on what Bistha's partner in crime showed the teacher, as also to all other teachers. Diana fell from the sky almost and asked the teacher if she herself believed it. That teacher used to love Di very much, like all other teachers - she saved Diana's life that day by divulging the actual information, the behind-the-scene drama – that one particular girl was defaming her by impersonating to be Di.

Bistha could never imagine in her wildest dreams that Di would come to know of the conspiracy, as she had requested all the teachers not to tell Diana about her friend's showing the text messages to them! It was a near perfect plan, which went sour due to the passing of the info to Di by her teacher, who trusted Di and knew she wasn't capable of such heinous acts.

Di immediately sent an email to Mrs. Raha narrating the ordeal, and the latter replied instantly that she would look into the matter upon her return. In the meantime, Di and her family lost sleep over the next few days, thinking what grave consequence the forgery could have on Diana, had the godly teacher not mention anything about it to her! Her aunt from Florida, Riya also suffered from anxiety attack, as the entire family knew of Di's horrible friends at that new school - all were very worried for Di's safety and mental well-being.

Vicky, in the meanwhile sent a request to the Director of the school, detailing what transpired in Diana's class, seeking an immediate appointment, pending which he would have absolutely no alternative but to lodge a FIR against Bistha and unknown persons in her class for criminal conspiracy, maligning, fraud and cheating – it was up to the police to find out who aided and abetted Bistha.

Mrs. Raha called Ritu thereafter, and expressed her grief and apology over the incident, and assured Diana's safety from the evil souls – she also gave an assurance that justice will prevail, and she will do everything required to unearth the ploy, so as to put the culprit to final warning. However, this was another dirty ploy sought by Raha in order to kill two birds with one stone – to show Di's family that she was going to take some action against Bistha (to pacify the situation), and also to get Bistha more close to her (so that she can play dirty games with Di at a later period of time). Raha was a demon in real life situation – her external appearance was completely deceiving! She had slimy mind, evil spirit and unholy attitude to anyone she didn't like. If you keep buttering her and shower her with gifts and material bribes, you are on her good side; however, if you are morally and ethically strong, she's your worst enemy.

Vicky understood that if he pursued the matter with the police or IB Board, then the competency of the authorities will be put to question, as some of the basic requirements of IB were caring, sharing and sympathy – the authority who were involved in the selection process of those girls would have definitely questions to answer; since it was the first batch of IB for that school, their fate in imparting IB would also hang on a wire – all because of a few devilish and evil-minded young girls who couldn't control their jealousy over a new entrant to their school, scoring higher marks than them consistently, getting praises from all the teachers!

Vicky had inculcated many values and wisdom into Diana as she was growing up. By virtue of spending a majority of his time in the US, he told her not to try pleasing others, before pleasing herself first. He quoted a famous psychologist by saying that not pleasing others enough amounts to surliness, while pleasing too much makes one obsequious – you have to be friendly, but not too friendly. The sweet spot in the middle is where you may want to be. Vicky also told his niece the famous American saying which goes like "what goes around, comes around". Mrs. Raha had also told Diana to perform well in her studies, so that the tables may turn – another of her apparently harmless gesture, while damaging Di's career was always on the back of her mind.

Thereafter, Di started to ignore those wiseacres around her and behaved politely to everyone, while keeping mostly to herself in class. She had lots of respect and affinity towards most of her esteemed teachers, with blind eyes to her classmates' routine mocking, humiliation and ignorance towards her. As a matter of fact, many well-wishers told Diana that her classmates' actions against her might work out better for her, as no company was always better than bad company. Many of her classmates performed poorly in the final examination and received negative feedbacks from IBO.

What was mind-boggling was that, two classmates scored 2 out of 7 in mathematics test during the first-year final exam, combined with averages of internal assessments and periodic tests throughout the year. As per IB rules, any student failing to obtain a minimum of 3 out of 7 will have to be removed from Diploma Program (into Certificate Program) if it was a SL subject; in case the subject was a Higher Level one, then such student would have to be demoted to SL from HL. This was a strict universal rule promulgated by the IB Board across the world. However, those two girls who secured 2 out of 7 in Maths had magic wand, and their final scores were doctored by certain official of the school!

One of the girls who failed to obtain the minimum requisite marks belonged to a booming real estate developer's family, and her mother was the Director of many shell companies – those companies were used to convert the black moneys made by the father in his real estate deals across the State, with paybacks to political figures, to legitimate money, by virtue of reporting fictitious profits of those shell companies to SEBI and IT- the black money earned though the difference of paper money and actual cash received in the real estate deals were funnelled through those shell companies in crores!

That girl always showed off her persnicketies and snooty attitude, coupled with hifalutin and bumptious arrogance – most girls hated her for this, but didn't say a word in front of her, due to the fact that she used to throw regular high-flying parties with scrumptious food and expensive foreign liquors.

Teachers hated her too - but didn't dare to open their mouth in her presence, fearing backlashes from one of the invisible hands positioned quite highly in the school. That girl also bunked school for more than a month, on the false pretence of suffering from pox, while she actually went to China with her supercilious and pretentious family – that way the family could dispose of some of the huge cash they accumulated through their unscrupulous business practices.

The invisible hand in the school, in exchange of a handsome payola or inducement, returned the favour to that girl by jacking up her marks obtained in mathematics, thus helping her illegally to retain her SL subject. As for the other girl whose father was a successful businessman, an all-expense paid trip to South Africa to Dr. Mukherjee and a trip to USA for Raha worked as wonder to help his daughter retain her subject in IB, through the same invisible hand!

Diana was the only girl in IB from that school who belonged to a simple middleclass family. Plus, she was a hot favourite of Mrs. Sanyal. Mrs. Chakraborty, Mrs. Swati Dam and some other teachers, which was an eye-soar to most students, as well as to that invisible hand. Mrs. Dam was the Senior School Coordinator for ICSE students of the school – she loved Di very much; as a matter of fact, she was the one who kind of forced Raha to sign the documents to be sent to Oxford by Di, after she applied there without Raha's knowledge. Raha couldn't stand the fact that Di was applying to the premier institute, and refused to sign the mandatory documents, when Mrs. Dam pitched in for Di, so as to get those papers duly signed and sent to Oxford.

So, Di was punished by the invisible hand through strict instructions to some teachers from that invisible hand to reduce her marks! While Diana deserved at least 6 in three subjects, only Pampa Sanyal dared to disobey the invisible hand and gave Diana a straight six. In all other subjects, she either got four or five, which was less than alright as per IB standards. Dr. Mukherjee, Mrs. Chakraborty and Mrs. South – all were forced by Raha to reduce Di's grades, as the spiteful animal wanted to spoil the predicted grades at a later stage, when Diana applies for foreign studies. Such was her dirty vision and unlawful mission, coupled with unethical objective and unholy purposes.

However, Diana had studied very hard to make sure that the tables turned around with her securing high marks in all subjects; after the papers were shown to her, Di got very frustrated to find out that her answer-sheets were scrutinised 'differently' than most other girls – even in English, her answer script was marked by a different teacher, who apparently acted on the behest of Raha to give her lower marks than she actually deserved.

She never came into terms with how unfair discrimination caused a dent in her career, as she had planned to use the marks in her application for colleges abroad!

At her previous school, Diana was discriminated because she didn't attend private tuitions offered by schoolteachers there. In her senior school, she was discriminated because she wasn't liked by her classmates as she didn't join their routine partying and under-age drinking, and abstained from all get-togethers those students hosted to flaunt their power, etc. – to make matters worse, the invisible hand acted as Di's worst enemy after the former got influenced by rich parents of some of those spoiled brats.

Few months before the results were out, Vicky had written a strong letter to the school against many irregularities, pointing out what some of those girls do in class; they used to pen foul and dirty languages aimed at teachers and director of the school in the WhatsApp group of the school itself, and Vicky wrote about it; they used to bunk school to attend parties and sleep-overs at boyfriends' houses (on the false pretext of doing homework with classmates); some of them used to watch X-rated movies at class, when teachers weren't around; some even copied assignments from external sources (boyfriends from other local IB schools) and used those pirated versions for their school-submissions. A parent of one the girls even forced liquors on other girls on the occasion of the former's birthday party – Vicky also wrote about it.

The officials chose to ignore all those, and informed Vicky that school had no control over students outside school premises – this was despite Vicky's writing to the school that classroom and school learning tools were used to plan for the party aforementioned!

What was unthinkable to Vicky that the invisible hand poured everything down the ears of the parents of some of the girls in question, who instantly became Diana's worst enemies. A few of them gifted expensive bouquets and ancillary items to the invisible hand on the occasion of Diwali and convinced the latter to act in vengeance towards Diana! The chain-effect followed from the invisible hand to downwards, to cause trouble to Di.

One good thing which transpired out of the unholy saga noted above was, Diana became a stronger girl. Although she was very frustrated and depressed initially, after she found out how the girls, aided and abetted by their parents, were able to coerce and influence the invisible hand to cause misery to Di, however, she recuperated from her mental shock quickly.

At first, she was telling Vicky that she didn't want to continue her studies; she dealt with the year-long false accusation from school and constant aggravation, insult and ignorance from her classmates – but now, she was fed up about the fact that her arduous and diligent studies went in vain. Vicky and Ritu constantly provided words of encouragement for their only asset.

Riya and her daughter called Diana up repeatedly to inspire her; Riya gave the final vocal tonic to her beloved niece; she told Di to forget about the school performance, and prepare for SAT. That way, if she can score high in SAT, she would be able to prove to the school that they were wrong in assessing her. Many of the classmates appeared for ACT and SAT before, with disastrous results. So, it was Diana's turn to show to the world who the real boss was!

Vicky got his loving niece-cum-daughter-cum-best friend registered for SAT, after a short trip to New Delhi – that trip was really a boon for Diana to get rid of her pain and sorrow, and was also a blessing to Ritu to get some rest from her hectic and extremely hard-working routine life. At the age of 81 years, Ritu used to do everything for Diana which a mother, a father and a maid would jointly do for their kid. Diana regained her positivity and charisma soon - she was determined to get very high scores in SAT, which she did eventually. Her scores in HAT for Oxford, as well as ACT for US colleges were very good too – she got interviewed by Oxford later, a feat which no one from that disgusting school ever obtained! Di would've gotten into Oxford too, but Raha pulled some strings there, in order to deny her admission. As a matter of fact, Oxford couldn't even provide a 'reasons for denial' to Di, sharply in contrast to their announced policy of doing so for every rejected candidate!

Things weren't easy for the family during the time Randi stopped to pay anything for Di. Vicky had to cope with increase in tuition fees, to bear substantial expenses for SAT and AP registrations for different subjects, to deal with various expenses related to extracurricular activities – all those, while the criminal father abstained from complying with court orders to pay maintenance monthly even after execution of the order! Ritu had to pawn out some of her jewelleries in order to raise money; Vicky had already exhausted all his savings and was by then practically a broke! Riya used to send money from USA in order to keep the tuition expenses online. They couldn't express their grief and sorrow to anyone, as the family always held their heads high – they wanted no sympathy from anyone.

Diana, on the other hand, was such a nice and understanding kid that she completely stopped ordering food from outside – her most favourite passion, she gave up! She didn't even tell her family that she needed books for her studies – her German teacher used to regularly pester the students to buy certain books and take certain tests from outside, for reasons known best to her. Even when she went for maternity leave, she had her successor continue the onslaught of pestering students with forcing to buy newer books frequently.

Di started to borrow books from various libraries – where borrowing wasn't permissible for certain books, she took pictures of all those pages which she needed to study, upload those pictures from her phone to hard-drive, and study that way. She never even asked for a single dress or fancy stuff, until situation changed with sale of Vicky's bungalow.

Back to school, many of those girls failed to make up the lost days at class due to excessive absences, which should have gotten reflected in their Report Cards; the School itself mandated a 80% minimum attendance for any student to get promoted to next class – that requirement was clearly stated in the school diary and other places.

The management of that school chose to ignore the rules mandated by them earlier, to loosen the noose so that the girls who failed to qualify for the minimum attendance were allowed to get promoted to IB2 – probably the 'hand of god' or same invisible hands worked in their favours!

The bestiary saga of that mysterious school didn't end at that! Some girls who performed miserably on their promotional tests and IAs (internal assessments) were soon felicitated by the school authorities through Merit Certificates, on the annual prize day!

Vicky felt that the school deserved a special prize for being unfair and unbiased – he got really shocked to see how such a great school was becoming a gazing ground for spoilt affluent girls gradually, with some of their super-rich parents apparently showering the invisible hand there with gifts and other favours, so that the smirch acts by their spoilt kids don't deface the parents; apart from that, nix!

None of the girls Di knew who really deserved prizes were called during the brouhaha ceremony! Di decided not to care for the melodrama that was going on – instead, she was better off focusing on her education and enlightenment. The world had started to become a great place for the morally and otherwise corrupt and evil people; it wasn't possible for any single individual to change that; so, it was better to focus attention on positive sides, and ignore the rest!

Bistha tried to take revenge by not informing Diana about participation opportunities in various important extra-curricular activities like debate, quiz, etc. By dint of her long-standing past reputation at junior section of that school, Bistha became a popular student in the past before Diana joined – soon after Di joined the school and started getting praises from all her teachers,

That evil girl Bistha started to develop malice and invidiousness; if she wasn't a berk, she would had been better off competing with Diana in a fair manner, for mutual development; but she chose to outwit her competition by unfair means, thereby destroying her own reputation and career.

Critically belauded at her school during the past in her hay days, Bistha was being overlooked basically by not only her teachers, but also many of her peers ultimately, as they realised what kind of fractious young girl Bistha had become, especially after her slapdash performance on a school event, when Bistha lost her focus and displayed arrogance – her fervid dance-show was a flop, and she became an object of laughter to most, including her coevals.

She had been chary to tell everyone the truth about the WhatsApp message scandal made her an object of shame, and she was literally doomed. In addition, her long-standing tactics of buttering teachers for personal gains got exposed.

On the other hand, there was nary any complaint against Diana from any corner – even other subject teachers who did not take any class in which Di was ever present, started conversing very nicely with her, realising the harm intended to be inflicted on that innocent girl could have easily been seen as a ground for her rustication from school, had she not discovered Bistha's virile attempts on time.

Encouraged by the success of her first published book, Diana started writing a novel, which was always one of her unfulfilled dreams till then. Unlike most other girls at her school, Diana didn't waste any of her precious time during Senior years – she used spare times to put together her inborne talent and power to shape disparate things into a unified whole in an esemplastic imagination.

She even used non sequiturs intelligently in her writing, for comedic use in compiling her novel, apart from implanting some archetype characters which seemed to reflect universal patterns of human nature; few characters were depicted a bit maudlin self-pity, and efforts were made to alleviate banal or repeated words.

The novel was written over a period extending to more than one year – from beginning of summer of Diana's first year at her senior school, till midsummer of the following year; what Di used to do during her spare times in between, was to jot down the points on her smartphone, assimilated her thoughts and then composed few paragraphs – though it was kind of difficult to put cohesive sentences together at different period of time for a particular chain of thought, Di used to write down few sentences in her laptop relating what came up in her mind, leave those until the next time, and returned back to the composition which she was initially focusing on.

Instead of dawdling or going out with friends on weekends and holidays for partying and hanging out together for some impermissible actions like under-age drinking, etc., Diana had a positive frame of mind to utilize the time in the most effective and constructive manner, not only for personal enlightenment, enrichment and improving vocabulary, but also to pursue her noble efforts of helping out disadvantaged kids with the financial gain she would have after publication of her novel.

She also got continuous motivation from other family-members, her teachers and friends from her previous school. Diana was unfortunate not to have a single girl from her senior school to call a friend, but she accepted it with open hearts.

Soon after her first novel got published, Diana received many positive comments and feedbacks from various corners; most people who read her novel seemed to love it, as it was kind of unusual, and not a stereotype composition. Her characters were sometimes fakir, sometimes farceur – she dominated her composition on a few strong characters.

Diana melded her talents with traditional values, and projected few strong characters in her novel, and made conscious efforts to reach out to people she was fortunate to come in contact with, in order to market her novel pan India, as also across the globe.

She even delivered a breathless and effortless spiel to promote her first novel and went through the rigmarole of getting it published on her own, based on her bitter experience in publishing her first book, when there were some kerfuffle over some words she had used in her unedited version from a few of the world-famous publishers, who made unwarranted fuss about usage of those words, and demanded that Diana alter those terminologies.

Di refused to give in, as changing those words would have defeated the main purpose of the articles concerned - Vicky had to write to Bloomingdale County Sheriff's department and other regulatory bodies in the US, to have the money paid in advance returned by one such internationally-reputed self-publishing house to Diana.

Vicky was the one who suggested self-publishing her first book, when Diana made several futile attempts to have her book published through proper channel, meaning through some of the famous publishers; most established publishing houses required at least one full year's time to publish any book, for reasons known best to them!

Vicky and Di were constantly searching for self-publishers across India with mostly positive feedbacks from budding authors, following publication of their books with them – the search revealed while many self-publishers claimed that they publish a book within one or two months, and offered various packages to choose from, a few of them actually deliver on their promises. So, the job became more difficult to find a good one.

Diana contacted one of the self-publishing houses in Chennai after short-listing them based on positive feedbacks and sent the soft copy of her book. They started making various hanky-panky requests to persuade Diana to go for a higher package – Vicky spoke to them over the phone many times in the months to follow; it struck him when the same person answered all his calls – he contacted one of his college buddies who was settled in Chennai, to discover that the publishing house was a one-man army, although they had profiles of various fictitious persons on their website, aimed at misleading their clients.

Thereafter, Vicky started surfing the net over the next several weeks - he finally selected a local self-publishing house, working out of an office at Nager Bazar, Dum Dum. They didn't appear to be a pother initially – however, as discovered later, the owner of that place was kind of a conman, trying to bully budding authors into going for expensive packages that many of the authors didn't actually require, to begin with!

Vicky was no fool – he realised that this guy was nocuous in the sense that he would accept the initial deposits from authors gracefully, and then delay publishing beyond reasonable period on various false pretenses, causing some agita to the inexperienced clientele. So, he made up a concrete plan.

Di and Vicky started visiting them regularly, along with Ritu, after signing the agreement and paying for the package to publish Di's book – Vicky also ensured the firm's compliance with pertinent provisions of the agreement, by threatening to expose their imprudent business practices. Thus, he was successful in getting Diana's book published within a couple of months – it was later revealed that the self-publishing house was notorious in their dealings, making up all kinds of excuses to coerce clients into spending more!

They didn't take any initiative in marketing of the book, contrary to what they claimed before – when confronted by Vicky on that issue, they claimed that by marketing, they meant handing over posters, leaflets and tee-shirts to clients, in order for them to do marketing of their books themselves.

Vicky chose not to pursue the matter further, as he already had his hands full – he had enough lawsuits to deal with at that time; however, he made sure to write against their deceptive practices to the concerned authorities later!

Diana scored decent marks in her first year of IB and then further improved her score to near perfection at the end of the second year – she scored a whopping 42 out of 45 in IB Finals, thus making everyone around her proud. Mrs. Sanyal was prouder than anyone else, as she was the pivoting factor behind Diana's continuation of IB at that institution – thereafter, she did retire in style. Di, on the other hand, would be ever be grateful not only to Mrs. Sanyal, but to all the teachers of her high school who loved her unconditionally, including her favourite Mrs. Dam; she would maintain frequent contacts with all of them in the future, especially with Mrs. Sanyal and some of her more favourite ones.

From the varied experience that Vicky had in India and the US, he thought it would be best for Diana to leave her motherland and get admitted in a US college. However, there was huge costs involved - Diana's father blatantly refused to bear any expenses for her higher studies abroad. As a matter of fact, as soon as Di started her high school studies in one of the best girls' school in

Kolkata, the evil father Randi stopped paying for everything, which caused tremendous financial impact on the family, along with pain and suffering for the little kid who lost her mother already so early in her life.

Randi had meanwhile started living together with Suparnakha and her daughter, who was also a sleazy woman at Diamond Harbour, and stopped visiting Diana completely. Vicky initiated lawsuits against the absconding father of his darling niece, and even after Court ordered Randi to pay monthly expenses regularly after some time, the sociopath liar didn't, citing his no income – he falsely filed an Income Tax return showing his annual income to be less than Rs 2 lakhs, even after pocketing the full family pension of Diana's deceased mother!

So, the only option left for the family at that juncture was for Vicky to sell his huge property so that Diana's college expenses could be met. After a great deal of work, that plan finally materialised - Di flew off to study in Yale University. She was initially home sick and used to miss her family a lot, especially her grandma – she was the one Di became more closer to down the road, as she was growing up. Ritu was her heart and everyone else came after.

God had always protected Diana from all evils, and so did few of her teachers, including very pretty Maths teacher and and English teacher. Even some of the teachers who didn't teach any subject to her, knew her well and always inspired her to perform better. And, who else could have been happier than Mrs. Sanyal to see her favourite student excel?

Di never forgot any of her esteemed teachers from her high school and maintained contacts with them long after she passed out from the school. Mrs. Sanyal had a special position in her heart always, and no one except her own mother could take her place, in the minds of Diana. Many teachers from her primary school and junior school also maintained very good relationship with her, and rendered their best guidance to Di, whenever she needed it.

Bistha and some other girls continued to get some 'blessings' from their old school – they sometimes got away with some heinous crime against Diana, sometimes they will use their inveterate skills of unctuosity & oleaginousness to butter-up some teachers, in order to get higher marks than they really deserved; it paid off, especially for Bistha and the other Bengali girl, as few teachers and officials who fell for those smug self-servicing earnestness or smarminess however, when Vicky decided to complain to IB Board about the dereliction of duties, breach of ethics & gross negligence in awarding marks discriminately, Di didn't let him file the complaint until she completed her studies there, fearing backlashes and adverse repercussions.

As it turned out later during the IB exams, none of those foul plays worked for those girls; Diana obtained 42 out of 45, thereby becoming school topper. Vicky understood the reasons behind the school's initial attempts to lower marks for some girls during IB1 very well – as it was the first year of that School in IBDP, they wanted to show to the IB Board how strict and efficient they were. In addition, the witch Raha and her pet teachers conspired against Di so that her chances of getting into reputed foreign universities get marred.

By lowering marks for few students during the first year, the authorities wanted to prove to IB that their teachers were instrumental in developing IB skills amongst its student's gradatim, in piecemeal manner, from bad to better. That way, competency of their teachers will be proved beyond reasonable doubt - they will be able to get their coveted renewal of IB programs!

Inexperience of many teachers there caused widespread panic and chaos amongst the students during the first year of IB, as areas needing drastic improvements (like proper planning, organising and implementation) were not rectified in due course. The school got rid of the inefficient and corrupt DPC and some officials shortly, as the number of intakes were getting drastically reduced year after years.

And, the invisible hand behind not permitting some of the teachers to grant proper scores to Diana during her high school tenure also subsided over time, due to the direct threat posed by Diana's uncle waiting for opportunities to expose the attempt to victimise the innocent girl, to bring matters to the attention of IB authorities, denuded of evil intentions by the person concerned in position.

It was never unravelled if any exceptional benefaction behind the scenes attributed to reasonably good scores for some, and more so when attendance of some of the girls were beyond par – IB rules were very specific regarding minimum attendance. There were some students who did not officially meet such requirements but were still promoted to IB II! Mrs. Raha chose to turn her head on other side in matters pertaining to such anomalies, apparently as she succumbed to pressures of influential guardians of notorious students, as well as to gifts and articles 'donated' by those students. She also didn't want to rock the boat, as she was going to retire soon thereafter. That was of course a demotivating factor for Di; but, the young girl garnished enough courage and fighting spirits by then, so as to keep her going.

It may have been a combination of several evil intentions working in tandem behind the scenes, coupled with concocted efforts to traduce Diana, as she felt later. The invisible hand was instrumental on one end to vilify and besmirch Di – on the other hand, some classmates led by the daughter of the land-shark turned promoter, and Bistha were after Diana to decry and calumniate her; some even vilified Di for certain ulterior motives – they were all out to anathematize Di like scroungers to fulfil their dubious intentions.

However, God had always been protecting the demure, reticent and righteous young girl with pristine soul and clear mind – Diana's few teachers mostly acted as her saviours, shielding her from the constant wrath of those guileful and crooked girls. Mrs. Swati Dam was one such guardian angel for Di; although she never taught Diana directly, but the wise lady recognised the innocence and potential of the young girl, and decided to be on her sides.

Mrs. Sanyal was a super-educated, bright and quick-witted young lady with a perspicacious and canny mind – she was an astute person and there was no fooling around with her. Most girls hated her strong personalities and witty acumen; Diana loved her though! She dreamt to be half as bright as her role model when she grew up – she was full of compliments to that great lady - most of her classmates openly maligned Di after class, falsely claiming that she was buttering the teacher; but Diana continued to love and admire her.

It was quite evident by the way she carried herself that Mrs. Sanyal had a rock-solid background with great values inculcated in her by her parents. Her daughter was also very bright and intelligent, with great stature and pleasing personalities – she was pursuing undergraduate course from Ashoka. Her friends spread all over the world, and the mother-daughter duo would naturally become globe-trotters. Each time they returned from their international trip, Diana would anxiously wait to hear about the experiences of her favourite teacher-cum-friend-cum-sister.

As a matter of fact, Diana used to make life difficult for Vicky and Ritu each time Mrs. Sanyal would go on a trip, asking them frequently what her idol would have been doing periodically throughout the tenure of the trip. Vicky used to get irate by the continuous questions posed to him regarding someone he knew very little about – he would sometimes ask Diana: "How am I supposed to know what Ma'am is doing sitting thousands of miles away from her". That way, Di could be stopped bugging him with questions from the innocent and sinless young girl.

Mrs. Swati Dam also liked Di so much that she often invited her favourite student to participate in debates and discussions relating to a club where Diana wasn't even a member of! The duo seemed like two sisters with so much liking for each other, and those evil girls who were Di's classmates got even more jealous. They refused to let Di join them in various groups they were part of, thus making life more difficult for Diana.

Di's flair for writing, her creative activities and community services were adored by Mrs. Sanyal, who subsequently issued a super-duper letter of recommendation to Diana for use during her college application processes, which helped Di very much – she always maintained regular contacts with her favourite teacher down the road.

Another strange act of nepotism and favouritism by the Principal of that school was observed when she refused to hand over the internship certificate Di earned through hard work at The Telegraph, towards the end of her first year in IB. None of the other girls from that School who were selected for the internship attend the final day of the program there, for which the career counsellor felt insulted (as she was the one who arranged for the said internship at The Telegraph). The Counsellor by the way was a good for nothing person, with very little efficacy in her job.

As regards the Telegraph incident, for an eyewash, the virulent and rancorous Principal called all the girls in her office and told them that they will never be sent for any internship program down the road, for skipping the last session of the program, resulting in ill-reputation of the school! However, Di found out that one of those girls with affluent family was again selected for another internship during the next summer, while Di never received her certificate – the acrimonious lady kept promising her handing over the certificate 'shortly', which never materialized. Thus, it was a clear-cut case of discrimination and one-eyed action from the highest authority of the school, duly implemented by the DPC and her group of pet teachers.

Furthermore, within a very short span of time, the Principal called Di for a discussion at her office, when she was made to wait 45 minutes standing at the corridor without even a fan or seat, while she was sick at that time which the Principal was very much aware of. After that, the mentally ill lady called Di and started scolding her for making a hue and cry over not receiving the aforementioned certificate.

The wicked Principal used filthy languages towards Diana's guardians, as they requested the lady to hand over the internship certificate to Di without further delays, pending which they were going to inform IB about the matter. She told Di point blank that she was going to mess up Diana's letter of recommendation if she told her guardians about that incident. The pernicious influences of Di's guardians' requests took a pestilential turn when the Principal called the Head of Finance into her office – both of them started grilling and pestering Di for an earlier email by Vicky to handle the billing of the school with more care.

The Finance Head, one Gopal Popatlal was an inept and most ordinary accountant with less than desirable background, who was selected by the Principal for reasons known best to her. He didn't have more than one clerk to handle in his finance unit, although his designation was termed as Finance Head

– whether any of those two persons involved had any real head is a matter of debate. Anyways, Popatlal's inefficient handling of accounts had created duplicate billing for Di, which Vicky had righteously complained about; that complaint apparently opened up a Pandora's Box in terms of unholy nexus /collusion between the two involved, and things turned pestiferous soon.

Popatlal joined the Principal in hurling abuses towards Di's maternal grandma and maternal uncle continuously, while the poor girl was made to stand and listen to all kinds of nuisances. She was also touched inappropriately by the nasty animal while Di was returning back to her classroom. However, Di never confided in Vicky about the latter issue up until many years later, as she was scared that Vicky would drag the beast out in the street and hand him over to the cops. Di also didn't tell anyone about the entire incidence at the Principal's office before her school was closed for summer vacation. Although Vicky wanted to lodge a formal complaint against the school to appropriate legal forum, but Rebecca and Di persuaded him to refrain from doing so, fearing ugly retaliation from the evil lady and her partner in crime.

After summer vacation, the fees were paid by Vicky in the scheduled time, although the server-connection from the school host was poor, which resulted in some wastage of time. After the payment was successfully transmitted online from Vicky's bank to the school authority's designated banker through the school-designated third party e-billing company (which was again a brainchild of Popatlal and his evil brain, apparently after getting a sizeable commission from the deal), Vicky ended up paying penalty for being late by few minutes, which he naturally protested in writing.

The slipshod Head of Finance wrote back to Vicky the next morning, referring him to the guardian portal of the school's website. Realizing the fact that the incompetent guy would not care to look into the issue further, Vicky decided to forego the penalty he paid, thinking that it was useless to deal with someone as inefficacious as Popatlal.

Due to some glitches in their system, the school authorities did not post the payment made by Di's guardians duly, and Popatlal jumped the gun at Vicky the very next day, without waiting to see if the delays in posting was a result of their own fault or so, and issued a notice of late payment, asking Vicky to pay the tuition fees immediately, failing which actions would be taken against the student.

This infuriated Vicky so much that within minutes of receiving the notice, he wrote a strong email to the slipshod knucklehead and his mistress, attaching a copy of successful transmission receipt, asking them to exercise more care and be more efficient next time. He thought the matter would end amicably there, as he already did forego the penalty charged by the School.

However, the devil and inept combo decided otherwise – Popatlal called up Vicky in the afternoon, trying to convince him that the payment did not go through due to lapses on the part of Vicky. Being an educated and polite gentleman, Vicky did not tell the lousy guy that the number of postgraduate degrees Vicky had will exceed the number of letters of Popatlal's name; instead, he told the inept guy that he should check with his banker if they have indeed missed the payment. To this, Popatlal told adamantly that he had called up the head office of his banker in Mumbai, and have spoken to their top management, who confirmed non-receipt of the fees.

At that point, Vicky got little confused – he didn't realise that the third-party vendor appointed by the school after Popatlal took over, had almost the same level of efficiency as the Head of Finance there (birds of a feather flock together type of scenario). It was eventually found out that the e-billing company's system somehow didn't post the transaction on the guardians' portal of the school website, resulting in all the chaos. The same evening, Vicky noticed that the payment was updated successfully by the third-party vendor post facto, showing the date of payment as the retroactively the exact same date the payment was made by Vicky.

Since Popatlal suggested to Vicky to wait for two more days and remit the fees again (earlier during the same day), Vicky forwarded the screenshot of the posting referred to above to the wiseacres (the mistress and her servant) in the school thereafter, adding a comment saying that "this was exactly what I meant to be more efficient…."

God knows what transpired next in the devilish minds of the made-for-each-other duo at School, as Popatlal sent a reply to the above-noted email to Vicky next morning, stating that it was lack of Vicky's understanding of the process! The stupid clown didn't know that Vicky had a M.B.A. in Finance from S.U.N.Y. at Oswego, and was a Certified Public Accountant (equivalent to Chartered Accountant in India) from USA, apart from being a Certified Financial Examiner from The American College, and had six other postgraduate degrees from the USA, apart from few from India!

Vicky wrote a very strong email back to the devil duo at school, pointing out the blatant lies told by Popatlal during his telephonic conversation the day before (which was thankfully recorded at Vicky's end), apart from the outright lying by the inept guy that he had checked with his banker's H.O. about the non-transmission of the payment. Vicky wanted the weirdo to tender a written apology within three days for all his lies and slander, pending which he threatened to file charges of defamation and other criminal acts against the incompetent guy decorating the chair as Finance Head!

As usual, the school didn't respond to Vicky's mail, in the same exact fashion that they preferred to during the past – there were three other occasions in the last one year when Vicky pointed out the anomalies and misdeeds of the school authorities to the Principal in writing, when the latter chose not to respond back, apparently as she knew what kind of ammunitions Vicky had to substantiate his case to disrobe the evil woman.

At least on two occasions, Vicky also had informed the Director of the school about the above-noted matters, when he noticed that the incompetent Principal chose silence over writing back to Vicky, clearly as she had no case at her side. Her futile attempts to warn off Vicky failed repeatedly – she didn't realise that a couple of jackals cannot chase off a matriarch lion!

It became gradually evident to Vicky that the Director, being an old lady with partially incapacitated brain, preferred to be on the jackal's side instead of being an impartial lady, probably as she didn't want to face the raging lion who was being wounded by backbiting of the two omnivorous canids, by sneaking in from behind. So, Vicky waited till Di finished her courses with that lousy school authorities, and then sent all supporting documentation to IB headquarters, asking them to send in their own examiners during all upcoming exams conducted by that school, as they were leaking exam papers to candidates of their choice, through the school's office (in exchange of monetary gains, which Popatlal carefully side-lined in sundry accounts for deposits and withdrawals at his convenience, flouting all norms, in direct collusion with the Principal and the DPC).

Vicky had also written to IB regarding the fact that classrooms were shared between girls studying different subjects and in different batches, as the infrastructural development promised to IB by the school were not completed in a timely manner. Also, the students had to sit on the floors to eat their lunch, as the school didn't have any dining hall; their canteen was a defunct one too, with very limited vegan snacks. Classroom air-conditioners were not turned on regularly, discipline was not enforced on selected students, nepotism and favouritism was the order of the day, and about many other issues which were in direct violation of the norms and standards of IB.

They didn't have a single dedicated IB teacher, and even the DPC was forced to teach ICSE students from other classes, while IB rules clearly stated that each school should have dedicated IB teachers who will spend all their duty hours for programs related to IB only. Subsequently, IB had issued final warning to that school, and being the only IB school for girls in town, they faced a bad rap! The Principal and her accomplice Popatlal were fired, and so was the DPC – the trashy lady was shown the door once dusts settled following IBO investigation with appropriate 'cease and desist' order to the school!

Interestingly, many colleges subsequently outright rejected applications of those students with questionable background from that school, when they failed to meet the predicted scores during their final examinations. Diana, on the other hand, was able to obtain admission to the college of choice with no problems at all – thus, it was again justified that justice can be delayed, but it can't be denied.

Diana's grandma and her uncle used to feel very much secured with Mrs. Raha around their ward all the time, acting as her guardian angel. Di was extremely saddened by the news of her demise decades after she passed out – she made it a point to ask for leave and visit Kolkata to pay her last respect to this great human being. She cried like a baby at her funeral, and felt like losing her own mother once again!

What Di missed more than anything else in her High School was not having a true friend – she used to have many friends from her primary and junior schools, who she was in touch throughout her life. But there wasn't a single girl in her high school who she could call a true friend.

Most girls there were obnoxious and superficial – they used to lie a lot about almost everything and used to be mongers of gossips, criticising and badmouthing others, including their closest friends! Di wondered what type of circumstances during childhood can turn girls at such young age to be like them!

One of her close friends from her primary school, named Atreyi belonged to a poor family – her father used to work in a bicycle repair shop, and her mother used to be a homemaker. Atreyi was a sweet young girl, very honest, upfront and talkative – there were times when Diana and Atreyi would meet after a long time, exclaimed with joy, and start asking questions to each other – without listening to the answers the other girl was rendering, the friends would holler and scream with joy and used to go back asking the same question again! Ritu used to take Atreyi and Diana to South City Mall sometimes, and the girls loved each other's company so much.

Atreyi's mother unfortunately fell sick of pancreatic tumour, which rapidly spread all over. She couldn't attend to any household chores for a long time, being completely bedridden. Atreyi used to take care of all the domestic work on behalf of her mother, after returning from school. Her father used to help as much as he could, but he had to work harder to meet the rising medical expenses of his spouse. Things were quite bitter and sad for the family.

When Atreyi was appearing for her Board exam, her mother passed away – she was extremely saddened for quite some time, until Diana met her routinely and encouraged her to prepare well for her upcoming exams. Atreyi managed to get good grades and sought admission into a City College to pursue her bachelors.

Atreyi used to live in a town near Burdwan during her early childhood days, with her grandparents and their extended families. They had fresh vegetables and fruits grown in their own farm, got fresh fishes from their own ponds, had fresh milk from the cows they reared, and fresh chicken and eggs from their own poultry.

She was around four years of age when they moved to Kolkata for better prospect sought by her father, as farming wasn't an attractive mode of income anymore with rising costs of fertilizers and high cuts taken by intermediaries to sell produces. In addition, the parents wanted their child to have good educational opportunities.

Atreyi used to love watching the trains from the field adjacent to her house –she knew the train timings by heart, especially for the express trains, and loved the sight of long trains storming through the rail lines with loud noise. She used to run on the field along the tracks sometimes, to see if she can outrun the passing train, but in vain.

Sometimes she will jump and clap to see people in the train waving at her, although she couldn't make out why most compartments were covered with glass-windows through which she couldn't see anything except at night times. She made sure she reached the field along the tracks in time not to miss out on viewing passing trains, and always wondered where so many people travelled in those trains every day, throughout the year! Maybe they don't have houses to live, she thought and felt sorry for them.

After the family decided to move to Kolkata, Atreyi was in for a big surprise – she was in the train herself with her parents! Alas, she couldn't see the field where she played and ran every day, nor can she see her house; dad said they lived far off the nearest station, and that's why they had to take a bus to the station from home.

It still didn't make sense with her, as in her mind, irrespective of where they lived, the train had to cross the same route so that she was able to see her place! It took her many years to realise that her grandfather's home was on the route beyond Burdwan station, when she travelled to Asansol many years later to visit her maternal uncle's house.

It was quite a change for Atreyi when she reached Kolkata – how can a city be so big that you end up spending hours in bus to reach from one place to another? How so many people are travelling on buses, cars and all types of vehicles all day long – where are they going?

Back in her village, people were out on streets only at certain times, some going to fields, some to work in nearby towns and the rest to school. They used to come back at scheduled time too; those leaving for fields used to come back before noon, those to work – by evening, and the school kids by 3 in the afternoon. Other times, roads were nearly empty, except some cars plying to God knew where! And, people used to go for shopping only on Sundays and Thursdays, mostly in early evening hours.

But in Kolkata, it seemed tens of thousands of people flocked the streets all day long for reasons beyond her understanding. Many of them spoke different languages, while everyone in her hometown spoke in Bengali! Many eat food which were completely unknown to her – vendors out on the streets were selling so many different types of food and other items.

She saw people eating food all day long at different stalls, whereas back home, people only eat twice – lunch and dinner; for breakfast, they always had handmade bread and milk. But now, she was seeing people munching all kinds of food all day long! Maybe they were poor and didn't get square meals in the past – she thought in her mind.

The dresses people at Kolkata wore really shook her terribly. Back home, men usually wore dhoti, and women wore saree – now, neither did she find any woman except elderlies wearing saree, nor any man clad in dhoti. Most women were wearing trousers, skirts, salwar suits and even shorts; Atreyi couldn't believe that some of the grown-up girls were wearing low-cut tops and short-length skirts!

Maybe their parents couldn't afford to buy those girls full-length regular clothes, the little mind reasoned. Guys wore trousers and shorts, and some even wore jackets and ties – things were completely different here, she thought!

Another matter which amazed her and was a kind of rude awakening for her was, lack of affectionate public conversation out on the streets. Unlike her hometown where everyone spoke to each other, exchanged greeting, etc., in Kolkata hardly anyone acknowledged others – they were busy speaking on their phones or listening to God knew what with wires plugged in their ears – it took her sometime to find out that people use headphones to listen to music and stuff, unlike back home, where people listened to music on radios – they didn't have any television back at their village; mobile phones were used by affluent people only. But in Kolkata, everyone had a phone or two, sometimes three - with multiple numbers and carriers!

Anyways, her parents got her admitted to the same primary school Diana was attending, as the authorities waived the tuition fees for Atreyi, being a Catholic school. It was here that she met Diana, and they soon became good friends. Diana loved the simplicity and innocence in Atreyi, and in case of the latter, Diana was a very innocent and loving girl,

Their friendship grew stronger over time, and they maintained regular contact with each other even after the two friends chose two different paths of education after completion of junior school,

Rittwika was another great friend from Diana's junior school – she joined the school from another institution located close to where she lived in Garia up until class four. Her father abandoned her mother, and her mother worked very hard as a nurse to bring up Rittwika.

She was a sweet little girl, as much fun loving as Diana, and their bonds grew strong from the very first day Rittwika joined Diana's school – the latter found her to be alone and shy; so, she went up to her during break and introduced herself. Diana thought it was somewhat unfair of her other friends not to speak to the newcomer, and she decided to take the lead to do the required introduction, so that Rittwika felt welcome at her new school.

At the behest of Diana, other girls started welcoming Rittwika, and pretty soon she became a part of the gang of the little monsters at school, laughing and playing at free times, pulling each other's legs, passing jokes and sharing food, etc. If someone missed classes due to absenteeism or otherwise, others would call up the girl who missed the classes and kept her abreast of home-works or other pertinent information.

Most girls in Di's junior school came from middleclass families, and some belonged to economically less privileged sections, while a few belonged to affluent classes. However, there was not a single boasting of wealth or showing off, or shameless buttering to earn any undue advantage, which were the qualities rampant in Di's senior school.

When they were in class eight, Diana came to know that Rittwika got into an illicit affair with her next door neighbour, a married young chap, who used to sneak in after Rittwika returned from school, in her mother's absence, and use her to gratify his unholy physical desires. Di vehemently protested against such matter, cautioning her friend that she was playing with fire, and she would get into serious trouble in every which way.

She also warned Rittwika that she was seeking an impossible venture, as the guy was married – he would definitely leave her as soon as matters go further, and Rittwika would be harmed in many ways. But the latter chose to ignore her friend's advice, and sure enough, had to face severe consequences.

One of the other neighbours found out what went on inside Rittwika's apartment after the guy used to sneak in and informed her mother. She was heartbroken, as she was working like an ox to make ends meet, and there, her very own daughter put her to shame. She didn't have enough resources to send her daughter off to a boarding school; nor could she afford the risk of letting her daughter stay alone in her apartment, following the horrible discovery!

Finally, she managed to convince Rittwika to go back to the local school where she was going before, because the school timings would allow her mother to return home by the time school ended, unlike the school she was in.

Sadly enough, the friends had to part ways, although Di told Rittwika very clearly not to call her ever if she saw that guy again. No complaints in police were lodged by Rittwika's mother, fearing adverse consequences from the guy involved – he used to be the son of a local land shark, with an array of influential and politically well-linked connections.

Rittwika married another guy with no income two years later, upon successful completion of her Board exam – her husband had finished college course in a lesser known college in Kolkata and was unemployed for few years. He was living off his elder brother's income, thus giving his brother's wife enough ammunition to launch domestic missiles on the new bride, acting as a crusader. Rittwika had no other choice but to listen to her constant raps and shed her tears silently.

Eventually, she couldn't take the constant verbal and physical abuse at her in-law's house anymore, and jumped from her roof one afternoon, thus ending her life. Her body fell on the iron fencing on the road, thus piercing her torso into two. Di wasn't made aware of that terrible incidence until years later, when she was enquiring about Rittwika from a mutual friend at a tennis club, who happened to reside in the same area the beautiful girl used to!

Di was devastated on hearing the news, as she knew very well that Rittwika wasn't a bad girl at all, in any manner – it was just she fell into a trap at a ripe age, when someone took advantage of her loneliness. She contacted other girls from her junior school, and they all went to Rittwika's house on a Sunday morning, to see and console her mother.

Alas, she was gone too – she couldn't bear the loss of her only child, her only lifeline, and jumped at a metro station in front of an incoming train! The girls wept together for hours there, until they realised that the person standing next to them was the same piece of junk who abused Rittwika.

The old friends decided to confront the guy in front of his family and neighbours; so, they teamed up and went to Rittwika's in-law's place - one of the girls videotaped the entire conversation with the evil family secretly. The guy initially refused to admit his fault but succumbed under pressure. Then he started weeping aloud - Diana called the police and handed over the videotaped recording for further prosecution. He and his family were arrested on the spot, but later released upon showering bribes – the usual nine yards!

He got bail soon, as the main witness and victim were both dead; the local police and the Investigating Officer assigned to the case did not put appropriate sections of IPC for obvious reasons; no charges for culpable homicide leading to prison terms were induced. In addition, the public prosecutor on the case gratefully accepted a lump sum payola from the accused, thereby not pleading for cancellation of bail, or not even pursuing the case properly. So, the girls decided to pray for their deceased friend's soul, instead of uselessly pursuing the case.

Di sometimes wondered if there was any existence of God at all, with so much sins and inhuman acts getting unpunished day by day! Maybe God decided to stay away from its finest creation after a certain time, upon realising that the finest creations were not the finest anymore! Maybe God had also started accepting bribes – felt the little girls!

After completion of her college, Di got a good placement on campus hiring, and moved to UK to start working for a broadcasting company. It was a very good and reputable media house, and Diana was thrilled to have finally taken the first step towards fulfilling her ambition to be an anchor! Her boss was very cordial and supportive, and pretty soon Di learnt the tricks of the trade and got promoted – she was a very likeable person all along her life, and all her peers and superiors liked her very much.

Her soft-spoken attitude and good mannerism were admired by her subordinates too, and Diana never treated anyone with any lesser respect than she herself would like to be treated with – she even shared her home-cooked lunch with some of her colleagues, who reciprocated fairly well too. She loved the British culture and mannerism too and used to take short vacations intermittently to visit Ireland and Scotland – she took Ritu along with her after some time, and the duo loved each other's company so much!

Di always remembered the good old days when her demon father Randi stopped contributing anything towards her living or educational expenses, while she was pursuing IB. It was extremely difficult for her guardians – Vicky, Ritu and Riya to take care of recurring expenses, apart from her hefty tuition fees and allied expenses.

Vicky exhausted all his savings by the time Diana got promoted to next level; he had to take a loan from his life insurance policy to pay off the school tuition fees for the last quarter of first year. Thereafter, he had no other option but to sale his house and make ends meet.

Even after the court ordered Randi to immediately pay the monthly maintenance and save her from vagrancy, the monster father didn't – he was willing to go to jail after the necessary execution processes; in his evil mind, he thought that a few days' jail term will let him get away with non-payment, considering the loopholes in Indian laws existent at that time.

Properties of Randi couldn't have been attached, as he had transferred his moveable and immovable properties to his paramour and her daughter's name before the court cases were initiated, and he produced false documents at court.

Being a lawyer for a considerably long time, he was well conversant with limitations of prevailing laws & regulations and acted accordingly. In addition, his flat at Ballygunge was not gifted by his father Harini despite many requests by Vicky and his mom to do so – that would have at least given some consolation, because the flat could've been sold to pay off the maintenance accruals, or help Di take coaching classes for SAT, AP, etc. – but, she couldn't, as luck played havoc on her!

After his father's death, the heir of the flat were Randi, his sisters and a cousin brother who also inherited a part of the flat due to Harini's unlawful action of depriving him of a part of sale proceeds from the Diamond Harbour house! An injunction against selling the flat at Ballygunge was therefore considered a futile attempt by Vicky; so, it was not pursued further.

Vicky had to cut down on his expenses substantially thereafter, and so did his ailing mother, who curtailed on many essential items like milk and newspapers, in order to save money to meet the required expenses for Diana. Ritu even stopped obtaining outside help for domestic works, as they were forced to cut down on expenses.

Their lawyer at that time, one Deba Banerjee played foul on his clients and made arrangements with Randi in exchange of some monetary benefits to prolong and delay legal proceedings. Other lawyers' high fees and charges for court appearances, etc. could not have been afforded by the victim's family, and they had no remedy.

Although providing timely and effective relief to clients should be the sole motto of advocates, but very few of them followed such ethics. The other advocate for Di's family, one Shraboni Roy was worse! She used to be a highly respected and reputed lawyer of her time and was selected to represent the State on numerous high-profile cases, including a very infamous and highly publicized case - Park Street assault on a woman by affluent goons.

Roy was chosen by Vicky to represent him and his mother on an array of false criminal cases lodged against them by the two werewolf cousin brothers of Vicky, aided and abetted by officers of local police stations, who were 'friends' with those furious and criminal minded werewolves.

Since Vicky and his parents didn't budge into those culprits' pressure to sell the ancestral property and hand over to a promoter known to them, that two persons' untamed wildness made lives for Vicky and his family a living hell.

So, they chose Roy to represent them at courts of law, not realising how crooked and miser Roy would prove to be – she asked rupees twenty from Vicky to give to the court clerk after obtaining next dates, etc., gave rupees ten only, and pocketed the difference. This was in addition to her daily fees of two thousand rupees!

Initially, Roy was very efficient and honest in handling the cases. Her resolutely firm and unwavering attitude caused immense damage to the culprit cousin brothers – she was quick to clearly establish at court that those two were making frivolous allegations against the innocent family. She even compared the educational and social standards of the two families in public to convince the Judge to order the two evil complainants to appear without fail for interrogation, pending which non-bailable warrants would be issued.

Vicky did his Diploma in Management from IGNOU after passing out from St. Xavier's College, Kolkata – he also completed the intermediate of Cost Accountancy and also a Certificate Program in Marketing Management from Jadavpur University, before migrating to the USA. Over there, he not only attained his master's degree in Business Administration from State University of New York, but also successfully completed six post graduate programs during his employment with the government there.

He had also undergone a course in Leadership Excellence from Indian Institute of Management Calcutta – so, he was academically a brilliant student with lots of rich and varied experience at work. But her never boasted of his education or job and maintained a simple living high thinking principle.

His two cousin brothers did not even complete their schooling and were never employed anywhere in their lives. They lived off the ill-gotten money their father Sunny earned all his life in the form of bribes and easy money, before he was suspended from Motor Vehicles Department, few months before his scheduled retirement. But, in the meantime, he had amassed crores of rupees, which his 'ideal' sons spent lavishly all life long after Sunny's death!

Advocate Roy was inching towards convicting the two complainants and freeing her innocent clients from false charges, when those two devils approached her and offered hefty sum to get their backs saved. Vicky couldn't understand why she was repeatedly skipping her scheduled interrogations and court dates with various excuses and reasons.

Sometimes she will state that she fell down, sometimes she wasn't physically well, sometimes she had very urgent court cases to appear, and sometimes she couldn't come to court due to traffic jams after the collapse of Majerhat Bridge. However, she charged her full fees from Vicky and there was no relaxation even when Judges would be absent, or court-functioning interrupted by some unrest or political movement or otherwise.

Eventually, Vicky started smelling the rat; so, he asked Roy if she wanted to pursue the cases for them or not, diligently and without any disruption – she apologized and continued to harass and victimise her innocent clients even after that. Vicky had not much option left, as no other established lawyer would accept cases taken over from such a reputed and senior lawyer; going for junior lawyers at that crucial junctures might prove costly to them in terms of expertise and charisma.

At the same time, other lawyers known to the family were not an iota better than Roy or Banerjee – so the decision wasn't easy; Vicky believed in the old saying that a known devil is better than an unknown devil, as one can anticipate probable moves from a known devil, but with an unknown one, everything will have to be left to chances!

There were times when Vicky contemplated taking laws at his own hand and end the long-drawn battle abruptly and with precision, as he had not much faith left with legal systems prevalent at that time; but, his unfettered, untrammelled and unbridled love for Di forced him to hang on till she emigrated to USA for higher studies. However, his darling niece being a very optimistic and intelligent young lady, she made him promise holding her hands that he won't do anything like that ever.

Therefore, the ongoing legal battle lasted till the very last day Vicky was around! Maybe his soul was more powerful than his body, as it transpired later that both of those cousin brothers died a horrible death by asphyxiation from an accident resulting out of exploding gas stoves shortly after Vicky's death. Maybe Vicky took his ultimate revenge against those two devils. Many Hindus believed that people dying of accidents end up going anywhere except heaven – so maybe they would rot in heaven along with their evil father!

Randi too, was subsequently killed in prison by other inmates when they found out the real reason of his conviction and serving jail-term – Suparnakha died a horrible death after suffering for a long time, after her daughter left her unattended. She wasn't even around when Suparnakha died – there were no rituals performed for any of those four evil souls!

Vicky used to be in constant touch with Diana over facetime, google duo and WhatsApp video calls, and so did Rina from USA. Di used to take her grandma to fine dining restaurants in the evenings and used to travel to nearby exotic locations during breaks or long weekends. Di became more like a mother to Ritu from this point on, taking care of all her grandma's needs – she was around 87 years of age by then, and was still as energetic as always. Both of them had gala time with lots of fun and travelling.

Diana was very close to one Jane Whitaker who used to work as an intern with her at a British broadcasting company based out of London for few months during College breaks. However, Jane never returned to UK after her internship and moved back to the USA from where she belonged; Di gradually lost touch with her, until one summer weekend, Di called a common friend in New York to get another huge shock in her life.

Life can be full of surprises – but to some, it may turn out to be disastrous in just few days. Everything so happy and sweet may change to completely shocking and sad in matter of minutes, and dreams can be shattered in a whisker, as it happened to Jane on a nice summer Friday night.

Jane and her husband Joe were having a time of their life just few hours back, in a nightclub with friends dancing to the heavy metal and gobbling their favourite snacks and drinks; but now, everything is changed. Joe is no more, dying on the spot behind the wheels; Jane woke up in her house after returning home from the hospital, after getting emergency treatment for few hours there.

She opened her bleary eyes when the cat, all seven pounds of squirming flesh, climbed onto her belly. Squinting into the sunlight streaming in from the open window, she discovered that she was now the weary possessor of a pounding headache, and at some point, had managed to lose both a tooth and a spouse. Jimmy, as Joe had named the Siamese kitten when he first brought the cat in, had no idea that skies fell down on the head of the happy couple, and that his master would not be returning again to feed him or play with him. And, Jane will never be the same merry and spirited young lady again, for the rest of her life!

Jane was brought up in an orphanage, as her teenaged mother dumped her right after she was born, and she was never able to find out who her real father was. She used to miss the warm touch of a mother that most kids get to cherish when they grow up; however, with the passage of time, all her wounds were healed – she never looked back at her past, as the Father of the Church she frequented as a child had advised her not to dwell in the past, and live the life that God has bestowed on her. She was a very religious person from her early days, and always made it to the Church on Sundays, if she was around.

Time flew by as she graduated from school with reasonably good grades, and was soon adopted by her foster parents, Jim and Kathy. They didn't have any child of their own and had accomplished almost everything in life that most people eye for, except that God didn't destine a child of their own to this highly established couple. But they were blessed with Jane, as she became an integral part of the family within a few weeks of her adoption. Both her foster parents were extremely busy executives with long hours at work – however, they made sure that they spend quality time with Jane during the time they were home.

Weekends were always fun for the entire family from thereon, as Jim would run all errands on Friday evenings, and made himself available for the next two days. Kathy, on the other hand, will ask the nanny to take weekends off, and will do everything for Jane that a good mother usually does, during the weekends.

Most of the time, the family will fly out to exotic places on Saturday mornings and fly back Sunday night, after spending superb time filled with luxury and leisure; the weekends that the family decided to stay in, they will go out for breakfast at a nice diner near their house on the hills, go golfing or playing tennis in the country club few miles from their house, and have lunch there – on Saturdays.

During the weekend evenings, either they'll host a party at their farmhouse, or they'll be invited to a friend's or colleague's house. Both Jim and Kathy were very fun-loving people - they used to make everyone around them burst in laughter with jokes and funny conversations.

Sunday mornings were spent between running chores and visiting Church; the rest of the day used to be a private moment for the trio – they used to sit either on the plush leather sectional on their huge living room in the afternoons, or out on the patio or in the garden, and used to giggle and talk. Kathy used to cook herself on Sundays if they were in town, and all three had a marvellous time with mouth-watering food and heart-soothing discussions – they were just a very happy family.

Pretty soon the high school days were over; so, Jane had to relocate to a distant city for her college. Initially, it was sort of painful for the whole family, but soon they got over it – they used to meet up during holidays - Jane used to travel back to her home on vacation times. She became friends to many students in the college, and she had a very good time between studying and time off.

Her friends were from different parts of the country, with diverse backgrounds and cultures. Jane pretty soon started speaking a little bit of foreign languages with her friends from different countries in her college. It was fun, although Jane made sure she studied well and score good marks, which she always did.

Time flew and Jane got a campus placement during her third year in college, which she stuck to after she completed her graduation. Her employers were very fond of her, and Jane used to enjoy most people's confidence due to her sheer dedication, hard work and strong discipline. The inevitable happened, and Jane superseded quite a few employees at work when the time came for promotion, and everyone around her accepted Jane as their new boss very sportingly.

Although Jane did go out on many dates during her college years, but she was very focused on her career path, and didn't want to have her mind distracted until the right time approached. It was in this Company that Jane was working for, where she met Joe. He was from Hungary and had an accent. Jane liked him very much from the day she first saw him at a conference, as Joe seemed to be a very honest, decent, straight-forward and down to earth type of a person – his background was humble; he always spoke about his parents and siblings back home - he missed them dearly, but couldn't bring them along due to various family constraints and obligations.

He was a great sportsman too - Jane used to play tennis with him a lot during time off. Soon, they fell in love and decided to tie the knots after getting their parents involved - Joe formally proposed with an engagement ring which Jane delightfully accepted.

Jane kept very close ties with her foster parents all along, and she visited them during holidays and special days like Thanksgiving, etc. Christmas was knocking at the door, and Jane decided to introduce her fiancé to Jim and Kathy – so they flew over; they were greeted very cordially as usual.

Jim and Kathy wanted Jane to get married soon, as they weren't growing any younger; they wanted to see her settled in family life! Joe spoke to his parents over Skype and introduced his would-be in laws - the next spring, they were married on an island near Hawaii.

Their wedding arrangements were overseen by no one else that the old Jim and Kathy. They didn't leave a stone unturned to make it a gala event – an event that will be talked about in years to come for all the 400 guests there! Jane made sure that the children and the people from the orphanage where she was brought up, attend their wedding ceremonies, with all expenses borne by the family.

The kids' eyes glittered with surprises - most of them were spellbound to witness such a top-notch wedding ceremony, with food served from a five-star facility on mainland Hawaii. The wedding cake was a seven-tier one, with a height reaching almost ten feet!

All present had a time of their lives there. And guess what the great foster parents gifted the newly wed! A vacation house spreading over an acre of beautiful land on a small island! Indeed, where else Jane and Joe needed to go for honeymoon, when they had such a heavenly place belonging to them?

After they returned to reality from the wonderland, Jane and Joe bought a fairly decent house on the outskirts of the city they worked in; they politely refused to take any financial help from anyone on buying the property. Jane felt that she had already gotten much more than she deserved from her parents - she didn't want to drain their wealth further; plus, the couple felt that they needed to be independent in all respects from this stage of life - they'll not go beyond their means in terms of expenses.

Sure enough, this wise decision helped Kathy in the long run, as Jim left for his heavenly sojourn a few years later, she had enough money to fend for herself. Jane insisted that her foster parents bequeath all their wealth to the orphanage after their demise. They appreciated her good hearts and made out a Will duly notarized to such effect.

Joe got a promotion soon - this wasn't a blessing in disguise to the couple, as he had to relocate; Jane and Joe discussed about it a lot. After a fairly prolonged and amicable discussion, they felt that Joe shouldn't refuse the promotion. They agreed that Jane will put in a resignation right after Joe assumed his new role in the far-away city – she could easily get a suitable job for her down there, with her kind of qualifications and experiences.

Her colleagues and friends all hosted a brilliant farewell party to Jane after that. She flew back to join Joe, and spent few months hunting for a nice house there; they sold off their other house, and pretty soon, were able to find a wonderful house on the beaches. Commute time for Joe was less than half an hour's drive; Jane was confident that she would find something suitable within the vicinity, which she eventually did.

That wasn't a huge corporation that she used to work for, but still was a fairly good-sized company in the allied sector – this helped Jane negotiate on her benefits, etc. - her new employers were happy to welcome her on board too. With the kind of young lady that Jane was, she took no time to make new friends. They used to hang around for a drink or so after work, as Joe used to return home late.

Jane liked to cook for Joe, but he wasn't too thrilled at this idea during the weekdays, as Joe wanted his wife to relax after returning home from work. They used to be a really lovey dove couple, understanding each other's needs and respecting each other for how they were. There were some minor cultural differences, which were sorted out in no time, to each other's satisfaction.

They used to spend the weekends pretty much home, if they were not travelling to see Kathy. Joe brought a small kitten one fine morning, a stray one, and named him Jimmy. He used to play around with Jimmy every now and then; he used to make sure that Jimmy ate and drank from his dispenser routinely. Jane also took good care and hygienic requirements of this new guest. Soon, he grew big, weighing more than seven pounds. He used to purr when his masters hugged each other – he even used to lay next to Jane at their bed.

Joe was working on complying with procedural requirements to bring his younger brother as an immigrant, as promised to his father on his dying bed. He had lost his mother earlier from cancer! Joe wanted to take Jane with him to Hungary when his father died, but Jane was pregnant. So, they decided that it was safer for her to stay home and not take such a long flight.

Jane could feel the baby inside - right after Joe returned, they started attending counselling sessions for first-time parents. They dreamt big about this baby; Jane was contemplating quitting her job for few years, just in order to be with the baby during infancy stages – Joe was so happy about it that he kept kissing his wife over and over, until she was blushing and all!

So, it was decided that after the completion of eighth month, which was coming up, Jane would ask for maternity leave, and if not allowed, will quit her job. Joe had already begun shopping for the would-be mother and the baby - their lives were all full of dreams and aspirations. But, man proposes, God disposes.

On a fine Thursday evening, Joe returned from work; after the usual hugging and kissing between the two lovebirds, Jane requested him to join her friends for a quick drink at the nightclub located very close to her office. Joe was reluctant, but Jane didn't want to miss out her friends' bash - so, Joe agreed; but, he said, "Honey, please remember that no drinks for you tomorrow night: remember what the doctor had suggested?" Jane smilingly agreed – she wasn't drinking after she learnt about her pregnancy either.

Right after work, Joe picked up his beautiful wife from her office, and went to a hairdresser. Jane wanted to look perfect; she had even picked up a brand-new gown for her earlier! From there, they went to a common friend's house to get refreshed and to change over to party clothes. That friend was supposed to join them in the party too, but as luck would have it, she backed out in the last minute for cramps!

Anyways, soon the gorgeous couple were at the nightclub, reserved by Jane's friends mostly - they were in the dancing mood. Joe made sure that his wife didn't dance to heavy metal or rock bands and sat with her on the corner during those times that fast numbers were playing. Whenever they played slow songs, the couple would hold each other, caress, smile and dance slowly with the tune.

One of the friends there wanted to play some dirty tricks; so, she wanted Joe to keep on drinking. Jane was taking diet coke - Joe was poured pegs after pegs of whiskey. He initially refused - but thinking in his mind that his wife can get hurt if he refuses to her friend's request, Joe obliged.

Soon, he was almost drunk, when Jane had to take a stand at that finally – earlier, she thought that a few pegs won't be that harmful for Joe, but what she didn't realise was, her friend was pouring raw whiskey – immediately, Jane raised an alarm, politely telling her friend to back off. Joe realised that Jane has become furious - he didn't want to risk ruining her friendship; so, he politely excused himself as he wanted to sit down with Jane to sober up a bit.

Suddenly, someone there started smoking cigarette; thus, Joe saw no option than to leave the place right away, as the smoke was going to be dangerous for his wife and the unborn kid. He didn't pay heed to Jane for the very first time during their marriage, as he walked out of the building and started the car.

Jane wanted to drive, but Joe didn't apply his mind, probably out of frustration at what transpired that night – so, he started driving. Jane was going to try and stop him, but he had already pulled out and was approaching the highway.

What happened next was the inevitable. All Jane remembered was seeing very strong lights as soon as they approached the highway - the crashing sound thereafter!

When she woke up in the middle of the night in the emergency room of the hospital, Jane saw grim faces of some of her friends - she knew right away that something horrible had happened. They didn't tell her anything, but a sobbing acquaintance's mild words entered her ears – "I can't believe that Joe is gone".

All that happened to Jane was her losing a tooth in the front due to the collision and the deployment of the airbag, after the truck hit their car on the driver's side that night. She was brought back to her home towards the dawn; a friend of her decided to stay with her until she fully recovered.

Jane was given strong dosage of painkillers and sedatives, which made her fall asleep soon. She had to idea that the world around her had come crumbling – that all her dreams were shattered. She was back to square one of her life; from where she started as an orphan.

She was once again an orphan, as she would lose her baby in her womb soon - Kathy had died a few months ago, too! Therefore, there wouldn't be anyone Jane can call family, one more time in her tragic life! A full circle had been completed!

Does life always traverse full circle, like that? Who knows – thought Di! She tried contacting Jane many times thereafter, but none of Jane's friends knew anything about her whereabouts after the tragic incident. It was another shocker for Diana, as she really wanted to sit with her at least once and share some private moments with her; but alas!

Di told herself the same old phrase over and over – oh well, life goes on! But she always cherished the short little time intermittently which she got to spend with Jane during her internship; but she decided to move on.

Diana finally moved back to New York when she got her coveted job at a world-famous television channel as editor. She got her own office now; it didn't take her more than a week to familiarise herself with this operation – she did great during the orientation and training program. She even got 'political desk' as her first assignment, working with renowned anchors – her ultimate dream of becoming one someday. She also learnt quite a bit of technology there, as they were on top of technological developments.

Di had once told her adopted children who relied on technology for almost everything that 'until we are all brain patterns on programmed computers, there are still forces that don't bend to our wants, including senescence and death – so you children will keep on talking like this too, until you grow old and become wiser, and begin to think rationally.

The old saying about a halo around the moon portending rain has some truth to it – the halo is caused by cirrus clouds drifting 20,000 feet or more above our Earth, and high cirrus clouds often precede stormy weather. Therefore, it is advisable to you children, to use your technological depth with inner values and beliefs.'

Diana had a neighbour in the next block who became very close to each other – her name was Nisha. She was quite popular in the area; she was the one who introduced Diana and Ritu to many other families of Indian origin, who were either first-generation immigrants or otherwise. Nisha's husband Raj was very active in organising social and cultural events in the neighbourhood. The couple seemed like made for each other – however, their love story was not full of roses – it had more thorns than flowers.

Life wasn't ever easy for Raj - three siblings back at his home in Shyambazar, abusive parents; he only hoped his situation could have been much better! A class X dropout, Raj being a hardy guy with a stout figure at 6 feet 2 inches I height, he worked at a small restaurant in central Kolkata as a cashier.

A job which fetched him only Rs 3000 per month and consumed his whole day, leaving him no time to work for another job in order to at least provide a nutrient-enriched meal for his siblings. Despite hailing from an economically disadvantaged background, Raj was always keen to learn more about mathematics, a subject which enthralled him even though he couldn't afford high-priced tuition!

Going to work on a routine manner each and every day was monotonous for him. Walking in the sweltering heat for half an hour took a toll on his health very much. He soon developed white patches throughout his body, especially on his face - he was ashamed of himself looking like that and was literally frustrated. He knew what the consequences will be; still, he was in the midst of a dark sea – it seemed like that to him each time he thought about it!

One lazy summer day when most of the people in the neighbourhood were sleeping and the weather seemed dull, there was a large scream heard close to the restaurant where he worked! Raj came out with his dirty hands, when to his horror, he saw an elderly man aged around 65 being beaten mercilessly by a mob. To his astonishment, there was a huge crowd around him as mute spectators - their task was just to take videos and selfies, whilst an old man was crying for help!

Raj couldn't even get the time to think about his probable course of actions - he quickly took a stick which was lying nearby, rushing forward to the man's rescue. The inevitable happened – the mob left the old man and started beating up Raj heinously, causing profuse bleeding and several injuries to Raj. The crowd still did absolutely nothing, but to keep watching the onslaught!

Within a few minutes, police arrived at the spot. An ambulance took Raj and the old man to a local hospital. Raj's spine was broken - he suffered lots of wounds all over his body. However, financial and family woes worried him a lot more than his pain from his injuries at that time. Who is going to look after his siblings? Who will pay for them? How will his siblings be surviving without him? He got even more depressed thinking about all those uncertainties.

Raj ended up spending more than forty-eight hours in the Intensive Care Unit of the hospital, where a Medical Board was formed to treat him in the best possible manner. All he was given as food was saline, as doctors didn't want to take any chance with his condition.

About a week later in hospital, Raj was given snacks to eat. Green tea didn't sound good in this state, but yeah it could make through. Just as he had the last sip of tea, the door slid open. The old man whom he saved just a few days earlier entered the room in a well-dressed business attire, accompanied by a sweet, cute looking girl of around 14 years of age.

Raj already started to feel better as they approached the bed! He had never seen such a beautiful girl like her - she was a shy, tall and slim girl, with curly hairs and dark eyes! He simply couldn't take his eyes off her - it was like love at first sight for him!

"Glad to meet you man. You are a true brave-heart! You saved my life; I will never forget your deed ever" said the old man, coughing as he put his hand inside his pocket to get a handkerchief, which left Raj wondering about the old man's mysterious cough. After a brief pause, Raj replied "It is my pleasure. I wouldn't have resisted myself in protecting my own family members in this type of a situation; why should I then not save you?"

The old man said: "It seems you are from a very educated and noble family. I believe your upbringing was excellent, though I noticed that you wore rugged clothes." With tears in his eyes, Raj decided to tell the old man everything about him – an honest confession followed thereafter.

"You are a true soul. I will pay for your medical expenses" – said the old man. These few normal lines seemed like magic to Ra! He exclaimed in joy and thanked the old man in every manner that he could possibly think of.

Amongst all the sadness and happiness, there was something constant - the eye contact between Nisha and Raj! "Here's my daughter, Nisha. She is excited to meet you" said the old man.

"Hi Raj. I am Nisha. I am grateful to you for saving my father." said Nisha in a happy mood. "I will pray so that you feel better soon. Best regards for you." Raj felt so happy to hear the sweet girl uttering those kind words. He said "Thank you so much Nisha - it is a privilege to be able to save your father. Maybe we will meet up later." Nisha returned a cute smile and a willing nod.

The visiting hours were over; so, the father daughter duo soon left the boy. The whole night Raj dreamt of the girl. It seemed that life has a completely new meaning for him now – he started dreaming about Nisha day in and day out!

After a few more weeks, Raj was discharged. As promised the old man paid all his hospital expenses. Everything seemed well for Raj, at least momentarily. However, he started missing the cute little girl – every minute that he kept searching for her seemed to pass so fast; he desperately wanted to see Nisha – her dream girl!

Minutes became days, days turned into months; months turned into years. The physical complications from the previous accident seemed to take toll. Raj, now a mature boy, could not walk properly. His siblings got married and went off to far off places, leaving behind crippled Raj - the one who worked relentlessly for them.

Raj started realizing that it was high time for him to face the harsh reality. Nobody was with him. He lost his job due to underperformance because of his physical constraints. Raj was extremely sad – financially broke and more importantly, heartbroken.

Many days he sat with a picture of the early happy times, cherishing those nice moments, and hoping that the happy times would be back again. He went without proper food for many days.

As time flew, he learnt to live with his happiness and sadness - his happiness that he was alive. Sad not to see his dream-girl again! Eventually, he gathered hope; soon, he started to work in a café. He also desired to pursue higher studies - he enrolled himself in a good institution.

He also took up a job at banquet hall, helping in the improvement of the services provided. Raj began to work harder - there was a determination in him all of a sudden, which he had lost long back - many decades ago.

After a few years, he obtained his degree - a bachelor's in fashion. He had an offer to work abroad in England, but for that it required him to pass several English proficiency exams. So, he got enrolled in an English-speaking institute and continued his part time work at the same time.

Months passed - Raj began to pass the lower levels to move on to the higher ones. Everyone including his teachers were extremely delighted at his performance. Day by day, the once poor boy finely turned into a handsome, educated and well-mannered man.

One fine evening, there was going to be a fashion show at the banquet hall where Raj worked. It was basically a fashion promoting event. Different models, different mannequins and different types of attire and stages - everything was well organized. Due to Raj's high interests in fashion, and his inclination towards mathematics, the organizer allowed Raj to be the head of the event, which was a remarkable achievement without much prior experience. It was a committed, passion driven job.

Raj was hesitant at first, but after several persuasions by the organizer, he eventually agreed. Seeking god's blessings, he set out for the most rewarding experience of his life. With his academic career blooming at an unprecedented pace, Raj could not wait for the other exciting things waiting to happen down the road – marriage, children, house, car and all the other luxurious things once deemed unattainable by him as a teenager.

After days of hard work, unlimited phone calls and sleepless nights, the final day had eventually come! Raj was ecstatic and was proud to host the event – he put in his best efforts to ensure that the event was a gala success and had left no stones unturned in any manner. He slowly moved towards the hall entrance, getting gradually mesmerized by the live models, as well as the beautifully dressed mannequins.

Amongst all the tall, beautiful, amazingly dressed girls and statues, he desired something else. He was looking for a girl, who did not know he existed, or the story that had brought him there. He had no reasons to be discreet but still he had to be careful. He was standing near the doorway, surveying the golden banquet hall, which was filled with refined bodies in saris and jackets, apart from beautiful young women with straight hair who never had much facial expressions. But they will, soon - any moment now.

The event started soon - huge applauses; kind words of appreciation for the wonderful management and the settings; unbelievable response and feedback from the organisers and the audience! Raj was the man of the event – what more could he have dreamt of?

Walking his way down, after having completed a survey about how many people had turned up, he really felt proud of himself – around 12,000 footfalls. He could not believe it - his past bad days were just a flashback for him right now!

His eyes suddenly fell on someone - a girl in a black sari. Everyone was talking to the girl; many gentlemen were crowding beside that astoundingly beautiful girl! Raj knew who she was though - despite having important work to touch base on, people to meet, he stood there waiting for the reporters and the crowd to move away.

The girl, moving her head here and there, finally looked at Raj - it was the same eye contact which had happened several years ago during his fateful stays in the hospital, after he tried saving the old man from being lynched by a mob.

"Raaaaaaaaj" came the girl running, then tightly hugging the gentleman that Raj has now become! "You are unrecognizable. You have changed a lot. You look so accomplished!" - said the girl moving her hair locks behind her ears in the same pink blushing face, smilingly. Raj in a broken voice, could not limit his joy to his smile; his cheeks were full of rolling tears, as everyone stood amazed.

"From the first time I met you, I never thought even once of making someone else as my own, Raj", said Nisha wiping tears of joy from her cheeks. She stated that she even went to his last-known address but to her despair, Raj had already moved out by then! "Papa did not allow me to visit you when he was there", said Raj's dream-girl.

"Oh my god! Did he die? I am so grateful to him - because of him, I met you! You inspired me to work harder. Today as I stand here, I want to say something", said Raj.

Everyone kept staring at the happy couple - the ladies and gentlemen who gathered around, kept wondering who was going to marry their most lovely model. "Nisha, you are going to be my wife and today two of my dreams came true - first is getting to see you and having you as my own, and" he paused for a bit, as everyone looked at each other wondering what was coming next; "I am going to England as the Head of the Fashion department of The Globe!" exclaimed Raj - everyone clapped as the couple kissed and danced.

After a few months, they got married - the happy couple moved to New York, with their two children and a dog. Many people including Nisha were still somewhat unaware of Raj's story of perseverance and zeal - his straightening his acts, facing the challenges the world around him had once posed, with no fear and no negative vibes.

All those hard works had finally paid off, as he considered himself to be one of the luckiest guys in the world, especially after he met Nisha. Soon after meeting Nisha, Diana became close friends with this family. They used to take turns to host parties on weekends, when Di and Ritu would join them – they all used to enjoy a lot, especially the love-story of Raj and Nisha.

Time flew there as well - Diana soon got quite a few promotions successively, and sure enough, the day soon came when she was accorded the position of staff reporter, helping out the Anchor here. Things were moving perfectly for her, until the day came when she was denied the most coveted position of her life – Anchor! It changed her life completely! It was a denial of promotion on the ground of insipidity!

Di wanted to be an anchor with ANN from her early childhood days – she was mesmerised and very excited to see her favourite anchors on Television. Many of them used to motivate her online, either through Instagram or by email, so that Diana can become one of them down the road.

Bill Ripley was her most favourite television host – she would drop everything around the time when Bill used to appear on ANN, and she fantasised to be co-hosting TV shows with Bill one day soon. Di fixated her aim from her high school days; so, she started her focus on Journalism and Mass Communication, with special emphasis on Media, during the same time she was preparing for her IB finals.

After a few months, Di was assigned for international reporting from the Asia office in Bangkok! But unfortunately, Bill had left ANN for ABD News by then, and Diana had a very hard time accepting such a disaster for her. Anyways, she was happy that she could see her grandma now more often, flying back to

India on off days and so on. Ritu had chosen to go back to her ancestral house in Kolkata after Di moved to Bangkok, as her new role entailed prolonged hectic tours.

Following a couple of years of jostling around as a staff reporter, Di was transferred back to London office with a promotion. She was thrilled due to the fact that all that was needed then was, an opening of the position of an Anchor with her dream-company. Time flew - soon she learnt that one of the senior anchors was retiring soon; she called up her boss in the US who confirmed the vacancy – the boss suggested that she put in her application right away.

With the kind of education and experience she had under her belts, Diana was confident that she would get the position with no problem. There wasn't any competition per se for this position too; so, she was ecstatic!

Wasting no time, Di forwarded her application to her boss Peter, who recommended her right away; all that was needed at that point, was the big boss's concurrence. Although many of her colleagues suggested that she call up the HR and request them to expedite her application, but Di didn't do it, partly due to her instilled values and ethics, and partly because she didn't like the idea of solicitation – the latter was against the company policy too. She was confident that she will get the job that she had been aspiring since childhood; therefore, she decided to wait until the higher ups reverted back to her.

It was a Sunday evening right after New Year's Day - Di was on the telephone with her grandma at India – she routinely called her up on every holidays and weekends, inquiring about her health, talking about the good old days, about their trips to various parts of the world together, as well as other stuff. Di used to rent a small studio apartment in Nottingham; she used to save her salary for taking her grandma for nice and exotic vacations once a year, without fail. They had visited most of the world by then - life had finally started looking good for Diana finally!

Di's laptop was on and she suddenly saw an incoming mail from her employer – she told her grandma that she was going to call her back soon, as she jumped on the couch to retrieve the email. Yes, it was from ANN HQ! She couldn't breathe properly; she was so excited and so happy – the day have seemed to surface – the day she was waiting for all her life! She offered her prayers to God and opened her inbox; her heartbeats were so rapid and loud that she could almost hear the thumps. She started reading the mail of her life; wait a minute! What's written there?

It said on the first paragraph of the mail: "Thank you for your application for the position of Anchor with ANN". But what in the world was written on the second paragraph? Di's head started spinning like the rotors of a drying machine. It said: "We deeply value your service and your dedication. You have been an asset for us so far; however, we regret to inform you that your application could not be considered due to the insipidity of your profile and background. The management wishes you best of luck."

She stared at the email message on her computer, her mind racing so fast that the words blurred together and no longer made any sense. Just three lines, but enough to make her life--the life she'd worked so hard and sacrificed so much to build - begin to crumble around her.

Diana began to wonder what exactly in her profile reflected on her as being insipid! Was she really devoid of qualities that made her spirit and character inane? How can they think that she was a lady without distinctive, interesting or stimulating qualities? Was that a fair assessment of her resume or her background? Or, was it her gross misfortune striking her once again at the most crucial juncture of her career path?

Thousands of questions jumbled up on her brain. Di laid down on her little couch that she bought from a flea market at a bargain – soon she fell asleep; drops of tears came down on her ragged pillow. Sheds of moonlit skies could be seen through the small window, some of the light reflecting on her wet cheeks like falling petal from drying rose. There was nothing much she could've done to alleviate that situation; she gave it a hundred per cent in life, in order to achieve her desired passion in her dream-job! It was just not happening – what else could have been done?

Was that whole thing a denial on the ground of insipidity, or just her continued bad luck that she had been 'endowed with' from her childhood? Who knows?

Di woke up in the middle of the night, with strong headache and weakness all over her body. She didn't know what to do; she looked at the clock to figure out that it was Monday morning for her grandma – so she called her and broke the bad news.

Both of them started crying aloud, and asking the same question again and again: how come God be so cruel? She had done absolutely nothing in life which may be considered as harmful or sinful. Still, the Almighty had not blessed her with the most coveted job in her life, the one she was dreaming for years! How can that be possible?

Anyways, pretty soon her grandma started consoling her, telling Diana that it was not the end for her career; Ritu suggested that Di call up her mentor, Bill and speak to him. So, Di took the next day off from work, calling in sick – she indeed had an acidic stomach and intermittent headaches and trauma.

After taking few over the counter medications for pain and inflammation, along with a digestive enzyme, Di called Bill. He couldn't believe that either, but soon thereafter, he advised that she flew down to New York to meet him at his office the following Monday morning. He didn't elaborate any further; but Di started feeling a positive vibe from the conversation.

So, she went back to work the next day, as usual, keeping a low profile – many of her friends came over to her and consoled her during lunchbreak; Di thanked all of them for being there for her in such difficult times. However, she didn't divulge the information pertaining to her scheduled visit to NYC next weekend though – instead, she took a casual day off for the following Monday.

Although Di was in a kind of double mind at the onset about flying down to NYC, disrupting her routine work with ANN, however, the thought of getting to meet Bill after a very long time, especially with his kids and family-members around for a Sunday night dinner at his place in Long Island, gave Diana enough inspiration and motivation to go ahead with her planned visit.

She reached NYC in late afternoon, checked in at her hotel in Manhattan, had her routine conversations with grandma, and left for Bill's home by Long Island Railroad. And guess what? Bill was waiting for her at the station! They had a wonderful time there for few hours, after which Bill's wife dropped Di after dinner at the hotel. All of them had a really fascinating time there at Bill's house.

Di woke up early the next day and checked out of her hotel after complimentary breakfast, so as to take a cab to ABD's HQ – she reached there sharp at 9 am, went straight to the Reception area, where Bill came over to receive her. They had some preliminary discussion about the modus operandi of his organization, along with the tiny winy differences in their operation, etc., as distinguished from ANN, so that Di could be better equipped to answer any query, if needed.

Thereafter, Bill asked Diana to walk towards the President's office; she was really surprised at that gesture. Why in the world will the President of such a large conglomerate and reputed media house want to meet a reporter like her?

Before she can think further, she found herself walking like a zombie, entering the humongous office of the President. Bill introduced her - as soon as she was seated, the President gave her an envelope, welcoming her on board as an Anchor! The rest was history.

Di became an internationally acclaimed anchor for ABD News Corporation - all her dreams became reality. Even ANN wanted her to return as an anchor there, which she politely refused, stating that ABD was there for her when she needed it the most; therefore, she shouldn't be unfaithful to them. And speaking of Bill, who else can be happier than a "guru" to see his 'bhakt' attain whatever s/he deserved in life?

All of those unimaginable achievements were possible due to Di's belief in herself and on the Almighty, her relentless work, dedication, sincerity, honesty and ambition. She couldn't thank her grandma for all that she accomplished later in life, as she was the real inspiration behind Diana's success. She was the one who always stood by Di thick and thin, continuously boosting her morale, providing her guidance and building up her confidence. As a matter of fact, Ritu was the reason why Diana became who she was!

Di was relieved so much to realise that her work and personality was not insipid; the denial on the ground of insipidity was just a lack of proper HR skills that the concerned department exercised, it seemed, by the turn of events. She had always believed that if you keep working hard and focus on your priorities, nothing is impossible in this world.

Earlier, Vicky and his mother moved to Puri after their beloved Diana's travel abroad. They were able to finally dispose of their share of the ancestral property after a lot of trouble.

But the court cases kept haunting Vicky back, although all the allegations against him were false and fabricated. The local police aided and abetted the criminal duo to such extent that Vicky was contemplating leaving the country for good. He got completely frustrated with most of the scenarios and prevailing conditions there in his hometown. He even started repenting his decision of returning back to India.

Vicky always cherished his stays and his life at the US, as he spent the best moments of his life there – he even brought his parents and his younger sister there several times, when they all had wonderful times. Leaving US for Vicky wasn't an easy decision at all, but deep down his mind, Vicky loved his motherland. He knew that he had to come back there to safeguard his parents and his only family left.

It wasn't an easy decision for him, but he had to choose between luxurious and prestigious life on the one hand, and his love for parents and his motherland, on the other - the latter prevailed. He had to ride his way all alone, especially after his father's demise, because Vicky and his father used to be very close – his dad was his mentor, his guide. With him gone, Vicky had been riding life all alone practically.

Di had successfully completed her UG and became an anchor in a top-notch broadcasting firm in the USA, after completing her internship in the UK, and after several years had elapsed, with her gaining more insights and experiences at her profession. She and her grandma used to live together in a nice condominium on the west coast.

They frequently visited India to see Vicky. He lived in a seashore property off the coast of Bay of Bengal; he was pretty happy that Di had achieved her dream. But, what about Vicky now? What was there left for him now? Was he of any use to anyone anymore? What else was the purpose of his life, now that Di had already seen her dream coming true?

Those were the questions that came creeping on Vicky's mind that day, in the middle of that damp and rainy winter day – he was the lone rider now - he had to ride it along – alone, all by himself! He achieved so much in life; but, was he able to lead a peaceful life for which he returned back to India?

Suddenly, Vicky felt that he had severe chest pain and heavy sweating and excruciating pain on shoulders and chest. All he wanted to do was to drag himself to the corner table where his expensive gadget gifted by Di had been charging – but he couldn't.

He wanted to hear the voice of his world's best daughter/niece/friend /sister for the final time over phone – her cuckoo voice always soothed Vicky and healed all his wounds; but that day, he couldn't reach the end-table; the stultified man finally fell down – was he tired of fighting all his life? Was he sent to earth by the Gods to protest against evil and protect the innocents, as some sort of messiah? The answers will never be known!

A flung of rain pattered against the window of the living room; soon, rain stopped outside, and darkness prevailed – Vikram came to this world alone crying in his mother's womb, but smilingly left alone to join his favourite younger sister and his loving dad up in heaven!

His eyes were kind of pink and lachrymose – was he going to miss the sweet little girl she raised all his life, who had then become an internationally acclaimed news anchor, far from where his body was lying? It seemed that the lion-heart did cry at his last minutes! He was mortal alright!

It was kind of tragic that no one was around Vicky when he breathed his last. Even after his demise, it took almost a day for anyone to find out that he was no more – thanks to the milkman the next morning that his neighbours came to know of the death; the milkman saw Vicky lying dead on the floor through glass window. He raised an alarm thereafter – the next-door neighbour called up Di to give the shocking news.

News of his death devastated Di – she had lost her dear brother. She had been constantly dealing with painful demises from her childhood days – her own mother, then her dear grandpa Biman, and now her best friend in life – her uncle Vikram. Upon regaining her senses after hearing the news of her Dada's death, when she froze temporarily, Di called back the guy who called – she wired money to him, so that he can pay for preserving the body at a mortuary till they arrived.

She wanted to hide the devastating news from her granny; but the constantly flowing tears down her cheeks couldn't be controlled - Ritu knew right away something terrible had happened with her son. But, being a strong lady that she always had been, bearing all pain and enduring all losses, Ritu hid her true feelings. She told Di to get tickets to fly back to India right away, so that last rites could be performed for her dear son, who was no more!

Di and Ritu flew back the very next morning; they took care of all the customary rituals and ceremonies during the next few days with heaviest hearts anyone can possibly have. But they were little consoled to find out from the post-mortem report that he died quickly of a massive cardiac arrest – he didn't suffer more than few minutes!

So, Di and her granny had found reasons for some consolation after all the pain they felt about the great loss - Vicky had left for his heavenly sojourn in peace, without any suffering and ailments!

He always used to refer to death as just a change of clothes – he stated to Di many times over the years that life cannot be complete without death: 'Older generations need to pave ways for next generation for betterment of world. Just as one changes clothes without change in anything else in him, souls change body to transform into someone else down the road.'

Diana would obviously miss his constant guidance, unselfish love and continuous support; but she decided to face life again normally, with the courage bestowed upon her by her dear brother Vicky.

However, with Ritu, the matter was completely different. She had dealt with all personal losses in death till now reasonably well - but with Vikram gone, she seemed to lose her ultimate will to live.

Ritu could never cope with her beloved son's death; she had endured many untimely demises in her life, which included her younger daughter, her younger brother, her husband, and now her only son. Soon she got bed-ridden and became sick. Pretty soon she died of pneumonia from the cold that she caught while performing last rites of her only son! Maybe she wanted to join her son up there, along with the rest of her family!

Maybe God was finally happy with Ritu's constant redemption for something bad she must have committed in her previous life! She lends her helping hands to anyone in dire danger, sometimes at the cost of her own family's betterment – she never stopped helping people even when age was taking a toll on her health! But, in return, she seemed to have gotten absolutely nothing – most people didn't even acknowledge what the great lady did to support them some way or another! Now, maybe she rests in peace!

That was the penultimate blow to Di – now that she had lost everything, she had no one else to rest her crying face on. There was absolutely no one to call her own left in this world now, except her cousin sister Rina and the bed-ridden ailing Riya. This loss was unbearable for her – but she had dealt with enough blow life had to offer by then – she made up her mind to focus on devoting her life to what she always aimed for, instead of grieving.

Who was going to yell at her to change her clothes, to eat her food, to do her hair, etc.? Those thoughts jumbled up in her minds sporadically, but being a strong lady, she quickly came to her senses, making up her mind to get to her desired destination. After all, that's what Ritu would have wanted her most favourite girl to do, if she was alive! With a shattered heart, Di gradually tried to be herself once again in life!

Earlier, when she used to visit her uncle Vicky for summer vacation during her second year of college, Di received some invaluable insights from her dear uncle about life and death - why people should focus on not keep grieving out of any kind of delusion in life. Vicky had gained such insights from visiting one of his friends in Behala few months ago, which he wanted to share with Di.

Vicky had reminded Di the basic fact that grief over any matter was born out of sheer ignorance. To him, there was a marked difference between concern and ignorance. Those were his exact words:

"A person can weep because of the loving relationship with a departed soul, or as a result of personal attachment to the departed soul. Or, the person may decide to cry simple out of the social expectation to cry when someone close departed – crocodile tears or whatever form and manner it maybe!

If the person who died lived an unrighteous life, there could be concerns about his fate. Rituals for departed souls were prescribed by almost all religions across the board for one reason mainly – so that the departed soul may live a better after-life, or whatever happens to our soul once we die.

Even if a good person dies, there may be enough cause for grief – we fear for our own selves in the absence of wise counsel of the departed soul. While there maybe various reasons for morning for those who have died, but why do we sometimes mourn for living persons? Many of us who are alive can cause anxiety in various ways – certain times, we cry out of love or attachment; sometimes, we grief over fear of events that have not happened yet.

In that context, it may be interesting to note that some men aged 20 years or so do not care or worry about what the world thinks of him; after a decade or so, he may start thinking what exactly the world thinks of him. But, in his forties, he may start to realise that the world around him do not care of him at all!

So, it is always better to deal with a tough situation aptly, rather than keep on grieving over it. We have to accept sometimes the basic fact that we cannot change a particular situation, no matter how much we try; so, it's more fruitful if we start finding a way to deal with it, instead of complaining or crying over it.

Decisive actions are needed most of the time to deal with changing world around us. Nurturing worries, tensions, fear or grief to deal with past or future anticipated situations & events may be complete waste of time & energy – it's an ineffective way to deal with life. It's better to deal with situations at hand at present, in the best possible manner, without worrying about the outcome.

Lord Krishna said the following through our Bhagwad Gita, in order to lift Arjuna's mind to the highest spiritual standpoint, at a time when Arjuna was fearful of losing his loved ones over waging war:

'There was never a time when I was not there; there was never a time when you were not there; there was never a time when these kings were not there. Even after the war, we will not cease to exist – we will be there.' Thus, He explained the reason why we shouldn't grieve over the dead, or over those who are about to die. He stated that nobody really dies; so, there is no need to lament over the deceased.

Our essence is eternal; the only oneself (atman), present in the heart of all beings is immortal. The atman which enlivened the body does not cease to exist when the physical structure perishes – it is imperishable and is eternal. So, the real 'I' or our Essence never dies – why grieve for it then? Apart from this eternal truth, there is one more reason not to mourn.

The body experiences changes over time, and undergoes several stages – childhood, adolescence, youth, adulthood and old age. However, the in-dweller, the Self, remains changeless – it is the same at all stages of life. The physical or other changes over time materialises only on the body; they do not affect the immortal Self.

When our body changes from one stage to another, say for example, from adolescence to youth, none of us either crave for the past or grieve over the change. In the same exact fashion, through death, we leave one body and take on another. It may also be compared to change of clothes, which we all do several times a day throughout our lives – we don't grieve over it, do we?

The people who are wiser than others are not deluded by the death of his own body, or that of someone else close to him/her. There's no grief where there is no delusion."

The above explanation and simplification of life and death provided by Vicky to his dear niece years ago, proved to be very efficacious and puissant for her in overcoming all odds, melancholy, despondency and lugubrious mood at various stages of life. Although Di might end up having a doleful look sometimes (like upon finding out about Vicky's untimely sojourn to heaven), but she managed to come to terms – to quickly adapt to the warranted situation and move on!

But, with Ritu gone from her life, the wretched young lady found it extremely hard to deal with it; however, with a disconsolate and crestfallen look on her beautiful face, Di called up Rina who immediately rushed out to JFK airport in NY, to be on her cousin sister's side.

Rina flew back to India the next morning; the two ladies joined hands to finish the rituals and fly back to the USA, after taking care of the loose ends in India. Diana's fortune, however, took a gigantic turn at this juncture, probably with blessings from her recently-deceased 'parents' – the true guardian angels!

She got an unbelievably surprising offer from another top broadcasting corporation owned by the Warner Group to become the President of International Desk. Who in their normal mind could refuse such a lucrative offer? After all, that was like the highest step on Di's career-ladder!

Her new office there was bigger than some people's homes – it was a huge room with private meeting room in one corner, a relaxing couch with all kinds of cold cuts and beverages on the adjoining area, a huge ladies room with wardrobes and dressers on one side – on the other side was her gigantic desk overlooking the Hudson river through panelled glasses with private balcony. Her salary and gross emoluments were nearly twice as her last employer paid her; there was not one perk or fringe benefits in this world, which wasn't included in her current package.

Di believed deep down her heart that this couldn't have possibly happened without the showering of blessings from her brother-cum-uncle Vicky and Grandma-cum-mother Ritu, as they had become God themselves, showering upon their most beloved Diana everything she deserved. Di kept some pictures of her uncle and grandma on the edge of her desk facing her; she always made sure that she sought their blessings before venturing into any strategic meetings or major events.

With big positions came bigger responsibilities – Diana was the number two in the entire Corporation. She worked diligently from early morning hours till late at night. Soon after joining there, Di bought herself a mansion with acres of lands, with golf course, swimming pools, horse track and fabulous lawn and garden. Since her palatial house wasn't far from her Head Office, she used the company-provided limousine or alternatively, her chauffeur-driven Mercedes to commute.

Since her duty encompassed a lot of travel to other cities and destinations, she converted a part of her huge lawn on the back of the mansion to a helipad – she used that pad for landing and take-off of choppers to fly her to and fro nearest airports, from where she flew first class to her destinations, unwinding a little bit en route.

Most of her time was spent in procuring new businesses, reviewing and changing company policies and practices, planning and implementing projects and newer shows, complying with laws & regulations, statutory reporting, presiding over meetings and host of other activities.

In order to destress her mind, Di used to visit Broadways for watching theatres once in a while. After watching the first show of a very popular theatre there, she called up one of her close friends at work and narrated the following lines to her: "putting on shows at the amphitheatre takes a large cohort of people, each rendering their own expertise, and I began to see that theatre is a veritable smorgasbord of various options – lights, sounds, costumes, props, actors, director, stage manager, etc."

Thus, it was evident that apart from being a very efficient professional in her own field, Di had developed profound management skills by virtue of her previous close association with her uncle Vicky, so that she could see the whole picture in almost everything, be it theatre or something else. She learned to deal with any adversity as a pleasurable challenge, rather than something to be tholed.

Even knowing fully well that her broadcasts or shows probably were being monitored by the despots around the world, she always held her head high to render her honest opinion on any event, be it political or apolitical.

Almost all people who used to view her shows, her investigative reports in particular, soon became her fans – they loved the straight-talks Di used to have with her guest-speakers or in-house experts. One of her very close associates, Janet Levy, got much inspiration from Di regarding honest, unbiased and fact-based reporting – she kept in close touch with Di even after Janet decided to call it quits there, in order to become a freelance reporter.

Janet heard many stories of West Bengal from her mentor Di – so, when an offer came to her from an internet-based organisation called American Thinker to conduct some deep research in the field of biased government in Bengal, Janet jumped on it.

She was very excited about it – she called Di to pass on the great news; Di congratulated her and wished Janet all the very best. Di gave Janet with some very pertinent input as to the manner in which she should conduct her research back in India and helped her with contact numbers of people there.

After incredibly deep research, aided with interviews of people from all facets of life, Janet compiled an article titled 'The Muslim Takeover of West Bengal' – it was blogged with incredible laudatory response from most people. The article read like this –

"Riots, restrictions on speech and religion, and the takeover of politics and law enforcement are just a few of the unwelcome changes that can be expected in non-Muslim societies as Muslim immigrants increase in number, according to Dr. Peter Hammond. A Christian Missionary based in South Africa and author of 40 books, Hammond delineates how Muslims change societies in his book, *Slavery, Terrorism and Islam*. Citing examples of countries worldwide, Hammond outlines typical activities that occur as the Muslim percentage of the total population increase. It is a warning bell about the gradual, step-by-step changes that can be expected in other countries still undergoing significant Muslim immigration.

These societal changes occur because devout Muslims are bound by a 1,400-year-old doctrine of immigration originating in Islamic scriptures and based on Mohammed's migration from Mecca to Medina. Under the religious edict of Hijra, Islamic expansionism and submission of all non-Muslims to shariah or Islamic expansionism and its counterpart, Jihad, are first expressed as Muslim demands for special status and privileges within the host country. A higher percentage of Muslims in the host country can soon translate into Muslim control of political processes, law enforcement, media, and the economy, as well as restrictions on freedom of movement, speech and religious practices. The appropriation of goods and property, as well as violence with impunity, can also occur.

The situation in at West Bengal in Hindu-majority India, bordering Muslim-majority Bangladesh, illustrates the inherent problems to non-Muslim societies of a growing Muslim population.

Bengal, an ethno-cultural region, was politically divided in 1947 during the partitioning of British India and Pakistan. Under this arrangement, the Bengal province was carved in two: the predominantly Hindu West Bengal, a state of India, and the predominantly Muslim East Bengal, which became a province of Pakistan and, in 1971, the Muslim-majority country of Bangladesh.

At partitioning, the Muslim population of West Bengal stood at 12% and the Hindu population of East Bengal 30%. Today, with massive Muslim immigration, Hindu persecution and forced conversions, West Bengal's Muslim population has increased to 27% (up to 63% in some districts), as per the 2011 census and Bangladesh's Hindu population has decreased to 8%. While the situation for Hindus in Bangladesh is certainly dire, life has become increasingly difficult for Hindus in West Bengal, home to a Muslim-appeasing government and a breeding ground and safe haven for terrorists. For several years, West Bengal has suffered under apparent Muslim-planned riots designed to implement shariah, extract government concessions and grab more territory.

In 2007, a violent protest broke out in Kolkata (formerly known as Calcutta) against Bangladeshi feminist author, physician and human rights activist, Taslima Nasreen. The demonstrations against Nasreen were a thinly veiled attempt to institute Islamic blasphemy laws and curtail freedom of speech.

Nasreen, who was born a Bangladeshi Muslim but chose atheism, had witnessed the horrific treatment of Islamic women in her medical practice, and advocated for freedom of expression, women's rights, non-Muslim rights and abolition of shariah law. In 1993, she published a novel, *Lajja (Shame)* about a Hindu family persecuted by Muslims. The novel ignited a furore in the Muslim community, which called for a ban on the book and offered a bounty for her death. The novel was subsequently banned by Indian authorities. Nasreen was physically attacked, went into hiding and escaped from Bangladesh to Europe. After 10 years' exile, she returned to the east and settled in Kolkata. Her Bangladeshi passport had been revoked and she waited several years for a visa to be able to visit India. While in Kolkata, she continued to write articles of Islam despite renewed threats and calls for her beheading.

In November 2007, a protest organized by militant Muslims against Nasreen led to riots as Muslims blocked traffic, pelted police and journalists, torched cars and damaged buses. Similar to the justification for the *Charlie Hebdo* murders in Paris, West Bengali Muslims protested the violation of shariah blasphemy law, which mandates death for anyone who dares to criticize Islam. The army was forced to intervene, Nasreen was placed under house arrest and later forced to leave the area. The banned Student Islamic Movement of India (SIMI) and the Pakistani Inter-Service Intelligence (ISI) were believed to have fostered the mayhem.

In 2013, Muslims in West Bengal were actively lobbying for a second partition of India to create an Islamic super state – Mughalistan – that would incorporate Pakistan, Bangladesh and parts of India. Meanwhile, ethnic divisions were also stirred up by an upcoming local election. Into this charged situation, the murder of a Muslim cleric by unidentified assailants sparked outrage among Muslims, as thousands mobilized for rioting in the Canning District. An article in a popular weekly publication, *Organiser*, called the attack 'a well-organized and meticulously planned attack on Hindus.' Over 200 Hindu homes were looted and firebombed, hundreds of temples and idols destroyed, and vehicles set on fire amid shouts of 'Allah-hu-Akbar!' Repeated calls for help by Hindus went unanswered by the police. Local residents claimed the authorities were complicit with the Muslim mobs.

This January 29th, in a market in the Kolkata suburb of Usti, more than 50 Hindu shops were ransacked, looted and gutted by rampaging jihadists. Police mostly watched as bombs were hurled at Hindus indiscriminately. They fired a few random shots into the air and detained victimized Hindu shop owners while their attackers roamed free. A legislative assembly member and the state minister for minority affairs reportedly demanded that local police release the few rioters held in custody. There was limited reporting by the mainstream media that didn't specify the Muslim identity of the perpetrators and West Bengal's Chief Minister, X (left blank intentionally), issued no statement about the violence. Independent sites, *Indiafacts* and *Hindu Samhati*, reported the incident with numerous photographs.

With a 27% Muslim population, enough pressure exists to tip the scales for elected officials precariously toward advancement of an Islamic agenda and make Muslims the most privileged class in West Bengal. In some areas, such as the border district of Murshidabad, which is over 63% Muslim, de facto shariah is imposed on all residents. The vast majority of political candidates, elected officials and law enforcement leadership are Muslim and the economic prospects for Hindus dim as Muslims refuse to patronize non-Muslim businesses.

Chief Minister of Bengal (code named X), who has received official visits from Hillary Clinton and several U.S. ambassadors, offers a prime example of a political leader who expediently favours Muslim constituents, capitulates to their many demands and entices them with special benefits and privileges. The reality of Muslim vote bank politics, whereby an entire Muslim community votes along lines dictated by the local imam or religious leader, adds to the problem and furthers Muslim control of the state. X has gone so far in her Muslim sympathies as to publicly recite the *Kalima Shahadat*, the Islamic conversion prayer, in front of an audience of imams.

Because West Bengal's Muslims were largely responsible for her election as chief minister, X has made substantial payback. She approved and validated the academic degrees of 10,000 previously unrecognized Saudi-funded and controlled madrasas (Islamic colleges) four minarets (Muslim towers), honorariums for imams and an exclusively Islamic township. X called for establishment of Muslim medical, technical and nursing schools with special subsidies for Muslim students, as well as Muslim-only hospitals. She has favoured Muslims to the extent of distributing free bicycles and rail passes to female Muslim students and laptops to Muslim boys. X's political party will most likely send more Islamists to serve in parliament in the future. Reportedly, jihadist sleeper cells inhabit the area under her protection. Meanwhile, the needs of Hindu refugees from Bangladesh are ignored, even as they continue being victimized in West Bengal.

In June of 2014, X made a highly questionable appointment, Rajya Sabha, to the upper house of the Indian Parliament. Despite multiple warnings from the District Intelligence Bureau that had red-flagged him for instigating violence against Hindus, including alleged participation in the Kolkata and Canning riots and sheltering known terrorists, she selected Pakistani Hassan Imran to serve as MP. Imran is a founder and self-admitted member of the radical student group, the Student Islamic Movement of India (SIMI), a recognized terrorist organization banned by the Indian government. He founded and edited a radical weekly magazine, Kalam, which he later turned into a daily newspaper, Dainik Kalam, and sold to the Saradha Group, a financial conglomerate with ties to West Bengal government officials. The publication has advocated for the establishment of Muslim-controlled areas in the state under shariah.

Hassan has close ties to local Islamist leaders and has worked with Jamat-e-Islami (JI), a pro-Saudi jihadist group supported by Pakistan's Inter-Services Intelligence (ISI). He also has ties to a chief official of the Islamic Development Bank, a Saudi entity that has financed Hamas and the Muslim Brotherhood affiliate, the Council of American Islamic Relations (CAIR), an unindicted co-conspirator in the Holy Land Foundation terrorism funding trial in the United States. JI and the ISI have been linked to efforts to take over the Indian state of Assam and separate it from India.

The Saudi-funded terrorist group, Jamat-ul-Mujahadeen, also linked to MP Hassan Imran, has a major base in West Bengal, including bomb-manufacturing units, and has used Wahhabi money to build mosques throughout the state. The Muslim call to prayer is blasted by loudspeaker from early morning to late at night and some thoroughfares in the Muslim districts of Kolkata are closed for all traffic for Friday prayers.

Recently, Hassan and other associates of X were implicated in a financial scandal – a Ponzi scheme with the Saradha Group – and things are starting to unravel for the chief minister. A major investigation of a consortium of 200 private companies that collected between $4 – 6 billion from over 1.7 million before it collapsed, may bring down her reign in West Bengal. Her MP appointee, Hassan, is believed to have acted as a liaison between Jamat-e-Islami and the money launderers."

The blog released in the year 2015 received lots of positive feedback for Janet. Too bad that she stopped writing or engaging in any occupation soon after he married Stuart, a physically disadvantaged man whose lower limbs were paralysed from an accident. He made a fortune as compensation arising out of his insurance claim – Janet came to know about it, and jumped at the offer of marrying the billionaire, just out of sheer greed to enjoy high life – a life offering a bed with roses!

She was also getting threat calls after her blog made it rounds, from certain corners. Igniting communal tension was never her intentions – she just wanted to express whatever truth and data she gathered during her investigations and research. But, to some, she was an evil person – they wanted to behead her. Stuart convinced her to take a quick exit from her profession to start enjoying a rosy life.

Life at that point had somewhat become a bed of roses for Di too, until the point that she started becoming an eye-soar to her colleagues, most of whom eventually became her subordinates, although they had been working for the company for a much longer period of time than she was - they felt that they were denied promotions to the top Executive rank, for which they started blaming Diana.

They wouldn't have mustered enough courage to say anything on her face, or being insubordinate directly; however, they started criticising her, depicting her as a lady from the third world country trying to rule their lives, and so on and so forth.

Diana was fed up with all the growing turmoil and office politics on the one hand, and was getting anxious to materialise her ultimate dream of parenting few underprivileged kids from the streets of Kolkata – she always had a love for the City, although the place had not accorded her with the best life had to offer; her childhood days were not the most glorious days of her life, though she had the best guardians anyone can dream for, in Biman, Ritu, Vicky and Riya. She always nurtured a strong urge hidden inside her evergreen soul to give back to the society - to make life really happy for some kids in distress back home.

It didn't take much thinking after that, as Di sold off everything she had in the US, to bid adieu to the great country that gave her the best time of her life, in every material sense. She hosted a big going-off party, where almost all her friends, co-workers, neighbours, et al were invited – Rina was there too, and she helped out Diana a lot.

Her mother Riya was no more – after her father Sam passed away, Riya headed for her heavenly sojourn too, leaving their surviving daughter Rina to be the only close relative to Di. The cousin sisters kept in regular touch with each other; they became very friendly over time, as they were the only immediate family each of them had in the world anymore!

When Mary and Subir were in eighth grade, the remaining kids staying with Di at Alipore were taken back by their natural parents or guardians, as they had already graduated from school, and were ready to help out their aging parents who had to put them up at Homes shortly after birth, due to financial constraints.

Although Di and all her foster kids felt very sad, but they were consoled by the fact that those kids would get to grow up with their natural parents, at their own homes. Diana contacted some people in power and got the kids some benefits under various governmental available schemes that they would be entitled to, with potential for future employment opportunities for the kids down the road.

However, as luck would have it, situation of one of those kids named Nisha, who used to be little arrogant, wifty and ditzy young girl right from her juvenile days, got worse after she went back with her parents, leaving Diana's home.

Her natural father died few months after Nisha went back to her biological parents, when her mother remarried a guy named Tim – they knew each other while Jose was still alive, and it was said that Nisha's mother had extramarital affairs with Tim, who was an incorrigibly fractious, irritable and peevish guy. People in the neighbourhood also claimed that Jose and his wife used to quarrel quite a bit at nights; the marital discord escalated after Jose found out that his wife was cheating on him.

Jose was a vagabond in his younger years, as he established political connections at a very early age, to subsequently become an active member of a students' union at his college, although he actually never crossed the boundaries of school-level education – some hooligans known to him helped Jose get a false Secondary Certificate, which he used unlawfully to get admission into a local college.

He spent more time lollygagging in different places, thanks to the money he used to make through students' admissions & some other unscrupulous methods. He even faked his college degree to get himself a job in a local private hospital as a maintenance supervisor.

He had absolutely no knowledge of electrical, structural or civil matters when he started out with his new job! Jose used his political connections to get the coveted job at a lucrative salary; soon, he begun wasting money on alcohol and other substance abuse habits. He met Nisha's mother at his place of employment; he didn't divulge the fact that he killed his former wife and made it look like an accident.

Nisha's mom was employed as a nurse in the same hospital - they soon started dating and thereafter got married. Everything was fine until Nisha was born, when Jose started to doubt his wife about her character – he had earlier caught her fondling with an affluent patient at the hospital! He knew deep inside his mind that she was not a loyal wife anymore.

After Nisha's birth, Jose started abusing Nisha's mother on a routine manner, delating her of infidelity and bigotry. He even challenged his wife to go for DNA tests to ascertain the paternity; when she refused, Jose got mad and persuaded his wife to abandon the child on the streets, or face desertion.

So, the wretched mother had no other choice but to agree to the evil plan of abandoning the child with woebegone face. Next morning, Jose wrapped the new-born in a towel and dropped her near Shyambazar crossing, far off from where they lived near Ultadanga.

The Chairperson of West Bengal Commission for Protection of Child Rights was on her way to her office in the vicinity of Ultadanga, when she noticed some stray dogs barking and hovering around a suspiciously moving object. The lady named Bonnya, was a very noble and kind-hearted lady, who used to be a rebellion from her early childhood days, protesting against social injustice and crimes.

Whenever challenged by any vested interest groups, Bonnya would deliver fervid and efferent speech defending her actions and protests; any dust over the matter will settle soon. She was nominated to the Chairperson of that Commission much later in her career - she gracefully accepted it, knowing fully well that she might have to work within constraints of political boundaries, etc.

As soon as Bonnya heard the commotion, she asked her driver to pull over – she got down, had a slum-dweller standing there pick up the strange object, and sure enough – it was just what she thought it would be – an abandoned baby girl! Immediately, Bonnya took the infant to the local government hospital, identified herself in order to make sure that proper care be given to the baby, and got her admitted there in neo-natal care unit.

After some time, Bonnya would arrange for safe transfer of the baby, who she named Nisha, to a reputable orphanage known to her, where Nisha was growing up well – it was here that Diana first saw her when Nisha was around five years of age; Di adopted her with Bonnya's help.

When Jose and his wife met Nisha at Di's bungalow after a long time, she was around 16 years of age; they were mesmerized by her beauty and her mannerisms, etc. – those were the qualities that Di had inculcated in the precious girl Nisha.

That was one of the best things about all kids under Di's care at her home. She made sure all the kids become very disciplined, polite, obedient and smart as they were growing up, with impeccable mannerisms - although sometimes, some kids had to tolerate each other's' little foibles, as few of them became different in their attitude.

Subir was little hyper - one of his little idiosyncrasies was always preferring to jump in the car before anyone else could. But all the kids mingled well; they were a happy extended family.

Anyways, Jose was spellbound as Nisha was coming back home after her Board exams were over, and the couple wanted to take Nisha to her parental home – Diana and other kids weren't thrilled at the idea, but after they got Bonnya's nod on this, Di decided to send Nisha back to where she belonged.

After Nisha returned home, Jose did everything possible for him to make up for his sins in abandoning this beautiful girl years ago – he wanted redemption and prayed to God for forgiving him. God had something else in mind, as Jose died of a liver dysfunction soon thereafter. Nisha wasn't very sad, as she hardly had any affinity towards any of her parents, as she rarely saw them – it was only maybe once in two or three months that the parents would visit her at Diana's.

Some time passed and Nisha's stepfather Tim showed some signs of affinity and care for Nisha – he soon gained her confidence. Tim used to be a lawyer in Sealdah court, who belonged to a decent family. He first saw Nisha's mom when he took his father for treatment at the hospital she was working and met her at his father's cabin there.

Soon, they were in a relationship, meeting frequently after her duty hours would be over, spending time together in various places, until Jose found out about their illicit affair – he became desperate after this, and started visiting his paramour at Jose's house. If Jose confronted him, Tim would threaten him with false cases and other dire consequences.

After Jose's death, Tim moved in there, started cohabiting with Nisha's mother – he had eyes on Nisha too, as the latter was turning into an alluring and slinky young girl. Nisha was an incorrigible and inveterate flirt, and her habits couldn't be changed. The inevitable happened - they developed one of the most unholy relationships that anyone could think of around Kolkata in those days.

Tim would skip attending courts, get dressed and go out on the pretext of going to court, and will return home soon after Nisha's mother left for her work. Nisha became pregnant within a short period of time; her mother couldn't take it anymore – she walked the train lines when a moving train was approaching on her direction to wait until she got hit, and her torso was in pieces on impact!

Nisha did not have much remorse - neither did Tim – but, they decided to go for abortion of the baby illegally, and got away by paying bribes to the concerned clinic – they separated their ways thereafter, and Nisha became an escort, enlisting her name to a high-end escort service centre operating out of New Town.

It was nothing less than simple harlotry or whoredom – the oldest profession of archaic courtesan ship changed into a sophisticated term, where eyebrows won't be raised often. Her pimp would call her up whenever he got contacted from a prospective client; he will pick Nisha up and ferry her to a predetermined apartment (typically a rented one at posh neighbourhoods), where the client will arrive soon - then the pimp will make sure that Nisha returned safely, after extorting more than fifty percent of what she made at one sitting.

Physical and mental abuse by the pimps were also included in the package, to which the police and other authorities preferred a blind eye to these kinds of booming flesh-trade in the City – the pay-out they would receive from their sources associated with those pimps and girls were substantial, or at least enough to turn their heads away, as if nothing was going on.

Diana wasn't aware of that horrible turn of events, until there was a headline in a local newspaper someday, with a picture of a call-girl murdered in a Salt Lake residence, which caught her attention – it was Nisha!

Di rushed to the local police station, identified the body, and took it from morgue after the post-mortem procedures were concluded - she made sure that Nisha got proper cremation. She brought a handful of ash to her bungalow, put it in a corner of her garden, and had a beautiful headstone placed there.

She would routinely go there to mourn and commiserate with Nisha's soul for her premature departure – after all, Di played the role of a mother for the unfortunate girl for more than a decade!

Another of the kids who left Diana's sacred home after attaining majority was Robin – he got himself a job somewhere in Chennai where his employer permitted him to complete his college. Robin evolved later as a success story for all kids, as he worked very hard during days, studied at nights, got very little sleep, and completed his graduation.

His employer gave him consecutive raises, and even sent him to Australia for further training at company expenses, and after he returned back to India, Robin became the Chief Administrative Officer of the company. The only sad part relating to Robin, in the minds of Diana was, he never called or came over to see the great lady who changed his life!

Being faithful or loyal used to be a quality which many kids from that generation were devoid of, felt Di. But she was very happy of how Robin turned out in life and refrained from making any quibble about it. She seemed to belaud one of her foster children's success to many known to her and felt very gratified to have been a part of it.

Down the road, Robin would migrate to Canada to settle there with his family, who had no knowledge of his childhood or where he grew up! Robin told his wife and kids that he was brought up in an orphanage, sponsored by some reputed organisations, apart from the fact that he had a nightmarish past – no questions were ever asked of him on that one.

That way, he thought, no one needed to know about Diana – he was worried that if people find out that he was the son of a wagon-breaker and a maid, then his social esteem would be jeopardized. He used to be opportunistic from his early days! Di realised it long time ago, but chose to ignore his crooked habits – however, she continued loving him in the same manner she loved all her kids.

Robin had an elder sister named Soma – she used to look after Robin whenever their mother wasn't around. Soma got married to a rickshaw-puller in Bowbazar at an early age; after there were few attempts by hoodlums in the locality to outrage her modesty, her mother thought it would be in the best interest of the teenaged girls to get married soon.

Soma moved to Bowbazar and started leading a life typical with slum-dwellers – working hard from early morning till late night, attending nature's calls before wee hours of the morning in shared toilets in order to evade prying eyes, taking care of the household in every possible manner with limited resources, etc. But she loved the rich traditions and history of Bowbazar, as she heard from her in-law and friends.

Bowbazar was known as a grey area sandwiched between White Town in the south where the British stayed and Black Town in the north, meant for natives. As a result, migrants from China, Iran, Portugal and even Italy made Bowbazar their home.

Bowbazar was not a typical swanky neighbourhood by any stretch of the imagination, with squatters and eateries gnawing into the pavements, a figurative as well as literal veil of dust covering its old buildings and a cacophony of sounds from shops selling anything from spectacles to ply boards. It was anything but a peaceful neighbourhood that Soma was used to, although it clearly illustrated and dispensed some lessons in tolerance, harmony and peaceful coexistence.

During the early 19th century, Kolkata, the second-most important city of the British Empire, used to be divided into the British 'white town' and the native 'black town'. Those who didn't belong to either of those two categories ended up settling in Bowbazar, turning it into a melting pot of cultures, cuisines, habits and languages.

Bowbazar's gravestones would bear a rare assortment of Italian, British, Buddhist, Jewish, Armenian, Chinese, Iranian, Parsi, Scottish and Portuguese names. Behind the veneer of the government offices which sprung up lately, buildings with unexciting architecture & dull colours, were the memorials, monuments, markets and even a mortuary which bears testimonies to the cosmopolitan past of that small pocket.

The red buildings of Bow Barracks, mostly occupied by the Anglo-Indian communities since independence, used to catch Soma's eyes every time she sashayed along the road. Tiretta Bazar, known by some deformed name, used to be her biggest attraction there, with magnanimous volume of fruits and all kinds of stuff selling there year-round.

The place, one of the most congested and chaotic as it connected Dalhousie with Sealdah station, used to be a treasure trove of Chinese goodies, though Chinese faces were few and far between. There were shops selling noodles, incense sticks, sauces, pork and strings of Chinese sausage. A deluge of people could be seen on weekends to savour Chinese breakfast and slurp soup sold in a broad alley behind a building named Poddar Court, which used to be a heaven for buying electrical and other products at cheap prices.

Soma could not come to terms when one very old and famous mortuary was shut down. The collective whirring of five freezers where dead bodies used to be preserved at L. Madeira, a 200 year old unit, ceased to exist one day all of a sudden – the signboard outside against a white backdrop, with austere black lettering, gave way to a new banner announcing new ownership of the building.

Soma couldn't believe her eyes, and she rushed back home to tell her family and friends about that! It was the same place where her husband's body was preserved after he died from a road accident years ago!

She heard that the place was set up by Henry Joseph and Joe Charles more than 200 years ago and has witnessed both World Wars! The coffin made for Mother Teresa (Saint Teresa) was even made there. One of the retiring owners, Florence Madeira lamented that they were the only ones who knew which chemicals to use to preserve dead bodies for a prolonged period. The same magic of chemistry was perhaps needed to preserve the cultural and religious diversity of Bowbazar, thought Soma!

Subir was less meritorious than Mary and other kids – he often needed his mother's help with studies. An essay competition was coming up at his school, for which Mary had already submitted her chosen essay on the topic.

But Subir started pestering Di to do it for her – the angry mother told him that was the last time that she was going to write for him, as she never liked those sorts of unethical practices (although she used to witness these 'external helps' from parents all along in her own senior school, where her classmates would go to attend parties, compelling their parents to complete unfinished homework for their kids' school)!

Di always thought of those as not only unethical & imprudent, but also as ghastly and loathsome. Diana was a born rebellion and challenged everything that sounded unjustified or inequitable for her.

This was even reflected on the essay she helped her adopted son Subir write for the competition, for which Subir received various accolades. The essay was titled 'Transforming India – Quick Fixes'.

"I love my country, the world's largest democracy and a very diverse country, with 22 different languages written in 13 different scripts, with over 720 dialects. Naturally, there will be many challenges poised when a country so huge and diverse is on its coveted path of being a developed country – I believe we're treading on the right direction, as we constructively deal with some of the grave social concerns that we are facing today; let us discuss those concerns in a nutshell, and try and address those with suggested solutions that may help us attain our greater objective of transforming India.

First and foremost, I'd like to initiate this process by addressing the biggest social concern that we have been encountering for a long time – illiteracy. Although our governments over time have tried to alleviate this major social evil, however, there's lot more to be done, in order to ensure that fair education is imparted to all at every level. Education leads to awareness, which in turn makes us better. The easiest way to ensure free and fair education is uniformity of contents of study between different boards, across the platform, and also making it mandatory for kids to go to school up to a pre-determined level, say minimum Std. X.

Apart from this, we should also do some research and brainstorming to ensure that our education is scientific and advanced, and let us put to side-line any thought which spreads repugnance and anathema by a few. Let us throw out the anachronism that has survived since medieval times, in order to help usher in healthy changes to our education system as a whole.

The next social concern is alleviation of poverty from grass-root level. We can easily take lessons from the USA, where food-stamps, shelter and financial support are provided by the government for displaced persons, or persons with no income. Our employment exchanges should be more proactive and efficient. At the same time, people should be more conscious and wiser not to waste food, and to help others in needs.

More orphanage and NGOs should be set up to deal with extreme situations, and they should be monitored closely, in order to ensure that apart from providing proper care, those bodies are also enabling kids access to schools and higher education. I also feel that our taxation system needs to be revamped a little, in order to levy some taxes for social development to the wealthy.

The huge multi-national corporations doing business in our country should also be paying something for the corpus meant for poor classes and the disabled sections, either as a tax incentive or as part of the existing CSR programs.

Inequality should be eradicated to the extent possible by fair means, in all the fields including employment, retirement, gender-based, religious practices, sexual preference, etc. We should be enlightened enough to realise that all men are created equal, and should be treated accordingly, and not treat others on the basis of caste or other evils noted above.

A case in point may be, mandatory contribution from mega events like IPL to this particular cause, that is, removal of social disparity. This contribution may be used to provide neonatal and antenatal care to pregnant mothers and infants, so that the death-rate due to malnutrition can be controlled. Equitable health-care availability even in remote areas is a must. Rising costs of private healthcare and it's unaffordability by the poor is another area of concern here, which should be regulated strictly.

Crime towards women are on the rise, and even children are not being spared by some of the demons. We have been experimenting with amendments or enactment of stricter laws and regulations, but in vain; the number of predatory incidents is still on the rise, and maybe we need to explore alternative avenues like the ones successfully implemented by some countries.

Same modus operandi can be followed for corruptive practices, another greatest social ill - corruption at all levels is costing our exchequer deeply, and this can be eradicated by harsh enforceable punitive measures, as well as social awakening. Same is the scenario with child-marriage practices still prevalent in many parts.

We also apparently seem to have been treading far off from knowledge explosion and technological innovation that's sweeping across the world. Our complacency, and somewhat irrational suspicion of modern thinking and technology, still holds the country back. We need to inculcate a changed perspective with positivity in this aspect now, and more and more people should get global exposure and experience.

The young generation should be more apt to act as change agents, and work on increasing tangible performances and productivity, in line with the global workforce. Few small-minded Luddite resisting changes or progress should be ignored. And, they should refrain from denigrating everything Indian, and not imitate those quality of other nations which aren't rational for us to adopt.

Population explosion is another biggest social concern that has been a monumental challenge for us, and maybe we should follow the example of China, who has been able to mitigate this problem successfully. Our mind-sets need to be changed regarding birth-control mechanisms, by spreading more awareness, as also by proper education.

People are the greatest natural resources of any country, and it is the people of that country who both define and determine the strengths and weaknesses of their Nation.

Thus, in my opinion, it is the obstinate or anachronistic mind-set of many of us, aided and abetted by our lack of awareness of our rights and responsibilities, our unwillingness or helplessness to fight for social emancipation and economic empowerment, our increasing non-tolerance, etc. -are some of the very basic issues, underlying the more visible symptoms like caste system, illiteracy, crime, corruption or poverty.

Governments should also work closer towards providing adequate nutrition and health to all – this is what economist term as human capital. Let us forge our own future, free from the trammels of materialism, and excel in everything we do.

What is needed is a paradigm shift in the way we think and act, and this is possible only when we enjoy a fair combination of the solutions cited above, in addition to other tangible developments like infrastructure, science & technology and economic advancement. I do believe deeply in my heart that situations are changing, and we can transform someday soon".

Subir transformed into a better student and an avid learner while he was growing up; he hardly scored less than average marks in any subjects throughout his school life from that point on.

However, he begun to associate with wrong kinds of friends during his high school days, hanging out with them on dark corners of alleys and engaging in inhaling forbidden articles - Diana warned him many times about the probable outcome of his poor habits and offences. But he started to accuse Di of being over-protective and sometimes, he even went on to remind his mother that she was not his biological mother, and therefore, she better not tries to command his life.

Diana was heart-broken - but couldn't argue on that painful and heartless allegation; though true, she never thought of any of her kids like that before, that she wasn't their real mother!

The outcome was very much foreseen – Subir dropped out of College during his first year and could never ever go back to studying. Seeing no other way to stop her son from wasting his entire life this way, Diana set up a courier company serving on domestic front for him, so that he can manage operations with not much difficulty.

She used to manage the company during its initial stages and even thereafter intermittently, so that Subir could learn the tricks of the trade, and then silently watch him perform his part. Gradually, he picked up, and became a successful entrepreneur; he contemplated to go global - he even wondered if he should be going public for listing on national stock exchange, etc. but had to quit the idea due to lack of expertise and education on matters like stock companies, initial public offerings, prospectus issues, trading and statutory obligations, etc.

There were times when Diana used to have conflicting thoughts in her mind as to sending her kids to colleges in the US, vis-à-vis putting them in Colleges in India. Corruption, admission scams, dominance of students' union and its flexing muscles, unlawful donations and improper exercise of power by influential people to get their children admitted at elite colleges were some of the very common practices prevalent in India, at the time when Di herself left the country to complete her college in the US.

But, at a time when she was thinking of sending Subir and Mary to their choices of colleges in the US, something happened which Di could never have imagined.

About fifty people in the US were taken into custody, including two prominent Hollywood actresses, some sports coaches and many college administrators for a nationwide college admissions scam that stunned the nation. In one of the largest academic scandal ever prosecuted by the US Department of Justice, hundreds of FBI officers and IRS agents rocked the academic world in an operation titled "Varsity Blues" and arrested those culprits on charges of bribery and corruption involving intermediaries and parents, who purchased admissions of their wards in elite schools like UCLA, Georgetown University, Stanford, Yale and few others!

Celebrities like Felicity Huffman and Lori Laughlin were amongst those named in that scandal – Huffman had incidentally made some comments about her daughter's stressful college application process few months earlier, but chose not to mention anything about the unethical path she treaded herself in order to get her daughter admitted through back-doors!

Rich people buying their children admissions into elite schools wasn't new in the country – there had been allegations about one of the controversial Presidents of the US himself (along with his son-in-law) being involved in adopting similar modus operandi - they were scrutinised and pilloried over their passages to Wharton and Harvard respectively.

However, the new national scandal was unique, in the sense that it involved cheating, falsification and bribery charges.

Quoting an FBI officer who was briefing the media in Boston in less than 24 hours of unravelling that crime, "we're not talking about donating a building so that a school is more likely to take your son or daughter. We're talking about deception and fraud". FBI outlined a scheme where parents went to the extent of paying proxies to write tests and examinations on behalf of their children.

Several ACT/SAT administrators were also charged by the FBI for faking qualifications and scores of children who belonged to wealthy families, in order to get them in to elite schools. It was also alleged that some of the suspects paid bribes amounting to $25 million to get their wards admission in top-ranked colleges. According to the authorities, the scheme also involved parents paying William Singer, founder of a college prep business in California, to get someone else to take the SAT, ACT for their kids.

One of the high-profile celebrities accused in the case was Lori Laughlin and her husband, Mossimo Giannulli – they allegedly paid $500,000 to some of the intermediaries at the University of Southern California, in order to get their two daughters qualify as recruits to the College's crew team, although in reality, none of their daughters participated in the crew.

Another Hollywood star, Felicity Huffman allegedly paid $15,000 for a college entrance exam cheating scam, disguising the amount as donation for charitable purposes! As per testimonies of a witness, Felicity and her actor-husband William Macy met that person at their Los Angeles mansion, where that witness explained to the couple how he 'controlled' a testing centre, and could have someone secretly change their daughter's answers, to which the couple agreed.

The Head Sailing Coach of Stanford University, John Vandemoer was also charged by the feds, along with Rudolph Meredity, the Head Soccer Coach of Yale, and Mark Riddell, a counsellor at a private school at Bradenton, Florida.

As per documents revealed by the US Department of Justice, the above-noted conspiracies involved three stages – first, bribing SAT and ACT exam administrators to allow a fake test-taker, commonly Riddell, either to secretly take college entrance exams in lieu of actual students seeking admissions, or to correct the students' wrong answers at the test venue.

Second stage was bribing athletic coaches and administrators of the universities concerned to facilitate admission of students to elite universities under the disguise of 'athletes', which was one of the criteria of admission into those reputed institutions.

And, the third stage would involve using the façade of Singer's charitable organisation, to conceal the nature and source of the bribes.

Singer, the founder of college prep business, used to facilitate cheating on the SAT and ACT exams for his clients' kids, by instructing them to seek additional time during the exam, deceitfully under the umbrella of learning disabilities, etc. – he would also facilitate the process of obtaining those fake medical documents at extra charges.

Once the additional or extended time was granted through those fake documents, Singer instructed his clients to change the location of the test centres to either a public high school in Houston or a private college preparatory school in West Hollywood.

Singer had already established enough unholy relationships with some test administrators at both the above centres and paid them bribes to the tune of $10,000 per test, in order to facilitate the cheating scheme. He also paid Riddell another $10,000 per student per test, for taking tests on behalf of them. Singer typically got paid anywhere from $15,000 to $75,000 per test per student, the purported payment being camouflaged as donations to charity, thereby entitling his rich clients to take additional deductions in their income tax filings later!

After the scam was unearthed, Diana was really confused – she was in double minds; should she send her kids to US where corruption in academic institution apparently had begun to take off, or should she send them to reputable colleges in India? She obtained some help from some of the academicians she knew from her past. One of them referred her to an expert counsellor named Priya Banerjee.

Priya was an alumnus of Harvard, settled in US – she married a professor there and had two beautiful kids, both of whom were very established in life. The youngest daughter was an alumnus of Cambridge, while the elder daughter passed out from Oxford. Priya used to run a technical guidance service to international students seeking admissions in US colleges – as soon as Di found out about Priya, she decided to seek her help.

However, as it turned out later, this was another mini scam that Priya was running, as she would take an advance of five lakhs INR from a student at the initial stages, and then would seek humongous amount later, depending upon the college in which admission was sought.

So, Diana decided to send Mary for foreign studies and have Subir go to a famous college in New Delhi, under Delhi University. That way, she thought, she will have consolation in her mind that she tried both!

New Delhi was a city most favoured by Diana from her adolescent days – she used to travel to New Delhi at least once a year with her granny and uncle, sometimes accompanied by her aunt Riya. She loved almost everything about New Delhi, starting from its clean roads to the various monuments, shopping, travelling and most of all, eating out.

She used to stay at The Lalit located right on Barakhamba Road adjacent to Connaught Place, her most favourite part of the town, and used to walk around for shopping, eating and having fun.

The first time Di went to New Delhi with her family was when she was studying in seventh grade – they stayed at another decent five-star hotel at Connaught Place – it was an area full of actions, but was very clean, well maintained and great ambience - she fell in love with the area. Its impeccably clean roads, hundreds of fast food and fine dining joints, disciplined crowd, well-mannered businesspeople and the overall ambience of the heritage place amazed her.

She went to Dunkin Donuts for breakfast, Starbucks for coffee and appetizers, McDonalds for lunch and after munching some light food at Burger King in early evening hours, she would go either to Pizza Hut or any decent fine-dining restaurants there – she had huge options to choose from, and those detectable options solely pumped her adrenaline!

Vicky would definitely book decent airlines' tickets in advance for flying into Indira Gandhi Airport; he'll then book first-class coup in Rajdhani Express while returning back. Diana loved it more flying into New Delhi, as she liked taking flights; she also liked the Rajdhani for unlimited food they served, especially in AC 1 coaches.

It was more fun when Riya would accompany them, as they would get total privacy between four of them; at times when just three of them were travelling, sometimes a stranger would share their coup, or sometimes there won't be any co-passenger. They'll be happier if there was no one else in their coup.

If a fourth passenger would join the family in their coup, Diana didn't like it much, due to the fact that many highly-positioned government officials or ministers travelling on that train at the expense of public money would act rudely to the train staff, and would carry a big air around them.

Vicky used to act mischievous with some of them, making funny comments to aggravate them, or turning the air-conditioning vent secretly towards where that passenger was seated (so that the cold air will blow directly at that person), or by making noises when the person started snoring.

Vicky would tie a thread between the two flexible handle-bars dwindling from the sides of doors, so that with every jerking of the compartment, the handles will collide with each other, making a screeching sound; the person will wake up, look around, take a sneak peek at his fellow passengers (all of whom will appear to be in deep sleep), get up, drink glass of water, and then delve back in his heavenly sleep!

God forbid if the passenger passed any foul smell or worse, if he farted – Vicky would get up, grab a deodorant or room freshener; then, he will spray it aiming towards the hind side of the person, making it obvious that he knew who farted! If the passenger farted during his sleep, Vicky would somehow wake him up, by making weird sounds, or by dropping a water-bottle supplied by IRCTC intentionally on the floor and pressing on it with his fingers, to make a squelching sound.

If the fellow still didn't get up amidst all the turbulence, Vicky would fall on his side making it appear like an accidental fall, thus forcing the person to get up – he knew very well how to aggravate people who aggravated him, it seemed.

There were incidents when a fourth passenger in their coup depicted lack of mannerism by constantly gazing or staring at others' food-trays while Diana and her family were eating. Vicky would pick up an item from his own tray, say for example an egg, and would ask the person if he wanted to have it. As most passengers travelling first class in Rajdhani seemed to be vegetarian, they would get agitated.

Sometimes, they will ask the coach attendants or ticket examiners to change their coup, which will act as a boon to Vicky, as he always preferred quiet, decent and well-mannered individuals. Diana and Ritu would have really difficult time to control their laughter with all the nuisances Vicky would resort to sometimes!

The first time Di experienced the comfort and luxury at The Lalit was when the family was en route to Wagah Border - they decided to stay for a night at New Delhi. Diana was in eighth grade then, and they planned to visit Amritsar from

Delhi, to witness the border ceremonies, visit the famous Jallian Wallah Bagh, Golden Temple, etc. Beating the retreat and flag lowering ceremonies at Wagah Attari borders were enjoyed thoroughly by the families – visiting Jallian Wallah Bagh the next morning gave Diana goose bumps; she never forgot the trip!

Jallian Wallah Bagh massacre, which happened barely few months after the Armistice in November 11, 1918 ended World War I in Europe, took place on April 13, 1919 as undivided Punjab was struggling and was in ferment.

Earlier, Punjab had contributed a huge number of soldiers to the colonial government's war efforts – more than 3.5 lakhs of them over a four years period of conflict. Wartime sacrifices of those valiant soldiers from undivided Punjab was forgotten by the British rulers after their return home from all over Europe, to find unemployment in large scale at home. Failures in proper cultivation of crops thereafter resulted in more woes as shortages of food for consumption and skyrocketing prices of food grains added salt to injuries in the minds of people.

Concurrently, as the leaders of Indian independence called for peaceful protests against the draconian Rowlatt Act and a total strike was called on April 6th, a peaceful strike turned violent at the instigation of some sections.

On April 10th, about 20 people were killed when they tried crossing a railway bridge which led to the British-occupied areas – the crowd then turned more violent and some European civilians were killed as an aftermath. A harmless English missionary named Ms. Sherwood was beaten up by the crowd, and the turn of events shook up the British.

Reginald Dyer, a Brigadier-General, was sent to Amritsar with instructions to take a tough stand – he was the third officer sent within 48 hours! As British were panicking and feeling overrun by the Indian nationalists, there were lots of unrest.

Then came the most fateful day in Indian history – as Baisakhi approached on April 13, an enormous crowd gathered at Jallian Wallah Bagh – no clear estimates could be found on the actual number of people present there on that day, although it was evident that somewhere around 20,000 people gathered there.

The mood of the crowd was sombre, and fear was writ large on faces of the people as they started feeling trapped inside – every exit was guarded, and it was impossible for anyone to leave the premises without permission. Even a few who used to consider themselves as pretty close to the British, felt the sudden freezing up of their relationships.

Jallian Wallah Bagh was a garden only by name – it actually was a plot of wasteland, an irregular quadrangle surrounded by houses, and was actually a private property owned in common by several people. The main entrance was a narrow passage.

Dyer arrived at the Bagh with 50 armed soldiers and other personnel with knives and khukris. His soldiers immediately opened fire upon getting his order - 1,650 rounds were fired in ten minutes time, stopping only when they ran out of ammunitions. Dyer made no efforts to provide medical care to the wounded civilians, claiming that it wasn't his duty!

The senseless violence that killed around 600 civilians and wounded thousands later catalysed the Independence movement in India. But what was truly pathetic was the statement from one of the government doctors posted there at that time, who refused treatment to the wounded. That butcher doctor, Lt. Col. Smith, turned away the wounded people, calling them 'rabid dogs.'

The shooting had ended at 5.45 pm, and Dyer imposed a curfew at 8 pm, thus forbidding family members of friends to carry the wounded to hospitals after that time.

Many of the wounded died painfully after profuse bleeding through the night, crying out for water or praying for help. Many died of suffocation, buried under piles of corpses, or drowned in the well there. The next morning, due to intense heat, corpses started disintegrating – mass funerals had to be arranged. No official record of the funerals or number of bodies were maintained by the British – there was a marked disregard from them. None of the officials even bothered to visit the Bagh after the mass massacre.

It was later revealed that the age of those who were martyred on that day ranged from a seven-month old baby boy to an 80-years old man. At least 52 of those who were shot dead on that fateful day by those dirty monsters during those dreadful 10 minutes of mindless firing, were under the age of 18. Amidst all those horrors, rose a lion-heart named Udham Singh, the man who avenged the massacre by shooting dead Michael O'Dwyer at a meeting of East Indian Association in London on March 13, 1940 – around two decades later!

O'Dwyer, a former lieutenant governor of British Punjab, was at the helm of affairs in the undivided Punjab under British rule during the Jallian Wallah Bagh massacre – he had supported Dyer ordering firing at unarmed civilians.

Udham Singh, a revolutionary of Ghadar Party, shot him dead along with wounding two other British officials. His trial lasted for two days, and he was hanged to death in London. His statements before the British Judge will always stay remain a rich history for any nation struggling for independence from foreign rulers.

Transcripts from Udham Singh's trial indicated that he brazenly faced Justice Atkinson, and his last statements to the 'blind' judge went like this:

"I am not afraid to die. I am proud to die. I want to help my native land, and I hope when I have gone, that in my place will come some others of my countrymen to drive the dirty dogs... when I am free of the country. I am standing before an English jury in an English court. You people go to India and when you come back you are given prizes and put into the House of Commons, but when we come to England are put to death.

In any case, I do not care of anything about it, but when you dirty dogs come to India... the intellectuals, they call themselves the rulers.... And they order machine guns to fire on Indian students without hesitation.......killing, mutilating and destroying. We know what is going on in India – hundreds of thousands of people being killed by your dirty dogs… England, England, down with imperialism, down with the dirty dogs."

The family decided to halt for a night at New Delhi and Vicky booked a suite at one of the best hotels in Connaught Place (based on reviews on Trip Advisor and Google Maps) - The Lalit. He wanted his loving niece to overcome the shock she got by visiting Jallian Wallah Bagh that morning, reading all the inscriptions and articles written, and seeing the well and bullet marks all over the place. She always bore a soft and tender heart, feeling others' pain.

It was absolutely necessary at that point to heal her mental conditions by getting something which would divert her mind off the portentous and gloomy day in modern civilisation, especially when reports submitted by the authorities at that time were unpropitious and remorseless. Di wondered why a grandiloquent celebration to mark the event nationally was not ruminated by Indian government even after a hundred years have elapsed!

Vicky used to be a platinum member of Hyatt hotels during his stint at a highly decorated department of the US government in the past - he preferred to stay at Hyatt Hotels worldwide, in order to get access to the Club Lounge, and get complimentary snacks and beverages, amongst host of other benefits available to privileged members of the hotel chain. In addition, he used to get free room upgrades and complimentary pick-ups and drop-offs to the nearest airports.

However, after few years elapsed since his return to India when he didn't book any hotel, Vicky lost his elite membership status in Hyatt, Radisson and Marriott. His frequent-flier miles in US Air, Cathay Pacific and British Airways were already redeemed smartly before expiration though!

Upon arrival at The Lalit in C.P., the family was elated to find superb hospitality, conviviality and cordial welcome – it made them feel at home; they decided to make this hotel their destination in New Delhi for ever. Diana loved the complimentary breakfast buffet there, and she used to spend more than an hour running between the continental counters and a-la-carte stands with eggs and various items made to order.

While Ritu preferred typical Indian delicacies there, Vicky lived his old days with all American breakfast – he started out with fruits and cereal, then had a few of double sunny up eggs, bacon, ham, pepperoni, sausages, home fries, fruit juice and ended with Americano black coffee, his hot favourite in the past, though he was a fan of Brazilian coffee.

For dinner, Diana chose between a wide array of delicacies – Yorkshire lamb, chicken & cheese salad, baked potato & aubergines, peppered pasta salad, roesti & salad, batter fried fish, apple sausage plait, wiener schnitzel, chanakhi, chicken kiev, carbonara, beef stroganoff, chicken teriyaki, lobster, and what not!

As for desserts, she'll go for quiche, or black forest cake, or any of the available tantalizing items she normally would dream of, including chocolate Mikado Mess, Kimberly biscuit cake, apple gualette, chocolate raspberry ganache, pecan tart, tiramisu, marquise, mocha macchiato, red velvet, bacio cake, munster Indiana – just to name a few!

Upon her immigrating to US later, Diana would make sure that her taste buds remain active on one hand and treat her world's most favourite granny Ritu to nice restaurants, on the other. Depending on where she was travelling, she would go to the fine restaurants serving gourmet delicacies with Ritu for dinner.

While in NYC, she frequented to Reb Lobster, Katz's Delicatessen and the likes, but she took turns to get some authentic food from famous restaurants like Hudson Yards, Peter Luger, Akrotiri, Lombardi's, Keens Steakhouse, Tavern on the Green, The Rainbow Room, Totonno's, The Russian Tea Room, Delmonico's, Rao's, et al.

Diana used to love all kinds of food in NYC, and some of the specialties she craved for in specialty outlets, while in New York were fettuccine at Misi, folded cheeseburgers in pita at Miznon, devil in ganache at Mah-Ze-Dahr, wood-roasted mushrooms at Sunday in Brooklyn, malawach at Miss Ada, fried rice stuffed crispy chicken wings at Atomix (although there was no match anywhere for chicken wings at Anchor Bar in Buffalo in upstate NY, close to Niagara Falls), Spanish tortilla with trout roe at Frenchette, banana hotcakes foster at Bessou, Le Ravier at Bistro Pierre Lapin, sugar-cured bacon at Clinton St. Baking Co., Iberico katsu sando at Ferris, Kubaneh at Nur, pancakes at Chez Ma Tante, tater tots at Loring Place, spaghetti and meat balls at Pasta Flyer, fried shrimp tacos at Alta Calidad, braised lamb shank at Sofreh, vanilla soufflé or lobster quenelle at Manhatta, tomato pork noodles at Junzi Kitchen, egg rolls at Olmsted, smoked watermelon ham at Ducks Eatery, caramel stuffed snickerdoodle at Gramercy Tavern, amongst many others.

Back in India, while at Connaught Place, Diana and her family chose between the following restaurants for dinner, if they preferred to eat out: Ambrosia Bliss, Berco's, Parikrama, Peeble Street, White Waters, Ardor, Excuse Me Boss, The Host, Castle 9, and at Radisson Blues. The in-room dining in Lalit was great too, but they used to charge whooping service charges, for which the wise family chose to eat out – eating in the restaurant at the hotel there was problematic due to heavy inflow of local traffic during evening hours routinely.

While in Kolkata, Diana and her immediate family used to go to five-star restaurants and hotels only three or four times a year, to celebrate birthdays, anniversaries (of Ritu and Riya), or great news arising out of events related to Di's education, career and special accomplishments.

They switched between Eden Pavilion, Peshawri, Oasis, Peter Cat, JW Kitchen, Waterside Café, Dum Pukht, West View, Baan Thai, The Square, Mainland China, Vintage Asia, Pan Asian, and the ones at Taj Bengal. 6 Ballygunge Place was a favourite for Ritu, as she loved traditional Bengali cuisine.

Di loved chicken wings served with Jack Daniel's sauce at the outlet of TGIF located in Forum Mall – however, she always felt that the highest purpose of bar food, in all its cheesy, starchy, pinguid, deep-fried trashiness was to sponge up as many bad decisions as possible before one woke up with a katzenjammer.

So, she stopped visiting bars to grab food – the smell of liquor all over any bar used to make her dizzy too!

Di had visited New Delhi more than ten times and she became almost a known face to many in The Lalit; she even became a familiar face to many shopkeepers around C.P.

The longest she stayed there at one go was during their trip to Corbett National Park, when they stayed there for three nights due to inclement weather, before proceeding to Namah Resort in Corbett for two nights; that was followed by another couple of nights' stay at Ahana Resort. The shortest stay at her favourite hotel in New Delhi was for half a day, when they were en route to Prayag and Varanasi to perform periodic rituals for Diana's grandfather Biman and mother Gita.

She loved New Delhi, although there were some reservations and animadversions about extreme weather and rising levels of pollution amongst many about India's capital!

During some long weekends or short vacations, Diana used to visit some of the great places around Kolkata – she frequented Fort Radisson at Raichak, where the family will stay for a night or two, mostly at one of the sprawling bungalows owned privately by some prominent personalities, or at the hotel; Di would play tennis all morning long with her uncle, trying to win all the games.

However, Vicky with his old hands will win mostly, due to his agility and regular practice – Di would turn mad at him; he won't give in, until she won a few matches.

Sometimes, Vicky used to lose some games on purpose, faking double faults or faulty attempted returns; Di used to get back on him then, uttering the same words that Vicky would, when she missed a return or service! Vicky giggled and said, okay, will try harder next time! He had eternally loved Di all his life.

Some other times, they will take a tour to Bakkhali or Sunderbans, and sometimes to Jhargram or Murshidabad, after making reservations through the State government's online portal; the ruling party made conscious efforts in developing eco-tourism throughout the State, and Diana visited many places with the government-operated tour packages, primarily for safety concerns.

Although Mary completed her college with very good GPA, but Subir couldn't complete even his second semesters, as he got into unlawful habits and addictions.

After Diana got him some settlements in professional field, by forming the courier company for him to run, she hoped for the best, while deep inside her mind, she was prepared for the worst – knowing all about that wretched kid from way back when! She had pity for him, not much anger or frustration, as her nature was like that – to forget and to forgive!

Subir soon developed a relation with the lady secretary of his company; soon they got married without informing Di. She only learnt of their marriage once they entered her house after getting married in a temple. Diana was initially shocked, but she had to overcome her true sadness so that Subir's newly wed wife Lali didn't feel outcast – she appeared to be normal; Lali apologised to Di for not keeping her in the loops.

Di arranged for a gala reception for her son at Sikka Palace, near Ballygunge Phari, paying an exorbitant rental fee for booking the huge palace. She contacted the best caterer in town who served eight-course buffet dinner with varieties of appetisers, soups, salads and drinks. A four-tier pineapple cake was ordered from Flurry's in Park Street to make the special occasion a memorable event for all invitees.

Many talked about this grandeur reception for years to come, and the young couple were very excited with all the gifts and blessings they received from everyone. It was a boisterous jamboree, which many termed as one of the glitziest of wedding ceremony shindigs they had ever attended.

Lali was travelling from work back to her in-law's one epoch-making evening by a private bus, as there was a local strike going on and she had no other means of transportation at her disposal at that time.

As she boarded the bus, the conductor touched her inappropriately - Lali immediately raised an alarm. As no one there protested, she felt humiliated and distressed – she decided to get down from the bus in a hurry when she got run over by the rear wheels of the bus, as she skidded from the stairs – one of her legs got entangled between the rear wheels. She was dragged for few metres, after which she finally laid dead on the streets.

That almost cataclysmic tragedy turned into a disaster of apocalyptic proportions to the family. Di would be compelled to rotate her stays between her son and daughter soon thereafter, like a pendulum, making her feel unwanted by the same kids she had rescued and devoted her entire life on!

The incident triggered a panic button on the entire family, especially because Lali had delivered a boy few weeks earlier, and the infant was being breast-fed by his mother! Diana had no choice but to arrange for Subir's marriage again - this time, his wife turned out to be a mental patient, the fact of which wasn't disclosed by her parents or anyone else to Di's family deliberately; the bride's family wanted to get an opportunity to inherit the huge property that Subir would inherit from her mother some day when she's gone.

Diana took the matter less seriously, as she was always a kind-hearted person all her life; she didn't want to make matters worse for the new bride. Instead, she contacted the best psychiatrists in town to regularly attend to the bride and treat her. However, Subir won't be able to father any more child, as the bride was incapable of reproduction.

Thus, Subir accepted the fate and focused on bringing up his son in the nicest possible manner; but, he soon began to associate with street girls for meeting his physical desires, after his second wife had to be admitted to mental hospital after some time, when she wasn't responding positively to treatments at home.

In the process, Subir got addicted to commercial exchange of bodily fluid, and contacted virile diseases. He became so desperate at his newly found habit that he sold off his company to some bidder when he ran out of money to pay those girls. He didn't even change while he was in palliative care, it was evident!

Di wasn't aware of all that until she returned back from Singapore where Mary tied knots with her husband, Vivek. As soon as Di returned, she learnt about Subir's diseases; she had him fly down to the best hospital in New York City, where he spent next few months and returned home all cured physically.

Subir soon fell in love with another woman, with who he started living together. He couldn't marry this lady, as he wasn't divorced from his former wife who was in the mental asylum. She was a good mother to his son from previous marriage though - they lived a moderately decent life from that point on.

Di was somewhat happy to see Subir finally redeeming himself to become a changed person, although he had become infamous for all his poor habits, his repeated marriages and live together arrangement. But he didn't care, it seemed.

Mary had met Vivek, her husband while she was studying International Law at a prominent college in Singapore. Vivek was a business tycoon having an array of holding companies under his Group, in the fields of real estate, educational institutions and movie production.

Mary had consistently been a brilliant student since her primary days, just like her foster mother. Diana used to teach her at home every single day upon her return from school – she went to a famous catholic school for girls in Middleton Row area and always scored very high, sometimes ranking first. Mary had affinity towards tennis like her mother, and she used to go to CDFC near Gurusaday Dutta Road.

Di got her daughter enrolled in CDFC privately, without getting official membership of the club, as she wasn't into showmanship or being snobbish in any manner - she didn't want her kid to get influenced by 'suddenly rich' or 'non-holistically brought up' kids there.

The management of the club was very cordial; there were some famous sportspersons in their committee too. So, when one of the coaches imparting tennis lessons to private students misbehaved with Mary, her mother immediately brought the matter to the attention of the committee, in order for redressing the problem.

Diana was heart-broken when the committee tendered their apologies for the indecent gesture of the coach on one hand, but tactfully denied any involvement of the club in the matter, as Mary was not a member or child of a member of the club. So, Diana decided to take her daughter out of the place and got her admitted in the same club she used to play during her childhood – DCS in Deshapriya Park.

But she didn't forget to give a Parthian shot to the club executive who was present there, telling him that he was a churlish piece of crap. Di was becoming more aggressive as she aged, based on her bitter experiences which had been rocking her life from her days at her senior school, when some classmates got away with heinous crimes committed against her, against which the school authorities chose to keep tight-lipped; it was evident that Di was constantly being denied justice right from that point on, and she started protesting out against wrongdoers.

Mary was a very sociable, amicable and intelligent kid, just like her foster mother, who used to have lots of friends. But she chose only a handful to be her true friends, and treated everyone else as acquaintances, with the same level of friendliness, sharing and caring as she had with others. Mary also became a karate expert, as she got enrolled in a prominent karate club near Judges Court Road, and successfully participated in many tournaments.

As she grew up, Mary almost developed all the traits and habits of Diana, including her reluctance of wetting hairs every day during bathing. She was loved by almost everyone around her, although some of her classmates were jealous of her in many matters, which she chose to ignore. She ranked very high at both her junior and senior schools and got admitted in a very prestigious institution at Singapore.

She received acceptance letters from various famous colleges all over the world, primarily because of the excellent letters of recommendation she received from her school, coupled with her high scores not only at school level, but also in SAT and AP tests. Di let Mary decide on her college, because she had enough confidence on her daughter.

Di used to visit Mary every now and then, including the long weekends, and take her around to places of interests. The safety on the streets out there was probably the best in the world - Di thought of the city as one of the safest cities in world. They even went to Malaysia, Bangkok, Thailand on summer breaks together, and the mother-daughter duo were extremely happy – they missed Subir's company, but knowing his bad habits, they decided it was best if he wasn't around, for mutual interests.

Mary scored exceedingly well in her graduation too, after which, she obtained a very lucrative offer from a world-famous company as Legal Officer during campus placement, with a highly attractive package – Di readily gave her nod to that offer. So, Mary started with this company right away. She used to travel to many countries and places on business, soon becoming a famous young lady in corporate world.

Mary had met Vivek while in College – he used to be a faculty in Business Law - it was kind of love at first sight. His family was settled in U.K; it was a close-knit loving family of four persons. He introduced Mary to his parents and brother through videoconferencing after dating for around a year, following which their engagement ceremony took place in an informal manner, as he was pursuing his Ph.D. at that moment - he didn't want too many distractions. However, the couple agreed on an elaborate wedding arrangement in the near future – it was indeed a huge ceremony.

They eventually tied the knots in Italy at a villa by the sea, on an island by the coastal area. Guests from almost all over the world congregated for the elaborate ceremony – few were wearing brummagem tiaras and sashes, in an effort to conceal their haughty nature, without realising that many could detect the artificial ones from genuine ornaments.

An unbelievable sum of money was spent on the wedding reception, especially on the fabulous food that were served. Di felt that it was otiose to spend so much on catering when few people had responded to the invitation, due to the fact that many invitees couldn't turn up due to their pre-occupations or other engagements.

Diana was wearing a white silk saree embellished with vibrant embroidery – she was looking fabulous. As soon as Di reached the venue, she stated that she was really famished, and wanted to find out what was in the menu – she loved to see one of her most favourite dishes from Philippines there – an unlimited assortment of viands! She started digging in the sumptuous lunch with steamed rice and three viands – a meat, a seafood and a vegetable dish. She was so happy, as always, to have great choices for her food!

Di had always been a foodie since her early childhood days. She mastered the art of eating over time, be it Indian, oriental or western dishes. Her granny Ritu used to force her to eat more than she could handle, while Di was growing up, thereby enhancing her elastic appetite.

Ritu, being a lady from the old school of thought, used to think that more eating made kids healthy; so, she compelled Diana to eat more. In addition, Ritu was kind of an overprotective lady, who showed signs of mollycoddling in bringing up her loving granddaughter, Di!

After Diana's grandpa's demise, Ritu didn't feel like cooking anymore, as her husband Biman used to love every food that was ever served to him, be it a snacking item or lunch or dinner or anything. He cherished his food and preferred the idea of living for eating.

After his demise, Ritu used to feel very bad to cook anything, as she started missing her partner for over six decades. That was when Diana started getting the taste of outside food, as Vicky would order home deliveries from various outlets like Pizza Hut, Dominos, KFC, Spices N Sauces, Pao Chien, Hatari, Six Ballygunge Place, Bhojohori Manna, and other outlets.

Di loved pan fried farmhouse pizza with extra cheese, garlic bread and chicken wings – so anytime she would get an option to choose between various home deliveries, she would most definitely go for pizza outlets. Once in a while, she would go for oriental dishes – she liked mixed fried rice, chicken in white sauce and chicken sweet corn soup (if she ordered Chinese food, which will mostly be her choice of dishes).

However, sometimes she reluctantly agreed to order Bengali dishes because her immediate family loved it – Diana would order hilsa and bhetki only; other dishes would have to be ordered by Vicky, as she was not much of a vegan. She loved mutton curry and any item containing chicken.

As for desserts, Di had some special affinity for coffee and even caffeine-free lattes, especially after she visited Kentucky as a senior correspondent. She would describe the latte in one of her favourite joints by saying that though the taste was a bonus - the real draw in that caffeine free latte was the CBD, or cannabidiol oil; the CBD served in that lattes were derived from Kentucky-grown hemp, decocted from flowers and leaves with hot dairy or coconut milk.

Everyone who were present there used to have a heck of a time with her choice of words to describe her admirations; most around her loved the tone of her voice while she talked about food.

As for good barbecue pork ribs, Di used to tell the chefs that the litmus test of good barbecue was whether or not they had that moist-off-the-bone quality! She used to throw away conventional thoughts – she would defy traditional ways of events wherever she felt that any kind of cruelty to any living beings was being involved. She smashed all those superstitious talks to smithereens.

During her adolescence period, Diana was getting heavier gradually with all the oily, spicy and fatty food consumed by her. She was routinely engaged in various sporting activities like swimming and tennis, which kind of negated the extra fat absorption. However, it begun to show up on her teenage years - she never lost weight until she started going to college.

Food was like her best treat, and Vicky was kind of coerced to promise her great dining offers at star hotels and restaurants, if she did well in her exams, etc. – that was like a harmless bribe to get things done at Diana's end! Vicky somehow felt on some occasions, when he realised that his efforts to convince Di not to eat so much fat, were rather otiose or indolent.

In economics, that situation could have been coined easily as a zero-sum one, where the gains of one party, that is Di, were exactly balanced by the losses of another party, that is, Vicky – as no net gain or loss was created. Such rare situation arose as Diana got her taste-bud happy, but at the expense of her obesity, where Vicky ended up footing the bill; but he felt very happy to see the smiling face of her dear niece, especially after finishing her meal!

On a serious note, Diana's 'apple-pie order', meaning perfect order of food, was really articulate and carried a lot of wisdom. The only time she didn't like Vicky was when the latter would tend to speak in homiletic aphorism, which made Diana tiresome at times, although she knew very well that her uncle didn't mean any harm. He was merely trying his level best, as usual, to convey to Di some concise, terse, laconic and memorable expressions of matters relating to general truth and principles, so that she can become a better person in every manner, which she eventually did become.

She was always a foodie who enjoyed her favourite meal with her favourite television shows. While in India, she wasn't big on watching television; however, during her college years in the USA, Di used to watch various TV shows.

Amongst her favourite shows there, was the series Billions, which she later described to her friends at her college in a very interesting manner. She said that the show featured two outsized, magniloquent protagonists who were constant foils to one another: light and dark, good and evil, both cut from same ambitious cloth and therefore, destined to lock in an endless pas de deux of power.

Her observations were always admired by her professors and friends alike, especially when they boiled down to references to literatures or Greek mythology. She had special place in her heart for the Trojan War in Greece.

Her famous statements as to the characters on Greek tragedies were talked about in her close circles for years to come. One fine evening, during a great supper at a local Greek restaurant, when asked about Greek mythologies, Diana had said: 'Characters in Greek tragedies usually had a hamartia, or fatal flaws. Hubris, pride, presumption and arrogance were some of the chief traits that brought down peasants and emperors alike.'

As regards one of her friend's love life, Diana had made a far-reaching observation that touched everyone's soul, at her first job. One of her peers, a guy named Kevin was going through tough times in his relationship with his fiancée, as she was suspecting that Kevin was cheating on him. Di knew very well that Kevin didn't date anyone at work; after work, he used to go back straight to her, as they were in a live in relationship. Still, his fiancée will be sceptical of his whereabouts, apparently as she was leery and suspicious by nature.

Upon learning that Kevin had a fight the night before, Di called up his fiancée to request her to meet Kevin after work at the courtyard of their office building, so that the couple can sort out their differences in the non-avarice serene milieu. The quiddity of that place was surely to yield some jaunty outcome, which was resplendent in its luscious green surroundings – Di was almost sure that the conversation will transmogrify them to be imperturbable, which in turn will rejuvenate their sweet relationship.

Indeed, the plan was working well, until some nosy co-workers tried sneaking in, to lend their intrusive or prying ears to quest their nebby nature; as soon as Di observed those inquisitive folks gathering there, she stopped it.

Diana had told those overly-inquisitive friends / colleagues in a soft voice, that the couple had just went to talk, as they wanted to get it off their chests, which some people keep holding onto for years, just cankering their soul, but they won't know what to say. So, it was better if everyone laid off and let the couple chalk out their peace-talks silently and without any interference. The couple indeed sorted out their differences to lead a happy conjugal life thereafter, partly due to the observations made by their friend Di.

Di was never anywhere close to be a sycophant or flunky person – she fought for everything she accomplished in life; she earned it through hard work, tenacity, conscientiousness and firm resolve in a disciplined manner, with honesty and perseverance. The assiduity with which she could wear down her opponents was remarkable. Many of her friends from school, college and work tried to emulate her qualities, so that they can also excel in life as a person.

She wasn't big on junk food available on the streets, although some stalls selling egg-chicken rolls near Gariahat were some of her unplanned stop en route to shopping or leisure time walking.

Ritu was always an evergreen lady, with energies comparable to those of teenagers; she used to take Diana on leisurely walk on the streets when they felt like, weather permitting. Ritu never ever felt senescence – the process of becoming old. She always accompanied Di back and forth school and home; she always made sure she went with Diana on her various activities – in other words, Diana and Ritu were inseparable in mind and body!

It was always a dream that Diana kept hidden inside her heart, that someday, when she worked and became rich, she would offer the very best life had to offer, to her favourite granny. Di realised since her childhood that Ritu did much more than what a normal mother would do, despite her old age and ailments, especially with osteoarthritis and high blood glucose levels.

The dream did materialise later when Di reached the peak of success and fame, and she took Ritu to exotic vacations, royal cruises and to world famous fine dining restaurants. Vicky wasn't fortunate enough to join them, as he was dealing with unending legal battles at home.

After their honeymoon in Athens, the newlywed couple Vivek and Mary returned to Singapore; Diana returned to India. It was only then that she heard about the shocking news of Subir selling off his company and getting addicted to bad habits again.

Ultimately, she had no other option than to ask Subir to move out, as he was a big drag on wealth and reputation of Di – everything she worked for so hard in life could not have been spent on lousy addictions of her spoilt son!

She bought a two-storied house in Tollygunge for Subir; she also put her grandson in a convent boarding school in Kurseong, Darjeeling, in order to keep the kid away from his vagabond father.

Subir, in the meantime, started a live-in relationship with one woman who had kids from her previous marriage. He indeed proved to be a shame for Di, contrary to everything she had hoped for him when Diana adopted him. But she was happy that Subir was saved from his dangerous disease, thanks to best medical treatment at NYC at a state-of-the art facilities.

Mary, on the other hand, did well in career and family, balancing both in a nice fashion; she raised two kids – a son and a daughter. They eventually moved back to Kolkata after the nice couple retired – they put their kids to nice colleges in the USA, after they finished schooling at Singapore; both their son and daughter got married and settled down in the US.

Vivek and Mary both visited their children once in a while, when they spent quality family time together. They bought a spacious bungalow with lots of trees and landscaping in a place near Kidderpore, away from the chaos – their family seemed to be a very happy and successful one.

Even though they both had retired, the couple continued to be active in their lives by starting a franchise operation in financial management consultancy for elite classes spread throughout the globe, mostly online. Having lived and worked in different places, the couple adjusted well by dealing with polyglot clientele and businesspeople associated with them across the world - whatever they made through their business, it was deemed adequate for their survival.

Debt-financing, business plans, liquidation, amalgamation, bankruptcy proceedings, etc. were the lines of business chosen by them. They spent private moments in their Jacuzzi, hiding behind the long boundary walls – the couple's occasional rendezvous was a secluded bower in the garden; who said they were old?

As her children had already grown up and got settled in life, Di wanted to turn an unfulfilled dream she had been nurturing in her minds for years, a reality.

Diana wanted to take a closer look into the streets of Kolkata so that she can leave something for generations to come – she decided to write a few articles in one of the popular English newspapers about her detailed research, analyses and findings with solutions she sought to make streets safer and better. That way, she thought that her contributions towards the society will be found useful for people, as well as future administrations, so that positive changes can be made to make the streets of Kolkata safer, enjoyable and free of disruptive activities.

She was in her eighties but quite agile – she didn't have anyone to care for in her family. Her grandchildren from her daughter were all in reputed institutions abroad; Subir's son was also in a boarding school in North Bengal. Di felt that she had spent a bulk of her life devoted to her extended family with foster children – now she felt that it was time for doing commoners some good through her writings.

She also knew that only a few people manage to leave permanent footmarks on earth through their creation or activities; others leave earth without any major contributions. In the case of latter categories, their names would probably be remembered by their children, grandchildren or at the tops, their successive generations, at the most. But, no one after that will even know who they used to be, not to mention their names.

However, for those fortunate few who were able to leave some kind of footmark on common life, people will always remember them either through history, science, literature or performing arts and other notable fields. Name of Achilles, the Greek hero of Trojan War and the greatest warrior of all times, even portrayed as the greatest one in Homer's Iliad, will never be forgotten.

Similarly, names of Sir Newton, Einstein, Shakespeare, Tagore, Napoleon, St. Theresa, Swami Vivekananda and many legends in various fields will always be etched on human minds for as long as people roam the earth. So, she should also try to leave some kind of her footprint, contemplated Diana.

Initially, Di spent a lot of time speaking with pedestrians, cab drivers, bus drivers, passengers and hawkers relating to the problems they faced in their everyday lives. It wasn't that she didn't know about those issues, but she wanted to be sure, so that she can pen down facts based upon corroborative evidence and supportive documents, which can be further vetted by appropriate agencies, etc.

A lot of footwork followed for quite a few years, following which Di became very conversant with all the major problems and menaces faced by all sections of the community, except by those with vested interests, related to the streets. She also interviewed many authorities and councilmen, in order to derive a conclusive solution to the epic problems.

At first, she thought about writing a book about it, as she always had flair for writing – it wasn't anything new to her; however, Di realised that not everyone can afford to buy her book.

Thus, she made an informed decision to have her research work published in a reputed local newspaper in the form of articles lasting through several weeks, so that a bulk majority of literate people can derive the essence of her articles – she hoped some collective actions would be resorted to following publication of her articles; at a later time, she can compile the articles to publish a book, probably her final one, she thought.

She soon approached the Chief Editor of the newspaper, who already knew who Diana was – it was a moment of great pride for the editorial team there, as Di was not only a superstar during her prime time, but she had also done her high school internship for a week there decades ago. There was a picture of Diana in her school attire shaking hands with the erstwhile editor-in-chief, hanging on a wall across the main reception area, with a writing in bold: 'we are privileged to have you as our intern during your high school days, Diana Madam'! It was indeed an honour for the noble octogenarian lady.

After signing an agreement and complying with necessary documentation, Diana was invited for a pre-launch event party at Marriott Hotels, where the city's most influential and powerful men and women applauded the short and crisp presentation Di delivered, after the usual welcome speech and garlanding, etc. were completed.

The articles that followed over the next several weekends' special column on that newspaper were not only inspired by Subir's father's fate, but also a culmination of hard foot-work, interviews, researches and long hours spent by the old single lady – a classy, smart, eloquent speaker, soft-spoken but sharp and intelligent, and of course, highly educated and with treasure trove of experiences. Her entire writings on the topic were a big hit soon.

"Streets of Kolkata – Epic Problems:
Menace No. 1

Vendors / hawkers choking streets of Kolkata:

Street vending in Kolkata goes back all the way around the time of Partition of East Pakistan (now Bangladesh) from India, when lakhs of refugees swamped into Kolkata - they were forced to take street vending as a means of survival. The fortunate few were let in their houses by relatives and friends – but most refugees had no other alternative but to build shelters in various areas to have roof on their head; they took to street vending as a source of income to support their families.

Some of the privileged ones who got shelter in their relatives' or friends' houses in prominent areas continued to live there.

Eventually a few of those refugees became so very fortunate that they occupied the spaces either through meagre rental charges, or by virtue of various provisions under pertinent acts of tenancy et al.

The columnist personally knows of two such descendant families still occupying the spaces at a prime location, who subsequently took over almost the entire building by various means and turned those into two of the most popular Saree stores in South Kolkata – one of those now-turned billionaire pays only 800 rupees for two floors of one house as rent per month; the other one pays 1,200 rupees per month for four floors!

If the volume of space they occupy is evaluated in today's market value, the rental charges they are paying won't even come to a percentage of what it should have been in today's valuation!

Anyways, barring the fortunate few, street vending was one of the easier occupations prevalent at that time with minimum capital or no capital, as they would borrow stuff from local shops (either by pawning valuables or at high-interest rates borrowing), repay the creditors either at the end of the day, or at agreed-upon later times. Many local residents of Kolkata who failed to find a gainful employment or didn't have the means to start a business, eventually joined the people migrating from Bangladesh in street vending, finding it to be turning out as a lucrative business with gradual take-off.

Long after the British Raj ended, many Bengali 'babus' couldn't find a way out to come out of traditional office jobs their parents have inculcated their minds into over a period of time, generations after generations - they refrained from venturing out into business world. They were worried as to non-regularity of fixed income predominant in businesses in Kolkata at that time; therefore, they chose to stick to typical salaried jobs at public sector.

Those who crossed the maximum age limit typically imposed for government jobs in India, along with those who really excelled in their fields of education, mostly moved into corporate world or otherwise.

Another burning factor historically prevalent in Bengal is lack of proper employment opportunities. All political parties promise bundles of opportunities and employment assurances to the youths of Bengal through their election manifesto, with very minimal positive outcome once they were elected to power this has been going on since our Independence!

Educational system in this part of India needs complete revamping, with poor knowledge of English being a major lagging factor for less competitiveness in outside world for students of Bengali medium schools. Computer education was included in syllabi at a much later time; shortfalls arising out of those and other skills resulted in poor employability of many youths, especially those from rural Bengal.

No government till date has adequately addressed those issues - lack of industrialisation had a ripple effect on the once beautiful State. Agriculture had been a major occupation for rural families – but, increase in costs with lack of corresponding economies of scale, has forced many such families to resort to alternative means of income generation.

Education, like some other very important basic requirements guaranteed by our Constitution, is full of flaws and inequalities – it is only the very few privileged ones that gets the essence of true education, which is beyond dreams for the vast majority primarily due to its humongous costs and external factors. Reservations and quota systems may also attribute to lesser or rational employment opportunities. Those factors have all added up to the point where a common youth with average education will find it extremely difficult to earn a decent living in Bengal.

Many of those youths will definitely venture into one of the easiest ways of income generation through street vending and hawking. Once they can gather a few lakhs of rupees from some sources, they can set up a stall or 'Dala' on a street close to where they dwell, by virtue of association with some politically connected people, to start dreaming big. Their overhead expenses are minimal, due to the fact that a majority of them don't pay taxes, don't have salaried employees, don't have manufacturing or trading costs (other than payments to 'mahajans' – their debtors), etc.

And, the worst part is, none of their businesses are regulated; or is it better to state that, they don't fall under compliances to most laws and regulations, like Fire Safety certification, Environment Clearances, etc.? They don't have to file any reports to any authorities, thereby making them immune to most laws and regulations. They practically have no watchdogs over their businesses – only thing needed for them is a trade licence, which is normally available to all with certain add-on 'fees'.

Political parties provide backings to hawkers and vendors across streets of Kolkata to shield them from police or municipal bodies' corrective actions, if indeed they had the courage to enforce the law without political intervention or other undue motivation and/or vested interests.

The quasi-legal system prevalent here in sales and purchases of 'Dalas' (the sellers and buyers of open spaces on pavements and street-corners would sign a formal agreement on a non-judicial stamp paper, which itself is questionable in the eyes of law) have slowly transgressed into an informal system over the years, in which the buyers and sellers of said open space meant for public will execute an agreement with the dominant union leaders on such union's letterheads.

Thus, union offices who command the pertinent area, be it Dalhousie, Esplanade, Gariahat, Shyambazar or any other place, will offer their blessings to the occupants of those spaces through the signed agreement, either at the local offices of the unions, or at the house of various politically connected influential leaders, which in turn will give an extra layer of protection to those encroaching on our pavements and streets.

Add the woes of illegal parking under the protection of another wing of those unions (who collect hefty amount of monthly fees from their agents collecting parking charges from motorists, bikers, etc.), thus congesting the street further, resulting in almost no spaces left for pedestrians and common men – men and women to those belong these streets and pavements in reality.

The hawkers' union members maintain records of every hawkers, encroachers and parking attendants, with their names, addresses, pictures, location, dimension of area covered under its jurisdiction, etc. The sellers and buyers sign the notebooks periodically, as also when said 'Dalas' change hands – no transactions are permitted without the consent of the concerned union member or leader, who gets to enjoy a share of his chunk in addition to the 'officially agreed upon amount', in the form of donations, gifts and other unholy amenities and perks.

With advent of technology, many of these unions have started digitising notebooks, where serial numbers are assigned to the hawkers and vendors by identifying location of the 'shop' or 'Dala' by measuring exact distance of the spot from nearest street crossings. The database records the geographical position of the shop with landmark typically assigned to prominent, as well as, established shops and establishments in the vicinity.

Spaces thus encroached are even rented out by the actual 'occupant' to others, through an agreement signed in the union office where terms and conditions are formalised; rental payments, etc. are done formally through affixation of revenue stamps as validity semblance! After the advance or post-facto agreement, there is one essential element of transaction which is not recorded anywhere, either for purchase or sale or rent of those illegal encroachments – the quintessential part where a one-time payment (commonly referred as 'salami') changes hands from the new buyer/tenant to the seller/landlord/lessor!

This amount is undisclosed for mutual interests, as it is usually a huge amount of money depending on the area, location, proximity to landmarks, etc. To make it more interesting, a hefty amount of money goes to various vested interests' groups, who in turn, returns the favour by looking the other way around, when it comes to administration, law and order, or other issues. As has been noted and pointed out by many, most of the stalls draw electricity illegally from adjoining buildings and establishments, putting the entire neighbourhood at risks.

Drawing multiple electricity lines from a single connection to a business or household (with typically 3 to 5 Kw of load) through blessings of the concerned unions expose all the adjacent shops and establishments prone to fire and other hazards, as most of the hawkers use plastic sheets to cover their shops from rain and sunlight - many store various inflammable articles there too.

Utility companies in power sectors don't issue meters to anyone without a valid address. So, the hawkers take the easiest way out by having their unions attach wires to the meter boxes issued to adjacent shops and establishments, by paying certain amount to the union, who in turn pays some of it to those shops and establishments, primarily by coercing them to accept their 'proposals'.

The dedicated team of the union makes sure that for each four or five hawkers' stalls, a dedicated miniature circuit breaker on the switchboard is clumped for their stalls. No one can protest against these illegal practices - in case someone is 'out-of-his mind' to protest, s/he will be threatened with dire consequences; in some instances, those violators have even caused irreparable damages to the ones who did protest against any of the unlawful actions by hawkers' unions.

However, God forbid if a disaster strikes or mother nature fits into rage; if a devastating fire breaks out gutting many shops and adjacent business organizations or affecting many people, all those vested interests groups start denying having any allegiance or even knowledge of those hawkers/vendors carrying out their businesses therein. As a matter of fact, those groups will immediately try their level best to tip off the individuals whose negligence might have caused the devastation, so that something else can be blamed upon!

Despite civic rules allowing hawkers to occupy only one third of a pavement at a distance of 50 feet away from the nearest intersection, hawkers in Kolkata have almost occupied every nook and cranny of pavements, and even a portion of the street, with their structures. Although some authoritarian bodies have tried a few consorted efforts in the past to ensure compliance with the civic rules, but it was temporary, like anything else.

Things fall back to 'normal' once the special drive is over - it may be termed as an eyewash to public. More than half a million hawkers and street-vendors across Kolkata have turned the City of Joy to City of Bhoy (fear) to general public. Not a single government here has dared to lose votes by removing the illegally built structures and encroachments!

Pedestrians suffer a lot due to the ever-increasing encroachments on pavements meant for safe walking. Number of accidents will be more frequent, especially near major intersections and street crossings, as pedestrians are now forced to walk on carriage ways. For elderlies and differently abled people, it becomes a nightmare to walk on the pavements; for ladies, many indecent touches and gestures are noticed on crowded pavements.

In some cases, few of the hawkers were engaged in such misdeeds; if you have the power to engage in a brawl, go ahead to protest – or else, just deal with it and forget about it! The writer has personally noticed many hawkers glaring at girls while they were walking by those lunatic hawkers' stalls, especially during non-peak hours, against which the writer gave them a piece of her mind.

Running to police or civic authorities won't yield any positive resolution, for reasons stated above. Most Police officers in Kolkata typically won't help people who have no connections or who aren't politically or otherwise can be considered as an influential person – this is tragic but true. During the erstwhile regime of ruling party, many police stations will seek permission from local leaders when complaints were lodged by ordinary citizens against someone.

Under the current regime, many of those police authorities will refrain to take any conclusive action unless they get nods from local leaders of ruling political party, as if they were serving the party and getting paid from their party fund! It's the citizen's money that pay their salaries and other fringe benefits, but in return, citizens are turned away from filing complaints when they fall victim of a crime. This particular political party has been a shame on the face of Bengal! They came to power by promising positive changes, but alas!

The columnist personally had been a victim of police inactions, and in some case, their over-actions. Our house was under the jurisdiction of Lake PS until the administration changed it to Rabindra Sarobar PS. Many officers and junior staff in Lake PS are known to a local criminal who has several Court cases pending against him – he has spent some time in jail too – he is out on bail on at least five criminal cases, but gets away with almost everything only because he is 'friends' with many officers and staff of Lake PS (and now, Rabindra Sarobar PS).

The miscreant in question spends considerable time with those officers and even invites many of them to his house (lives on the first floor of the house we live in) - he has unholy nexus with them. Thus, when he assaulted my uncle on September 2015 along with his elder brother, after my uncle protested against their concerted efforts to steal our electric meter unlawfully, Lake PS was a sitting duck when my uncle went to report the incident after serious injuries.

The Duty Officer kept my uncle waiting for ever, while he was bleeding profusely from ears, nose, lips and whole body following the brutal beating he took from those two criminals. No inquiry was ever made, or no charge-sheets were filed before three years elapsed, until my uncle had to file a case in Court against police inaction. The charge-sheet the Police submitted following court order was concocted to suit the needs of the two criminals!

On the other hand, Lake PS immediately called the criminals who beat up my uncle after he went there to lodge a complaint, and had those duos file a counter-complaint. Lake PS was quick enough to accommodate their false complaints and submitted charge-sheet against my uncle in less than six months!

Things didn't change much after change of jurisdiction to Rabindra Sarobar PS, and the criminal duo are continuing to enjoy the unlawful hospitality and favours from the latter – complaints repeatedly to higher authorities went unheeded. This is Kolkata Police in reality. They won't act unless you are politically connected or are very 'pocket-friendly' to them!

Going back to the issue of 'dalas' swamping turning life in neighbourhood miserable, it also has turned life in upscale homes ugly. From making their neighbourhoods tinderboxes to making garbage dumps out of sidewalks, from making public urinals out of thoroughfares to making pavements dark and inaccessible during nights due to heavy plastic covers hanging under streetlights, these 'dalas' have become a number one nightmare for thousands of citizens. These citizens find it truly galling about the support these hawkers/vendors get from the system (civic, police, fire and other authorities).

Some house-owners from places like Rash Behari Avenue, Dover Lane, Lake Road, Gariahat Road and adjacent areas have even moved to different locations after they failed to live a normal hassle-free life in their homes. Some of them even failed to sell off their previous homes due to lack of legitimate prices, hampered by the hawkers' encroachments, often extending under the staircases and entranceways of their houses.

Some people find out in a harsh way that promoters and developers are not interested to deal with the hawkers, who have strong support of the 'system'; some find no one interested in renting those houses due to choked entry and exit points, and even lack of daylight inside the houses from plastics, tarpaulin and string of various objects used by the hawkers outside the houses, to cover up their stalls from rain and heat – they don't even care a tad about the house-owners and tenants therein – all they are about is to keep on carrying out their business as usual.

Many residents in those hawker-infested areas face problems driving their cars in and out of their houses, either because some temple or make-shift teashops or other stalls constructed by those hawkers right in front of their driveways, sometimes eating into the driveways. Some residents complain that they find it difficult to even avail of public transport, as police authorities erected guardrails to stop hawkers from spilling on the road - those guardrails hinder the normal ingress and egress of the residents from their houses to the designated stops for public transportation.

The situation worsens after dark, when the pavements turn pitch dark and filthy with litters and garbage dumped after closing of stalls for the day. And if someone gets hurt by accidentally tripping there, life becomes pathetic for the victim, as the doctors who will see the person will probably ask for all kinds of diagnostic tests performed before prescribing a single medicine – many doctors typically get 25% commission from diagnostic tests from the centre of their choice, and really gets upset if such tests are done from somewhere else.

If the victim of the accident goes to a government hospital in the city, he will be made to wait for some time in an unhygienic condition and in all probability, inaccurate diagnosis will be carried out – there have been incidents when a patient's right arm was plastered in government-run hospital, while the patient had a fractured left arm!

However, if the victim goes to a private nursing home, then he will probably get good treatments, but at the cost of a fortune – many privately-owned hospitals and nursing homes are known to randomly admit patients in order to inflate the bill; some even keep dead patients in ventilation for days, just to reap off as much as they can from the dead person's surviving kin et al. So, you're in a fix either way, as very few things are actually joyous in the great City of Joy.

The administration apparently wakes up from hibernation right after a major disaster strikes, and more so if the matter is publicised in news media and television channels. Some TV channels are quick to televise "breaking news" or headline news, followed by some shows where people from many facets of life, mostly unrelated to the actual victim, will sit and discuss various odds and ills of life on television channels over cups of tea, and render their expert opinion on the hot topic – but, like anything else, people will forget the tragedy shortly.

The topic will turn cold soon thereafter, with another major incidence or tragedy or breaking news in another part of the city! Some self-declared proponents of ruling political party are definitely going to voice their 'unbiased opinion' on the issue at hand, trying to fool the viewers into believing that the person is really not biased – and the saga goes on. The denegation or repudiation of facts gets distorted during their discussion, with no avowal.

As far as the Administration is concerned, all concerned departments will suddenly become super-efficient overnight. They will lodge suo moto FIRs (first information report) against 'unknown persons' or persons actually not the mastermind or in the nucleus of the cause of accident, just as sort of eyewash.

Political parties will almost immediately announce offering financial assistance to the victims or their families, notwithstanding the fact that tragedy might have been induced by direct or indirect actions of the 'victims' – hawkers ended up getting twenty thousand rupees after a recent fire in Gariahat where the cause of fire was accidental spark from illegal electrical connections by hooking done by the affected hawkers!

In Bengal, even if someone consumes country liquor known as 'hooch' and dies, his next of kin will get rupees two lakhs! One poor blacksmith said once that he'll consume such hooch when he gets old and die, so that his family can get the money from the government for their well-being! Again, tragic but true.

Some governments have tried to make streets and pavements clutter-free, but only temporarily. The vote bank and monetary gain are two of the major motivations for the governments which have worked in favour of the hawkers and street-vendors. In certain sections of the City, there were efforts to relocate the hawkers to nicely constructed supermarkets or buildings; however, after some time, the clutter-free pavements fell back to hawkers, many of them either related to the ones who previously owned stalls there, or to other groups of hawkers. Their steadfast loyalty to the ruling party pays off that way!

The transactional leadership behaviour is a hybrid between the nomothetic and idiographic leadership behaviours. These include the autocratic, democratic, and laissez-faire leadership styles, and the latest ruling party's style is more apparently leant towards a mix of autocratic and dictatorial style prevalent in 'Hi Hitler' era! The gargantuan appetite of some of the leaders from this party has blurred out some of the developmental works done during its regime and has drawn public ire.

Many of these leaders were farouche figures until the party was formed; they gradually started flexing muscles amongst primarily the economically disadvantaged classes, who have mostly been in an imbroglio state of perception as who to vote for! Many of these leaders became notoriously venal over time, although many of them were canorous initially – they subsequently started taking advantage of the enervate slightness of frail form of those poor peasants by luring them into dreamland and promising them rewards and benisons of better life! They started thinking that an opportunity has come, so that their hunger could be eventually assuaged.

A compendious study undergone on these poverty-stricken class in an abridged fashion by some NGOs have concluded that they tend to believe real apathy to socially or economically disadvantaged classes of our population is prevalent as a general rule, since the dawn of Independence.

The tomfoolery attitude of sitting members of parliament or lower houses of many ruling parties in the country during debates or question times at Parliament or other Houses, or even during interview sessions can be construed as buffoonery or skylarking. While their election manifesto and subsequent promises to voters to lower taxes for common people and middle-class taxpayers were well laid off, the only guarantees actually received after they assume power, are higher taxes and bureaucratic boondoggling.

Many of them are caught in financial shenanigan as they start dreaming quick and big, and video-tapes of some of them accepting bribes and resorting to unfair means divulge later on, creating momentary public-unrest and protests; however, with some media houses accepting gargantuan advertisements from the parties to routinely publish in their newspapers and televisions, the uproar wades away to some other insignificant event, either manufactured to distract attention or otherwise, unbeknownst to general public.

While it is very understandable that nearly half a million 'dalas' on the streets of Kolkata and surrounding areas provide income opportunities to nearly a million youth and several million of their dependants, the number one problem of Kolkata should be carefully tackled and monitored after providing rehabilitation to the hawkers and street vendors.

One approach to make the roads and pavements clutter free is to narrow the sidewalks and widen the roads, which will leave just ample space for pedestrians, but won't be enough for hawkers to set up stalls or carts. Another may be to set up fencing outside shops and establishments to discourage vendors from sitting with their 'dalas' on that spot.

The columnist personally thinks that the garden guard approach will be the best – that is, setting up a green patch on the pavement after leaving space for pedestrians, to ensure that vendors don't get enough space to put up their stalls. This approach will help our environment by mitigating levels of pollution in the City, which has topped the list of our country's most-affected cities.

Many preach to practice casuistry, the sense that the process of resolve they resort for moral problems through theoretical rules from a particular case to reapply said rules to new issues, which are somewhat tendentious. This method although applied in applied ethics and jurisprudence, and commonly used as a pejorative to criticize use of clever but unsound reasoning, may be more pertinent in sophistry, which relates to addressing moral questions.

When a principle-based approach may state that lying is always morally wrong, the casuist may argue that lying may not be unlawful or morally unsound, depending on details of the case at hand. The casuist may agree that lying under oath is wrong, especially in legal testimonies, et al – but, they would concur with the idea of lying if it saves a life; it might then be construed as a best moral choice! Such shift in paradigms are often descried in legal proceedings, when a person is betwixt between lying under oath and simply telling the truth! Thus, we may end up with results not favourable to an ethical person!

It seems that there is no strong political will to make Kolkata a better place to live and work. Each counsellor of Kolkata Municipal Corporation in each corner of the City should look up beyond personal gratification and gains, and should make the pavements safe, beautiful and clean. God only knows if that's ever going to happen!

Menace No. 2

Traffic snarls, road accidents and illegal parking on Streets of Kolkata:

For drivers in government buses, there's literally no impediment to drive recklessly and endangering lives of passengers and other people out there on the streets of Kolkata. They hardly care about safe driving rules, and frequently violate traffic rules and signals – they get away with it by virtue of their status as government staff, similar to the attitude prevalent in most government offices across the State. Accountability and dedication are something that many of those government employees, be it Central or State Government, are lacking in most spheres.

Introduction of incentive-schemes for government bus drivers recently have added salt to injury; they have more reasons to drive recklessly for gain. Also, an increased number of contractual bus drivers, instead of salaried government drivers, has resulted in more competition amongst those drivers to reap more profits for their respective contractors, who can replace the drivers at their whims.

Private bus drivers, on the other hand, work on salary plus commission, thereby inducing them to make more frequent stops at non-designated spots, competing with other buses to load more passengers. The onus of fines for violating traffic rules are on the owners of those buses - the drivers get away mostly with a caution from their owners. In addition, they have the backing of their unions and syndicates to shield them from further actions, etc. There is no commission system for buses beyond the five districts of Bengal or other states in India.

Private buses continue to be one of the biggest killers on the streets of Kolkata; three reasons are primarily attributable to this – racing for commission, helpers trying out their skills in driving, aversion to pay fines and overall tendency to break basic traffic rules. It is certainly a common practice when a helper or conductor of a bus is asked by the driver to get his hands 'fixed', so that they can become a driver someday. Maybe this is the biggest problem in accidents throughout India, be it a bus, a commercial vehicle – trucks, matador or minibuses.

In 2017, buses had claimed 77 lives in the city, trucks claiming another 74 out of the total of 329 accident-related deaths on the streets of Kolkata in the year 2017, thereby accounting for 46% of fatal accidents in Kolkata, between bus and truck accident deaths. Many times, a bus driver will start moving while a passenger has not yet boarded or alighted from the moving bus; often, bus fatality deaths result from this callousness and eagerness on the part of drivers and conductors of private buses to speed up, in order to chase a passing bus on the same road, for achieving economies of gain.

As per a report put up on the website by Kolkata Police in 2018, there were only 85 cases of accidents involving state bus drivers in the year 2017, whereas the number is 2,313 for accidents caused by private mini bus drivers in the same period, and the number is astounding for private bus drivers during the corresponding period – a whopping 12,353!

While state bus drivers are notorious for not stopping at designated spots or not plying through designated bus-lanes, the exactly opposite happens with private bus and mini-bus drivers; they make stops everywhere, at whatever point a passenger wants to board the bus - they won't move from a busy bus-stop unless there's another bus plying on the same route present there.

Many State bus drivers on local routes even smoke and chat on phone while driving, whereas many private bus and mini-bus drivers will apply sudden brakes while speeding, thereby putting passengers at risks of getting injured. In one respect only, they are the same, be it private or state bus drivers – not caring to bruise past a private car or motorcycle or even another bus, to hurry!

Therefore, as a passenger or driver in a privately-owned vehicle, and also as a pedestrian, you are always put to test by many of those errant bus drivers. If your vehicle is damaged as a result of such rash driving by a bus, or if you ever get injured, then you're most likely to get compensated from your own insurer under 'No fault' option, as it's a nightmare dealing with Police or Court. And, hopefully your insurance carrier is going to reimburse you for the losses legitimately, as many private insurers search for loopholes to deny claims.

Many police stations under Kolkata Police will make you feel guilty for the accident; many lawyers will make sure your pocket is harmed as much you got hurt! So, if you only carry third party insurance, then God bless you.

In all the Courts of Bengal, there are systematic approach to seek legal remedies. However, very few people actually use the cumbersome system, as the 'prevailing system' of bribing for almost everything, starting from obtaining a certified copy to getting a date from Learned Court is more effective. Even in the Honourable High Court of Kolkata, this same system is adhered to; unless you bribe the persons who take care of such matters, you are not going to get certified copies of anything in months – and without certified copies, your advocate cannot move your petition.

Many times, it has been noted that some advocates make a profit out of providing certified copies of orders or other documents, by pocketing the difference of money you pay them, as opposed to what they pay to clerks for obtaining those copies. It's very hard to determine if there are many advocates in many courts, who practice ethically and professionally to provide relief to their clients on a timely manner. All they care about is to maximize their gain by various means, and 'mutual understanding' between opposing advocates isn't very uncommon.

The most frustrating aspect of moving court is the waiting time – almost decades will pass before any adjudication is received, be it trial courts or most other courts, primarily due to the long pendency of unresolved cases. Legal fraternity blames this on insufficient number of judges, and the Judicial System blames it on frequent cease-work and other strikes, etc. called by lawyers.

It's sad to state that often court proceedings are halted due to death of a lawyer, putting into question the legal fraternity's accountability to aggrieved clients who have been going in Courts five or six times a year for the last ten or more years. It's indeed sad when a person dies; but calling off a whole day for it may cause 'silent death' to many!

During recent times, it has been noted that advocates will team up to cause harm and injury to anyone protesting their unlawful practices. While their profession entails providing timely relief and justice to their clients, many a times they don't even care to render timely relief, let alone justice. At Howrah, a group of advocates recently ended up in a brawl with corporation staff over petty issue as parking of their motorcycles.

It started from fistfights and blows, leading to pelting of stones, damage to vehicles, and what not – finally, they clashed with police when tear-gas shells had to be fired to disperse the mob.

However, the advocates from other courts soon joined the ruckus, resulting in road blockades, which caused tremendous inconvenience to general public. Advocates from all over will join the agitation the next several days, ultimately calling for cease-work throughout the state. This act of vandalism, hooliganism and organised show of strength resulted in thousands of already pending court cases to lag far behind; many aggrieved litigants ended up losing valuable time and money for those cease-work called by advocates from all courts in the state, causing vast inconvenience and denial of timely justice to those litigants and people dependant on those litigations.

What was confounding and ludicrous was, most of the advocates participating in cease-work called by their own bar associations, charged full fees from their clients; thus, it may be another form of extortion in the eyes of law. But who will dare to protest? Are those advocates who don't even listen to Judges, going to listen to common people?

The cease-work called by Bar Council and Law Association as protest against the hereinbefore noted incident caused misery to millions of people who were in dire need on various urgent matters relating to Court proceedings; but who cares? Nobody – it seemed. Judges from higher courts decided to turn their head from the untoward cessation of work by advocates around Bengal! Same exact trend followed with medical professionals soon thereafter, to which the local administration was also partially responsible.

Without a strong administration who will have the guts to render strikes by legal, medical or other emergency services professionals as illegal, matters will worsen day by day. Does any political party have the required stone buttress or stanchion to take any positive action in this regard? The columnist is of the unfortunate opinion that it may never be possible in at least Bengal!

People here are seemingly losing their backbone of spine to even protest against improper activities – so, how are they supposed to unite and thwart untoward incidents? Many people feel logy or sluggish to protest – so-called intellectuals walk the streets only when their own interests are at stake; administration has become toothless – they won't act unless the Supremo orders action!

Reverting back to the traffic mess, auto-rickshaws and other lighter vehicles are making streets more cluttered and unsafe day by day. Auto-rickshaws were initially meant to transport people from far-away places to central areas, from where other forms of public transportation can be availed.

With passage of time, autos have become a major form of transportation by itself, as some people find them quicker, easier and cheaper than bus or minibus. In addition, autos often ply through lanes and bye-lanes where buses usually don't, and in some cases, even if they do, the frequencies are lesser than the autos. Plus, people get to seat in an auto-rickshaw, which is considered a rare luxury on buses plying through the streets of Kolkata, due to increasing number of passengers with no corresponding increase in the fleet of buses.

Owners of private buses nowadays feel reluctant to add new bus to their fleet due to rising costs of fuel, insurance, salaries of staff and maintenance. Roads are not maintained well historically in the city, as the overseeing authorities fail to exercise proper care or monitoring over contractors' repair or patch work on the roads, either by sheer negligence, or for unlawful gains through cut-money received from those contractors and their agents.

Corruption is a real problem in our country, and Bengal probably will be placed amongst the top three states of most corrupt and imprudent practices, if there was a list of most corrupt states ever published. Such list may never be published in reality, as a thief will never badmouth another thief. While many government officials in other states do take bribes to get work done for the citizens, in Bengal the work is not done even after paying bribes. That's what causing profuse bleeding of our State!

There's no dearth of exemplum or aphorism in our rich cultural heritage – there are multitudes of great stories to illustrate some moral points – lots of pithy observations from pundits and experts containing general truth are readily available.

They were not only succinct, epigrammatic compendious, but also their statements and remarks were apropos of continuing the great legacy, starting from the Vedas, Puranas, Mahabharata, Ramayana and even greats like Somadasa, Shri Ramakrishna, Chaitanya, Vivekananda and the likes. People like Gopal Bhar and Birbal had quipped many witty remarks and epigrams to institute values in our life – but we practice corruptive practices; our moral turpitude leads us to where?

Who's going to protest against corruption without any adverse ramification? If you go to Regional Passport Office to get your passport renewed, after complying with online requirements, chances are that you'll be harassed at the Office unnecessarily for quite some time, apparently in an effort to squeeze some money out of you. If you refuse to give in, you may be assigned a different interview date for reasons known best to them. It appears that contractual workers have been assigned to perform jobs like initial screening there, and they have fallen into the 'system' quickly!

If you protest to central authorities, you may not get any remedies, based on personal experiences of many, relating to grievances and complaints. So, people choose to keep quiet and reappear on the next assigned date. Numerous similar examples of corrupt and imprudent business practices exercised at central, state and local levels of administration, as well as in some private institutions of repute, can be found as a prevailing practice across the State.

However, as were being discussed earlier, poor road conditions result in more frequent & unpredicted routine maintenance costs for private buses, adding to their woes of resultant increase in recurring expenses for owners, which also work as a disincentive for new entrants in the business. This takes a chain effect into lesser number of buses plying on streets of Kolkata, and more road accidents due to fierce competition to survive.

As for state-run buses, although there have been many additions to the number of government buses, but the number may be far less than actually required to cater to demands. Therefore, auto-rickshaws galore as another menace to Kolkatans.

Initially, autos were meant to reduce the burden on public transportation system. However, like anything else in Kolkata, as the number of autos started increasing, the drivers started forming auto unions. Subsequently most of the unions took shelter under ruling political party's banner, changing their allegiance with change of power in the state.

The obvious happened thereafter – union leaders, mostly connected to heavyweights in political parties, became errant; they started circumventing the existing laws and regulations by adding more passengers than permitted in the autos under their command, enlisting unlicensed autos under their leadership for personal gains, allowing or abetting auto drivers to change routes and drop passengers intermittently as per their own whims, etc.

As for example, an auto with permit from Thakurpukur to New Alipore will unilaterally decide on a truncated route, will force passengers to get off at Chowrasta, pick up a fresh batch of passengers and drop them at Taratala, and will do the same exact thing to ultimately reach New Alipore. This way, he's making more than double amount of money by cutting short the route and taking advantage of the fixed rates prevalent on shorter routes.

The worst part is yet to come – most of the auto-rickshaws plying through the streets of Kolkata will definitely take sharp turns and move like snakes especially on a congested road with heavy traffic, thereby increasing chances of a collision or resultant injuries, and in some cases, death of the passengers. There have been many deaths reported from various parts of Kolkata either as a result of auto-accidents resulting from the former cause or overturning due to such cause.

Infants have slipped from mothers' arms due to the same menace, at least twice during recent times, and have died on the spot. Union leaders disavow their association with the culprit driver momentarily when the heat is on; thereafter, they let the accused driver go back to his usual self after dusts settle.

If police are forced to take actions against these errant drivers due to public outrage or social media upheavals, the auto drivers will stage unlawful protests against 'police atrocities' on the entire route, blocking roads and pelting stones on passing vehicles, etc.

Another menace faced on the streets of Kolkata are from rogue bikers, uncaring cyclists and undisciplined crowd. It has been a trend these days for any guy going to college to persuade his parents to buy him a branded motorcycle – most of the time, the parents oblige; if they don't, there might be serious repercussions in their daily lives, including suicide. A motorcycle has somehow become a status symbol for the youths, so that they can flaunt their expensive and foreign made motorcycles on fairer sex to impress them, or to show off to their friends as to who they are.

It is very sad that the society has been turning more materialistic and less idealistic with passage of time. Qualities like ethics, principles, moral value and integrity are becoming obsolete, and are more often than not, ridiculed of! It appears that we are trying to adapt to western cultures without knowing the intricacy of their cultures.

Discipline and mannerism form an integral component of western culture; but we are not aware of it. We are very happy to imitate their dresses and fashions, not realizing what actually should be the combination to wear as per their standards. For example, we wear sneakers with salwar, dress pants and other formal outfits! Girls smoke cigarettes and consume alcohol in public here, and many a times, these are girls from orthodox families.

Many bars and pubs in Park Street allow under-age drinking, and my complaint to one of them with pictures of a group of girls studying in Class XI in their bar was ignored by the authorities. They probably don't know that a former US President's minor daughter was arrested in US for buying beer! We're just happy to imitate.

If it was in India, the girl would have definitely called her parents, friends or relatives, who in turn would have exercised their undue influence over the police authorities to let the girl go unpunished. A friend of distant niece of an ex-Mayor of Kolkata slapped a traffic sergeant who was performing his duties at Rash Behari junction few years ago; the sergeant rightfully stopped the vehicle with this "heavily connected" friend of ex-Mayor's relative disobeying traffic laws, for which the diligent sergeant was 'closed' subsequently.

Indeed, the famous saying by Alexander the Great and his troops upon arrival here centuries ago – which goes as – really Seleucus, what a strange country it is!

Performing stunts on Red Road by rogue bikers have been stopped after killing of an innocent serviceman performing rehearsals for Republic Day Parade near Fort William several years ago by a criminal son of a prominent businessman of Kolkata, with political connections. Of course, there cannot be any survival of most businesses here without political connections and undue advantages passed on to them by dint of such connections.

A guy whose son killed a defence person, during routine parade before Republic Day few years ago, rose to fame with political blessings to quickly become the biggest exporter of fruits - vending fruits from the streets of Mechua to becoming an elected leader of ruling political party; further expanding his wings as exporter (with offices spread across many countries) has blessed his family, in the sense that the family ended up owning a fleet of high-end foreign cars, including Porsche SUV, Mercedes, Audi, to name a few.

The obvious resulted when his spoilt son ignored multiple signs; he crashed many barriers to severely injure some Indian Air Force Officers and bludgeoned death to one of them -they were rehearsing for the Republic Day Parade on Red Road few years back. The father of this criminal apologised mea culpa in public; however, the cost of the valorous Air Force soldier's life was merely anything in his mind as compared to his recalcitrant and obdurate son's lethal fantasy to drive recklessly.

This defiant son of the fruit merchant spent couple of years in jail as eyewash. He spent his time there lavishly, singing and laughing in his cell defiantly - he seems to think that not singing soulfully is to whine and caterwaul tunelessly, as he considered himself to be a budding singer.

In addition, the tergiversates father-son duo lacked the wherewithal to pay the victims' families even a mere one lakh rupee despite Court orders; speaking of which, the Hon'ble Judge in this case observed in her disposition that a lot more was expected from the probing team and the prosecution!

It was a frantic search for the police that had earlier led to the arrest of the culprits. CCTV footage produced at Court clearly depicted the truth that the infamous son had broken barriers after leaving the metalled road on the fateful morning. He chose to drive on open grounds near the Hooghly bridge approach, immediately after he jumped the first warning sign posted there; he was warned the second time about the ongoing rehearsals for Republic Day celebrations up ahead, but he chose to break through a second barrier at South Gate.

Thereafter, he broke the third barrier at J.K. Island adjacent to Fort Williams gate on Red Road. When he finally decided to take a U-turn back on to Kidderpore Road, his imported Audi car hit the sabre of an Officer – however, he chose not to stop even then! Then he hit the young Officer of IAF head on, flinging him into the air; still, he sped up and drove off.

It was only after hitting another barrier near South Gate on the opposite direction that his airbag automatically inflated, after which he was compelled to stop. He called his friends from there to get hitched to a safe location where he was hiding for three days, until police arrested him (out of public out roar and pressure from the IAF). As luck would have it, the mere sentencing he got was for two years – he was released upon the verdict of lower court eventually, which may also be considered as questionable decision!

However, one good thing that happened out of that tragic event was banning of bike races along that stretch of road. But the hoodlum bikers shifted to other areas and less crowded stretches of roads to display their 'god-gifted' skills, which eventually turns out to be death-traps for them! National Highways are not even spared out of their chosen venue.

There have been many tragic deaths either due to over-speeding or stunts by bikers on the highway leading to Kolaghat – but, there's no stopping these youths, who also get into brawls and fistfights often due to their hyper attitude and frequent mood-swings. Some girls from affluent families also are somewhat of an incentive to these youths to showcase their masculinists' frame!

Bicycles are usually a blessing in disguise for streets, in the context of environmental friendliness, and as a means of transportation for the economically disadvantaged sections of our community. But, in the absence of dedicated lanes for bicycles, they tread in the same path taken by motorists, often accounting for minor traffic accidents. Some of the bicycle-riders also are experts in flouting traffic rules – they zig-zag across busy lanes, often resulting in accidents.

Matadors and mini-door vans are probably the biggest menace in suburban and rural areas, with no adherence to traffic laws, whimsical stopping and changing of lanes with total disregard to ongoing traffic, speeding and sudden brake applications - all these make up a sizeable congestion and accidents in those areas.

Last but not the least is, we the common people, more specifically the pedestrians on the streets of Kolkata, are another big menace. Many people don't understand the logic or rationale behind pedestrians crossing roads with incoming traffic from both ends. They keep waving at oncoming vehicles to stop and let them pass, sometimes letting some cars pass them by a whisker, and then running to the other side of the street.

What goes on inside their minds is something one may be very curious to find out about – is it the rush they're feeling to reach their destination on time? Is it that they've to reach a cremation ground on time, and are getting late? Or is it that they are simply stupid? No matter how late you're for work or School or business, how much fraction of a minute can you save crossing the streets like that, putting your own life at jeopardy? Is anything worth more than your own life? Can't you have a head start little early? The answer is remained to be found by many.

If accidents happen due to the above-stated careless and dangerous attitude depicted by general public on roads, then others will either stand as mute spectators, or will vandalise the vehicles at random, or will block the traffic for hours until some top-notch police official comes in and agrees to something which will never be done. In the meantime, thousands of other people en route to their destinations will suffer.

Ambulances with critical care patients inside being transported to hospitals or nursing homes will be left stranded for several precious minutes, thereby endangering lives of patients inside. Same exact scenario is noted when some students of colleges or universities choc-a-bloc streets of Kolkata for various demands, many of which are unfair.

As for instance, several colleges barred their students from taking tests due to their failure of adhering to the minimum attendance rules imposed rightly by the college authorities during recent past. Many students thus duly affected, chose to wrongfully take to streets in order to vent out their frustrations or angers, thereby making thousands of innocent people to suffer for hours.

Another university in Jadavpur is notorious for taking to streets for any type of agitation, which should be dealt with severe punishments for obstructing and denying rights of other people. Those halcyon days before turn of the century seems to be mythical now!

Similarly, unless a spot-fine for crossing roads while signal for traffic flow is green is imposed at all intersections diligently, in an equitable manner by the authorities, this in-borne habits of pedestrians in Kolkata to juggle through roads with least care for others can't be changed; along with this, social mind-sets need to change from within us —no one can inscribe values and discipline in us unless we change our own outlooks.

As for vehicles and buses and other modes of transportation, a digital card should be given to all drivers, so that data in central database could be monitored real time; thus, punitive measures can be taken appropriately in case of violations or any unlawful actions.

For people who keep on dirtying streets, immediate fines should be imposed on them based upon closed circuit television monitoring app; their failure to pay spot fines should tantamount to failure to adhere to rules, for which some time should be served by them in jail or police lock-up. These actions might work as a starting point to deter street nuisances to some extent.

Menace No. 3

Jaywalking and flouting of rules and civic norms on Streets of Kolkata:

Accident statistics collated by the Headquarters of Traffic Police at Lalbazar has time and again attributed jaywalking as the primary trigger for most accidents on our streets during the last several years. Be it crossing the road while speaking on a mobile phone with ear-phone plugged in the ears, walking on the roads instead on the pavements, climbing over a railing at the median divider, trying to hop on to a running bus on the middle of the road, or walking in the middle of the road with complete disregard to traffic signals or rules, jaywalking has resulted in a large number of fatal accidents in the city.

Nearly a third of all road accidental deaths involve pedestrians – dangerous behaviour of pedestrians, total flouting of rules and civic norms by a large section of our jaywalkers result in lots of fatalities, which could easily have been avoided.

Add the number of those youths with earphones plugged in their eardrums with high-pitched music playing, walking around the streets and trying to take short cuts for crossing to the other side – it's a very common sight on major intersections all around the city to see those weirdos zig-zagging between moving traffic and signalling moving cars and buses to stop, to make ways!

Some people dodge moving vehicles to get to the other side of the road in a rush, blatantly refusing to wait for pedestrian signal to turn green. Many prefer walking along the sides of the roads, instead of the designated pavements; they have the right excuses though – the pavements are full of makeshift stalls. This kind of sights are very common in most major crossings around Kolkata.

On Mayo Road crossing, people get off their buses on one side of the road and run across the road, climbing over median dividers even as traffic moves on. Some pedestrians have legitimate complaints though – signals change too fast! Also, at extremely busy crossings, cars come from all directions, and pedestrians have little time to keep tabs on signals. They end up merely looking around for oncoming traffic and darting across the streets.

Bus drivers also stop further away from designated bus stops, leaving their passengers little choice but to get on or off right in the middle of the road. Cops are busy keeping traffic moving with minimum disruptions and end up having no time to steer the errant buses away, or to ask pedestrians to follow rules.

Prosecution for jaywalking in Kolkata invites a bare minimal penalty of something ranging from rupees ten to one hundred, although there are hardly any convictions. Depending on the implication of the offence, many times the evader gets away with paying nothing, or even a nominal amount as settlement.

The current administration recently announced 65% reduction of traffic fines for all in Kolkata, thereby encouraging the routine evaders to pay a certain portion of the fines levied on them for various traffic offences committed by them in the past. While this practice gave a quick boost to state's revenue in terms of additional collection of fines and penalties, it also costs the exchequer 65% by way of waivers!

Many people wonder why in this era of digitisation, all traffic fines shouldn't be centrally computerised, processed and deducted directly from the bank accounts of the repeat offenders, if they don't pay in a stipulated period of time. One may argue that such practice will encourage some dubious traffic constables and sergeants to stash for cash in their pockets that way, by threatening to issue false challans, or threatening otherwise; however, the pros and cons should be weighed out and some concrete fair solutions should be arrived at.

What is more required from people from all sections in Kolkata is a simple civic sense – to obey signals, traffic rules and norms, and be respectful to others. Is it too much to ask for? Who knows – maybe it isn't, because of the simple fact that the current generations need to give back to the society what their forefathers had been taking from it, mostly pollution and environmental issues though!

Safety Issues:

As residents of Kolkata, we can proudly say that our streets are lot safer than many other places in our country that one may have visited. However, the following matters relating to safety should be reviewed and acted upon, apart from the ones noted earlier:

1) There have been a number of incidents of molestation and outraging modesty of women during the past several years, starting from the incident at Park Street, when a woman was dragged out of a moving vehicle after several guys of noted industrialists, or men of prominence were involved in kidnapping, raping and abusing her before deserting her near the crossing of AJC Road and Exide;

2) Ladies working in IT Sector and allied industries in the vicinity of Sector V of Salt Lake are vulnerable, as many of them work at shifts, and return home late at night. While most have now arranged for their companies to arrange transportation back and forth for them, there are many who still uses public transportation - there have been several incidents of molestation and other criminal actions against them by app cab and other drivers;

3)   Women travelling in buses and autos have often been harassed or abused by fellow passengers and others – while some of the victims had mustered up enough courage to bring the accused to Justice, many feel scared, and shy away from filing formal complaints, as the process is not only cumbersome and awkward, but also is quite embarrassing to talk about the experiences in public in front of other gazing eyes;

4)   There are still many lanes and narrow stretches of streets which are fairly deserted, especially after dark – those streets or by-lanes lack proper illumination, thereby making the anti-socials to choose those deserted and dark streets for their criminal activities, which include prying on innocent passer-by;

5)   Drinking alcohol on public places should be dealt with severely; it has been a recent trend of groups of young girls and guys loitering on some streets after dark with alcoholic contents in their possession, sipping in every now and then for pleasure; once inebriated, they can be vulnerable for criminal acts;

6)   CCTVs should be installed at all the streets at central points and monitored live round-the-clock at different police stations. Any suspicious activities seen on the monitor should be dealt with in accordance with law instantly, preferably through patrolling police bikes;

7)   Notices in bold should be pasted on major intersections of roads by the authorities to warn off intruders and perpetrators of crime, warning about strong punitive actions against street-crimes like mugging, molestation, etc.;

8)   A micro-chip should be installed on all vehicles, commercial & domestic, as well as on motorcycles, which should be readable by the CCTVs and police personnel on duty readily, with GPS tracking enabled;

9) Drivers of buses and any other vehicles should be fined on the spot, pending which their vehicles should be seized by concerned police authorities, for any violations and failure to follow traffic rules and regulations. The onus should not be on owners of the vehicles, as accountability that way can fall right on the driver; if the driver exceeds a specified number of violations, his driving licence should be revoked. Digital database of drivers is a must;

10) Police authorities, specifically traffic police, should exercise more care not to accept bribes and other favours from any vehicle violating norms; any refractions from this should result in suspension of the concerned officer;

11) The unofficial 'monthly' system of paying off some police authorities should be immediately regulated and dealt with strictly; and

12) Police and other civic authorities should be made independent of any political or unholy pressure from any quarter, so that they can perform their jobs in an efficient, transparent and fair manner – any violation of this should be dealt with accordingly, after the government makes an amendment to free police department from its clutches – who knows if it will ever happen!

Activities on streets of Kolkata:

A reputed English daily newspaper group has started an event mainly on holidays for children and others to enjoy the streets of Kolkata in whatever manner it please them, including dancing, singing, recitation, martial arts, drawing or simply walking and jogging. It is a wonderful start to make our streets more beautiful, with traffic halted during the even through diversion on alternate routes. People from all walks of life attend the programs with great enthusiasm and energy.

Similar activities are now taken up by several organisations; such activities should not be limited to central areas only - but should be extended to almost all possible corners. Awareness campaigns should be contemplated by all concerned, in order to address the current issues flooding our streets, including mob lynching, rumour mongering, bluntly forwarding messages, texts and images through social media without taking a minute to ponder over the authenticity or mere feasibility of issues described in those forwards, etc.

Educational institutions and corporate houses should join hands in organising various meets, events and seminars for social awareness, as also some issues of mass relevance. We tend to organize candle-light processions or agitations by so-called 'intellectuals' of our society for matters related to our own benefit, instead of organising those processions for greater interests or staging a mass protest against moral turpitude or aggression or other forms of butchering our society and our values.

However, we failed to organise a single procession when more than forty of our brave jawans were blown up in Kashmir by separatists and extremists – what goes in the minds of so-called 'intellectuals' who appear for sit-com or other televised shows, but don't have time to address a public rally or host a protest march, can be answered by them only.

Maybe the answer lies if the situation is affecting their earning bread and butter in any manner or not – who knows? Some may wonder if some of those so-called 'intellectuals' actually deserve to be called intellectuals or not! Can acting on make-shift stages (meant for viewing by certain section of our community, popularly called 'Jatra' in local terminologies), make one eligible to be called an intellectual? Is this a fair practice? Maybe it is, as one of such 'highly talented performing artist' became a member of our Parliament few years back. She is still serving our country, or maybe better termed as disserving India.

Quite a few of such 'intellectuals' are amongst our policymakers, fortunately or unfortunately, depending on which polarised section one belongs to! An actress who provided shelter to the main accused in the infamous Park Street rape case has been nominated for Lok-Sabha election! So, if she becomes a MP, should she be providing shelters to terrorists (as her domain would certainly expand)? Another actress whose mother used to be a stalwart in Bengali movies became a MP during the last election; she is also running for the upcoming elections. Her mother never wanted to contest elections, while she was a real performing artist; however, her daughter does, apparently because she is a better performer (maybe in some other evil senses)!

The columnist doesn't hold any reservations against any celebrity running for electoral contests. However, the columnist believes that nominations should not be based on publicity – it should be based on merit, inherent talents, etc. The person should be intelligent enough to stand up in our Parliament or Assembly to ask questions, to challenge wrongdoings, to foster in betterment in public life, etc.

What factor other than popularity prohibits a truly intellectual like a brilliant scientist or educator or accountant to get nominations for elections? Is it the popular face that a political party should look for when deciding on nominating candidates, for a quick win? The answer is probably in the affirmative.

We tend to outcast a man who has done considerably well to transform India in terms of development, digitisation, environment, science & technology, foreign currency reserves, international relations, taxation, banking, education, housing, rural electrification, and almost all spheres of nations wellness. The gentleman with a 56 inches chest has the guts to reciprocate with precision surgical strikes on a terrorist-infested country, by giving a free hand to our Defence heads, which resulted in unparalleled support from every corner in the world.

But, some of our mean-minded politicians are trying to crucify the gentleman for crimes he hasn't committed, just so that those bunch of thieves can outrun him! At least give him another term to see if he really can turn around our country to where he says he will! It's really tragic that all the three major faces vying for the PM's office are known to be involved in huge scams indirectly in the recent past. So, should we call a dubious person as a PM of our country, in the event any one of them wins the election?

The manner in which elections are staged by ruling political party in Bengal is despicable. They use the Panchayat members (who got elected uncontested to their seats by criminal acts) to bribe villagers in various means, starting from cash to distribution of poultry, meat, liquor and less respectable items. If bribing doesn't work, they will use force to threaten and scare off the voters; if that even work either, they will have outsiders flock to the polling booths on poll days to jam the booths, in order to start engaging in rigging.

Our existing laws pertaining to deployment of central forces should be immediately changed. Under existing laws, the State administration directs the forces to be located at places where they are least needed. Instead of deploying forces to sensitive booths, often they will be stationed at some building as sitting duck, with a fancy term called 'Quick Response Team'. God forbid if any quick response is indeed required in a certain area – they will reach there after few hours, almost always at the behest of the administration that's deploying them!

We should come out of the shells of our own mutual interest-clad minds once in a while for change and feel proud to be called Indian first and then called a Kolkatan next. There are many of us who consider people from other states as foreigners - some don't even know the topography of our own State. A niece of a sitting MLA stated recently during a conversation that Shillong is in West Bengal, and therefore, it is a safe place for our erstwhile Commissioner of Police to be interrogated by the CBI on a national Ponzi schemes scam!

The least we can do is to educate ourselves and stop humiliating our own selves! If each one of us, say for example, makes it a practice to teach the kids of our domestic helps, drivers, or gardeners at least once a week, say on a weekend evening, then we can at least garner enough strength in those kids to tell their friends and associates what they learnt from you, thus becoming more enlightened in the process. Instead of hosting various expensive Pujas and rituals at home and spending huge amount of money to pray for God's blessings, we can get more blessings for free that way – by imparting education and values in our kids – others' kids are after all our kids too, isn't it right?

Kids have a bigger role in educating their parents and others, in cases where the parents or acquaintances were found to be ignorant, or not knowledgeable enough in serious matters relating to pollutions, global warmings, civic senses, etc. If a kid practices what she learns at School through her Environmental Values and Science classes at home and ensures that her parents and others adhere to the same norms and practices, then at least a few people can change – they may act as change agents themselves easily. After all, it's their own future that's at stake.

Flooding on streets of Kolkata used to be a regular feature up until very recent years, especially during monsoon times. Thanks to good work by civic bodies, that nightmare has been partly mitigated, although there's still room for improvement in terms of maintenance, timely removal of slits, operational efficiency of pumps at different strategic points, etc. aided by a more structured early warning system for weather, etc.

Overall, streets of Kolkata are not only safe and going to be cleaner soon, but also is home to thousands of homeless people. Although the streets offer special delicacies in terms of food and income to privileged sections, they fail to provide basic amenities to homeless people.

The rich and affluent sections of our community should redeem their worth as human beings by diverting even a miniscule portion of their fortunes for causes of those kids. Who knows what will happen to us on our next lives!

Even if some of us may not believe in reincarnation, but they should believe in 'karma' – so, any positive action taken today might yield better results down the road for you, in this life only – right? Therefore, we should wake up from hibernations and be Good Samaritan right from this very moment – not tomorrow; who knows if there's going to be a tomorrow!"

Diana always had a special place in her heart for those underprivileged wanderers. She became a household name amongst the literates in the country after her articles were published in the newspapers, and she finally decided to write novels which reflected her own life, as also lives of people she came across – the success of her articles inspired her so much that she started writing a book while focusing on her novels in between. The book was a collection of opuscula written between scripting the two novels, which became a best seller.

As she had enough spare time at her disposal, Diana finished the first novel in less than a year, and even before it was published, she started scripting the second one – it took her a year and a half to get the second novel published.

Diana became extremely popular across the globe for her twin novels, especially after the first one was nominated for Booker Award – that novel was published in UK, as her surviving ex-colleagues down there arranged for almost everything for her.

However, Di couldn't survive long enough to see her novels receive international acceptance, as she was not only a nonagenarian frail lady by then, but also regular conflicts between her adopted son Subir and daughter Maya (as to who would take turns by rotation for Di's stays) became too much for the old lady to handle. Ferrying her from one place to another erratically took a heavy toll on her mental well-being – she soon went into severe depression, which aggravated her deteriorating heart conditions.

Di had earlier sold off her great mansion at Alipore before she turned a septuagenarian, decades ago, after Subir and Mary gave their nods, mainly because it was difficult for her to maintain the spacious place all by herself. In addition, she needed money to pay for her grandkids' weddings, keep on donating to orphanage, old age homes and other charitable organisations, etc. However, she made the biggest mistake of dividing the remains of the sale proceeds between her son and daughter, on the verbal condition that they will look after Di on alternate basis for as long as she lived.

Some of her old friends had advised Diana not to gift everything to her children at that moment – they suggested that Di retain the propriety of the money in her bank, duly nominating her children as per her wishes, so that they get legal entitlement or ownership of the huge fund only after Di's demise, whenever that arose. That way, her money could act as her shield against inhuman treatment or abuse!

But, going by her individual experiences in life, in particular her own life with her maternal grandparents, Diana was wrongly convinced that her kids will leave no stones unturned to keep her safe and sound. She was confident deep down that her children will take good care.

She wrongly thought that no children can possibly fail to take proper care of their ailing parent - she had full faith on her foster children, forgetting for the moment that even some own kids those days used to treat their parents really bad in many cases, against which the   Courts ended up having to intervene, in order to ensure parents' safety and security in terms of financial matters.

Little did Diana know that she had to pay dearly for her costly mistake – a mistake that may even cost her life, as she was not being treated properly at either of her children's home during her stays with them. They didn't even care to have any medical practitioner check on their frail mother to ensure that everything with her health was safe and sound!

Her intake of medicines were infrequent too, due to non-availability of medicines because "they cost a lot" – she was shocked to hear that coming from her own children, at least that was how she used to consider those foster children, whose perfidiousness and sort of trahison des clercs stunned the loving old lady, who had dedicated her life towards the cause of those treacherous & ungrateful foster son and foster daughter!

Di was already used to receiving Judas kiss from some of her school friends like Bistha – but little did she expect that sort of untrustworthiness and acts of betrayal from Mary and Subir! Had she not rescued them from their miseries long ago, they both would probably end up on the streets of Kolkata – they both would be wretched.

She could have spent a mere fraction of the money she spent on those two children, in order to get herself some domestic animals – they would probably have given their lives for their masters; but alas, human beings are different!

We call ourselves the best creation of God, although many of us have proved ourselves to be worst creation through our actions – those were the words from Rina before she passed away some years ago, to her loving sister Di. Maybe she was right, felt Di at certain times.

During the time that Diana did spend with Subir, it seemed like she was a big burden on him. His son or live-in partner didn't care about anything else other than asking Diana to cook varieties of dishes for them every now and then. Di obliged, partially out of sheer love, and partly because of her soft nature. She had hard time standing in the kitchen for prolonged period of time during cooking, as she had osteoarthritis on both her legs – her routine medication was also hampered during her stays with Subir, as they wouldn't care to ask if she needed replenishments of her medicines.

To add to her woes, Di had to wash clothes for the entire family, dry those out – putting a load of dry clothes into washing machines wasn't a big deal for Diana; but, taking out wet clothes and putting those out for drying got to her eventually - she tripped down quite a few times in the process, for which she had suffered multiple fractures.

Subir seemed like the classic underdog schlemiel – not only was he known by most to be a nincompoop living off his rich & famous mother, but also was perceived as an ignoramus and dullard guy who will let her mother do everything for him. There were times when Di used to feel frustrated about how dimwit he turned out in life, despite all her best efforts to give the very best support so that he didn't act like a cretin.

She tried everything she could within her reaches to show the dunderhead how things were to be handled in life, just so that the numbskull dipstick could get ahead in life – but all in vain. Apart from being a womanizer, Subir couldn't excel in any arena in life; plus, he was selfish, opportunistic, and sometimes abusive.

Mary, on the other hand, was much better than her brother in the sense that she not only replenished medicines for her mother routinely, but Vivek also helped Mary when she volunteered to cook for them. Mary would also take her mother to hospitals for diagnostic tests and MRIs, etc. as and when required, and would also help out her mother with her daily chores, at least in the preliminary stages when rotational stays of Diana with her children started.

As time passed, Mary also started misbehaving with her mom, especially after Di decided to gift the tangible and intangible rights of Gitalaya (her brainchild that raised so many kids, saved so many and enriched lives of so many destitute children) to an internationally acclaimed organisation. She wanted to ensure that her mother's name remain in history on one hand, and other kids around the globe get to benefit from it, on the other). Di was unsure if Mary or Avik could effectively manage it, let alone Subir.

The benefactor agreed to keep the name of Di's organisation unchanged – they walked the extra mile by extending a courtesy to Di by declaring in writing that the new entity would have Diana's Home for Children written on it. Di was really amazed – she thanked God and her elders for everything.

Mary sometimes expressed her resentment with having to spend time for her mother, and on one occasion, she even yelled at Diana, indicating that it was better for an aging parent to die than being a burden on the children! The orphan from the streets of Kolkata who would have ended getting violated probably several times before getting killed out there with no one noticing, if Diana didn't provide her care, failed to remember the past and used to delate the hapless old lady who always treated Mary as her own kid!

Thus, the message was probably received well at heaven, where Diana's uncle Vicky, her aunt Riya, grandma Ritu, grandpa Biman and mother Gita apparently called in a closed-door meeting to unanimously resolve that it was time for bringing Diana home – she was already a 97 plus old and ailing lady, who had lived her life full, won't probably miss her children or grandchildren, and will be a gifted addition to God's chamber.

The 'minutes' of the meeting was documented and ratified by the God, and passed on for immediate implementation – Diana's uncle Vikram was assigned to be the first to appear to welcome Di home, as he had always missed hugging and kissing Di from the time she reached her adolescence.

During her infancy, Vicky used to carry Diana everywhere, starting from bed, toilets, dining table, playground, school and almost everywhere. Di used to hold Vicky's neck with her right arm, and wave with her left. Vicky even used to kiss good night and good morning to Diana every single day until she grew up, when she became a young lady all of a sudden!

Thereafter, Vicky had to show restrain by holding his world's most favourite niece-cum-daughter's hands and rarely kissing her forehead. He had missed not being able to cuddle and hug Di since she became seven or eight years of age, when she used to jump every time on the offer of bringing her back home from school! Vicky's heart had Diana's name written all over it, and she meant the world to him – probably that's why God decided to send him to accompany Di back to Heaven!

After instructed by the 'Board of Gods', Vicky almost immediately started running towards seemingly where earth ended, sending summons to Gita that her dear brother was going to ferry Di back. Gita, in turn, sent messages to her parents and sister through the fairies, that their loving Diana was going to join them soon, and Vicky was on his way!

Everyone assembled in great joy and the countdown had begun. All four of them started walking towards the main entrance – Biman and Ritu first, followed by Gita and Riya. Sam didn't want to leave his couch playing video games; but he was excited too! Rina was hanging out with friends, as usual!

Randi, who breathed his last after taking gruel beating by certain inmates of the prison where he was sentenced to, following conviction for contempt of court order and failure to pay maintenance and other expenses the Court had ordered him to pay, was probably still burning in hell. He had turned into a grumpy, curmudgeonly and tetchy old man, and following his murder, he was still rotting in hell – Di or no one else from this disgusting man's family ever performed any ritual after his horrible demise, which actually saved mankind!

His corpse remained in the filthy morgue for many days, following which, it was sent to Medical College where his skeleton was preserved for training purposes. Di felt that anyone studying those skeletons may end up turning to be as ghastly as the man who ruined her childhood!

Back on earth, Di laid herself down on a piece of rugged cloth on the pavement, stroked her hair feebly & retired to cogitate - she started recollecting her memories about the day she first met Mary, her daughter who didn't want to let her in that fateful gloomy day, because she had a party to attend to!

It was exactly there that Di first met her - the susurration of the river flowing a few metres away seemed a nuisance as the little girl offered quite a few facts and description of events to the perspicacious veteran reporter that Diana was earlier – how Mary fondly remembered her father taking her on a boat ride along the Ganges sometimes, while he used to be a boatman for rent momentarily.

Di was confounded at Mary's description as to how she saw rich guys and girls lying on top of each other inside the boat, while her father used to divert her attention to something else.

The little girl seemed somewhat quirky about her attitude at that time, in a sense of idiosyncrasy; but what Mary really wanted to narrate to Di in her own ways – oh well, Di realised that the reality was something beyond the purview of Mary's little brain. Or, was it that the sanctity of the river was something Di considered as much larger than occasional abuse by some, and even above those kinds of fishy acts by certain people on its holy waters?

Ganges is hallowed as a sacred, cleansing river – it is also known as Hooghly River. Ganges entered the plains at Hardwar – a dip in the water at Har-ke-pauri ghat is revered and considered as a first step in washing away the sins and purifying the soul. It was quite amazing to note that it was the only place after the holy Ganges enter the plains where the waters were fit for bathing, per Central Pollution Control Board (CPCB), as waters in Ganges got polluted.

The level of pollution was not the same all along its 2,525 km as Ganga wended its way through five states, before flowing into the Bay of Bengal. CPCB had set up monitoring stations along the river, and data obtained from those monitoring stations consistently showed the progressive deterioration of the quality of water down the basin, home to some 50-crore people!

CPCB recommended that the river water should not be consumed directly without some kind of treatment, as it may contain dangerous levels of dissolved oxygen, coliforms, biochemical oxygen, pH value and other impurities. CPCB recommended that in order to be fit for drinking, water in Class A category (fit for drinking after disinfection) should have dissolved oxygen of more than 6 mg/litre and biochemical oxygen demand of less than 2 mg/litre, with total coliform to be less than 50 per 100 ml. As for Class C category (conventional treatment and disinfection), water was fit for drinking if it contained dissolved oxygen of more than 4 mg/l and biochemical oxygen demand of less than 3 mg/l, with pH range between 6 and 9 and total coliform below 5,000/100 ml. And, water that did not fall in Class A or Class C should be fit for drinking only after organised conventional or advanced treatment, including disinfection.

As for bathing, the water should have dissolved oxygen more than 5 mg/l and biochemical oxygen demand of less than 3 mg/l, with acceptable pH range between 6.5 and 8.5, and acceptable faecal coliform range between 500/100 ml and 2,500/100 ml. Anything not falling within the above ranges should be considered as not fit for bathing, as per CPCB.

About 460 km into its journey, the first spot where the water got unfit for bathing and drinking is Grahmukteshwar, where CPCB recommended advanced water treatment plants for making the water fit for drinking. From that point on, the waters of Ganges should be considered as unsafe for drinking, bathing and other domestic purposes. Next major bathing ghat along the Ganges was Ranighat in Kanpur, the first major industrial city in the river's path – the ills of dumping industrial wastes over hundreds of years had taken a dangerous toll, until the Central Government led by an ironman took a strong stand through its Swachh Bharat and other movements.

Allahabad is the meeting place of Ganga, Yamuna and Saraswati where the world-famous Kumbh Mela is organised, and Prayag is famous all across the world for pious dip, although few realised that the water there was teeming with impurities. Assighat and other ghats in Varanasi, where the Ganges flowed through its course to Bengal, had surprised many scientists after tests concluded on water there yielded safe results for bathing, despite all the impurities it had collected all the way!

However, there was no turning back from there, in terms of acceptable ranges for safe bathing or drinking in Ganges waters, from that point on – by the time the water flowed into Darbhanga Ghat in Patna, all kinds of impurities and bacteria were found, all the way to Garden Reach and Uluberia.

Despite all the above findings and recommendations, hundreds of thousands of people bath in the holy water of Ganges every day, and more so on occasions; many use waters from Ganges for cooking and other needs too! And almost all believers use the water for performing rituals at home or other places of worship, when it is often seen that small amount of such water filled with impurities are consumed during the puja services, as part of the rituals!

Diana always used to be very worried about the above issues of grave concern to common people; she tried her very best to spread the message amongst commoners, so that the sanctity and cleanliness of the river could be maintained well.

She was also able to get Mary on her side on that issue, as they often would indulge in active conversations with people they knew, as also with strangers, relating to the dangers posed to the waters of Ganga, caused directly by greed and ignorance of mankind! Be that as it may, the mother-daughter duo used to be firm believers in the legends and myths surrounding the holy Ganges - they always made sure to pay respect to Mother Ganga every time they passed the river anywhere in India.

It was no shocker that Mary chose to buy her house near the Ganges in Kidderpore, very close to Metiabruz, where the famous warrior king Wazid Ali Shah's more famous Begum, Hazrat Mahal rested in peace in an almost forgotten mosque named Sibtainabad Imambara. Wazid Ali Shah, the last Nawaz of Lucknow, was a true hero in the war he waged against the British invaders. He was en route to assimilate his forces from various parts of the country, while he was captured by the British in Kolkata, where he spent his last days in captivity.

However, his brave-heart wife, Hazrat Mahal soon gathered a small army to wage a short-lasting war against the British in Lucknow, and captured the Residency in Lucknow (then HQ of British Army) for a short time, until she lost the war – thereafter, she fled to Nepal with her kids and spent her remaining time there. Her body was brought back subsequently and put to rest in the aforementioned Imambara in Metiabruz.

Mary wanted to buy a house close to the Imambara, but she couldn't find a suitable property; so, she had to settle for the only available property located near it. She was also into History very much, just like her mother Di - both the ladies used to be overwhelmed with emotions and pride about their predecessors' freedom struggle, starting from Sepoy Mutiny in the year 1857 till Netaji drove the crusaders away by threatening to wage a war against the British rule in India.

Diana had told Mary many stories relating to Indian freedom fighters as she was growing up, upon finding that Mary had developed a true interest in History. Jallian Wallah Bagh massacre was one of the stories which brought tears down the cheeks of both the ladies, each time they talked about it.

Even after a hundred years from the date of that brutal massacre in Jallian Wallah Bagh, the British government refused to apologise for the massacre during a debate in the House of Commons recently, despite scores of their own MPs calling for a render of apologies from the House, before the centenary of the tragedy. The debate was organized by MP Blackman and was held in Westminster Hall in London.

After listening to impassive speeches, the British junior foreign minister, who was representing the government of UK, had said "It's not appropriate for me today to make the apology that many members would wish to come. I have slightly orthodox views. I would feel a little reluctant to make apologies for things that have happened in the past." UK's ambassador to India, however, was a man enough to condemn the attack!

Mary had special place in her heart for all the martyrs from India's struggle for freedom – she even celebrated the birthdays of the famous heroes who gave up their lives in the cause of their motherland; she used to light incense sticks and candles in front of their pictures on their birthdays, offer her favourite sweets on plates towards their great souls, and used to pray for them. Of course, at the end of it, she used to gobble the sweets herself – like mother, like daughter!

That was Mary then, and this was Mary now – wow! As for Subir, nothing better could've been expected from him! His past history as a kid probably turned him into a psycho – Diana kept wondering if he was better off being sent to mental asylum, instead of giving him an ideal home, which he probably didn't deserve.

She tried all sorts of medical and psychological treatments and counselling for Subir at many stages, but it seemed all went in vain – Di sometimes felt that his attitude as a child was strange; many counsellors opined that he couldn't recover from his trauma as a kid. Diana felt that his young mind was like tender and mucilaginous leaves, hoping that he would heal over time.

Maybe she was wrong! Subir was described by many as a nebbish person, without the capability of earning money on his own, with no ambition – a pitifully ineffectual recreant – an apostate with no prestige or self-respect; above all, a perfidious son!

Di couldn't think anymore; her vision was getting blurry. She saw a cockroach crawling under the rug lying next to her - but was unmoved. This was really strange of Di, as roaches always gave her the howling fantods during her childhood days – she hunched up as small as she could out of fear, with an apparent premonition of imminent danger to her life!

After watching the roach crawl few centimetres, she would scream at the top of her voice, calling her grandma frantically to come and kill the devil; even if the roach was half-dead due to some reasons, Di used to be scared like hell during those days. Many a times, she woke up poor old Ritu from the middle of her sleep, if Di noticed any cockroach, however small in size it maybe!

She would often describe the insect as a flying monster, with long and poisonous tentacles on both ends (probably some traumatic observation or phobia), with hump – Vicky never understood how a cockroach can have a hunchback though! Nevertheless, if he was around during the 'doomsday' (as Di would often coin the day when she got petrified), he would love to see the giggle of heavenly gratification on his niece's face, when he killed the devil – mostly by stepping on it hard.

But now, she was in a vegetative stage - she couldn't even move her fingers. She kept gazing until the devil disappeared, just like her father did – she thought! Maybe it hoodwinked her into thinking that the roach may have been the afterlife her evil father rightfully deserved to be – payback time for the monster in this life to be reincarnated as a roach! Even during this difficult time,

Diana prayed that her devilish father and the lady he eloped with years before, comminute and triturate into something even smaller and nasty in their next life – something like an ant getting crushed under people's feet!

Suddenly, she could hear a very familiar voice – that of her dear uncle Vicky in a distant! Was he extending his arms towards her to carry her on his shoulder? It seemed that Vicky was running with open arms towards Diana, in an apparent fashion as if to indicate that he was going to lift his 'baby' on his shoulder again – like old times' sake! The next moment, Di felt like she was walking inside a huge pipe-like structure with lights sparkling on the other side of it.

She also felt that Vicky was holding her arms, like the way he used to when she walked out of her school, upon reaching her teenage years. But, she couldn't see Vicky clearly while she was traversing down the tunnel – she had a misty vision of a giant nebulous glow on her side, making her warm – giving her a sense of safety; Di felt Vicky was walking alongside her, holding her hands, so that she didn't trip or had an accidental fall.

An imperturbable tranquillity and phlegmatic peace culminated on her face, as Di walked out of the roseate and brightly illuminated pipe-like structure, holding her world's most favourite uncle's hands. Her glabrous palms and smooth fingers interdigitated and interlocked - she started looking around the beautiful place she had never even imagined before - the state of being satiated, surfeit was glowing on her cheek; her long white dress sparkling.

The quiddity and unusual enigma of the surroundings confused her a tad initially, until Di noticed some vespertine shadows at some distance, in front of a thickly wooded declivity – she saw her favourite grandma, grandpa, aunt and of course, dear Mom – smiling and waving at her from a recumbent position, by the edges of an awesome fountain!

She came out of the bright tunnel with her uncle and glanced at her mom first! Her dying mother's memory was so painful to the kid that Diana was left with no other options than to obliterate her sweet mother's memory from her mind forcefully – she had no other alternative than to ensconce her mind only up until the point of time when her mother got sick.

All the memories she had retained in her resilient and soft heart about her mother were pertaining to those good times Di used to enjoy with Gita prior to the latter's getting sick.

Di took a jaunty walk with her uncle on the very scenic path alongside a beautiful stream flowing out of the adjacent hill, as her dear family rose up, and started walking towards her. There was not a nary of any pain or sorrow as she drew closer to something like a bascule or draw bridge which was being lowered for her to cross over and reach them. She easily descried the four dear members of her lovely family waiting there on the other side - Diana gradatim wended her ways towards them gingerly, in an ingratiating manner.

She was rapturous, altruistic and ecstatic - Di put a commendatory subtle grin on her face – she was never an eccedentesiast, but was perpetually known to be a very convivial, gregarious, jocular, affable, mirthful and benevolent lady, who always had gleaming smiles on her beautiful face.

Diana was really surprised – how come all her dear and loving family lost so long ago were looking exactly the same when she last saw them? How come her mother was looking so young and vibrant? Diana started to get really embarrassed to feel her own wrinkled skin, dry lips and unclean clothes she was wearing, which got soiled on the streets down below; whereas, all her family members were glowing in pure white ensembles! Their appearances were exactly the same as Di saw them last, before they got sick!

What really took Diana by surprise was all of her near and dear ones waiting there for her were dressed in white cap-a-pie! And, how come all of them were smiling and asking her to go jumping into their arms? Can they lift a nonagenarian lady like her now – she's not a kid anymore; don't they get it?

Everything other than her loved ones are different here – the tranquillity, essences emanating from the pure white flowers, sounds of water flowing down stream and the soothing air that was blowing around are all much too different here. Gentle zephyr danced around her in that serene and divine place - she realised that it is a propitious moment in time, when people here are way much different than those unsupportive & indecisive as those down in earth, fighting for power & fame, ignoring their loved ones and leaving them for unknown fate!

Di used to accept both the good and the bad with equanimity, in aplomb & sangfroid manner down at earth, when her phlegm & determination carried her through many difficult times. Now, she felt she is beyond all tests life has to offer – she doesn't have to deal writhe or squirm between her children's houses; no more mental agony or pain; no more dealing with corrupt people down there! Moreover, no more dealing with inexorable rise in costs of almost everything!

Diana became very happy a little later to find out that all her adopted children, who were still surviving, arranged for a grandeur condolence meeting at one of the most prestigious venues in Kolkata, where they adopted a joint resolution to carry on her legacy. People from various walks of life congregated to pay their last respect to the great lady who inspired thousands to be brave, honest and caring in life, apart from being a fine individual.

Some were enraged by the irresponsible attitude of Maya and Subir during the final stages of Di's life. One of them, of course it had to be Janet, who felt the fresh remembrance of vexation was still enkindling the rages inside her. However, pretty soon she started feeling exhilarated by the eloquent speeches given by some of the guest-speakers there, in fond remembrance of the Great Lady, their loving Diana. Her works were invariably imbued with a sense of calm, serenity and divinity – her devotion will permeate amongst many in years to come, bringing in winds of change!

Many people close to Di in any manner, either through direct aid or otherwise, would even host annual rituals of Di on her death anniversary, without any puja or prayers – that was her last wish conveyed through Rina, who made sure that her loving sister's wishes were fulfilled, even after Rina was no more.

All the people will assemble in Gitalaya on that specific day, exchange greetings, organise fund-raising and spend time overseeing matters relating to destitute children under others' care, etc.

However, Di wouldn't wait to see what would happen down on earth; she already had enough to deal with – now all she wants is to relax in peace with the ones who really cared for her, her real family!

How 'bout the streets of Kolkata? This place isn't Kolkata, the city she was so fond of! So, where was she? She didn't want to look below at a crowd in a razzmatazz, some gathering around a dead body of an old and graceful lady! Seeing people gathering at that spot, a police sergeant arrived there to call ambulance and notify the next of kin – her purse had a mobile phone with her children's numbers, etc.

Mary and her friends arrived at the hospital soon where Di was carried to by the authorities – it was CMRI, where she was born around ninety-five years ago! Life indeed traversed a full circle for the great lady!

However, Di didn't want to look what was going on down there – a world which caused her more misery than happiness. She has finally found her most coveted place, amongst her most favourite persons – she didn't need anyone else anywhere!

Maybe she was better off forgetting everything about her past and cherish the moment instead. She was little confused - but she was happy; Di was beaming a beatific smile and was ecstatic – a sublime and serene joy prevailed on her beautiful elegant face, as the universal mother approached heaven!

Another gloomy and sultry night prevailed on the streets of Kolkata, with the only exception that the lady who took great pride in it was no longer a part of it!

Life went on normal down there, as if nothing had changed – the streets were all well-lit, hustling bustling of cars, hawkers and peddlers in their usual businesses, crowd enjoying salubrious food or taking stroll on their usual habiliments – some scurrilous and some supercilious; various types of self-proclaimed leaders continuing to fool people with bi-polar politics; the rich and mighty continuing to exploit resources at the expense of the have-nots. The same brouhaha of commercials, the same hoopla around elections, the same old same old - nothing had changed at all down there, it seemed!

It was business as usual – life went on the same all around the Streets of Kolkata! And up in Heaven, the God's messengers were all together once again, enjoying the afterlife with complete tranquillity and divine peace!

The Poem

Streets of Kolkata hold their heads high through ages -

Battling and struggling to survive all kinds of rages;

Many says it all started from the arrival of Job Charnock -

Streets have strongly withstood many currents of dialectal mammock.

Despite many rulers' futile attempts of sequestering the City,

Streets of Kolkata have proudly survived; it's not a pity.

Chock-a-block with shops, restaurants and businesses,

Bustling and hustling of cars and all kinds of buses.

The streets beareth all and endureth all, to be minions,

Not the one subordinate, but like idol to few billions.

Starting from the golden era of Shri Ramakrishna,

With the rise of world-famous Swami Vivekananda,

Kolkata has been home to people like Rishi Aurobinda,

Our true heroes Netaji, Tagore, Bankim Chandra

Sarat Chandra, Hemanta, Manna and Iswar Chandra -

Just to name a few who teemed to teach us many mantra.

Seen by many as hallowed, inalienable and sacrosanct,

The streets have taught us lessons as professor adjunct.

Foods on the streets are multifaceted and multifarious,

Not only junk or fast food, but also wholesome & salubrious.

One may cherish the phoochka or jhalmuri in alfresco -

Or the best cuisine, best dining or maybe some disco.

You'll get everything in Kolkata - from rosogullah to slumgullion;

A pleasant, lively & placid city that has always remained halcyon,

Its vouchsafe residents have historically granted help in condescending ways;

The nuncupative gift of love to visitors charms all from times of chaise.

It turned our society plausible & this revelation is apodictic;

Many eulogistic oration and writings about Kolkata is panegyric.

From elucidation and explication from Vedic exegesis -

Beyond critical apprehension of cathexis and anti-cathexis.

Many homiletic literature starts from God Brahma,

Everything starts with zero and ends in Karma.

Creator of the universe is the first god of the Trinity -

Scientists couldn't disapprove of existence of infinity.

Zero-energy universe hypothesis has similar conclusions,

Positive energy in matter is cancelled by negative gravitations.

Going back to the streets of Kolkata traversed by men who're puissant,

Some are poor, majority are middle-class, and some are very affluent;

All dressed up in their usual habiliments,

As per their own values and sentiments.

Many return back home after dark stultified -

Some portraying their moments they enjoyed.

But many are not so superjacent -

They're better off not saying anent,

Of anything of rare naissant.

Head held high is incipient,

Of any person in their nascent.

Streets are full with ladies with great ensemble,

Where men from all walks of life also assemble.

It's strange that some are recalcitrant -

Although many of them are obedient.

Some sweat out as redolent,

A few nearly smelling like rodent;

They breathe out the air of halitosis –

Perhaps it's in their metamorphosis!

We can't blame any for not using fragrance,

Until they push out any smelly essence.

This is noticeable if you're on public transportation –

As not everyone can be beneficiaries of corruption.

However, some here are not easily enervated,

Vibrant souls also galore highly motivated.

Pompous few try hard to bloviate,

In a maladroit attempt they navigate,

A sycophantic attempt to ingratiate –

They can jeer and hurl epithet,

Act as much revile and vituperate,

To castigate, berate and calumniate;

They need to answer to the sobriquet –

If it traverses into legal scilicet,

Their offences cannot be extenuated;

Others may laugh cachinnated,

Eventually they'll be denigrated –

Then they will be severely debilitated.

There will be no time left for conciliation,

The time has already gone for propitiation.

They will feel remorse and will be contrite,

But the crack can't be fixed by Dendrite;

As time has passed in festinate,

They may get break if they're fortunate.

Gormless and feisty as they're in traduce -

Few friends stay with them forever in truce.

There's absolutely no dearth of those popinjays -

Their conceitful attitude will end up in hays.

They will certainly be paid back in their own coins,

They will end up eating banana, not tenderloins.

Perplexing or abstruse it may sound - to some, even esoteric;

Slake and satiate your thirst for verbiage - don't be a pessimistic.

Flattering will get you nowhere in the long run - the streets quipped;

You can berate, harangue, lambaste, vituperate or be ill-equipped -

Whatever goes around will definitely come around,

To haunt you and intimidate you round and round.

There might be people speaking in animadversion,

You're better off ignoring - without any diversion;

Some may accuse you wrongfully and delate -

Keep up your best efforts, leaving rest to fate.

As long as you lack moral values, ethics and be inflexible,

You'll end up seeing the world around you as unliveable.

Trees by the streets appear interdigitated,

But, their beauty can nowhere be obviated;

The memory can't be obliterated -

Its essence can only be eventuated.

In strong winds, the trees swing and dance as terpsichorean,

The soothing air & languorous leaves are left to perception.

Those fortunate kids go to schools with maieutic theory of teaching -

Less unfortunate ones are left with dealing with all sorts of preaching.

Many academic language is obscure and verbose,

Full of loquacious, garrulous and orotund prose.

Instead of using hortative sentences or statements,

They often end with absolutely no encouragements.

Some schools of thought believe and solicit casuistry -

Their process of reasoning to resolve matters is mystery.

It's not at all rodomontade -

This is like masses flocculated.

Noise of cars below will bombinate,

In the ears of all who're unfortunate;

Up and down so immensely disparate,

Peace-loving citizens chose to separate -

By confining themselves in their own self,

As there's not much to be done to delve.

It may be better to ensconce yourself in your house -

Unless you want to quip or circumspect,

You're probably safer holding your respect.

Any protest you raise may bring back yeasty days -

Not as a revolution, but as an evolution in many ways!

Street below may be circuitous,

Remember that trees are salubrious;

Wind blowing slow sad susurrus,

Despite routine falling in multitudinous -

Birds on the trees are euphonious,

Their chirping sound very canorous.

Migrating over the seas, they need a break on terra firma,

The flocks have to rest on land, and not get pachyderma.

Leaves seemingly so glabrous -

Glowing at sunset roseate glamorous.

Younger leaves are tad mucilaginous;

Despite the roads below in razzmatazz,

Echoing all that razzle-dazzle in Alcatraz!

Some people are doughty and valorous.

Few though transforming into querulous,

Some wearing dresses in diaphanous -

Maybe they want to be Croesus!

Few snooty girls on streets wear brummagem ornaments,

To expose their haughty attitude & poor predicaments.

A rare few of them are scurrilous -

Those strange folks so supercilious;

These are really nocuous,

Their voices are so stridulus.

They look little too crapulous;

Their faces are more lugubrious,

As they realise they're fugacious -

On the whole it appears holus-bolus,

Without construing it as hocus-pocus!

It's strange that some girls don't believe in their muliebrity -

That way it yields some repleteness, or maybe it's satiety.

Very few remember how the world for women changed with suffragettes,

It was their revolution which produced great ladies like Melinda Gates.

Be apologetic when confronted by an angry occidental -

Unless you're the archetype of somewhat sacerdotal;

Especially if he's a contemporary as you are - coeval.

Try pacifying him with a horseradish sorbet quenelle,

Lest you're betwixt iron mask and rugs made of chenille!

Streets of Kolkata display many anthropomorphic hoarding -

Displaying ads which passer-by's eyes are caught while fording.

Some hoardings below probably read boustrophedon,

Unless its sophistry compels you to take Saridon!

The brouhahas over the infamous commercials on neon -

Those former era without commercials seem to be halcyon.

Down the street, customers expect some lagniappe,

Shopkeepers oblige, smiling & grinning like a pet ape.

They want to make sure there's nary murmur or complaint -

So that bureaucracy or legal system don't make them lament.

Tourists curiously wend their ways across the City,

It's amazing to watch their precipitancy and legerity.

Peaceful hours of sacred nights demand refection;

Let's enjoy the night devoid of any untrue denegation.

Foreign cars pass by - from Mercedes to Volkswagens,

Some carrying perpetrators of financial shenanigans.

Many political parties get away with things mindboggling -

Their actions cause higher taxes and bureaucratic boondoggling.

Before most of them are elected to power -

There's absolutely no dearth of promise-shower;

Once they start their coveted regime in the State -

Everything else for commoners is left to poor fate.

The escape of Fleance is peripeteia in Macbeth's tragedy -

Bardolators idolising Shakespeare will always admire His comedy.

It's ludicrous when a CM claims the Great Man and Tagore were friends;

The hypocrisy, idiosyncrasy, ignominy or mere doltishness - where it all ends?

She's self-professed doctorate who thinks the Great Men were contemporaries;

Despite born three hundred years apart, she's unaware of it, clad in her sarees.

Another ex-CM had banned English and computing from government schools -

Sent his own son to UK for studies - no one thinks he was amongst the fools!

Some leaders portray themselves as experts of ratiocination;

In reality, experience with them turns out to be some illusion.

Call it delusion, apparition, chimera or hallucination -

The end-result is lack of governance & poor administration.

Public money is whimsically dispensed with such largesse;

Is it munificence, bounty, bride, charity - or spreading cheese?

Racial hatred has always been anathema to our great City,

Streets of Kolkata will always stand spirited with doughty.

The City that boasts of intrepid, unabashed, gallant men & women -

Will always ensure they strive together, live together and say omen.

Our City will tread on like a caravanserai -

Our children will ensure that they fructify.

Be that as it may, streets of Kolkata are always in hype -

Something always comes up to change the stereotype.

Winds of change blows through its many corners,

It's yet to be seen whether it can add more feathers -'

To the great and fun-filled streets of Kolkata,

You always have love and regards from Dipeeta!

This is an informal request not through any causerie -

Not to construe this as awkward act or gaucherie;

The poem here is to be purely read as a retrodict,

Some may differ on any phrase or may contradict.

If anything I wrote here doesn't suit you -

Call me names, curse me, but please don't sue.

Acknowledgement

The minor author wants to deeply acknowledge the support, motivation and help she received from the following persons and entities, without whose constant words of encouragement and direct/indirect support, publishing this second book within one year's time span wouldn't have been possible:

1) First and foremost, her loving and caring sweet Grandma, Mrs. Rekha Mukherjee for all her inspirations & help - making her who she is today;

2) Mrs. Sampa Sanyal, Swati Das and Indrani Chakraborty of Modern High School for Girls, Kolkata for their confidence in the author;

3) Mrs. Ananya Chakrabarti, Chairperson, WBCPCR, Government of West Bengal, and all esteemed Members of WBCPCR for their support;

4) Amazon Kindle Direct Publishing, as well as M/S Gouri Press;

5) Author's aunty, Mrs. Jaya Chatterjee and her family for unselfish love;

6) Shri Sugata Bose, M.P, Government of India, Shri Dilip Mondal, M.L.A. (W.B.) and Shri Baiswanor Chatterjee, M.I.C. (K.M.C.);

7) Smt. Sagarika Ghose, ex-editor, Times of India Group;

8) Messrs. Will Ripley, Max Foster, Frederik Pleitgen, Kristie Lu Stout, Clarissa Ward and other great Anchors of CNN;

9) Ms. Ningning Tomiyama, Head of Asia Council, YGLP - Oxford; and

All the friends, teachers & office-bearers of all the institutions (barring a few) the author ever attended. The author would like to thank her Dada, Victor Mukherjee for his constant guidance, support, motivation and protection……

N.B. All proceeds received as Royalty by the author from sale of this book will be distributed amongst recognized charitable organisations working towards betterment of children, women empowerment and destitute kids in dire need of financial assistance, during the first year of publication of this novel.

Anyone interested in viewing receipts or details of donations stated above, is requested to drop a line to bhatumukherjee@yahoo.com

Thank you. God Bless.

Made in the USA
Coppell, TX
06 March 2025

46738882R20188